ISBN# 978-1-063572-14-8
ISBN #978-1-963572-15-5

Cover by: Josh with Pro0Design-X

Dedication

To the one and only kind person in the operating room that day: The anesthesiologist who could see the fear in my eyes and detect my anxiety. I told him to just be sure I woke up.His smile reached his eyes above his mask as he told me as long as I was going to be out, he'd like for me to bring him back a cheeseburger and an order of onion rings. Nothing like a laugh before your world goes black. Sometimes it's humor, sometimes compassion, and sometimes simple reassurance that someone's got your six.

Contents

But I Kissed A Cowboy

Annie Mick

Chapter 1

Reece

God, I love my job! Admittedly, there are days and nights my body aches from the push and pull, the lifting and carrying, the shaky climbs, the risky descents. But no greater satisfaction can be found than knowing you've saved a life. The sound of breath being sucked back into someone's lungs after you've pulled them out of a burning building, a baby's cry when the mother goes into early labor after a car accident. Yeah, that only happened once, but have you ever delivered a baby in the midst of chaos?

The accolades don't hurt either. But honestly? If I never receive another pat on the back, another 'atta boy', another 'well done', I'll be good. The adrenaline rush alone is enough for me.

That's not to say there aren't nights I would like to bury my head in a pillow and wake up with a happy case of amnesia of the day before. The days when the *Jaws of Life* were used to no avail. The days when there was no hope even before we arrived. It happens. There is no such thing as a one hundred percent success rate. It's something we're trained, conditioned, taught, and warned about before ever being put in the field.

Not everyone can be saved.

And yes, it is true. Every once in a while, we do get the innocuous call to rescue the feisty feline that has climbed the neighbor's tree in order to avoid the supposed vicious dog on the ground. I often would like to sit back with a bowl of popcorn and a beer and wait for the scene to unfold. Take the damn dog inside and observe as the cat skillfully climbs back down, then sits outside the window watching the dog go nuts, while it licks himself in honor of winning the battle once again. I swear to God, you'll see him smile as the dog goes crazy. Had cats been given the capacity, I'm sure they would laugh. Instead, they purr, melt hearts with those cute little meows, and convince even the cruelest of men of their innocence.

Having been raised on a horse and cattle ranch in Texas, I watched it all the time. Those cats are hardly helpless. If they can get up, they can get down. They're very independent creatures. Those claws are like ninja knives. Why do you think we wear thick gloves to snatch them out of the tree? They were built to be mean, cunning, stealthy. Besides, have you ever seen a cat land on anything other than its feet?

Once I learned the only felines that truly needed rescuing are the kind that leave scratches on your back while squeezing your dick, cats became the least of my concerns, and pussy became a high priority.

The only exception I ever encountered was a girl I gave a

horseback ride during one of my last summers on the ranch. *My kitten.* It was also the last time I ever let a girl ride in front of me on a saddle. I've had plenty ride *on my* saddle since – just never while riding a horse. Not that she was supposed to ride there in the first place. But when you're seventeen years old and the world's finest ass shows up in denim cut offs and a tank top, well – let's just say I was stiffer than the saddle horn she was instructed to hold onto. Long, shiny brown hair, beautiful silvery gray eyes, a cupid's bow above pillowy lips, and the perkiest little tits I'd ever seen.

Her dad had brought her to Texas from North Carolina for vacation that summer; apparently doing his best to make up for being a part-time parent. We'd encountered it many times over the years. When Disneyland lost its sparkle, or affordability, parents would bring the kids to a dude ranch where they could ride 'real' animals. If only the dads knew . . . the moms were sometimes looking to ride the dudes instead of the horses. But my mother knew, and having birthed some rather genetically blessed sons, she would take the reins and lead a trail tour herself before letting one of us loose with a cougar – the two-legged kind.

Ninety-seven thousand acres and we used one tiny portion of the ranch to provide an entertainment area in the summers from early June through August. My family-oriented mom's recreational hobby. It cost a small fortune to build; the barn to keep the horses, generators to keep it cool, water tanks, transport of hay and grain every day. Not to mention the insurance premiums. But all the woman had to do was drop a kiss on my dad's cheek and maybe bat her eyelashes a time or two, and that man would crumple at the knees and indulge her every whim. *Still does, actually.*

Open five hours every morning, three of our mellowest horses, three of the boys to work it *while mom supervised,* and the trail was only two miles long. Two miles of which she could see every inch with high powered binoculars. "For safety reasons," she would tell us, followed by a stern clipped, "Yours."

"Horses! Dad! What made you think this was a good idea?" the sexy little fireball had protested as my two older brothers snickered. "They're huge, and . . . dirty! I'll fall off."

"Bug," her dad nearly pleaded. "I'm doing my best here to make a memory for you. Indulge me, please?"

"Indulge you? Aren't you riding too?"

He shook his head, wincing. "Sweetheart, not with my back the way it is. This is all for you."

She was torn, conflicted; the look in her eyes a mix of resentment and concession. Divorce did that to kids. We'd seen it many times. *Please the parent and get it over with.* "Fine, let's do this. Which one am I riding?"

I bit my tongue, the overwhelming urge to volunteer myself squashed by my mother's glare. Intuitive woman, that one.

My brother, Ronan, didn't hesitate to take the necessary steps to get close – asshole – and wheedle his way into her good graces to be her scout, giving her a choice of the three horses we used for customers.

We had Lightning – a name the horse had outgrown, as her speed had settled more into a painful trot – saddled up tight and ready. Demon was also prepped – another that had earned his name back in the day, *fourteen years prior*. Beelzebub was the other choice and he was growing impatient, but only because if he wasn't working, his preference was to stand in the shade and munch on carrots and dry grass. His protests usually started with a high pitched whinny and harmless snorts that had a tendency to scare the shit out of the rider.

After Ronan voiced the prospects for her, she glared at him before shooting her father a look of disdain that may have made me sweat a little if she weren't so damn cute. "Lightning,

Demon, and Beelzebub? It sounds like a one-way trip to hell!"

"I'm on Lady Luck." I patted the shiny black mane of my favorite prize-winning mare, then proffered, "You can ride *with* me. I promise I won't let you fall."

My brothers snorted in unison as my mother cleared her throat and tossed me a look of skepticism coated with warning. "I'm not sure that's necessary."

"She's skittish, mom." I shrugged, feigning innocence my brothers couldn't have paid for. They'd had their pants down so many times, the women in town knew whose dick was whose just by feel, because they'd been feeling them for years. My intentions may not have been of the saintly variety, but my game had never made it beyond third base. This girl was different though. I wasn't really looking to play ball – I simply wanted to replace her discomfort with a smile. "I want her to have some fun." Echoing her father's words, I added, "It's her chance to make a memory." *It was mine too, but some things you just don't share.*

The little knockout studied me with wary eyes. "What if I fall off the back?"

Waving her over, I reassured her, "Come on. You're not riding on the back. My saddle isn't dirty and I'll ride behind you." It took everything in me not to boost her up by that cute little ass into the saddle; instead letting her independently struggle as she threw her leg over and settle on top. Waiting until she was steady, I placed my boot in the stirrup and easily straddled myself behind her. As I reached around her small body that fit against mine like it was made for it to grab the reins that were wrapped on the horn, I smirked at my brothers and mouthed, "Fuck you." They only chuckled and went to work on my behalf, reassuring her father that his daughter was in good hands.

She was in good hands, too. I would never take advantage. They knew it. I simply enjoyed the company of a pretty girl, and she was much closer to my age than theirs. I'd tolerated the whole season entertaining kids and little old ladies on this trail. It was my turn to enjoy one last day.

And that is how it came to be that the little spitfire ended up on the horse with me. It was the end of summer, the height of the season over. School would start in a week and *"Bug"* would be a pleasant memory.

We rode at a slow pace, light generic conversation; the only riders on the trail. Lady Luck stopped to snatch some grass from the edge of the trail when we reached the turn-around point – her usual spot in the shady grove of trees. The one tiny slice of heaven that couldn't be spotted, even with my mother's high-power binoculars. As she did, the girl fell forward with the unexpected movement and my hand found the perfect resting place on the flat of her taut stomach and held her to me. She was perfect. Soft and smooth; my little finger dipping into the crevice of her bellybutton as if it had found a home. But hers had a shapely little roof on it in the form of a curved barbell piercing in the skin above the crevice. Delicate and tasteful. Her hair smelled fruity and light. Not the overpowering flowery crap other girls' used that attracted every bee and fly within a hundred miles. Thank God for tight Levi's – I didn't want to scare her. I was pretty sure the blood supply was taking a hit, but she was like an aphrodisiac.

"You alright?" I chuckled as I held her close to me, upright in the saddle. "I told you I wouldn't let you fall."

"Yeah," she answered weakly with a nod that made the scent of her hair waft toward my nose. "I didn't expect her to do that. I should squeeze the horn tighter."

Head out of the gutter, Reece. She meant the saddle horn.

"This is the end of the trail," I reluctantly told her, though in no hurry as I allowed Lady Luck to continue her snack as my reason to hold her close. "As much as I hate for this to end, we need to head back."

She twisted her upper half and tilted her head up to look at me; one hand on the saddle horn, the other gripping my wrist to assure I didn't let go of the hold I had over her stomach. *As if.* "Thank you. This wasn't so bad after all."

She had the sweetest smile I'd ever seen. Full, plump, kissable lips. Unique light gray eyes with tiny green flecks that would taunt my dreams for years to come. The innocence of an angel, but the curiosity of an inexperienced young woman.

Not something that was easily found around those parts. The girls around home loved saving that horse and riding the cowboy instead. Hence the reason my brothers were already leaving sloppy seconds in three counties.

"How old are you, *Bug*?"

She rolled those gorgeous eyes and groaned lightly. "Only Dad calls me that. I'll be sixteen in two months."

"Sweet sixteen," I whispered, my pulse quickening, the desire to kiss this girl overwhelming. She wasn't *that* young. "Have you ever been kissed?"

Her pink tongue darted between her lips and my eyes followed its path. *No, she'd never been kissed.* She shook her head slightly, her eyes fixed on mine. "Would you let me be your first?" She nodded slowly as I leaned in, one hand on the reins so Lady Luck wouldn't bolt, the other still on her midsection.

She was delicious. Lips smooth and soft, pliant against mine. She tasted like cotton candy. No gaping hole begging for my tongue. An innocent yet breath-stealing kiss. I'd never experienced anything like it. The slightest, happy, little purr vibrated in her throat, transferring all the way to my dick. Someday, that girl would be a lucky man's wildcat.

As I pulled back from the kiss, I winked. "It's definitely not Bug. You will forever be my Kitten. That was the sweetest purr I've ever heard."

She giggled as her cheeks turned a beautiful shade of

pink. "Then you will forever be my cowboy."

I took my cowboy hat off my head and plopped it onto hers. "Yours to keep to remember today."

She adjusted the hat on her head and acquiesced, "I don't have anything to give you."

"Kitten," I adjusted her in the saddle once more, gently drawing her into me, then tugged on Lady Luck's reins to turn us around, "you gave me a kiss I'll never forget. Now lean back on me for the rest of the ride so I'll remember the way you feel against my body."

Best. ride. ever.

I loved growing up in Texas. Open land as far as the eye could see. I'd never been allergic to hard work, long hours, getting dirty, or callused hands. But working with horses and cattle and eating dust for breakfast, lunch, and dinner wasn't what I wanted to do for the rest of my life. I have five brothers who love it a whole lot more than I do.

The need to make a difference consumed me after losing two college friends and watching two others be saved as the firefighters used the *Jaws of Life* to extricate them from the nearly crushed vehicle that had been hit by a drunk driver. It was devastating and a driving force at the same time. You can say, "I want to" or "I should" forever, but wishes and time are thieves. Do it or don't. And that is why I am a firefighter, in Phoenix, Arizona, in the prime of my life, enjoying singledom and a healthy libido.

My downtime usually comes in the form of a few beers, hot wings and pizza, a good steak on the BBQ now and then, football games, good friends, and some good sex when the tension gets too high. Unfortunately, the sex provides only short term relief so I probably enjoy it more often than I should. It's physical, mechanical, unemotional, and hot. A simple way to blow off steam and relax a body part that weightlifting and cardio workouts don't seem to relieve. Get in, get off, get out. Not to worry, the ladies enjoy themselves. Quite often three or four times in one session.

I make it home at least twice a year to see my folks and brothers. Lady Luck still gets a daily visit from her favorite rider while I'm there, though I swear she still gives me a side-eye identical to the one she shot me the day I watched the girl get in the car with her father and drive away. The day I neglected to ask for her name, a phone number, an address; a way to keep in touch. The side-eye that literally speaks: *"You are such a dumbass, Reece"*.

It may have been her first kiss, but I've always considered it my best kiss.

Chapter 2

Mallory

Liberty Collins and I sit in a bar after a full week of our parents having been in town to celebrate us receiving our masters' degrees. Years of school and hard work, and the only thing left is for her to decide her place of employment. I've already taken a position at Banner Medical; the largest hospital with the most sought after positions in the city. I would love to have Libs join me, but the final choice is hers. She has four offers sitting on our dining table awaiting her decision; Banner being one of them. I'm a nurse anesthetist, Libs is a nurse practitioner.

Liberty and I have been best friends for fourteen years.

Inseparable since high school. We've lived together since the first year of college. I came along when she needed somebody to fill in for what was missing. She came along when I needed somebody I'd never had. A real friend. A secret keeper. Like a diary you can talk to instead of simply write in. And I'm the same for her.

The bartender serving us isn't actually a bartender. He's the son of the owner, and a doctor at Banner, here helping his dad due to being shorthanded tonight. My bet is the sick call-ins are probably at the big concert in town and shaking their asses to music instead of here shaking the cocktails they should be. I'll admit though, the doc/bartender does fix a pretty good margarita.

"Okay, potty break's over. What did I miss?" I tease as I cross the bar on my way back to where Liberty and the handsome bartender/doctor discuss what I hope is a future date. She's been in a dry spell for years. Between school, clinicals, and searching for a lost boy from her childhood, she's been too busy to give her personal life any attention. I've done my best to convince her if she doesn't hop on the live pony, she'll never know the difference between a stallion and a gelding. Yeah, she didn't appreciate the analogy either.

"Us!" one of the grinning morons at the end of the bar yells on my way past. Lovely, a double-mint duo. The kind that don't have enough stamina to get the job done on their own, so they depend on a partner to finish the task if they fail. The sure thing. They call it kink. I call it blink. You know, blink and you'll miss it because it's over before it started. Not quite inability, not really impotence; simply incompetence.

Turning to indulge their frat boy fantasy that is never going to happen, I watch their eyes light up before I tilt my head and study them for a quick minute. "Dumb and Dumber at the same time, huh? Sorry guys, even I'm not that charitable. Go home, call your mothers and apologize."

"Apologize for what?" the brunette of the duo asks defensively.

"For not being man enough to get the job done solo."

They stare, slack jawed, before I turn and make my way back to where Liberty sits. I take a long sip of my margarita and set the glass down hard. "That'll teach them."

"Teach them what?" the doc/bartender asks.

"Emotional impotence." I nod in satisfaction. "Threesomes will forever be accompanied by thoughts of their mother, therefore preventing them from being able to perform. My job here is done. Just watch."

The two idiots start to argue about who made their last conquest come harder, before one storms toward the door. I call out before he gets too far away to hear, "Be sure to tell mommy I said hello."

The handsome blonde remaining at the end of the bar glares at me. I tip my head toward the door. "Well, go on. Call your mother. Wouldn't hurt to take her to brunch on Sunday either." He's of the gorgeous variety – blue eyes, well-trimmed facial hair that would feel really good between . . . Hard to believe he needs a partner to get anything done behind closed doors. But then, looks can be deceiving.

He narrows his eyes and throws some cash on the bar. "You did that on purpose, didn't you?"

I match his steely glare with the advantage of one lifted brow, keeping my tone light, my question sincere, prepared to give him a little food for thought. "You got a sister?"

His brow pinches as he hesitates. "As a matter of fact I do."

"Younger?"

"Yeah," he answers, though it sounds more like a question, as if maybe I'm asking for a new friend.

I nod slowly as if pondering his answer. "And just how many would you want *doing* her at the same time?"

His mouth opens and closes, a little like a fish out of water, incapable of a response.

"Thought so," I nearly sing. "Do better. Be an example, not a hypocrite."

He saunters toward the door, but in my usual form of smartassery, I can't help myself. "Little sisters like brunch too. A new Gucci bag if she's too busy to fit it into her schedule."

He stops at the threshold and turns, the heat in his eyes enough to melt the panties off a nun, before the corners of his mouth twitch and his face softens. "Well played." He winks. "I'll remember this."

Hello? That was kind of my point, dumbass.

Liberty's doc/bartender returns from serving customers in another area of the bar. "Are you ladies ready for another?"

We respond with a resounding yes, though after that heated gaze from the handsome stranger, I'm ready to have him just bring me triples.

"So." He grins impishly as he asks, "Did you put Eric in his place?"

That usual form of smartassery I mentioned above? Every once in a while it has a tendency to get me in trouble or bite me in the ass. An ugly sense of apprehension creeps over me as I inquire, "Eric?"

"The blonde guy." His lips tip slowly as he tries to hide a grin. "He's the head of radiology at Banner. Sounds like you two haven't seen the last of each other."

I drop my forehead onto my palm and groan loudly, "Oh, fuck me sideways."

The doc laughs. "Pretty sure he would if you asked him to."

Lifting my head, I scowl. "I don't do doubles and I definitely don't do players."

He grins as he lifts a brow. "You sure about that? It would seem you just played right into his hands. That was a test."

"A test of what?"

"Your integrity," he says with a nod. "You'd be amazed how many offers he gets in a week."

Narrowing my eyes, I ask, "And just how full is the good doctor's schedule?"

He shrugs. "No clue. I'm not his secretary."

The following Friday, Liberty is on her date with the bartender/doctor and I'm on the sofa watching Netflix, munching on a tasteless fortune cookie while pondering the words on the little scrap of paper I'd removed from the inside:

One can only ride off into the sunset if they mount the horse

What the hell is that supposed to mean and why is this in a fortune cookie? Chinamen use rickshas, don't they? I've been on a horse once in my life. And truthfully, I would have rather mounted the cowboy. My first kiss and I never even got his name. I do still have his hat, though. Cream colored with a leather band, complete with traces of Texas dirt. I've struggled to remember what he looked like, other than hypnotizing icy blue eyes that took my breath away, soft lips that molded to mine better than any description in the romance novels I used to read by flashlight – once my mom thought I was fast asleep. Sweaty blonde curls on the nape of his neck that only made him more rugged. Spending a week at a dude ranch is on my bucket list now that school is over and my paycheck is going to be rather hefty. Levi's, beefy thighs, and cowboy rides. I'm a strong believer in animal rescue. Someone has to save those horses.

Oh, and the romance novels? I read smut these days.

It was the summer before sophomore year, my last away vacation with my dad. Little did I know, it was his way of trying to soften the blow of informing me he was getting remarried. He pretty much destroyed any good memories from that trip with his news; putting to rest the kid fantasy I'd held onto that someday he would come back home to my mom and me. It was also two weeks before I met my best friend. We went for burgers and shakes after the first day of school. She wasn't just new at school; she was brand new to my neighborhood. We simply hadn't met yet.

Within two hours, I knew I'd made the best decision of my life approaching Liberty Collins after our last class. She didn't begrudge me my cocky attitude and I didn't let her shy away.

"I'm so mad at my dad for marrying that witch," I grumbled as I shoved another fry in my mouth. "I hope he doesn't plan on any more visits from me. I don't ever want to talk to him again. I hate that woman."

"I get that you're mad at him and you don't like her," Liberty said softly, staring out at the Atlantic as we sat on the bench outside the beachside burger joint. "Probably don't like him very much right now either, but he's your dad, Mallory. You still love him, don't you?"

I snorted and rolled my eyes. "Of course I do. I'm just . . ."

"Tell him, Mal." It sounded like a plea as a lone tear rolled down her cheek. "Tell him every chance you get. I would give anything to tell my dad I love him. I'd give even more to hear him tell me the same."

"Oh," I whispered as my heart broke for her. "Is your dad gone?"

She answered wordlessly with a slow nod, the agony of the loss painted in her eyes as the unique colors of blue and green turned nearly translucent with her tears. "My best friend was taken away after his mom was murdered. I never got to tell him goodbye. Then my dad died. And now I've had to move here. All I have left is my mom. Never neglect to tell the people you love how you feel. You may never get another chance."

I was stunned at her openness. I was crushed by her pain. I was struck by her wisdom. That girl needed a distraction and a friend. And so did I.

"I'll be your best friend . . . if you want, Libs," I offered with a shrug. "I'm kind of a smartass, but I'm really brainy and I will take any secrets you share to my grave. If you need a tampon, I'm your girl. We can study together. I only read about sex. I've only been kissed once and it was at a dude ranch this summer, so I've lost all interest in jocks for a while. I doubt I'll be having sex until I'm at least a senior."

Her tears had dried up by the time I caught my second wind and before I could continue, she giggled. "A dude ranch?"

"That's all you got out of that?"

She waved her hand at me as if it was a foregone conclusion. "I'd love to be besties. Now, tell me about the cowboy."

"Oh thank God," I groaned. "I've been dying to tell somebody. He was . . ."

Her interest that day gave me clarity that the anger toward my dad had washed from my mind. The bright blue eyes, the slight bump on his sleek nose as if it were hereditary and not from an injury. The playful smile when he called me "Kitten". I held onto that memory for a very long time, wishing I'd taken a picture when the vision started to fade. But if I close my eyes I can still feel the kiss, his hand across my stomach holding my back to his front, the way his pinky dipped into my bellybutton. So protective and romantic at the same time. It was the perfect first kiss. I haven't had the pleasure of one like it since. Men have a tendency to shove their tongue halfway down your throat as if they're searching for your depth capacity and gag reflex in anticipation of, well – we won't go there.

Opening my eyes and shaking my head at the wayward thoughts living rent free in an already overloaded brain, I mumble to myself, "What the hell is wrong with you, Mallory? A fortune cookie makes you think of horses and cowboys?" I crumple the tiny paper in my hand and throw it into the empty carton. "You've got orientation and people to put to sleep come Monday. Get thy shit together."

The deadbolt on the door clicks as Liberty turns her key in the lock. What the heck? It's just shy of nine o'clock and her date started at seven. All that work put into makeup and hair, and she's home before most people get started? The doc must have been a dud.

I glance over my shoulder as she walks in the door. "Tell me you at least got a meal out of him. What did he do? Talk with food in his mouth and spittle across the table? Chew too loudly? Dribble wine into his whiskers?"

Libs is a little anal about table manners.

She glowers before setting two bags on the counter. "No, smartass, he didn't talk with food in his mouth. He was a true gentleman with impeccable manners. He's also a cardiothoracic surgeon. Got called in for an emergency and had to end the date early."

"He took you on a date when he was on call?" I howl in disgust. "How rude! Good thing he didn't pull out in the middle of sex. Can you imagine the blue bits he would have left you with?"

She reaches into the fridge and grabs a bottle of red, then two glasses from the cupboard and two forks from the drawer. "Keep it up and I'm not going to share the cheesecake with you."

Hopping off the sofa, I make a mad dash toward the

kitchen, my mouth watering in anticipation of my favorite dessert. "You brought cheesecake home?"

"Complements of Michael." She sets the wine and forks on the counter and opens the bags to reveal two takeout containers with cheesecake from the fanciest Italian restaurant in the city. At a hundred bucks a plate, we've only been once. That'll change soon with the advantage of paychecks. "He ordered us dessert, paid the bill, called a Lyft for me, and left for the hospital."

"Wait a minute," I snap in disbelief. "He didn't even bring you home first?"

"Hospital is in the opposite direction." She shrugs one shoulder as she starts to pour the wine. "It was an emergency. Saw to it I had a ride and that we have dessert. He was thorough."

"He was thoroughly a jerk!" I snatch my glass, draining it of half the contents. "Did he even kiss you goodnight?"

She shrugs again, her head tilting with the movement. "On the cheek."

I fan my face and dramatically feign a southern accent. "Oh, Betsy Sue, be careful. Your virtue is on the line. That man is only out for your . . ."

A large blob of cheesecake lands in the middle of my forehead then plops down into my wine glass. I glare at a smirking Liberty who stands with the fork in her hand, tines up, as if ready to sling another bite at me, then reach into my wine glass with two fingers, scoop out the soaked bite of cheesecake, and slide it into my mouth. It's a bit . . . mushy, but I manage to choke it down.

Nodding slowly, I smack my lips as if savoring. "Not bad. Adds a little tang. Reisling might have been a better choice. We should probably just dip it one bite at a time though. It got a bit soggy." I swipe a finger across my forehead to collect the remnants left by the initial hit and deliver the creamy goodness to my mouth by licking it off with my tongue.

Libs looks mortified as she watches the last of it disappear from my finger. "That was disgusting!"

Lifting a brow, I grin. "Never waste cheesecake from Mancusso's." I walk to the sink and rinse my glass, then reach into the cupboard to grab a clean one. "Now pour me a fresh one and tell me about Dr. Michael Knight."

Chapter 3

Reece

Slipping out of bed in a well-practiced, clandestine maneuver, I reach for my clothes on the floor and gather them in my arms. Someday I'll learn to leave them strung across a chair so they'll be easier to find in the dark. The busty blonde in the bed is fast asleep, as well she should be. Four orgasms and a physical workout strenuous enough to give her a pass on yoga for the next week ought to keep her in sated slumber for at least a few hours.

Softly closing the bedroom door behind me, I stuff the two used, tied-off condoms in the pocket of my jeans, dress quickly in the living room – a stealth art you acquire as a firefighter – and lock the front door on my way out. I'm not big on repeats. Scratch that. I hate repeats. Half the time, I struggle to remember their names the next day. I love women. I love the women's movement – the bounce, the wiggle, the sway. Oh, you thought I meant . . . never mind.

I'm not a pig, nor am I a chauvinist. The ladies and I enjoy each other's company. Expectations are limited to phenomenal sex for one evening; quite often into the early morning hours. Okay, maybe I'm a bit of a pig. But I'm a gentleman pig.

The lady I just left behind that door had asked if I wanted to stay for breakfast, right before I smiled and rolled over and said, "Sounds like an invitation."

It wasn't exactly a lie. I do love breakfast. It was an invitation. I never said I would join her, nor did I have any intention of doing so. She'll figure it out when she wakes to an empty bed. God, I hope she didn't plan on me cooking for her. Poor thing's going to starve. See? Gentleman. It may have been an afterthought, but it was thoughtful. It wouldn't matter anyway. I don't ever stay the night and they never stay . . . with me.

My condo is my sanctuary. I cohabitate with several coworkers for 72 hours at a time at the firehouse; sleeping, eating, cooking, and running drills when we're not saving lives in one way or another. When I'm off, I live alone. I don't mind company that I know is going home when we're done watching a game, playing poker, or just having a few beers. I share a *building* with some of my best friends, not my home.

It's two o'clock in the morning when I pull my truck into the parking lot of our complex. Lights flash in my rearview mirror and I grin when I see Roger, a fellow firefighter and a best friend, arriving home at the same time I am. We've worked the same shift at the firehouse for the last five years, live in the same building, and are four years apart in age, him being older. We're virtually brothers from another mother.

He grins knowingly as he climbs out of his own truck once parked next to mine. "No breakfast, huh?"

"I'm up for breakfast." I chuckle as I sit and wait for him to climb in. All night diner it is. "Just not at her place."

He hops into the passenger side and closes the door. He takes a deep breath, blows it out with a heavy sigh, and rolls his shoulders. "Biscuits and gravy at the Happy Chef?"

I shoot him a cocky smile. "Didn't get your fill of muffin with cream tonight?"

He groans low and shakes his head. "I got plenty, but now I need sustenance. You know I don't like mixing my meals with sex. Stop the euphemisms with my food and just say pussy or tits." He shoots me a glare. "And don't do it at the table."

Shrugging one shoulder, I put the truck in reverse and back out of the parking spot. "You could always go for pancakes."

"True," he agrees. "You can't do much damage with those."

"Unless you put a blueberry in the middle and think of it as a nipple."

"Asshole," he grunts and flings his hand across the console to smack my arm. "Fine, I'll order a dinner meal now that you've ruined breakfast."

I laugh as I pull out of the parking lot. "Just don't make it tacos. I've got a million of them for those."

He chuckles, knowing the battle is lost. "Good God, are you ever going to grow up?"

"Not 'til Peter Pan is six feet under."

He rolls his eyes. "Or until you get into Tinkerbell's panties."

My laughter bubbles out of me at the memory. "Been

there, done that. Costume party in college. Believe it or not, she was more tempting than Jessica Rabbit."

"What? Who turns down the bunny?"

"Me," I deadpan. "My brother had already had her."

Half an hour later, we've ordered; Roger settling on a plate of spaghetti with garlic bread – yes, it's an anything/anytime diner – and me having ordered an omelet with a side order of bacon and toast. From the kitchen sounds a loud crash of dishes and a whole lot of swear words. The waitress arrives at our tableside soon after, her chin tucked low as she wrinkles her nose at Roger. "Would you be willing to order something else?"

A hesitant Roger narrows his eyes. "Why?"

"Did you hear that crash in the kitchen?" She winces. Roger nods. "That was your spaghetti and we don't have any more."

So much for me stealing some noodles from his plate and building a model of a string bikini on the table top. My brothers would be so proud. My dad? He'd tuck his chin and hide his chuckle. My mom? I can feel the sting from the snap of the dishtowel. She never missed.

It's all I can do not to laugh. He only ordered spaghetti because of me. He's also an anything/anytime eater. I look to the waitress and order for him, "Bring him steak and eggs, sunny side up. Put it on my bill." She rushes off to put in his order, relieved with a solution to the problem.

I won't mention flat chested women with big nipples, until his plate is on the table in front of him.

Two days later, we're called out to a three-car accident on one of the overpasses on I-17 where we find two slightly crumpled vehicles containing five victims, all being tended to by EMS. Our concern is the third vehicle – a good portion of which is hanging over the edge of the bridge after crashing through the guardrail – the weight of the engine being its greatest enemy. Screams can be heard from inside the vehicle as well as a baby's cry.

"We gotta get the cable on that back axle!" the chief hollers. "Get those cars moved and get that tow truck over here, now!"

There is traffic backed up across three lanes, mostly due to the ever curious rubberneckers, and the truck with the steel cable cannot get close enough. It sits in the emergency lane on the inside of the interstate while the cars sit bumper-to-bumper. Roger and I look to each other, Boonie and Vic right beside us.

"If they ain't gonna move, we move 'em," I growl as I head toward the stalled cars. "They don't need those bumpers to drive."

"Let's do it," Roger says as he storms beside me toward the vehicles.

Tanner Carson and Mike Carny, as well as multiple other uniforms are doing their best to direct the drivers to move into the emergency lane in order to make room for the truck to get to the other side, but there's always that one asshole. The BMW driver refuses to inch forward in order for the car behind him to get over far enough to move into the emergency lane. There is more than half a car length between him and the car in front of him; enough to make all the difference in the world.

"Turn it into the emergency lane!" I yell as I reach the side of his car. His windows are up, doors locked, but I know he can hear every word. "Move the car!"

"No!" He stares straight ahead, holding fast to the steering wheel with a tight grip. "There's not enough room!"

I pull the window breaker from the pocket of my coat and without hesitation smash it into the driver's side rear window.

The glass breaks into the expected shatter pattern and I smash it once more until it collapses and I'm able to pull a few sections out. Reaching inside toward the front seat, I grab a handful of hair and give it a good yank. "Open your fucking door, now!"

It works. The driver's door is open in no time. I use the cutter from the tool to slice through his seat belt, then pull him from the car and drop him onto the ground. I don't think I step on him to get into the car – can't say as I much care. I put it in gear and drive it over the emergency lane and into the median. Had he done what he should have, the underbody would be intact. As it is . . .

It leaves room for just enough cars to be rerouted from three lanes in order to let the cable truck through to where he needs to be. One asshole is all it takes to make the difference between life and death.

Fortunately for this particular asshole, the cables are attached in time and the car does not plunge over the edge onto the highway below. Mom and baby are saved, though not unscathed. Thank God for child seats and seat belts – not to mention people that actually utilize them.

Once the rescue is complete and the ambulances have been loaded, the traffic is starting to flow slowly. As we're loading up, the chief approaches.

"Didn't see a thing," he mumbles, then grabs my coat sleeve and slides it up. "Get your ass to the hospital and get that arm looked at. You need stitches."

I raise my hand to see the torn, blood stained sleeve as well as bright red blood still dripping from underneath. Huh. Hadn't felt a thing. Come to think of it, the lower half of my arm does seem to be a little numb.

"Hazard of the job, I guess," I say casually. "Probably bumped it on something."

His brow arches and he narrows eyes. "Yeah, I see it all the time. Maybe a car window."

My lips tip in a smirk. "That is what we were working with."

"Don't make it a habit, Callahan," he warns. "I'm letting it go because of the circumstances. Mr. BMW is probably a lawyer. Get outta here before he can ID you. As it is, we can all play stupid."

"Only play?" I grin cockily.

He scowls before a devilish smirk crosses his mouth. "You just got yourself cooking duty for three shifts. Get your ass to the hospital and get that arm checked."

"But . . ."

"Better buy yourself a recipe book, Callahan. Maybe call your mama to see if she has any suggestions. Texas chili sounds good for a start." He ignores any protestations he knows are on the tip of my tongue as he flags down an EMS worker near the last, and empty ambulance. "Got one more for you. Take him to Banner. He's one of ours."

"I can drive over from the station once we get back, Chief," I grumble.

The stern eyebrow he lifts and tone of his voice leave no room for misinterpretation. "I don't believe I stuttered, Callahan. Get on the bus."

I reluctantly saunter toward the ambulance, my boots scuffing heavily on the concrete below them. The outer edges of my vision start to darken and my head feels lighter the farther I walk. It's the adrenaline wearing off, I'm sure of it. I begin to shed my bunker coat that is starting to feel a lot heavier than it did five minutes ago, and the torn sleeve sticks to my arm. Pain shoots up to my shoulder in the most excruciating way and nearly makes my knees buckle.

"Holy shit," Roger's murmur echoes in my ear as he grabs me under my shoulders from behind to keep me on my feet. "What the hell did you do, Reece?"

Chapter 4

Mallory

"Tompkins." Dr. Evans' deep, gruff voice from the doorway makes me jump as I'm scrubbing in at the sink outside OR-3 to prepare for a cholecystectomy. "I need you in OR-2."

He steps beside me at the neighboring sink to start scrubbing in. "Who's in on this one? I've been on the roster since yesterday."

"Not your problem," he replies tersely. "I already notified Hawkins. You're with me in 2. Move it."

I'd toss him a salute if my hands weren't already sterile

and the room entrance weren't feet away. Geez, doc, a please and thank you now and then is not going to ruin your reputation. Oh wait, yes it would. You're the Grinch who stole Christmas . . . and Thanksgiving and Halloween and, you get my drift. I've worked with the man for nearly a year now, and while his bark is worse than his bite, I would be hesitant to give him mouth-to-mouth for fear of losing half my face.

Elbows bent and hands in the air, I enter OR-2, butt first, so the attending nurse can place my mask, gown, and gloves.

"You're gonna love this one," she whispers as she works the gloves onto my hands. "Every nurse in the ER has been vying to jump his bones for years. Firefighter, Reece Callahan. Wouldn't mind taking him for a ride myself." She winks and bobs her eyebrows.

"Trish," I scold and crinkle my nose, not that she can see it as the mask went on first. "Aren't you married?"

She snort laughs. "I didn't say I would, I said I wouldn't mind."

"Do the numbers, Tompkins," Evans calls from the doorway where Trish is now gowning and gloving him, as I stand at the end of the bed to check the chart for procedure, weight, and to double check for allergies. Evans is ortho. It could be any number of procedures he's performing. He knows I'm already on it – determining the dosage of propofol as he speaks.

Yeah, doc, like I'm going to inject the patient willy nilly and guestimate the drug dosage.

"Mr. Callahan, do you have any allergies?" I ask the still alert yet tranquil patient whose right arm is laid out on an operating table extension, draped with a surgical wrap, awaiting the skillful hands of the surgeon. It's a habit of mine. Always be thorough; double check on the off chance he'd forgotten any on intake. The patient has been given Midazolam to relax, but he seems pretty coherent.

He takes in a deep breath and blows it out slowly. There's a hint of remorse in his sigh, soon replaced with stubbornness. "Yeah, stupid people."

I make my way to the head of the bed and lean over him. "They have a tendency to give me hives, too. But I'm actually asking about anything that might be detrimental to your health if I shoot it into your blood stream."

"Wow, you got gorgeous eyes," he says with a dopey grin and a southern accent. "Do I know you?"

"If you knew me, you wouldn't have to ask." I pat his uninjured, and very muscly arm. "Now tell me if you have any allergies."

"Damn, baby," he mutters. "Kiss me and I'll tell you anything you want to know. I'd whisper sweet things in your ear that . . ."

"I think we're good here," Evans growls while Dr. Hayes, the anesthesiologist, snickers as he double checks my measurements and timing estimates.

"Good work, Mallory," Hayes commends me as he picks up the syringe and hands it to me. "Would you like to talk him down?"

"I can do that." I redirect my attention to the patient and slowly inject the propofol into the IV. "Mr. Callahan, would you count backwards from a hundred for me, please?"

He winks before he starts, never taking his icy blue eyes off mine. "100, 99, 98, 97, 96, 95, 94, 93, I think . . . I'm . . . in . . . lo . . ." His eyes roll as if he's fighting sleep and I carefully close them and place the tape with Vaseline over them to keep them moist.

"Let's roll, people," Dr. Evans snaps as he removes the drape from the patient's extended right arm. "We've got tendon repair to do."

"Seems you have an admirer, Mallory." Dr. Hayes chuckles as he monitors vitals on each screen.

"What else is new?" Evans grumbles as he begins to carefully remove the shards of glass and repair the damage. "That's why I use her in my OR. She's a good distraction for the patients."

That pisses me off. I'd like to think I'm in this OR because I'm good at what I do. I never wear makeup to work. My hair is always tied up and covered in a cap. Perfume is an absolute no-no. It's not like scrubs are flattering – more like flattening. Can't tell whether or not we have boobs under these gowns. Not that it matters. I'm here to do a job, and I do it well. If a patient tells me I'm pretty or compliments me, it's not my fault. But Evans is an insolent asshole.

The gash is nasty with one large and multiple small thick shards of glass embedded deep within the wound and the muscle. The tendon is damaged; requiring Prolene sutures to tack the tears.

Surgery lasts approximately an hour and a half. Evans places the final sutures to the top layer of the skin, applies glue to the more vulnerable areas for extra stability, and bandages the entire forearm carefully. "We're done. Take him to recovery and I'll check on him after my next surgery. Tompkins, monitor him for pain control when he wakes up."

As if I don't know my job.

I follow Evans out of the OR and toss my gown in the same bin he does his, as well as throw my mask and gloves in the hazardous waste bin.

"You use me as a distraction for your patients?" I huff, resisting the temptation to slap him. "Could you have been anymore insulting? I'm damn good at what I do, Dr. Evans, and if that isn't the merit you *use* me for, then use somebody else."

He looks as if I've slapped. *Damn! Too bad I wasted the opportunity.* He shrugs. "I didn't say you weren't good at your job. I implied you added a little something extra to it."

"No you didn't! You said I was a distraction!"

"Which is good for the patients' anxiety," he says casually. "It keeps their attention away from what's going on."

"That's not what it sounded like."

"Hang on," he says, holding up a finger as he steps toward the OR door and cracks it open, poking his head through. "People, Mallory Tompkins is also an excellent nurse anesthetist." He turns back to me and smirks. "Better?"

My narrowed eyes follow him as he saunters to the exit door, shooting daggers with his every step. "Mallory," he pitches with a lilt before turning back with a grin. "Those *gorgeous* eyes look better when they're wide open."

I clench my fists as the door swings on its hinges. "And yours would look better black and blue, asshole."

"I heard that, Tompkins."

"Anybody know how it happened?" I ask upon entering the recovery room.

"Story has it they were doing a rescue on I-17," Trish offers. "*Gossip* has it he put his arm through a car window to yank a driver out." She smirks. "Because he wouldn't move his car out of the way to let the tow truck through to hook up the cable to keep another car from going over the bridge."

I stare at the slowly waking Mr. Callahan. My shocked and wide eyes must say it all. "That's what he meant by stupid people."

"Saved a woman and her baby today. If I were you," she nudges my arm and winks, "I'd let him tell me anything and whisper those sweet things in my . . ."

"Stop," I scold her before I step to the left side of the bed where all the IVs are located. "How is your pain, Mr. Callahan?"

He rolls his head to the side to see who's asking and his lips tip in that same dopey grin he had in the OR. "There she is," he says dreamily, lifting his left hand to reach out and take mine. It's not uncommon for a patient to do – sometimes for comfort, sometimes simply for reassurance. I place my hand in his and he tugs a little harder as if to beckon me closer to tell me something.

"I'm highly trained in CPR," he utters once I'm close enough. "One kiss, Sugar, and I could resuscitate you."

As I attempt to remove my hand from his, I inform him, jokingly – sort of, "And I could *de*suscitate you in thirty seconds or less. Behave yourself."

He grips my hand a little tighter, his sleepy eyes twinkling with mischief. "Would you do it by sittin' on my face? I'd die a happy man."

Three peals of laughter fill the room because, you know – that's how many attendants are in here, and they've heard every word.

I've been openly hit on, discreetly flirted with, propositioned – Dr. Eric Hanson, head of radiology, being rather persistent in his pursuit – but I will admit none of them have made me laugh like this guy does. Even in his half sedated state, he is gorgeous. Like a sleepy Adonis. The kind that rolls over in bed and makes you forget all about brushing your teeth before you repeat the prior night's activities. Solid pecs and ripped arms. Thick lashes women willingly pay for, icy blue eyes that dance with mischief despite his dopey condition, and a level ten grin that probably drops panties everywhere he goes. At least according to the smut books on my shelf. I'm an avid reader; not so much a participant.

"Pain level, Mr. Callahan," I repeat, ignoring the snickers

in the room. "Zero to ten. What would you rate it?"

"If I said ten, would you kiss it and make it better?" he drawls, Texas style.

"No," I deadpan.

He breathes a resigned sigh and slowly blinks those extremely thick lashes. "I'm good. It was so worth it. Bet he listens next time." He chuckles and releases a few coughs. That's what we need – clear lungs. I slowly raise the bed a few more inches to encourage deeper breathing.

I nod at Trish as I reach for the curtain to leave. "Looks good. Evans will be down as soon as he's done in surgery. Page me if you need anything. You can move him to a transition room. Not sure if Evans will want to keep him overnight."

"His partner, Roger, is waiting for him," she says, grinning. "He won't have to wait alone."

My brows lift in surprise, and a bit of disappointment. It never fails – always the handsome ones. I've just been played. "His partner?"

She giggles and her face lights in amusement. "Aha! I knew he got to you. His station partner, honey. Both straight as an arrow. The ER nurses call them Rough and Ready. If you ever feel the heat rising or detect the strong scent of testosterone from the ground floor, you can bet they're in the building."

Behind us, Mr. Callahan's groggy low voice indicates he's fighting sleep as he asks the nurse, "What's her name?"

Rory is at his bedside adjusting the IV tubes before transport, and chuckles. "That's Mallory."

Mr. Callahan waggles his weak good finger at Rory as he narrows his already droopy eyes, seemingly deep in thought. "I've kissed her before."

Rory glances at me, his brow arched in curiosity.

I shake my head, roll my eyes, and mouth, "Propofol."

"Ah," he returns with a laugh. "The drug that dreams are made from."

Waving my hand in dismissal before sliding the curtain open, I bid them farewell. "See you guys later."

Chapter 5

Reece

"Go find her," I beg of Roger as he sits at my bedside. It's more of a cushioned cot – on wheels – in the curtained off cubby they put me in after surgery. I'm waiting for the surgeon to hopefully release me to go home. I want my orthopedic mattress or my recliner. "Her name is Mallory. I know her from somewhere."

He snorts. "Pretty sure you've entertained at least one Mallory along the way, Reece. What difference does it make? You don't do repeats."

"I'm afraid she's Karma come to bite me in the ass for all my one-night stands," I grumble, fighting sleep as my eyelids grow heavy once more. I refrain from confessing the jumpstart she gave my heart in the operating room with only her eyes between her mask and cap. And her hand on my arm? Electric. When I saw her whole face in recovery – the pert nose, the porcelain skin, the kissable lips – I was dumbstruck by her beauty. But those eyes. They were like a trip back in time, though I couldn't figure out to where or when.

Roger smirks. "Karma by the name of Mallory. You can check your ass cheeks for that bite mark another day. Lay your head back and get some sleep, dumbass."

"What if I don't remember her when I wake up?" *My biggest fear. Apparently it's happened once already. I'm good with faces; names, not so much. A little more time and a lot more visual and I'm sure I would remember. She was sassy. God, I love a sassy woman. I'll take that bite in the ass, so long as she lets me nip hers.*

He looks at me as if what I've said is the most ludicrous thing he's ever heard. "As if that's anything new, Reece. Could have been a one-nighter where you failed to impress, or she would have remembered you. Probably a fantasy. Go to sleep."

My head spins as I try to tip my chin indignantly. "I've never failed to impress. She is a fantasy, Roger." I put full effort into shifting on the bed to face him. "You gotta see her. She has these silver eyes that you'll never forget and these pillowy lips that you just want to . . ."

"Reece," he growls in warning.

"What?"

"I'm gonna put a pillow over your face if you don't shut up and go back to sleep. I gotta take care of your sorry ass until we figure out who can do it while I go back to work." He shakes his head and swipes his hands down his face. "I'll wake you when the surgeon gets here."

"I fucked up today, didn't I?" I lay my head on the pillow once again and stare at the ceiling.

"Yeah, right," he snaps back. "I'll take you over to Abrazo to visit the woman and her kid so you can tell them they weren't worth saving. How's that, idiot?"

"They going to be okay?" I glance in his direction and see him grin.

"They're going to be fine." His grin turns devilish. "Seems there's some asshole on social media who was crying about being assaulted and his fancy car being destroyed by a rescue worker. Didn't take long for a whole lot of people to destroy his version of the story and volunteered to show up in court on behalf of said rescue worker should he decide to pursue any charges." He nods in reassurance. "Gotta love social media. Now lay your head back and get some rest."

My eyes close as I think of this afternoon and all that happened. Mom and baby are okay. That, in itself, is peace of mind. My eyes don't open again until I feel Roger's hand on my shoulder and hear his voice alerting me to the surgeon's presence. I find not only the surgeon in the room, but Wiley and John, two of our building buddies, in the room as well.

These guys are some of the reasons I don't miss home as much as I was afraid I might. We're like family. John and Wiley are a bit older – okay, a lot older – but we all blend well. Tanner Carson is the other misfit of the group. A cop.

"Where's Mallory?" I ask Dr. Evans after he's checked me over and given me stern discharge instructions and told me the nurse will be in with the paperwork.

His eyes narrow and he folds his arms over his chest. "Her job with you ended with pain management. Follow up with me in two weeks in my office and we'll see if you need any physical therapy."

"B-but," I stammer, searching for an excuse to see her again. "I wanted to thank her. She was, she was . . . just so. . ."

He smirks and arches a brow. "Mmhmm. She's that way

with everybody. I'll be sure to extend your gratitude. See you in two weeks, Mr. Callahan."

"Prick," I utter after the curtain slides closed.

"I heard that," he says cockily from the other side.

I hold up the only middle finger that is functional at the present time. "Can you see this?" I grunt as my cohorts snicker.

"My imagination serves me well, Mr. Callahan. Just don't try it with the right hand," he warns with an air of arrogance I'd like to deflate. "I'd hate to have to patch you up again. Good evening, gentlemen."

"Damn, Reece," Wiley whispers. "You can't talk to your surgeon like that. He's the guy holding the scalpel."

"Not anymore. I only gotta see him for follow-up." I scowl, staring at the closed curtain, willing it to open so I can see the face that has my insides churning and my brain scrambling for a memory. If I had had that woman in bed, pretty sure I would have never forgotten her, because I would have gone back for seconds, and thirds, and . . .

"Who's Mallory?" John asks.

"Apparently a new conquest." Roger rolls his eyes. "Though I will admit, this is a new low for Reece. On the table, about to go under the knife, and he was still thinking with his dick. Probably went to sleep with a hard-on."

"I was on my back! I couldn't even see her tits and ass!" I defend myself through gritted teeth.

Roger snorts then mocks my earlier description, "No, it was her *pillowy lips*. One can only imagine where you were picturing those."

John and Wiley enjoy a laugh at my expense while I glare at Roger. "Asshole."

The nurse arrives with my discharge papers and written instructions shortly after they've finished their ribbing session over my *obsession* with the unforgettable nurse, and has me clumsily sign here/sign there with my left hand. As I do, it occurs to me I'll be wiping my ass with my left hand as well. *Sonofabitch.*

She then helps me with my clothes. My button down shirt accommodates one arm, while the sleeve on the other side hangs freely. Roger also brought me sweats and sneakers from home. With the sling my arm is in, this is as good as it gets for a while. I'll go shirtless at home. It's Arizona, for crying out loud.

"Is Mallory still here?" I ask the discharge nurse, hopeful the dicky doctor was being just that; a dick. In my periphery I see Roger roll his eyes.

The nurse ducks her head around the edge of the curtain and calls out, "Hey, Mal. Got somebody asking for you."

My heart races as the sound of jingling keys grows louder and the curtain flies open. "Oh yeah? Whatcha need, big guy?"

In the opening stands a woman, approximate age of fifty or so, approximate weight of two-fifty or so, and a ruby red stained smile that is pleasant, but definitely not the one I'm seeking.

Wiley sputters openly behind me but tries to hide it with a cough. *Choke on it, asshole.* Roger drops his head so low, I'd swear it's between his knees. John has the dignity of a gentleman and simply stands stalk still. His girlfriend, Ava Mynx, would kill him for anything less. She's an erotica writer – includes various body types and sizes in her books.

Think fast, Reece.

"Uh . . ." I stammer, "are you the one that brought me a juice earlier?"

"No," she says slowly. "But I can get you one if you want. What flavor?"

"Um . . ." I twist my mouth to the side as if pondering my choices. It's not her fault she isn't the Mallory of my dreams. And she is really pleasant.

"Prune," Roger tells her, then flashes me a wry look and utters, "That is what you drink when you're full of shit, isn't it?"

"You got it. I'll be right back, handsome." She winks and slides the curtain closed once more.

"You motherfucker," I mutter to a grinning Roger.

He shrugs. "Might as well get a head start. Those pain pills wreak havoc on the colon, my friend."

"He's not kidding," Wiley starts with a groan. "Back when I had my . . ."

"Shut up, Wiley," we say in unison.

I gag down a sip of juice and thank the nurse, wait for her to exit the room, then toss the rest into the trash. "Can we get the hell out of here?"

Reluctantly, I take a seat in the wheelchair, knowing it's the only way I'm allowed to leave, due to protocol. Once out of the elevator on the ground floor leading to the ER exit, I stand to my feet, and my shirt falls off my shoulder. "I am not being wheeled through there like an invalid. I can walk."

"Reece, you know the . . ." Roger falls silent with my glare. "Fine," he groans and waves his hand, leaving the chair with the nurse. "He's a stubborn ass. I'll make sure he gets out okay."

Wolf whistles follow me as I head for the automatic doors. On any other given day I would play along, give as good as I got, charm the panties off of them. But my mood is foul, I feel like crap, and now I can't even have a beer due to the pain medications I'm stuck with for a few days. All that and I still can't get her out of my head. I don't play where I work. We're not in the hospitals often – only on emergency calls that

BUT I KISSED A COWBOY

require the extra manpower – but the one thing I never do is mix work with pleasure. I may flirt and enjoy the banter, but it ends at the door – *the exit door*.

With that being said, *where the hell do I know her from?*

"I prefer this over your fireman's gear, Reece," Tara teases on my way through. "Less to get off when you're in a hurry."

"I've always wondered what was under that gear," another adds.

"If you need a home nurse, I'm your girl," Alecia calls out. "I'm really good at sponge baths."

"Gray sweats," another singsongs. "My every dream come true. Turn around one more time. Maybe jiggle those hips a little."

"Get me outta here," I snarl at Roger once out the doors on the way to the parking lot.

"Feeling a little naked, are we?" He laughs as he spins his keys on his finger.

John and Wiley walk behind us. "Is it always like that?" Wiley asks.

"Never a dull moment," Roger quips.

"Damn, I chose the wrong profession," Wiley acquiesces. "Think it's too late for me to switch?"

"Wiley," Roger spins and walks backward, not missing a step. "You need that hedge fund manager job. You got three ex-wives. You couldn't afford to be a firefighter. You'd be living in a cardboard box under a bridge somewhere."

"Yeah, but I'd be getting the ladies."

Roger spins back, continuing his forward trek with a quiet chuckle. "Do you wanna tell him?"

"Never kick a man when he's down, Roger." I laugh for the first time today. It's not Wiley's fault. He's not a bad looking guy, but how many women want to live with a man who can fart the alphabet song without missing a beat, drinks his soup from a bowl because it takes too long to use a spoon, and once tried to buy firewood for a camping trip from the Tinder app? He honest to God googled campfire supplies and was advised to use 'tinder' as the best fire starter, followed by two-foot logs to keep the fire burning in a manageable fashion. Never go on a dating site and request 24-inch wood. I think he's scarred for life. Maybe even intimidated a little.

Three wives, people. Roger was not kidding.

Chapter 6

Mallory

"Tompkins!" Evans catches me five seconds before I push the bar on the exit door to the employee parking lot.

Damnit! I was so close. I wonder if I could pretend I didn't hear him and make a run for it.

Squaring my shoulders before I turn around, I take a deep breath and spin to face the culprit who has disrupted my leave. "Yes, Dr. Evans."

"A word," he demands.

Oh the possibilities.

"Did you have a particular one in mind or am I supposed

to choose?" Yeah, I know, I'm probably poking the bear, but I'm hungry, tired, in need of a hot bath, a tall glass of red, and a good dose of Ava Mynx – my favorite smut writer.

He takes the final steps that he thinks gives him the intimidating stature he's going for: a head taller, arms folded over a well-defined muscled chest, narrowed eyes, shadow cast over me under the fluorescent lights above, sexy cologne within whiffing distance, five o'clock shadow that some women find attractive. Sorry, doc, I like a mix of soft and scruffy. Not a fan of whisker burn, visible or otherwise.

Don't speak, Mallory. First one to open their mouth loses the battle.

"How did he get your name, Mallory?"

My nose scrunches in confusion. "What? Who?"

He smirks. "Your adoring hero firefighter."

"I didn't give it to him. One of the recovery nurses did. And even if I had, what difference does it make to you?"

"He's your patient."

"Not anymore," I protest. "He's yours. There's no ongoing treatment. I was attending in the OR, by your demand, I might add." I tip my chin in defiance. "During which time you went out of your way to insult me."

"It was a compliment," he scoldingly reminds me. "Something which you apparently don't know how to take. Unless, of course, it's your gorgeous eyes."

"I don't need compliments, Dr. Evans, offhanded or not." I grin wryly. "I need for the patients to survive whatever it is I'm shooting into their veins."

His expression softens and he shakes his head. "You have no idea what you do for those patients, do you? The eye contact, the human touch, your voice, your humor, the reassurance. Most patients don't even know who's putting them to sleep. But you," he chuckles, "you go out of your way to make them comfortable."

Do not cry, Mallory. It was a long time ago.

My eyes drop to his chest. "They're scared, even if they don't know it."

He tips my chin with two fingers. "No more offhanded compliments. I wish I had a hundred more just like you, Tompkins. Mr. Callahan wanted to express his gratitude, but I told him I would do it for him. Go home, get some rest."

"Gratitude for what? I was just doing my job."

He taps the tip of my nose with his index finger. "Exactly." He turns to walk away; the classic saunter that is his and his alone with every step. "Pretty sure those *gorgeous* eyes may have had something to do with it, too. If having you in my OR weren't my top priority, I'd ask you out myself, but I don't need the distraction. Watch out for him, Tompkins, he's a player."

Thanks, doc. As if his offer of a seat on his face wouldn't have clued me in. A very comfy looking seat, I might add. The finely groomed facial hair with a perfect balance of soft and scruffy. Worse yet, vaguely familiar eyes that I cannot place, and an easy smile that I wish I could. He told Rory he'd kissed me before. No, Mr. Callahan, if you had kissed me, I'm pretty sure I'd remember it.

Whoa, whoa, wait a minute. Did Evans just say . . .

"So, we meet again." The velvety smooth voice of Dr. Eric Hanson sounds close to my ear before I can get out the door.

Speaking of players. Head of radiology, doctor from the bar the night Liberty met Michael. Of all the nerve! Testing my integrity by pretending he wanted me to participate in a menage a ` trois? Well, I've heard all about Dr. Hanson's *legacy*. Seems he's held in high regard by all of his colleagues. He's also held in high regard by all the lady leagues. Word has it he also scores pretty high with them.

My life as the product of a broken home may leave me single forever, but I will never settle for a cheater. Nor will I settle as second best to a goodwill dick. Be charitable with your assets, not your appendage. I will either be my husband's top priority – only sharing a spot with our children in our white picket fence-happy home – or I will end up a spinster. Better a spinster than the cellmate of a mutual murderer. A strong, independent, but unwounded spinster. Might have to home a few cats . . . maybe a rottweiler or two. Possibly even a horse. . . you know, to ride off into that sunset.

"Join me for a drink?" he whispers in my ear, reaching around me to open the door to the lot, his chest brushing my back as he does. "I'll even buy you dinner. If you're a good girl, who knows where it could lead."

"It's not leading anywhere, Dr. Hanson." I push the door hard so it flies out of his control, and step through to the other side. "I don't do doubles. I would rather pleasure myself than waste my time with someone who has an iffy stiffy."

He gently grasps my bicep to halt my footsteps and turns me toward him. His eyes are heated but there's a flare of mischief as he growls, "You wouldn't know pleasure if it bit you on the ass, little girl. Give me one night and I'll show you pleasure beyond your wildest dreams. Just so you know, the only doubles I've ever done are coming twice before I pull out, and the only *iffy* you need to worry about is how much of me you can take and how many orgasms you could tolerate before you beg for mercy."

Bit me on the ass? Little girl? Somehow those phrases sound sexier in Ava Mynx's books. Right now it simply sounds . . . condescending.

At the slightest tug of my arm from his grasp, he releases it immediately. "You know, I like a confident man," I say casually, "but I can't stand an egotistical one. Good night, Dr. Hanson."

"Mallory, wait," he says, then dips his chin and shakes his head. "Maybe I went about this the wrong way. I thought..."

"No, you didn't think," I interrupt him. "Had you thought at all, you might have aimed for my appetite instead of my ass. I am hungry, but I'm going home to eat. Again, good night, Dr. Hanson."

"It's Eric."

"Really?" I feign surprise, eyeing him from his head to his toes, then shrug. "I would have guessed asshole."

He pinches the bridge of his nose and chuckles. "And you would be right, but it's a temporary condition. Give me a chance, I'll work on it."

"You're a doctor." I grin wryly. "Try curing it instead. Did your little sister appreciate her Gucci purse?"

He narrows his eyes. "She wanted Chanel."

"And?"

"It goes wherever she goes," he grumbles.

I nod slowly. "Good boy. Did you tell her why you bought it?"

"Of course not, but it serves as my reminder whenever I see the damn thing." He huffs in frustration. "It's been over a year ago, Mallory. Are you going to have dinner with me?"

"Nope," I tell him. "I'm going home for a hot bath, red wine, and Thai food."

"I have all of those things at my place," he offers, then flashes a sexy smile and winks. "I could even toss in some bubbles, scrub your back..."

So much for working on it.

"Did you ever take your mother for Sunday brunch?"

He blows an exasperated sigh and rolls his neck. "Yes, Mallory."

"Good for you." I smirk before turning toward the parking lot. "Try a Sunday service this weekend. Might want to sit in the back though. Quick exit in case you burst into flames. Save the congregation and all. Goodnight, Dr. Hanson."

"I haven't been in a church since the last wedding I attended!" he shouts after me, as if the very thought is unthinkable.

I turn slowly and smile cockily. "How many bridesmaids did you entertain before the reception was over?"

He stares at me, jaw set hard as it tics, gearing up for a smartass retort. I give him a moment before breaking the silence. "Still counting or reminiscing?"

"I said I was working on it," he grumbles.

"They have confessionals in those churches too," I say lightly. "I'd pass on dipping your fingers into the holy water if I were you. I hear the sizzle can draw unwanted attention."

His lips tip as if he can't help it and he slowly shakes his head as his eyes study mine. "I've never had to fight for it, Mallory. I'm up for the challenge. I wouldn't be this persistent if I didn't like you."

Flashing him my best snarky grin, I fire off one last retort, "And I wouldn't be this *re*sistant if I did like you."

I didn't say it to challenge him, but he must take it as one, because before I know it his hand is in my hair and his mouth is on mine in one searing kiss I didn't see coming. To say the least, I'm startled. But unfortunately, I'm also . . . stimulated. The man is good with his mouth. I fall into the kiss as if it's second nature and give as good as I get. He moans as if he's tasted a delicacy, then dives in for one more taste as our lips part a millimeter or two. My breaths are shuddered as he draws back, his hand in my hair, and studies my face, then smiles cockily.

"But you don't hate me. It's a start." He winks, then pulls

his keys from his pocket and turns for his own car. "Goodnight, Mallory."

Chapter 7

Reece

"What are you doing here, Callahan? You haven't been released for duty." The chief doesn't bother to raise his head to see me poking mine in the door of his office. I swear he's memorized the sound of my footsteps. "You've got two more weeks."

"I can't take it anymore, Chief." My voice is near pleading and I'm ready to drop to my knees and beg if I have to. It's my sixth trip to the station in two weeks. My theory is if I make him sick of dealing with me, he'll just let me stay and ignore my presence. "I'm going crazy at home. Let me get two of my shifts of cooking out of the way. I'll make your favorites. I'll do paperwork. I'll hose down the floors. I'll – I'll do the . . ."

My offers are met with a slow headshake and raised bushy eyebrows. "Nope." He stands and crosses his arms over his chest and takes a few steps toward me as if to walk me out the doors of the station . . . backwards.

"Can I sit in the breakroom and do crosswords, sudoku, solitaire?" I beg, taking a backwards step with every one he takes forward. "I'll even do word search puzzles, improve my vocabulary."

I am not a sit at home kind of guy. It's been four weeks now and I am going batshit crazy. The guys visit sporadically, Ava and Shelley have cooked some meals for me, out of pity I'm sure. But it's involuntary confinement; a bit like a jail cell. I need structure, direction, and until Dr. Dick has released me, and my arm is at full strength, I'm stuck. Sex doesn't even sound inviting. I'm kind of an all-in, full force type, and until I get her face out of my head, it wouldn't be right to pretend with other women. Total lie. I have no interest in other women. Taking care of business in the shower with my left hand is bad enough.

I swear if the chief doesn't let out the laugh he's holding back, he's going to release it in a blast of noxious gas while lying in his bunk later tonight. He'll probably blame me for that too, and I haven't even fixed my Texas chili for the crew! I'll give him credit though. He stood behind my actions at the accident scene. It's not like we could have picked the car up and moved it, but it didn't make him any less angry about being down a man at the firehouse. It also lessens our chances of the yearly award for least amount of job injuries in our district.

"Two more weeks, Callahan. Got it on paper in my office. And that's only if you're released." He smirks. "It's called following the rules."

He's goading me, testing my temperament, and right now my foot is itching to rise and fall in a stomp of petulance. I feel like I'm getting my ass chewed for breaking my brother's Tonka truck. A very pricey Tonka truck with a label that looks an awful lot like BMW. No charges have been filed and no claims have been made. Word has it the driver was the son of a high profile businessman who didn't want his name smeared. Which would explain the sudden absence of social media whining. Had I been that son, my dad would have seen to it I'd be a pedestrian and user of public transportation for a year after an incident like that.

Drinking and driving? Reckless behind the wheel? More than ten miles over the speed limit? Being stupid and not obeying the law? We had one warning: *"You see them boots on your feet, son? They were made for walkin'. And that's exactly what you'll be doin', right after you get done cleanin' up horseshit, balin' hay, and polishin' saddles. Understand?"*

It was said with love, and a strong determination to teach us right from wrong. If we were going to drink, it was to be done around a campfire on the ranch. If we wanted speed, ride a horse. And women? *"If you're gonna tap it, you'd better wrap it. 'Cause otherwise, you're gonna marry it."*

Dad didn't just put the fear of God in us; he dished out reality. Happiest guy I know; strong credit given to my mom.

"Why don't you make a trip home while you have the time?" the chief suggests. "Get a few of those Texas recipes from your mama while you're there." He snickers. "You're not getting out of cooking, Callahan. You're going to need them when you get back."

It has been a while since I've been home. I'm doing independent PT with simple band stretches now. My final appointment is in twelve days. Dr. Dick barely spoke to me when I saw him in follow-up. Made me sit in his waiting room for forty-five minutes, only to then sit in the exam room for another ten while his nurse flirted with me as she removed the bandage. Ten minutes later, he honored me with his presence for all of two minutes with a poke and a prod and said, "Looks good. I'll see you in three weeks. Schedule on your way out."

"That's it?!" I'd asked, irritated and . . . oh, who am I kidding? I was pissed. He'd made me wait for over an hour for two minutes of his time.

The asshole smirked with his parting remark, "We pricks are efficient, Mr. Callahan."

Geez, grudge much, doc? Maybe Wiley did have a point. I should have waited ten more seconds.

"Can I travel while I'm on medical leave?"

Chief pierces me with a scowl that would melt Satan's toes. "You're traveling right now, Reece. In dangerous territory because you're driving me nuts. Show up here again before you're released for duty, and I might inflict an injury that keeps you out for another six weeks." He narrows his eyes and inclines his chin. "Picture my boot up your ass."

Rather than call one of my brothers to pick me up at the airport in Dallas, I rent a pickup and make the drive north to Denton. Totally unnecessary, as there are half a dozen available for use at the ranch at any given time, but I wanted my visit to be a surprise. The air is cleaner once out of the city. Still hot as hell, but it's not Phoenix, and the closer I get to home the more open the view becomes.

River and Ryder are the first to see the truck pull in the long gravel driveway at ten in the morning. I've been kicking up dust under the tires for the last mile, so I'm sure they've been keenly watching to see who the visitor is. I purposely slam the brakes a little hard so the dust flies heavy through the air as I come to a stop only yards from the first barn where they both stand.

"What in the holy hell!" River shouts as they both head in my direction at a fast pace, not appreciating the reckless arrival of whoever is behind the wheel.

"Hang on," Ryder grabs River's shirt sleeve on the way. "There's only one little pissant I know of would try that shit." He yells back toward the barn, "Ronan, Reid, we got us an ass to whoop! Better call Russ. He won't want to miss this."

I laugh to myself as I watch the dust begin to settle when the door of the truck is suddenly yanked open and River is pulling me from my seat. "Whoa, whoa, take it easy," I caution him as I shield my right arm. It's mobile, healing well, feels good, but still in the sling for protection and to prevent me from twisting the forearm.

"What the hell did you do, boy?" Ryder demands, eyeing me cautiously yet taking me in a one-armed hug on the left and tousling my hair in the same irritating way he's done since I was little.

As the other two reach us, they pass out one-armed shoulder hugs and hair tousles at the same time I answer, "A little incident with a car window."

Russ appears behind us, his boots heavy on the gravel, and in his deep rumbling timbre vibrating the mere air around us, "I take it the car won. How you doin' little bro?" He squeezes the back of my neck then pats my shoulder before he leans in and mutters, "Abbie follows social media pretty close. I know damn well that was you due to the call I got. Knock out the whole window next time before you reach in. You shoulda called me. I'd'a been happy to come babysit your ass for a week or two."

I turn to meet his eyes and shoot him a wry look. "I was on pain meds. I couldn't drink."

He grins cockily. "*I* could have."

Six boys in eleven years. Russ is the oldest, the overseer, and probably my favorite. But don't tell the others. Then there's Reid, River, Ryder, Ronan, and me. I'm the baby, and they've never let me forget it. They don't begrudge me leaving, but I sometimes miss the camaraderie that goes with a family business and working together day in and day out. They've never complained of boredom, but I'll never grow bored of the adrenaline rush and satisfaction of making a difference.

Ryder and Ronan are the only ones not married yet – other than yours truly. They share the east wing of the main house. Pretty sure their sloppy seconds have spread to five counties by now. The other three all have houses here on the ranch – spread far enough apart for full privacy and close enough for convenience. The main house is large enough to accommodate every one of them, but mom and dad believed in building a nest, raising the flock, and kicking them out when they were ready to fly. *Their words, not mine.* Ryder and Ronan apparently haven't grown wings yet.

"Reece!" Mom shouts as she rushes across the yard to greet me. She is still as stealthy as she was years ago; hasn't lost a step. Her shoulder length hair may carry more gray highlights, but it only enhances the bright blue in her eyes that she passed on to each of her boys. We all inherited the bump on our noses from Dad as well as the dimples in our cheeks. Our hair color varies from a slight shade of reddish brown to blonde and our body habitus is tall, built like brick shithouses, and muscled.

"Oh no! Reece, what happened to you?" she cries when she sees the sling on my arm. In spite of it, I take her in my arms and squeeze. The one woman in my life that has never asked for more, never demanded what I couldn't give. Only expected my best efforts and accepted the results. She never compared us boys. There was no competition between us. We were brothers, blood, family. And we were expected to support each other in our endeavors, no matter what they were – with the exception of Ryder and Ronan and their sexual exploits.

"I'm fine, mom. Just a little accident," I tell her as I pull back from the hug, but tolerate the virtual pat-down she gives me as she checks my cheeks, neck, shoulders, chest, etc.

Russ squares me a look over her shoulder from behind and rolls his eyes, then grins and mouths, "Mama's boy."

I flip him off with my left finger. "Hey, Russ, could you grab my bag from the back seat and bring it in the house for me?"

He slips by my side and grumbles, "Pansy ass."

"Be nice, bro," I utter back. "I'm wounded."

"That's nothin'. You ain't had my boot up your ass yet," he warns with a chuckle.

Still my favorite. He didn't really mean it.

"Come on inside." Mom wraps her arm around my waist. "I'll fix you a nice lunch and then you can choose your favorite for dinner. It's so good to have you home."

"You got us here all the time!" Ronan whines. "How come I never get to pick no favorites?"

"Because you'll eat anything I put in front of you, Rone." Mom shakes her head against my chest.

"Well, that don't make no sense," he protests.

She halts her footsteps, therefore halting mine in the process, and smirks at him. "Neither does your grammar, but we love you anyway, don't we?"

"It's my Texas drawl, Mama!" He bobs his eyebrows. "The ladies love it."

She arches a brow and dips her chin as they go eye-to-eye – give or take ten inches difference in height. "It's your southern lazy. And it makes you sound stupid. Speak proper English and I'll fix your favorite once a week. Deal?"

He stares as if he's been slapped, before his jaw drops. "Is that why we ain't had no barb ribs and beans for . . ." He clears his throat loudly and swallows hard, looking thoroughly chastised. "I mean, is that why we haven't had barbecued ribs and baked beans for a long time?"

"Who said your daddy and I didn't have them a week ago when you and your brother went into town for the night?" She smiles slyly. "Tell me, Ronan, what did you feast on while you were there?"

Rone looks mortified and ready to cry while the entire circle of our brothers sputter with laughter. Had it come from one of the brothers, he would have elaborated right down to the last lick, tug, and nipple (*whoops*) nibble of everything he feasted on while he was in town. Mom's aren't supposed to know about . . .

"Work on your behavior," Mom tells him, "and I might consider adding in some desserts that are actual food." We turn for the house and she mutters next to me, "I really wish your daddy and I had passed down an ugly gene to a couple of you. Word travels faster than a race horse on a track around here. We're just waiting for that first baby mama to show up at the door. Tell me you'll announce at least a fiancé before a grandchild."

"No foreseeable plans for either, mom." I chuckle and pull her toward the house. "I'm married to my job. One flame burning at a time is plenty."

Though there is one little spitfire I wouldn't mind warming some sheets with.

Turning my thoughts to the man that's missing, I inquire, "Where's dad?"

"Monthly lunch with the guys." She smirks. "Followed by a few hands of poker, I'm sure." She glances out toward the roadway as a dust cloud kicks up in the distance and waits to see the vehicle turn into the long drive. She laughs as we watch dad's pickup make the trek toward the house, then looks to my brothers. "Which one of you contacted your daddy?"

Ronan's eyes twinkle as he grins, proud of himself. "I did. Do you really think he'd rather play poker than see the prodigal son?"

"Hey, Reece!" Reid calls over as we watch the approaching pickup. "Think you can ride with that bum arm? I shoed Lady Luck last week."

My easy smile can't be hidden as I picture riding my favorite, prize winning mare and do a quick calculation in my head. She's nineteen now; a little past prime but still a winner. "Try and keep me off her. Thanks, Reid."

"Did you and dad really have ribs and beans last week?" I murmur to mom, knowing it's not just Ronan's favorite, but everyone else's as well.

"No." She chuckles. "I just love to get under your brother's skin. He can talk all the stupid he wants around those women in town, but I will not tolerate it at home. College educated and he insists on sounding like an idiot. For the life of me, I will never understand why they think it's cute."

"He did call Dad for me," I remind her as the pickup comes to a stop.

She sighs and drops her chin to her chest, shaking her head. "Barbecued ribs with beans it is."

Squeezing her tighter under my left arm as we head back toward the truck, I drop a kiss to the top of her head. "Just put me in the west wing, please."

Dad hops out of the truck as if it takes no effort at all. "Reece! My boy! How the hell are ya?"

It's good to be home.

Chapter 8

Reece

I spend my first night home reacquainting myself with four nephews who are spitting images of their fathers, and three little princesses who all take after their mothers, gorging from a table full of good food. The conversation and the usual rounds of laughter, as well as the never ending questions that go with every visit range from:

"Do you slide down the pole in the fire station?" (Little Rachel)

"Do you get to blow the horn on the firefuck?" (Little Rafe – minus two front teeth)

"Do you carry people down ladders like they do in

movies?" (Little Reagan)

"What month is Roger posing for in the charity calendar this year? I hope it's December. Save the best for last. A Santa hat and nothing . . ." Adult Abbie's teasing statement is halted with a tight growl and a glare from Russ. Someday I'm going to have to bring the live version home with me to meet the fam.

Ronan and Ryder build a fire in the pit after dinner is over. Once the kids have enjoyed their s'mores, Mom and Dad call it a night, and Russ, Reid, and River deliver the kids and their wives back home safe and sound. One pickup returns and three able-bodied men hop out; a pony keg that will be dry within an hour and a couple bottles of whiskey in hand.

"Ryder," Reid orders, "go grab the Solo cups."

"I'm always the errand boy," Ryder complains, but complies as he jumps to his feet and heads for the house. It's all of fifty feet away, the cups are right inside the kitchen in the pantry. However, given the opportunity Ryder will bitch about anything. I truly believe it's a complex he developed as a middle kid. Wants to be sure he's acknowledged for putting in the effort.

Good God, I hope he does better with women. Never rush. A cramp in your tongue is not the end of the world. Staving off your own pleasure to deliver one more for her is an accomplishment; not a punishment.

Halfway back to where we sit, he holds up the cups. "Got 'em."

"Yeah, well, backtrack." Reid points to the sliders that Ryder left open. "Go close the door. You born in a barn?"

"Matter o' fact I was," he says, tossing Reid a cocky grin and Russ the cups. "And seein' a horse's ass like you makes me homesick."

It really is good to be back. Can't say I'm not a little grateful to be in a sling. It keeps me out of the wrestling match that Ryder was begging for and is now taking place between four willing participants while Russ and I enjoy the first of a few beers and a good shot of whiskey, straight from the bottle.

"So, tell us, little bro," River starts once he's caught his breath and sat back down, "what did you do to that arm?"

I glance at Russ and he arches a brow and rubs a hand over his chin. "'Fess up. I'd kinda like to hear the whole story myself."

"Wait a minute!" Reid snaps. "You knew about this?"

"Only what Abbie got from social media and that he was okay. That's all that mattered. I figured when he was ready, he'd tell us his version."

My head whips toward Russ. "How did you know I was okay?"

He smirks and rolls his eyes. Typical Russ. "Who's your emergency contact?"

Oh.

"Hang on!" Ronan protests. "He's your emergency contact? Why not me? He's old!"

Russ sets his eyes on Rone in a heated glare, his voice deep enough to rattle the leaves on trees. "What did you just say?"

"Oh shit," Ryder mutters and tucks his chin.

"I – I meant ol – older. Yeah, definitely old*er*," Ronan stammers, emphasizing the last syllable. "Not – not old, Russ. You know, older than us."

"And wiser," Russ advises stiffly.

"D-d-definitely," Ronan agrees awkwardly, eyes wide as if waiting for the bear to pounce. "You're smarter than any of us, too."

Russ bursts into laughter and lifts his glass. "Now that we

have that cleared up, tell us what happened, Reece."

I explain the circumstances; the urgency of the situation, the stupidity and stubbornness of the driver. I really do believe any of my station mates would have done the same thing – I just happened to be there first. All told, it took me one beer to tell the story, but my brothers have each finished at least two.

"Tendon repair?" Reid furrows his brow. "Not cool, Reece. Russ was in that contraption for weeks and they had to pin him and put screws in the elbow. You can't go doin' that shit."

I wave him off with my uninjured arm. "Mine was nothing like Russ's. He damn near detached his. I didn't do battle with a horse; just a car window." I toss Russ a grin. "Next time I'll be sure to knock out the entire thing before I reach in."

"Still rescuin' those sweet pussies from trees?" Rone asks with a laugh.

"Not too often." Flashing him a cocky smile, I finish, "I prefer rescuing them from bar stools." Her face flits through my mind as I stare at the fire, apparently a little too long as Russ holds a freshly poured brew in front of me that I don't notice until he taps my arm.

"Got one that left a lasting impression?"

"Not from a bar stool," I utter before taking the glass and savoring a long, cold swallow. "A nurse from the OR."

"You tapped a nurse from your operating room?" Ronan howls, holding up a fist to meet mine in victory, as if I could reciprocate. One in a splint and the other holding a glass. "Nice score, bro."

"No, dumbass," I huff indignance, shooting him a look to match . . . twice. "I didn't tap her. I found her fascinating. She was funny and sweet. She put me at ease. The most gorgeous eyes I've ever seen."

"Oh shit, here we go again," Ryder groans, throwing his

head back. "Anybody else gettin' a flashback? It only took him two months to shut up about her eyes."

Ronan joins in quickly. "I remember that. The wet dream from the horsey ride. The brunette with the perky tits." He starts in a mocking tone, "My horse isn't dirty. I'll let you ride up front, little girl."

Ryder smirks. "She came back wearing your hat and you came back wearing a shit eating grin, trying to hide the hard-on from hell. Told mom the hat was a memory from the day. I still can't believe she ate that shit up."

"What the hell did you do out there on Lady Luck?" Russ inquires.

I shrug easily. "Just kissed her."

Reid's eyebrows head for his hairline. "You kissed a customer? How in hell did mom miss that?"

"We were in the grove of trees that Lady liked to munch in."

Ronan snort-laughs. "Yeah, like that wasn't planned. You were droolin' over that tight little ass. We kept her daddy busy so he wouldn't worry about her."

"He had nothing to be worried about," I defend myself.

"We knew that." Ryder rolls his eyes. "He was more worried about some news he had to give her. That's why mama let it go." He snickers. "Somethin' tells me you made it memorable, and it had nothin' to do with the horse ride."

"It was her first kiss," I confess, forgoing admission I haven't had the pleasure of one like it since. It was like a first one for me too. It was special, untainted.

Three "aws" ring out in unison and I flip them off. Reid and Russ just smile, before Russ reminds me, "You're still lucky mom didn't find out. She ran a tight ship on that business."

I shrug once again. "They were from North Carolina. It's

not like I was ever going to see her again. Like Rone said, teenage wet dream."

"So, why not ask the nurse out?" Russ says. "Quit messin' with barflies."

My mouth twists and my nose crinkles as I stare at the fire. "I might have pushed my luck a little bit with her." I scrub my hand over my face because, well – I have only one I can use.

"What did you do, idiot?" Russ asks, his laugh on reserve because he knows he'll need it.

I bite the inside of my cheek as I recall the *idiotic* behavior I would like to think I can't be held responsible for due to the drugs. But I know better. It was classic Reece Callahan behavior; the one that usually gets me laid in ten seconds or less. "In recovery, I told her I was highly trained in CPR. Offered to resuscitate her. She told me she could *de*suscitate me." I return their curious looks with a sheepish one of my own. "I told her if she did it by sittin' on my face, I'd die a happy man."

The spewed beer from a couple of mouths is enough to create a sizzle on the fire as their laughter fills the air.

Russ looks to Reid before dropping his forehead onto the heel of his palm. "Thirty-one goin' on thirteen. When is he ever goin' to grow up?"

Chapter 9

Mallory

Cardiothoracic rotation with Liberty's boyfriend and the witch known as Dr. Arseen – more appropriately named by the rest of us as Dr. Obscene or Ass-seen, because if her skirts got any shorter it would be – is not my favorite. Thank God for scrubs in the OR. Her unprofessional behavior is not the only reason we don't like her though – just one of many on a long list. She's egotistical, narcissistic, condescending, and quite frankly, a bitch. She's an adequate surgeon and gets the job done. She's also gorgeous – so long as you give credit where it's due – AKA the plastic surgeon. However, she's got a severe lady boner for Dr. Michael Knight, regardless of the fact she knows he is Liberty's boyfriend. If she stood any closer during consults she may as well be humping his leg. She giggles, touches his arm, his shoulder, even rubs his back. He does move away from her advances . . . most of the time. As he has publicly declared his love for another woman, it should be *every.single.time.*

Libs is well aware of the pursuant behavior, and I don't add to her angst, because I have no proof of infidelity. But you can bet your sweet ass I will be monitoring. I have a few observant coworkers in the OR that will keep an eye on the pursuer as well. Liberty is loved by everyone who works with her while Arseen is disliked by most.

I've watched Liberty search for the boy from her childhood for years without success. She is loyal to a fault. I've seen her cry, heard her call his name in the dark. It's no wonder she never had any boyfriends in college. Michael is the first leap she's taken since I've known her. I'd like to think he's man enough to catch her before she falls and not the reason she tumbles. I'm not being a mother hen, I'm simply being a friend and returning a few favors.

Knowing Michael and Dr. Hanson are good friends, I've taken it upon myself to try and glean a little insight from a different angle. Hence the reason I'm sitting across the table from the handsome head of radiology at Mancusso's this evening. If nothing else, I'll get a good meal out of it at my favorite restaurant.

"Why anesthesiology?" Eric asks after handing the menus back to the waiter once we've ordered.

"Why so curious?" I bat my lashes and smile cockily. "Got a procedure coming up that you're afraid I won't let you wake up from?"

He sighs heavily and narrows his eyes. "Do you think you could drop the sass for one night, Mallory? I really would like to get to know the real you. You haven't exactly made it easy, but I do know from Michael that Liberty thinks you walk on water. It was dinner tonight or take you swimming to test that theory." His lips tip in an impish grin and he winks. "Thought I'd go for your appetite instead of your ass. Seeing you in a bikini might be rather distracting."

I roll my eyes and shake my head. "You just can't help yourself, can you?"

He reaches across the table and takes my hand in his. "You make it hard."

My expression is as flat as the tabletop as I pull my hand back and wait for him to correct his Freudian slip – or double entendre. *'You make it hard'.* He either corrects it or I'm out of here. Cheesecake be damned. If he would just put a little effort in, convince me I'm more than a meal – literally and figuratively.

"I'm sorry." He holds up a hand in surrender and chuckles. "You make it a *challenge.* We've been bantering forever and I really would like to try a serious conversation. You fascinate the shit out of me and I just want to know why. Start over?"

"So long as I get cheesecake."

His laugh is one I could easily get used to. Not too loud, not over the top; confident. His smile is obviously well used; matching the crinkles around his eyes. "You can have anything you want. Now, tell me. Why anesthesiology?"

"One of the scariest things about surgery for some people is being put to sleep against their will," I explain with a shrug, "and the fear of not waking up again. I like putting the patients at ease and hopefully taking away some of that fear before their eyes close."

His gaze is set on me as his lids flicker the tiniest bit before he knowingly asks, "What did you have done that scared you?"

"Appendectomy." I stare at the glass of wine in my hands. "I was ten years old. It was so cold in that room. I remember shivering, the bright lights. I could hear everything; the beeps, the metal on metal of the instruments, the voices. But none of them were aimed at me until out of nowhere I heard 'Mallory, count backwards from ten'. No faces, no touch, no comfort. Just a ceiling with a light on it." The ever familiar burn behind my eyes every time I relive those moments strikes again. "I truly thought I was going to die. Alone."

"I'm sorry," Eric whispers. "No kid should ever have to go through that."

"Age doesn't matter." I scrunch my nose at the mere thought. "Fear affects everyone. It's the approach that makes all the difference in the world. You can use whispers, sarcasm, humor. A simple touch. Depends on the patient."

"That's why Evans loves to work with you." He runs his hand through his hair as he drops his chin and mumbles, "Ethics. His OR is more important than his bed."

"What?"

He's rescued from elaborating by the waiter returning with our food. Recalling a long ago conversation with Dr. Evans, I decide not to pursue it. Apparently Evans' conversation with me was garnished with eloquence. The one with Eric was most likely done around a poker table, or at a bar; maybe a strip club. One more reason to stay out from under the sheets with the doctor across the table. If I've already been a topic of conversation between those two, it wouldn't take much to be fruit on the grapevine. Gossip moves faster than Arseen's mouth during a blow job in the chief of surgery's office at quitting time. So I've heard, anyway – grapevine and all. I don't repeat what I hear – I make mental notes – blackmail material is a goldmine for revenge if needed. Best part? It can be done without ever being traced to the avenger . . . if done the right way.

My point? Arseen has a target on her back as big as Hal's birthmark. If you know, you know. She'll lose her job. Michael Knight? He's one of the best cardiothoracic surgeons in the country. The hospital needs him. If he screws up, he'll simply lose the best thing that's ever happened to him: Liberty Collins.

"How long have you known Michael?" I ask, dipping another bite of bread into the seasoned olive oil. Carb overload tonight, ass in the gym for two weeks to make up for it. It's all good; the gym is in the basement of our building. Besides, this food is too good to turn down. Pasta, bread, sauce that I'm tempted to lick off the plate, but since I'm in public, I refrain.

"Years," he replies easily. "We met in college and have been friends ever since. I've never seen him so happy as he is now. He's spent so many years working and being the best at what he does, he hasn't put much into his personal life. It's nice to see him start."

"Was he a gadabout before?"

He nearly chokes on the sip of wine he's just taken and puts the napkin to his mouth as he laughs. "A gadabout? That's kind of a grandma word, isn't it? Ranks right up there with gigolo. Are you asking if he got laid a lot?"

I nod. "Something like that."

"I never shared a bed with him, sweetheart. Didn't make it my business to keep track."

Yeah, he told me he wasn't your secretary either. Must be bro code.

He eyes me skeptically. "Are you asking on Liberty's behalf or yours?"

Head on, I meet his gaze. "If Liberty had questions, she would ask them herself. She's also a very trusting person, much more so than I am. How familiar are you with Dr. Arseen?"

71

He snort-laughs. "Not as familiar as she would like to be. Look, Mallory, I don't . . ." he hesitates, ". . . I'm selective. I'm sure the rumor mill has me bedding half the nurses and a quarter of the doctors. I assure you, the number I've fucked is minimal. It would be a disaster in the making."

"So this dinner is not a date?" I wave my hand over the table. "And that kiss in the parking lot?"

Reaching across the table again, he takes my hand, lifts it to his mouth this time, and kisses my knuckles. "No. You are a temptation I cannot resist. I've spent over a year trying to talk myself out of it, but you just keep sneaking back into my thoughts. I'm jealous of Evans and Michael, and Hawkins. They get to work with you. I get fleeting glances if I'm lucky."

"I'm still a coworker," I remind him. "One of those disasters in the making."

"No, Mallory." He kisses my knuckles again and flashes me a heated look. "You are the reason I want to break all my rules."

He is good, convincing. Sweet talker, tempting, goosebumps, thigh-squeeze inducing. First date, Mal. Not a snowball's chance in hell. You have rules, too.

I pull my hand back and pick up my glass of wine, tipping it to my lips. "I'm not sleeping with you tonight."

His chuckle is so low, I feel the vibration from where I sit. The look in his eyes nearly takes my breath away. "Mallory, if I took you home with me, we wouldn't be sleeping." He arches a brow. "Not until sunrise anyway."

Do not whimper. Do not fan your face. Do not give in. Breathe, idiot!

He grins cockily and winks. "Eat your cheesecake, sweetheart. The heat at this table is going to melt it."

Just so you know, I did not go home with the good doctor . . .

72

that night.

Chapter 10

Reece

I am currently standing in a dumpster in the alley at the back of our building searching for a little white box. The contents? Not a clue. Does it matter? Not to me. Is it imperative we find it? Damn straight it is. Because Tanner Carson is on his knees on the concrete tearing open every bag we toss out, desperately seeking whatever is inside. John and Wiley each stand in the other two dumpsters while Roger joins Tanner on the ground, sifting through the garbage bags one by one.

"Tanner," Roger calls out to him as he holds up what looks like the lid to a jeweler's box about four by four inches in size. "Think I got something here."

Oh God, please tell me it's not a gift for the bitch that's sporadically invaded his condo over the last year. They're a horrible match; a lawyer and a cop. But that's the least of it. Tanner is one of the nicest guys you could ever know. Miranda would probably eat ice cream in front of a starving kid and lick the spoon with a smile on her face. Yes, she is just that wicked. Our theory is she must give awesome head or Tanner really pities her. Yes, he is just that compassionate.

Tanner nearly dives for the item in Roger's hand and examines it for only a moment before tearing into the contents of the trash bag. "The rest has to be in here."

The three of us climb out of the dumpsters and join Roger to stand over Tanner; flashlights on our phones shining directly into the torn bag, where he carefully sifts through the contents until he's found every item he was looking for and carefully packs them into the box. I've never seen a man look so broken as he does when he clutches that damn thing to his chest, crumples to the ground, and folds himself in half, sobbing. I don't know what's in that box, but whatever it is, I'm damn glad we found it. Apparently, it wasn't jewelry, as it looked more like a photo, a piece of paper and a couple other indiscernible items.

Giving him time to collect himself, I look to John and Wiley then nod to the multiple trash bags on the ground. We collect them off the ground and toss them back in the dumpsters just in time, as the collection truck enters the end of the alley.

In the process of getting Tanner back on his feet and headed toward the door to go back inside, we discover he hadn't thrown the box out by mistake. No, his extremely unlikable pain in the ass girlfriend had intentionally thrown it down the trash shoot after she went snooping. I never did like her. He was in such a hurry to get down to the dumpsters, he neglected to bring his phone or his keys to get back in. He had ordered Miranda to leave but wasn't sure if she had. After watching the man fall apart, we were more than happy to guarantee him an empty home by the time he got back.

Roger sends Tanner to his place for a shower to wash the stink off, while the four of us ascend one more floor via the stairwell. Even if given the choice, we wouldn't have showered before completing our mission. Miranda is a stuffy bitch. She'll run from the stench alone. If we're lucky, she'll toss herself off the balcony. Four floors up ought to do it.

Roger pounds on the door with a clenched fist while he covers the peephole with a finger. It flies open moments later and a scantily clad Miranda stands on the other side.

"Tanner, you know I didn't mean . . ." Her gasp and shocked, wide eyes stop her whining, but her attempt to slam the door shut is stopped by Roger's fast hand as he steps forward, the three of us following him inside.

His voice is so low it would put the fear of God in a seasoned atheist. "Go put some clothes on and pack up. You've got five minutes to be out."

John is already opening a cupboard door to grab some trash bags.

"I-I can't be ready in five minutes!" Miranda screeches.

Wiley glances at his wristwatch. "You don't have five anymore. Down to four and a half now. Best get to movin'."

She shoots him a seething glare. "I hate you!"

He looks unfazed as he shrugs. "Not feeling any warm fuzzies for you either. Four and counting."

John tosses some trash bags at her. "Pack your things in these. One chance to get it all. The rest goes to charity. Hurry up."

She looks as if we've threatened her puppy. But we know better. Even puppies wouldn't like Miranda. They know a kicker when they see one. Now a cat just may enjoy the competition – claws and all.

"Charity!?" she screams. "I have Louboutins in there!"

John narrows his eyes and growls so low, I swear the walls vibrate. "I don't care if you have La Perla in there. Pack it up."

"You wouldn't know La Perla if it bit you on the ass," she sneers.

He snort-laughs. "I don't need it to bite me on the ass. I know it quite well when I bite Ava on the ass. Go pack!"

In the midst of the arguing taking place in the living room, we've all neglected to note Roger's absence until he walks out of the bedroom, arms full of clothing that he tosses on the floor. He snatches a robe from the top of the pile and throws it at Miranda. "Put that on and start packing the bags. I'll get the rest of your stuff."

"You're ruining my clothes!" she shrieks.

"Reece." He waves me over. "Grab a bag. You can empty her shit out of the bathroom. Give her no reason to come back. Not even a fucking toothbrush."

It takes a total of ten minutes to clear every last item belonging to a female from Tanner's bedroom and bath. She was given the opportunity to claim an outfit and put it on before leaving. A total of four bags and another filled with bathroom items sits at the door.

"Where's Tanner's phone?" Roger demands.

"I don't know!" She looks around as if searching for it, though it's laughable as she tightens her grip on the handle of her purse and scouts the room as if it might be floating in space.

Good God! She's an attorney. I hope she's more convincing in the courtroom. She'd be an innocent man's nightmare.

Roger pulls his phone out and hits the number he knows

will give us the answer, provided Tanner didn't turn it off. Miranda's purse rings with Deep Purple's *Smoke on the Water*. Roger's ringtone. It's a firefighter's thing. Mine is Talking Heads' *Burning Down the House.*

Wiley slides the purse strap off her shoulder from behind before she has the chance to resist and hands it to Roger. "I'll let you do the honors." Roger opens the zipper and dumps the contents of the purse onto the counter.

I wish I could say it's the typical contents one would expect from a woman's purse. I know my mom used to carry a small wallet with her ID and cash, tissues, lipstick, a compact, etc. Embarrassed the hell out of us once when a tampon fell out, but Ronan should have handed it to her as asked, instead of tossing it through the air. Right there in the middle of the restaurant. Yeah, he paid for that. Shoveled horseshit for a month by himself.

No, Miranda has the usual things one would expect, along with the extra thing she shouldn't have: Tanner's phone. However, she's also packing one thing we definitely do not expect. A used, tied off, full condom.

"What the fuck is wrong with you?!" Roger stares at the unseemly item lying on the counter then shoots a seething glare at Miranda before shoving the other items back into her purse. He looks to the rest of us. "Set her shit outside the front door. Get her out of here. I'll call the super and have him change the code immediately." He grabs some paper towels from the holder and picks up the used condom, throws it in the trash under the sink, and washes his hands.

We escort her to the front door via the elevator, accompanied by her numerous trash bags loaded with her clothing and personal items, not to mention her whines and protests all the way down. Tempted to leave the bags outside the front door and make her load them herself – having been raised better – I just can't do it. That, and I want her gone as soon as possible.

"Go get your car, Miranda," I order once at the door. "Make it fast and we'll load them up for you." She shoves the door open and storms toward the parking lot.

Looking to Wiley and John, I roll my eyes and groan, "Let's just do it and get her the hell out of here."

Wiley snickers. "Is this the Texas gentleman in you coming out?"

I smirk. "My Texas gentleman gets them in bed, Wiley. I wouldn't touch her with a twenty foot pole. This is my *mama raised me better* behavior. Besides, I gotta wait for the super to make sure he changes the code and emails the other residents."

He bends to pick up a couple of the bags. "Well, let's do it."

John grabs his arm to stop him from gathering the goods. "Not a chance. She's going to park it and shut it off before we go anywhere near that car. She's nuts. I ain't looking to be roadkill tonight."

Wiley crinkles his nose. "What the hell do you think she was gonna do with that rubber?"

The very thought makes my stomach churn. There are horror stories regarding what scorned women accuse men of having done. John's right; she is nuts. Miranda is an attorney, and wicked. DNA evidence? And this is why mine get tied and tucked . . . back in my pocket before I leave. Maybe it's time I slowed my roll. Honestly, I've slowed it since the injury. Ah hell, that's a lie. I've been sitting in the pit while all the other drivers are running laps around me. I haven't been active since the busty blonde – what was her name – I left in bed believing we'd have breakfast in the morning.

Two days later I was putting my arm through the window of a car and hours after that I was staring into the most stunning eyes I'd ever seen. Unfortunately, I still see them . . . at night when I close mine. *Unforgettable.*

I'd finally gotten the opportunity to ask Liz, the knows-everything-but-lovable receptionist at the hospital, who she might be. Mallory Tompkins, nurse anesthetist. Hence the reason she told me she could *de*suscitate me. Sassy, funny, and so fucking gorgeous she makes my chest clench. But her touch on my arm in the OR, the sparkle in her eyes that let me know she was smiling when she joked about stupid people giving her hives, her voice when she asked me to count backwards. I could feel every muscle relax just knowing she'd be there.

"My best guess is a pearl necklace or baster filler for blackmail," John says.

"Huh?" My mind tries to recall what we were talking about before I once again got lost in thoughts of the spunky brunette.

They laugh as the car pulls up at the end of the sidewalk to the parking lot. "Where the hell did you go, Reece?" Wiley inquires. "You were a million miles away. I asked what you thought she was gonna do with the . . ."

"I don't care. As long as we found it." I reach for two of the bags. "Let's get this over with."

"Hang on. Crazy bitch hasn't shut the car off yet," John warns us once we're out the door, hands loaded with the bags. He yells out to her, "Shut the car off, get out, and open the trunk!"

She lowers the window and hollers back, "I already opened the trunk. Just throw them in!"

"Shut the car off and get out," John growls, "or you can come pick up this shit by yourself."

"The trunk's already open!" she shrieks. "What more do you want?"

John and Wiley both drop what's in their hands and therefore, so do I. She looks absolutely crazed; eyes bulging, teeth bared. She slams her hands on the wheel, shoulders rising and falling with deep breaths.

"Don't know about you guys," John says, "but I really want to keep my kneecaps. Let that crazy bitch come and get it. I do not trust her." He grabs Wiley's elbow and then yanks on mine, pulling us back toward the building. "Let's go."

Once she realizes we are not going to put the items in the trunk for her, she pulls the car forward, then puts it in reverse. She turns the wheel hard, hits the gas pedal and speeds toward us in reverse, up and over the curb until she hits the concrete barrier twenty feet from the entryway – her Mercedes Benz now with only half the trunk space she had before.

The super and his assistant arrive at the same time the last of the concrete chips are falling to the ground. "What in the Sam hell?"

"I think she might be drunk," Wiley says casually as we pass them on our way in the building. "You want us to call the cops or you got this?"

He already has his phone in hand and waiting for the call to go through. "I got it. Can I call you if I need anything, Reece?"

"You got my number, Arnie," I tell him. "Just don't forget to change the code."

The three of us run to our own places to grab showers before heading to Roger's to order pizza, watch a couple football replays, and end the evening with a few beers. Apparently the police don't have any questions. Arnie obviously had enough answers.

We don't question Tanner about the little white box or its contents, nor does he volunteer any information. Whatever it is, it's important to him. And while we helped him find what's important, we also helped relinquish him of a ball and chain he didn't know was holding him back. He'll thank us one day. He's younger than us; it's a learning curve.

Chapter 11

Mallory

Dr. Michael Knight proposed, on one knee, in a fancy restaurant in front of a crowd of people Libs didn't know. The rock is enormous, ostentatious – everything Libs isn't. She can't wear it at work. High prongs are a hazard. Truthfully, she's in no hurry to put it on at home either. The ring spends more time in her jewelry box than on her finger. He didn't call her mom or stepdad to ask permission either. Doofus. I don't mind an alpha male – prefer them actually – but some things in life require protocol. Asking for an only daughter's hand in marriage is one of them. I love Liberty's mom as much as my own. Respect is a must.

BUT I KISSED A COWBOY

Simply one more checkmark against the good doctor.

"So, when's the date?" I inquire for the umpteenth time before stuffing the last bite of taco in my mouth. We're at our usual Mexican restaurant after a long and arduous week. If you're going to suffer heartburn, may as well make it worthwhile. That, and they make the best margaritas north of the border. "We only have four months left on the lease. I don't need three bedrooms so if I need to start looking, you need to let me know. Do you plan to move in together before the nuptials?"

Another night without the ring on her finger.

Libs sips her margarita slowly, as if to stall for time. "We still haven't chosen one. I'm in no hurry, and definitely no plans to move in together." She jokingly tips her chin. "You'd better not start looking for a new roomie. We haven't even filed for divorce yet. There's property to be divided. Who gets the wine glasses, the corkscrew with the penis handle, the phallus design cakepan . . ."

"The unopened dildo is mine," I state flatly.

"Then I get the smut books," she counters with a smirk.

"Ava Mynx belongs to me!" I exclaim, a little too loudly; noted only after a couple ladies in the booth behind her turn in their seats and chuckle. "We're huge fans," I tell them.

Liberty dips her chin and mumbles as she scoots out of the booth, "Well, now that you've thoroughly embarrassed me, I'm going to pee."

I giggle softly and whisper, "Don't take too long or they're going to think you opened the . . ."

She narrows her eyes. "I'm going to murder you."

"No you're not. You wouldn't know where to hide the body. That's what I'm for. Your job is to wipe up the scene of the crime." I wiggle my fingers. "Teamwork, remember?"

She stares for only a few moments before her face splits in a grin. It is what we're here for – each other. And that is our age old promise in the scenario that someone hurts either one of us. I bury the body, she cleans up the mess. Libs has adermatoglyphia; lack of fingerprints. A weird and rare anomaly, but handy should we ever need it. Being in the medical field did help her obtain a passport – thank God – as we needed it for a vacation to Costa Rica last year. She simply shakes her head and walks away, a soft chuckle as she goes. "I'll be back."

"Make it snappy," I giggle. "Don't want anyone thinking you're . . ."

She flips me off.

There's movement behind me as the back of my booth teeters slightly and a large body suddenly slides into mine next to me. "Hello, Gorgeous."

It only takes a moment to recognize the handsome smiling face and the deep southern timbre. "Mr. Callahan." I lean away from him to get a better view and arch a brow. "Make yourself at home."

He grins impishly, giving him a bit of a boy-next-door look mixed with a more alert Adonis than the sleepy one I remember from the OR. He slides his arm over the back of the booth and winks. "Thank you. And it's Reece."

I crinkle my nose and tilt my head. "Reece. Like the peanut butter cup?"

He leans in close to murmur in my ear, his slight southern drawl feeling like melted butter as he chuckles and his breath tickles my skin. "Oh, baby, I taste a whole lot better and my filling is much creamier."

And boom!

Stepped right into that one, didn't I? Fighting the goosebumps that envelop my skin and the rush of tingles

84

that spread from my lower back to my neck, not to mention the urge to squeeze my thighs together, I push back on his extremely firm pec and utter, "Good thing I already ate. And I'm not in the mood for dessert."

"Did I overhear correctly? You're a fan of *toys* and Ava Mynx?" he asks playfully. My cheeks flush in heated embarrassment, which is a first. I've never hidden my love of reading, just maybe the genre.

"She's actually a fan of *me*. Who the hell are you?" The harsh growl is unmistakable as Eric appears out of virtually nowhere, a hard glare aimed at Reece, arms folded over his chest. Michael stands behind him, scouting the restaurant, obviously searching for Liberty.

Reece glances at me and winks before he looks to Eric. "Reece Callahan. Nice to meet you. And you would be?"

"Her boyfriend."

"No you're not!" I gasp in protest as I narrow my eyes and grind my teeth. We're . . . convenient, that's all. "What are you guys doing here?" It's not really a question, more an accusation. We had no plans tonight. Word had it a group from the hospital was meeting at *The Tempest*, a well-known strip club frequented by a few of the rowdier coworkers. I hadn't shared that info with Libs, but I'm not their babysitter either.

"We came to join you for, uh, dinner. We're, uh, running late," Michael contributes with a grimace, glancing around the restaurant as if it would be his last choice for eating establishments.

Screw you, pal. We like tacos. We also down margaritas like water after a shitty week of work. Even add salt to the rim when we plan on elevating our feet at the spa, such as we do tomorrow. Don't even think about changing her plans or I will forge your signature for two back-to-back, weeklong conferences followed by a two-week invitation for Liberty's and my mom to stay with us.

You won't be getting laid for a month. Just try me.

Reece places a hand on my thigh and squeezes gently before leaning in and speaking so only I can hear. "Wannabe boyfriends are a mere stepping stone. I think I understand why you're settling on *toys* and Ava Mynx books. If you'd like an introduction to the real thing, let me know." He studies my face as if trying to solve a puzzle, then whispers dreamily, "Those eyes."

Reece rises from his seat in the booth – a powerful presence that makes Eric take a step back. There's a good three-inch height difference, broader shoulders, probably thirty pounds as well . . . of solid muscle.

"Nice to meet you," Reece says with a chin tip and a smirk. "Don't need a name. I'm good with faces." He looks back to me one last time. "Mallory," he says with a wink, grins cockily, and runs his tongue along his bottom lip, "seat's reserved. I love tacos."

Screw the goosebumps; I need a cold shower.

Liberty arrives at the booth as Eric and Michael glare at Reece's retreating backside, as well as whoever else had been in the booth with him. It's men; their laughter echoing throughout the restaurant as they make their way toward the door. I'd love to take a peek, but I'd have to stand to do so.

"What are you guys doing here?" Libs asks, rising to her tiptoes and placing a kiss on Michael's cheek as he dips his chin, making the task slightly easier for her.

One more checkmark against the good doctor. He should have reached for her first, shown elation at seeing his bride-to-be; instead looking complacent with the results and returning a quick peck to her forehead.

Oh Romeo, Romeo, wherefore art thou . . .

I stifle a laugh at the ever growing *doofumisms* checklist – my title for Michael's shortcomings – and roll my eyes. I'll show it to her someday. Her avoidance of choosing a date, the lack of enthusiasm, the overall laissez-faire vibes are telling me she's more than hesitant. We haven't gone dress shopping, they haven't searched venue options. She doesn't even have a bridal magazine on the coffee table to flip through for ideas. I also caught her doing a search for the boy from her childhood a week ago.

"We've already eaten and we're on our way out," I tell Michael as I reach for my purse and slide out of the booth.

"How about we go for a couple of drinks, then?" Eric proffers.

"Get tired of the strippers, did you?" I deadpan.

Michael's eyes widen as Eric's narrow. "We weren't there for the show."

"Strippers?" Liberty's question is aimed at Michael, but Eric rushes to his defense before giving him the chance to explain, *as if he could.*

"We joined a couple of people from work for a drink, Liberty," he explains. "We sat with our backs to them the entire time."

I should have gone to the bathroom with Libs. It would make for one less person in this group ready to piss their pants: me from suppressed laughter, Michael from *oh shit* syndrome. I couldn't care less what Eric does, but Michael is supposed to be committed to one 90% naked body – his fiancé's. A faithful man doesn't get heated up in one place and go home to cool off. A weak man avoids temptation at every turn . . . until he doesn't.

Just like my dad. I've forgiven him after all these years. But forgiven doesn't necessarily mean forgotten.

Oohhh, Libs is pissed. She does not have a poker face. Her left eyebrow gives the St. Louis Arch a run for its money. The green and blue of her eyes turn nearly translucent. Her skin flushes from the neck up. The little blue vein in her left temple pulses. Thank God it's never been aimed at me, but if you know, you know. It feels good to see the lady balls come out.

Libs snatches her purse from the seat in the booth and slides it onto her shoulder. "You ready?"

"Liberty, wait." Michael grasps her elbow, but she yanks it from his hold.

"I've got plans already," she sneers then tips her chin. "Think I'll see if *Hank the Hung* is performing later."

"*Hank the Hung*" is a phenomenon of sorts who performs at The Tempest once a month for ladies only. Not that we've ever been. From the sounds of it, that thing could poke your eye out . . . or leave permanent damage. Thirteen inches and twirls like a helicopter blade. Damn thing could perform a hysterectomy without a scalpel.

Eric steps in front of me, blocking my pathway to the door. I tilt my head, batting my lashes. My smile is loaded with sappy sweetness, my tone anything but, as I keep my voice low. "Move 'em or lose 'em, sans the anesthesia."

"Who was he?" he demands.

"My waiter?" I look up, feigning puzzlement. "I think his name is Jeremy."

"Reece Callahan," he says venomously.

"Sounds like you already know him."

"I know *of* him."

I shrug one shoulder. "Well then, stop asking stupid questions and get the hell out of my way."

"Are you seeing him?"

"Probably not as much of him as you did the strippers," I taunt with a smirk.

He falters for only a moment. "I told you . . ."

"You ready to go, Libs?" I turn to see her falling for whatever lame-ass story Michael is feeding her as he tucks a wisp of hair behind her ear and flashes her puppy dog eyes.

Give him enough leash, Mal. He'll either run away or hang himself with it.

"Yeah, I'm ready," she says before leaving a kiss on Doofus' mouth.

Eric pulls me in for one of his own, though not nearly as gentle. He fists my hair and wraps a tight arm around my waist, pressing our bodies together to assure I know exactly what I – or maybe the strippers – are capable of doing to him. As much as I would like to resist, it's difficult. The physical attraction is strong between us, but the fundamental element of emotion seems to be lacking. Maybe it's just . . . me.

He ends the kiss with a harsh pop. "I'll call your Lyft. You're not going to the strip club." He closes his eyes, inhales deeply and releases it slowly, reconsidering his order and turning it into a plea, "Please?"

"Well, since you asked nicely." I shake my head and roll my eyes. "We're not going to the strip club. I need to go home, sleep for a hundred hours, and go to the spa tomorrow. We've had appointments for the last month."

He smiles, apparently feeling as if he's won a battle. "A spa day, huh? Waxing? How about tomorrow night? Pick you up at seven? We'll order in?"

*Of course we'd order in. That's the norm, isn't it? The sudden overwhelming desire to enjoy some Netflix, a glass or ten of wine, comfy PJs, maybe even an Ava Mynx book in the comfort of my overstuffed chair is too much to pass up. When's the last time I was actually wined and dined? Yeah, I think I'll start my period tomorrow. Maybe even add in some stomach cramps. Oh, I'll have to stop and buy some chocolate, just for the hell of it. Thai food sounds good too. An order for **one.***

Chapter 12

Reece

"So that's Mallory, huh?" Roger and I stand in the parking lot outside of the restaurant. "Cute. Hot, in fact. Who's the blonde?"

We've just said goodbye to Vic and Boonie after having dinner, post our 72-hour shift at the firehouse. Boonie has a wife to pick up at the airport in an hour, and Vic's fiancé had to work late so he was in no hurry to get home.

I glance back at the window and peer inside. "No idea. I can't even see her."

He laughs knowingly. "Dude, we could line up strippers

in there and you wouldn't see them if this Mallory were in the room. You were glued to the edge of the booth trying to listen in on her conversation. Reece, ask the woman out, get your rocks off, and move on to the next one. I just wondered who the blonde was. I only saw her ass as she was walking away. Don't think I'd throw her out of my bed."

Studying the figures inside the window for a moment longer – the stupidest thing I've done in a long time – I see the *non-boyfriend* pull her to him for a kiss that she sure doesn't seem to be objecting to. Yeah, I'm an idiot. I should have left ten minutes ago. When I told her to let me know if she would like an introduction to the *real thing*, I meant Ava, the author of the books she apparently likes. Okay fine. That's not the whole truth. I also meant my dick. What the hell? They're both impressive. And I do love tacos. Both kinds.

"Well, that's gotta sting a bit." Roger grimaces when he sees what I do, then slaps my shoulder. "Come on." He opens the door to the cab of his truck and I walk to the other side and do the same. "The Tempest has to have a better show than this. There's a whole selection of titties there."

"He's probably some doctor dick from the hospital," I grumble as I slam my door, hating myself for feeling a pang of jealousy. I so need to get laid.

"Hey!" Roger admonishes as he puts the truck in gear and pulls out of the parking lot. "They might be good at what they do, but we're damn good at what we do, too. We're the might and the muscle. They're the slice and the stitches." He scowls when he stops at a red light. "Don't you ever think you're second rate or second place to anybody. Besides," he grins cockily, "have you ever had a lady complain about your muscle? You can bet your ass our stamina is better than any MD she works with. Now, let's go get that picture out of your head and you can choose who to use your stamina with."

I'd already chosen, but I choose not to share that little tidbit with Roger. Mallory Tompkins has taken up space in my head ever since the OR, and like a fuzzy vision that haunts your dreams, I can't recall a clear memory. Just out of reach and the harder I try, the blurrier it becomes.

Tonight's view inside the restaurant window was like a splash of whitewash on a painting I was still trying to study. I was so close – just inches away. I know those eyes, those lips. One taste and I'm sure I would remember. But thanks to the 'non-boyfriend' I not only didn't get the opportunity, I got a quick kick to the balls and a strong blow to my ego. I didn't take my brothers' sloppy seconds. I sure as hell am not taking some doctor-dick's leftovers.

Three steps in the door of The Tempest and a loud, shrill screech rings through the air. "Reece!" The buxom blonde from two nights before the accident – I remember faces and boobs – bounds over as if we're long lost lovers and jumps into my arms. *Holy shit! She's a stripper?* "You didn't stay for breakfast," she whines, then juts her bottom lip and feigns a pout. "I was in the mood for your sausage."

Roger can't contain his laughter as my unspoken plea of *"get me the hell out of here"* spreads across my face. He reaches for her shoulder and gently pries her off of me. Straight-faced and flat toned, he tells her, "Reece and I are working tonight. We're searching for a friend before his wife finds him." He looks out across the room as if scouting the crowd. "I don't see him anywhere so we'd better keep searching. Let's go, Reece."

She whimpers – literally whimpers in the most irritating, skin crawling, nails on chalkboard decibel level I've ever heard, "When will I see you again?"

Instead of the tempting "hopefully never" that begs to leave my mouth – I am a gentleman – I simply shake my head and tell her, "No clue," and turn for the door.

"What about you, handsome?" she mewls behind me, propositioning Roger before he can get out the door. *Good grief, desperate much?*

"Sorry," Roger placates her. "Bros before ho...olesome women like you."

The door closes behind him and he shoves my shoulder. "What the fuck were you thinking? Her voice alone made my balls shrivel. I hope to God you either wore earplugs or you muzzled her. That'd be like bangin' Miss Piggy."

"Asshole," I mutter. "Sometimes you can't tell until you get out of the . . ." Car doors slam in the distance and two familiar faces come into view. I grab Roger's shirt sleeve and pull him behind an SUV parked nearby and duck down low, peering over the top of the hood.

"What the hell are you doing?" he growls, though with the forethought to do it discreetly.

"Shh."

Watching the figures as they move across the parking lot toward the door, I feel an overwhelming sense of satisfaction. She didn't go home with him. I pull my cell out of my pocket, zoom in, snap a few pics, then switch to video and record the two of them walking in the front door. So, the *boyfriend/non-boyfriend* likes strip clubs when he's not kissing Mallory. At the same time I feel satisfied, it pisses me off. How can he kiss a woman like her and then go watch strippers? The other guy isn't my concern. Don't have a clue who he is. Maybe Liz will when I send her these pics and video. She'll know how to get them delivered. Hopefully she'll show them to Mallory. I'll be sure to date and timestamp them for proof.

"What the hell was that about?" Roger demands once we're headed back toward his truck.

"That's the guy who was kissing Mallory."

He presses the button on the fob to unlock the doors and the lights flash. He pauses before opening the door and stares at me over the back. "Your point?"

"He was just kissing Mallory and now he's here at a titty club. Who does that shit?"

"You were propositioning her and telling her how much you like tacos, and now you're here at the titty club." He squirrels his face. "Well, you were, until little Miss Piggy came along. When's the last time you got laid, Reece? The porcine queen?"

"I was injured," I remind him with a scowl. Though his question does remind me, it was the porcine queen.

"Months ago," he states firmly, as if I don't remember. "It wasn't your dick, Callahan. Time and wishes are thieves. Your philosophy. Do it or don't. Are you that hung up on her?"

"No!" I deny vehemently. "I'm simply trying to figure out where I know her from. I'm good with faces, Roger. It's names I suck at. And neither one is ringing a clear bell with me."

He snickers as his lips tip. "Well, apparently yours isn't ringing any with her either. Maybe it was an epic fail and she wants to spare your feelings."

My words are spit as I glare at him. "I have never failed, much less epically."

"Well, you may as well have fun while you try to figure it out. So, do I drop you at home so you can watch your dick shrivel up, or are we going to Cranky's?"

He's right. And sex is one of my favorite pastimes. Pretty sure there's a barstool warmer waiting for me right now. Why I've been so hesitant is beyond me. If she didn't invade my thoughts and dreams like she does, I'm sure I would have been exercising my dick versus my right hand in the shower the way I have been. It's a form of physical therapy, isn't it?

Cranky's may not be fancy, but it's quiet, discreet, and clean. I'll be in and out long before daybreak. One drink, one smile, and we'll be rolling in her sheets in no time.

I pull open the door of his truck. "Drop me off to pick up my truck. I'll meet you at Cranky's. I want to make sure I can get out the door when I'm ready, and I sure as hell ain't stayin' the night."

"Atta boy." He chuckles and starts the truck.

"Have you ever had a steady girl?"

It's a long mile before he answers, his eyes set on the road before us, hands tight on the steering wheel. "Once," he says gruffly. "And once was enough."

He doesn't elaborate. The bitterness in his tone speaks volumes. He's still angry, maybe even a little bit hurt. But I'm not my brother Russ, so counseling isn't exactly in my wheelhouse. I am a good listener though. If he ever decides to talk about it, my ears are open.

The bar is full, the options are limitless, as is the usual. But I wait until Roger leaves with his flavor of the evening, and then I go home – alone. Just like I have for the past few months. He'll never know and I can pretend while I continue to solve the puzzle that is Mallory Tompkins.

Chapter 13

Mallory

"Mallory," Savannah whispers as she enters the locker room then glances over her shoulder, *both ways*. "Bathroom, now."

"You need a tampon?"

"No! I have news." She scowls, then points to the door leading to what she has apparently deemed the room of discretion.

Savannah is an OR tech who's been keeping her ears and eyes open for me. Shy, quiet, friendly if you approach her first. Otherwise, you wouldn't know she's in the room. The perfect spy. A little like a ghost in scrubs. Until you take her out for a couple of drinks – then she is the life of the party. Not that anyone else knows. Libs and I are the only ones she's ever gone out with so far as I'm aware. She presents as plain; hair always covered in a cap, eyes hidden behind big frame glasses, and she wears baggy scrubs. But when she lets her gorgeous red hair down, loses the glasses to reveal dazzling green eyes, applies a little makeup, and puts on a dress? Hot damn! The woman has boobs, a sculpted ass built by Buns-R-Us, and legs that shoe and boot makers would pay her a fortune to model.

We squeeze into the one-person bathroom and she locks the door behind us. She places a finger over her mouth and blows a whispered, "Shh."

I only nod because, well – I hadn't planned on talking. *Humor her, Mallory.*

"You know that bachelor party for Damon in Vegas next weekend that a bunch of the doctors are going to?" I nod again. "The one that Liberty's fiancé is going to? Dr. Knight?"

"Yes," I drawl softly, resisting a lip twitch at being schooled on who Libs' fiancé is, as if I needed a reminder.

"Well," she sneers, as much as a whispering person can, "Dr. Obscene is planning to crash it. I overheard her on the phone in her office. You asked me to keep my ears and eyes open."

My teeth grind so hard my jaw hurts. "What did she say and do you know who she was talking to?"

Her lip curls in disgust. "She said to consider it a last hurrah before the ball and chain and it would be a one-time thing. Nobody needed to know." Her eyes moisten and she swipes at them before she finishes, "Then she said, 'One time Michael. Get it out of our systems'."

My blood boils as the *doofumisms* checklist takes a backseat to the big red flag on a pole I want to drive through that asshole's heart, then his forehead, then his crotch. No, I'll cut his dick off first. Then I'll drive the pole through his heart . . . if I can find one.

"What are you going to do?" Savannah chews the inside of her cheek while puffing the other until I poke it with my finger.

"Stop that. It'll give you wrinkles. I'm going to do what a good friend does. Take care of it."

"Liberty's going to be so hurt."

"Only for a little while." My gaze is harsh as I recall my mother raising a child on her own, all those nights hearing her cry over a man who had chosen another woman over her. "Better she learn now rather than after he puts a couple kids in her."

"True," she agrees, as if enlightened. "What can I do to help?"

Pointing a hard finger, I make myself clear. "Make damn sure nobody else finds out about this. Can you do that?"

She slides a pinched finger and thumb across her lips. "Sealed. I promise."

I pull her into a hug – something I am not known to do. "I appreciate this. You're a good friend, Savannah."

Squeezing me harder than I expected, I hear the sincerity in her words. "You guys have been good friends to me. They're not easy to find. Give Liberty a hug when it all goes down. Don't tell her it's from me though, I don't want her to be embarrassed."

So the good Drs. Knight and Arseen are finally playing their cards. In Vegas, no less. Game on, assholes. Interesting, as Eric is attending the same bachelor party.

It didn't take too much coercion to get Liberty to make

this trip with me. With minimal explanation and maximum suspicion on my part, we head for the entrance to the tunnel to board the plane to Vegas.

"There's my favorite brunette from the hospital!" The now familiar voice that I'm unfortunately growing fonder of every time I hear it calls out from the other side of the terminal. *What on earth is he doing here?*

Reece Callahan is persistent, I'll give him that. Every time he gets an opportunity, we *run into* each other in or outside of the hospital. He's never obnoxious, never overbearing. He's rather comical most of the time. But it's the way he cants his head or studies my face when we banter back and forth, as if I'm a puzzle. It's not creepy. He's never approached me when I'm alone, i.e. on my way to my car in the parking lot. He's never asked for my phone number or address, nor has he asked me for a date; probably thinking Eric is my *boyfriend.*

"Check out the blonde," his firefighter partner, Roger, yells. "What's your name, sugar?"

Poor Liberty leans on the wall of the tunnel, her emotional state fragile at the present time due to what she's afraid we'll be walking into. "It's roll over and stay dead, Roger. She's unavailable. Don't you have a cat to rescue from a tree?"

"I've been offering to rescue your pussy for months, Mallory." Reece laughs. "Say the word, baby. I'm all yours."

I pierce him with a glare. "Still not looking to get hosed, moron."

The smirk leaves his face as a flash of regret replaces it. That was a little too forward, not to mention inappropriate in an airport full of passengers. Not quite his style. The offer of sitting on his face may not have been subtle, but it was discreet, and he was drugged. Roger laughs hard while a third, rather good looking specimen appears ill. I flip them all off then grab Liberty's elbow and lead her down the tunnel toward the plane.

It's said what happens in Vegas stays in Vegas. Which would mean if we catch Michael cheating, I can cut his dick off and leave it behind. That would be in keeping with the general rule. Right?

Fine. I didn't cut his dick off, but I did bring my friend home – minus one cheating fiancé and the risk of a lifetime of unhappiness. She deserves so much better. If I could wave a magic wand and find her childhood love, I would – because the detective I hired a year ago after my paycheck allowed for it found nothing. Just don't tell Libs. Hope is better than nothing, and if we didn't have hopes and dreams, what's the point of living?

Chapter 14

Mallory

"Mallory, wait!"

I've managed to avoid Eric since Vegas for the last month. I've asked for a temporary schedule change at work – much to the dismay of Evans – and I park my Rogue in the lot out front so it blends with the hundred other vehicles belonging to visitors. I've blocked him on my phone and don't answer any unidentified numbers, restricted him entrance to my building, rerouted flower deliveries to the hospital, and marked letters 'return to sender'. Libs and I haven't had dinner out for the last month; instead ordering in, because neither of us want to deal with unwanted dinner guests, for her or me. We've survived.

The art of making a good margarita wasn't that hard to grasp, and there's always wine.

Weaving my way around the ambulance and firetruck that sit at the emergency entrance, I hasten my footsteps toward the parking lot. It's been a long day, an even longer month. I'm physically and emotionally spent.

"Mallory! Damnit, wait!"

Spinning on my heel, because I can't take anymore – that and I'm done parking in a lot that gives me two thousand extra steps I don't need to take – we nearly go head-to-head. Okay, head-to-chin, as I yell, "What do you want?"

"You're going to hold *me* responsible for *his* behavior?" Eric hollers, pointing a thumb back toward the hospital we've just left. "I wasn't the one with my dick in somebody else!"

"I don't care if you had your dick in ten somebody elses," I grind out slowly. "We are not committed. Friends don't let friends be stupid. You were there, I watched you. You slapped him on the back and let him walk away with her knowing what was going to happen."

"What did you expect me to do?!"

Releasing a pitiful laugh, I stare at him. "You're kidding. You remember Libs, don't you? You've sat across the table from her when we've had dinner, you work with her, you've seen them together. What were you supposed to do? How about show a little loyalty to her, Eric? How about proving you can think with something other than your dick?" I shake my head and hold up both hands and take a step back. "What you proved is you're no better than he is. She is my best friend, and I'll be damned if I associate with someone who thinks so little of her and whose moral code is no stronger than wet toilet paper."

He grips my shoulders firmly and growls, "I'm not his fucking babysitter! It had nothing to do with us!"

"It had everything to do with us!" I snap back and twist out of his grip. "I'm just glad it happened now before she put any more time in with him and before I wasted any more with you. Stay away from me. Find someone else to play with."

"Damnit, Mallory . . ." He reaches for me again but the nearby growl of contempt halts his attempt.

"I believe the lady was quite clear." Never have I been so relieved to hear that southern accent, though the playfulness I've grown accustomed to is absent. Reece Callahan in full firefighter gear is a sight to behold – tan coat with yellow stripes and rubber boots. No helmet, but that golden blonde hair is mussed in a way that makes me want to reach for it and brush it off his forehead.

"This is a private conversation," Eric spits, hands clenched at his sides.

Reece tilts his head toward the gawking crowd gathered not far away, then arches a brow. "I beg to differ. A little unprofessional, don't ya think, doc?"

Eric takes note of the small crowd Reece has steered his attention to then glares at Reece before he looks back to me. "We're not done, Mallory."

"Yes, we are."

Reece extends his gear covered arm and smiles, his eyes lit with amusement. "Need an escort, Gorgeous?"

I really don't. I'm more than capable of walking to my car. I'm pissed; not fragile, and I'm sure Eric wouldn't hurt me. But for some reason, that elbow looks inviting.

"Sure." I slide my hand through the bend in his arm and avoid a last glance at Eric. "Thanks."

Apparently, Reece likes to push his luck – or someone else's buttons – because he flashes Eric a cocky smile. "I'll see to it she's well taken care of. G'nite, doc."

"Watch your step, fire boy," Eric sneers. "She's out of your league. She makes three times what you do. Stick with the bar flies and nurses."

"You asshole!" I spin back and shriek at Eric. That was low. Firefighters are first responders, the public servants who save lives in the worst and most dangerous conditions. They put their lives on the line every day for us.

Reece stiffens beside me before gently sliding my hand from the bend in his elbow yet smiles. "Give me just a minute, will you, Gorgeous?" He takes the three steps necessary to reach Eric and grabs the front of his scrubs and twists. His voice is so low and filled with venom, I feel it all the way to my toes. "I don't do what I do for money. I do it out of honor and service to the people. Can you say the same Mr. X-ray? Don't ever demean what we do over a paycheck. You can't buy class and I've never needed to buy pussy. The lady said you're done. Take a hint." He releases his grip on Eric's scrubs, but not before delivering a restrained shove to his chest as if he's made his point. "Don't make me reinforce it."

My eyes are set on Reece as he turns back to me and extends his arm once again, an inquisitive arch of his brow as he asks, "Ready, Sweetness?"

I couldn't hide my smile if you paid me to. That had to be one of the most gallant speeches I've ever heard, despite the pussy remark. But firefighters do rescue kittens from trees, don't they?

Sliding my arm through the opening he's offered, I grasp the bicep underneath and squeeze as we head for my car. "I'm all yours."

"Be careful what you offer, Mallory," he says teasingly. "I might take you up on that."

Once at my SUV, I hesitate before opening my door. "Reece, I don't judge a man by how much he makes. That was really shitty of Eric to say. When I found out what you did the day of your surgery . . ."

"Just doing my job, Mallory," he interrupts.

"No," I hold up my hand, "let me finish. You guys are heroes and if I ever need rescued, I hope you're on the team." My nose crinkles. "Kinda like today."

I tug on the front of his coat and rise up on my tiptoes to leave a kiss of gratitude on his cheek, but he sees it coming and turns his face just fast enough to meet my mouth with his. He doesn't want gratitude – he wants a taste. I would have expected Reece Callahan to be harsher, demanding, maybe even dominating. But instead he palms my cheek, tilts my head so we fit perfectly, wraps a claiming arm around my waist, and delivers a kiss that almost convinces me he's a gentleman. There's no tongue. No tonsil rescue mission. No teeth clashing. No gag reflex test. It's feels . . . vaguely familiar. And so good that a tiny groan leaves my throat before I can catch it and rein it back in.

He slides his fingers into my hair and gently pulls my head back, staring into my eyes with that puzzled look he often graces me with, then whispers so softly I nearly miss it, "Impossible."

Before I can respond, the radio on his hip is loud as it squawks and an authoritative voice informs him, "We're all done here, Callahan. Let's roll."

His eyes never leaving mine, he pulls the radio from the clip on his belt. "Be right there." He opens my door for me and softly orders, "Buckle up, Beautiful. Drive home safe."

Impossible? What the hell did that mean?

Chapter 15

Reece

She purred. She actually *fucking* purred. I wanted to eat that mouth like it was dessert; show her what my tongue was capable of, but something held me back. I've made women moan, groan, whimper, whine, beg for mercy, cry out in ecstasy. But only one has ever truly purred. The sweetest sound to ever reach my ears, and my dick. *My kitten.* All these years later, I've never forgotten it and never experienced the same pleasure since. The one I felt above and below my belt in unison. My dick is affected by many things – a pretty face, tits, ass, definitely blow jobs. I've never been one much for noise though. I'm not into women screaming my name, nor me moaning theirs. A few well-timed swear words have always worked. Reece Callahan: satisfaction guaranteed.

The angel on my shoulder is laughing in my ear. *"This is your conscience rearing its ugly head, Reece. Did you know Karma and I are friends?"* The devil on my other is cackling. *"Fuck 'em and forget 'em, Callahan. Who needs a name?"* My internal groan screams at me, *"I do! I need a name!"*

Actually, I *needed* a name. Fourteen years ago! What am I thinking? That girl was from North Carolina and it happened in Texas. So what if Mallory reminds me of the girl with silver eyes flecked with green, the soft lips that tasted like cotton candy. The innocence I got to savor in delivering her first kiss. How long did I get to study her face? Three minutes? I held her back to my front the whole ride with the exception of that kiss. I wonder if Mallory's bellybutton feels the same – if she has a piercing. My little finger itches with the thought. There must be thousands of women with silver eyes. Lip injections are a dime a dozen, but hers are real; soft and full. And that purr; the tiny vibration that went straight to my crotch. The way she looked at me after. It affected me today as strongly as years ago. Which is why I'm grateful my uniform isn't nearly as tight as my Levi's were back then.

"What was going on in the parking lot?" Roger asks from his side of the backseat of the engine on our way back to the fire station. We had been at the hospital due to an accident involving four vehicles, a couple of drunks; one who punched a female EMT when he missed his target. Restraining the drunks and administering extra medical care to personnel isn't typical, but shit happens. Administering a few bruises to the drunk in retribution can be done if you're careful . . . and discreet. I mean really, it could have happened when he tripped and fell . . . or took an accidental knee to the ribs on the way down. What can I say? I'm a justice kinda guy.

My tolerance and patience limits were already hanging

by a thread – the adrenaline still pumping through my veins – having had to apply ice to a woman's face after pulling a drunk off of her. Then I saw the dick doctor grab Mallory's shoulders, and her twisting out of his grasp. Women are not meant to be manhandled. *Ever.* But then to insult me about my earnings? I not only don't do what I do for money – I don't *need* to do what I do for money. I have a trust fund fit for a fucking prince. All of us boys do. Generous grandparents. But nobody needs to know that. I've never touched it and it's willed to my nieces and nephews in the event of my passing.

"Mallory was being harassed by the guy from the restaurant." I shrug, though the urge to put my fist through something is strong. But one quick swipe of my lips with my tongue calms me as I taste . . . *cherry.* "The dick doctor. I took care of it."

Roger chuckles and reaches across the seat, backhanding my arm. "By sucking on her face?"

"She was thanking me with a kiss to my cheek, asshole."

Vic's burst of laughter can be easily heard over the sound of the engine. "Last time I checked, cheeks are found on either side of the nose or the ass crack." He turns in his seat, grinning like a fool. "Which one of you missed the target?"

Still feeling and tasting that kiss and wanting to do it again, I smirk. "I never miss my target, Vic. I was just warmin' her up."

"Warming her up? Never known you to chase anything, Reece," Boonie contributes from the driver's seat as he pulls up to the station and begins to back the truck into the port. "Don't they usually come to you?"

"Reece has never been turned down," Roger teases. "Poor guy's being made to work for it."

"Word of advice, Reece," Vic says as he turns once more and lifts his brows. "I've been kissing Molly's cheeks for five years. Gonna marry her in a month." He winks and grins. "It's the lower set you wanna go for. Never have I enjoyed kissin' ass the way I do hers."

Three groans ring out in unison as Boonie shuts the engine off and quips, "Pussy whipped and spoken like a man in love."

"And lust," Vic adds. "That little ass is so fine and all mine."

I-17 is a disaster. This is the kind of accident that stays with you for days on end. The visual. The faces. The crumpled bodies that have no pulse; the ones that do. You've got your screamers who are trapped with minor injuries, screamers trapped with severe injuries, and those covered in so much blood you can't tell if it's theirs or the co-passenger next to them. If given a choice, I'd rather hear more screams up and down this strip of approximately thirty cars, because it would mean signs of life. But we don't get to choose; we only get to deal with what we have and seek the best outcome.

Every hospital in the city will be receiving victims. Families will be separated according to the degree of injuries – children from their parents, spouses from their mates. Firehoses spray foam on the ground as the *Jaws of Life* are used to cut the steel so the sparks don't start a fire.

More bodies are placed on stretchers than in bags, so that's a plus. Some are shipped to Abrazo, some to St. Joseph's, others to Banner Medical. Tanner and a good portion of the 98th district police department are here – redirecting traffic and assisting with rescue. We must have four fire departments involved, as well as half the city's emergency services.

Roger and I both end up at Abrazo and Banner on two separate trips to help with transport of victims. There are only so many EMS workers to do on-scene triage, so we help when the situation calls for it. Like a well-organized assembly line. I see her once in the middle of the mayhem; a cursory glance as she assists with hospital triage. Unexpected, as she works in the OR but my guess is they're using all available personnel for this. As I rush out the emergency doors on my way back to the scene, a fleeting thought of that kiss runs through my head. *My sanity amongst the chaos.*

Tow truck companies have called in flatbed trucks to place multiple cars on the beds because it would have taken for-fucking-ever to clear them out one by one.

It's five hours before we're given the clear to leave the scene. One more day before my shift is over. I don't think I've ever felt like I need it more. But there is no rest for the weary until the shift is over. The best I can hope for is amnesia when I lay my head on a pillow and close my eyes.

Who's going to take care of the two intact youngsters we pulled from the backseat after removing their lifeless mom and dad from the front?

The teenagers in football gear and cheerleading outfits. Will the guys ever play again? Will the girls ever cheer again?

The little girl holding her dog as it licked her face in the backseat – the only part of the car left intact. God, those tear-filled eyes.

I'm not sure which one of the guys took care of the asshole at the backend of the accident, shouting that he needed pictures for his insurance company before they moved his car. I just didn't have it in me. Actually, I did, but the morgue didn't need another body tonight. And going to jail probably wasn't in my best interests.

"I fixed you all some hot chicken soup and sandwiches," Burkey says as we enter the main room back at the firehouse.

Ah, nothing red. Nothing too heavy. Choice of hot or cold – both if we want. No distinguishable odor. Comfort food. Burkey retired two years ago but has a tendency to pop in when he knows he can be of help. Not actively, of course; more to lend a hand or an ear if needed, as well as a meal that isn't going to remind us of what we've just been through. I'm sure they'll be offering talk therapy through counselors. It's to be expected. We're a pretty tight-knit group around here and we've got each other's backs. We also have the Chief. Smart and seasoned. Handpicked his crew so we work like a well-oiled machine.

"I'm gonna grab a shower first, Burkey." I tip my chin in passing and a bead of sweat rolls down the nape of my neck. "I'll be down in a few. Thanks."

"I fucking hate days like this," Roger grumbles from the shower next to mine. The smell of diesel fuel permeates my nostrils as I try to scrub it off, the steam from the shower only intensifying the effects. It's not the worst smell in the world – death trumps everything – it's simply a reminder.

"Did you notice the new blonde in the ER?"

His timing is always spot on. My face under the hot water as I try to rinse off a shitload of soap proves it as I suck in a breath of air – getting water instead – and choke on it. Only Roger would notice a new prospect in the midst of disaster. Like I said, *sanity amongst the chaos.* It would never interfere with work, as we don't normally touch hospital personnel, but I swear his dick has radar.

I sputter through the last of my cough, then roll my eyes, only to get soap in them. This day just gets better and better. "Only you, Roger. An ER full of gurneys and bodies and you're still scouting for pussy."

"Actually," he drawls, "it was her ass I noticed first, but then she turned around. Have you ever seen anybody with two different colors of eyes? Damn, if I only looked at one at a time, it'd be like having two women at once."

I turn the faucet off, reach for the towel, and wrap it around my waist. "You've been reading Ava's books, haven't you? Is our resident erotica writer giving you fresh ideas?"

"Fuck no!" he shrieks, slamming his faucet off. "I don't need books and I sure as hell ain't going to read Ava's. That'd be like lessons from your mother." He steps out of his shower stall, towel wrapped around his waist.

I laugh. "You actually look in their eyes when you're having sex?"

"You don't?"

Clapping his shoulder on the way to my locker, I snicker. "Mine are so lost in ecstasy they couldn't focus if they tried, Roger."

"Fucknuts," he grumbles. "It's no wonder you can't remember their names."

"Yeah," I tease with a smirk, "but they always remember my dick."

Sanity in the chaos. I do believe I'm getting an appetite back. Tightknit group. Who needs talk therapy? We use diversion tactics.

Chapter 16

Mallory

I've been called many things in my life.

Immature *by the nuns who didn't appreciate my sense of humor.*

Imaginative *by the teachers who liked me.*

Impudent *by the ones who didn't.*

Incompetent *by the driver's ed teacher who felt I should have run over the squirrel in the street versus destroying the shrubs in the beautifully landscaped yard. My first experience in delivering vengeance. The ASPCA awarded me a certificate for animal awareness, and the school was shamed into paying* *for new shrubs. I also received my driving certificate.*

Insolent *by the referee who made a bad call. I thought "dumbass" was fitting. That player was off-side! I should know. I'd been gawking at his ass the whole game.*

Indecent *by the principal after a group of us were caught streaking across the football field. Oh please, it was dark and it's a rite of passage. Everyone knows that.*

But never have I been called *impossible*. And no one ever should be. We all have potential.

It's been two weeks since the parking lot incident yet I can still feel that man's mouth on mine. Evans's words echo in my head. *"He's your patient".* His parting remark of *"Watch out for him, Tompkins. He's a player"* hits a nerve as well. Would a player kiss like a gentleman? Are they chivalrous? Wouldn't he expect something in return for his heroics?

I've fended off Eric for the last time, making it clear it's over – unfortunately, under the guise the *fire boy* and I are an item. He doesn't know I haven't seen or heard from Reece since the incident. My best guess? Reece hated the kiss. Maybe that's what impossible meant: he expected more and was severely disappointed. It's not like I opened my mouth for him. I've never been told my skills were lacking, but it is a bit of a blow to a woman's confidence.

It's seven o'clock when Libs turns the key in the lock. The lasagna is warm in the oven and the scent of the best Italian food in the city fills the air. She breathes deep and hums in delight. "You fixed Italian?"

"You didn't order it?" I feign puzzlement and stuff another bite in my mouth.

"Uh, no."

"Huh, well you'd better dig in before a neighbor comes to claim it."

"Mallory!" she exclaims. "You're eating someone else's food?"

I love getting a rise out of Libs whenever possible. She'd probably walk the halls and knock on every door before eating a mistaken delivery. Me? Not so much. However, I know who this was meant for and who it was from, and it is sitting exactly where it is supposed to be. As well as the note that accompanied it.

Hey Gorgeous,

Things have been extremely busy and . . . complicated. I'll explain everything. Tomorrow night is the big reveal and I'm begging you to join me outside the emergency room at six o'clock. Hero's promise: a moment you'll never forget. Clothing of your choice. Scrubs, sweats, naked (kidding, save that for me), whatever makes you comfortable. Dinner was just to butter you up. I know you love Italian.

Please come. It's the only time I'll ask. Otherwise, I like to be in control. Read that again and think about it. Just like I've been thinking about that kiss. Where did you learn to purr like that?

See you tomorrow night, Beautiful,

Reece

I couldn't decide if I should crumple the note and throw it away or fold it and put it in a drawer somewhere. I don't purr, damnit. It's a little moan that escapes my throat when I'm enjoying myself. I'm not a screamer. Though no one has ever called it a purr except for that one time so long ago when . . . Then I read it again. Oh shit. Forget the purr. He likes to be in control? Hmmm . . .

"Come here." Reece takes my hand and draws me away from Roger and another man he introduced as Wiley; a guy who lives in their building. I have no idea what's going on as there seems to be no *big reveal*, nor does anything seem unusual. People sit on the benches chatting away, foot traffic is the same as always, no emergency vehicles or people rushing in at the current time.

I got off work an hour ago so I stuck around instead of going home and returning. The guys are in street clothes, so it's apparently a day off for them. And let me tell you, Reece Callahan knows how to wear Levi's. Low on his hips and molded to two defined cheeks above thick thighs. I don't understand why women go on and on about gray sweats. Maybe I could convince the cable company to air a rodeo channel. Pay-per-view tours of dude ranches. I'd rent them. Sweats are fine for easy on/easy off but come on! I do a quick calculation in my head for banked vacation time. I could book a flight to Montana or Wyoming for a few days. Bucket list checkoff. Tonight. Definitely checking flights and dude ranches when I get home. Liberty and I would have a blast. Riding a cowboy could be the cure-all to get her over the doggy ride she witnessed her ex-fiancé performing in that hotel room.

"What?" I demand, pulling my hand from his and spinning to tip my chin in order to make eye contact. Damn! He is tall. Unfortunately, he's gorgeous too and the megawatt smile he wears only enhances the features you picture your children having someday.

"Thank you for coming." He dips his chin, bends at the knees to accommodate my height, and lifts his brows. "I've missed you, Mallory."

"Ah." I chuckle sarcastically and nod slowly. "Would that be the impossible me or have you come back to do a risk reassessment?"

"What?"

"It's what you called me after that kiss," I grind out slowly, then enunciate, "*Impossible.*"

God, he's funny when he looks confused. Brow furrowed, mouth twisted, the way he cants his head as if his thought process might work better on a tilt. It must work because his eyes widen and he breathes a quick, "Oh, shit! That did probably sound bad, didn't it?"

I hold up my index finger and thumb, mere millimeters apart. "A little bit. Now, why am I here?"

He gently takes my shoulders in his hands. "Mallory, it was the kiss, not you. Let me explain . . ."

"Don't worry about it." I wave a hand in dismissal and step back. He's only making it worse. I'm pretty damn good with my mouth – so I've been told. That time spent perfecting my technique with my pillows as a teenager paid off. "Now, tell me why I'm here or I'm getting in my car and going home."

He takes a glance at his watch and another at his friends studying the exit doors of the hospital. "You and Liberty, you're good friends, right?"

"Best friends." My face wrinkles in confusion. "Since we were kids. We pretty much grew up together. What do you want with Libs?"

"*I* don't want anything, but I know someone who does," he explains with a chuckle. "And I thought you might want to be around for what's about to happen."

"What are you talking about?"

Roger turns at that moment and calls us over, "Guys? Shit's about to get real."

Reece takes my hand in his once more and leads me over to where they stand. "And Lucas has found his Liberty," he mutters next to me as we observe my best friend rush into the arms of the cop I recognize from the ER nights ago.

"Holy crap," I say as I peel my eyes away from the couple latched tighter than a magnet to steel and stare at Reece.

"That's Lucas? Lucas Monterrey?"

"Was," Reece states with a soft smile. "He's been Tanner Carson for years. He was adopted." He studies my face for a little too long and cants his head once again. "I guess sometimes all it takes is having a name."

"She's been searching for him since the day they were separated," I whisper in astonishment. I had lost all hope for her after the detective found nothing. So much for making reservations for two at the dude ranch. Ooh, Savannah might want to join me. If not? Oh well, that much more for me.

We walk toward the newly found happy couple and Roger and Reece applaud them in unison before Libs looks to me. "You knew about this?"

"Not 'til now." My voice cracks, tears edging near the surface. The last thing I want to do is cry – not here in front of everyone. I am so happy for my bestie I want to pull her into a hug and shed tears of joy for her. I want to congratulate her on finally finding her happiness. But that takes sentiment, and I am not an openly sentimental person. I'll take that journey with her when we don't have an audience. So, instead I buckle down and armor up, aka scrutiny with a side order of smartass.

Recalling a previous conversation with Liberty during one of her many searches for the man, I look to Lucas and remark, "Well, so much for a beer belly and a transmission in a bathtub in Kentucky. You got seven kids and a wife?"

His eyes flash with confusion before glancing at something behind me and he smirks. "Five kids and two ex-wives. Is that a problem?"

At the same time I shriek, "How many!?" a burst of laughter comes from the three morons behind me. I'm usually better prepared, but then I'm also not used to a gang war that's extremely unbalanced. "You assholes!" I bark at the men behind me.

"Aw, come on, Kitten," Reece wraps his arms around my shoulders from behind. "We were just teasing."

Kitten? Kitten!?!

"Come home with me and I'll make it better." He nuzzles my neck and whispers in my ear, "Daddy's got everything you need."

My elbow to his muscle-covered ribcage hits hard, merely making him flinch. "I would sooner squash your balls. I don't have a daddy kink. What the hell is wrong with you!!?"

Lucas' groan is loud. "Reece, it was a joke."

He lifts his head from my shoulder and I take my best shot with another hard hit to his ribs, duck out of his grip, and head for the parking lot as he yells at Lucas, "But I thought you said . . ."

It was a joke when I made the comment to Lucas in the ER! An offhanded, perhaps inappropriate, remark to get a cop out of the exam room. Proving once again my smartassery can get me in trouble sometimes and make me the subject of conversation.

Chapter 17

Reece

First on my list? Murder Tanner Carson. *"You could always let her call you daddy."* Real funny, asshole. I knew he'd had an uncomfortable confrontation in the hospital with Mallory the night he'd finally found Liberty, but he hadn't elaborated. I really should have investigated a little more rather than let my imagination get the best of me. I'm not one much for kink myself, but sometimes you do what you gotta do to get your foot in the door. Both he and Roger know about my slight obsession with Mallory. Fine, maybe more than *slight* but they don't know *why*. They think I'm simply horny and enjoy the challenge. I'm never not horny – that's a no-brainer – but the challenge is my moral compass. Yes, folks, I do have one. I've spent the last two weeks trying to disassociate Mallory from a wet dream of long ago. It wouldn't be fair to her, would it? And what the fuck was I thinking calling her *kitten*? It slipped out as if it were the most natural thing in the world.

That kiss is what did it. I knew one taste would jog my memory. She might not have tasted like cotton candy, but cherry was just as good. And those lips; soft and plump just like they were when . . . And those eyes. Damn, those eyes. But it's impossible.

However, I wish my dreams would tell me the same. One night I'm on the horse with the teenage girl, and the next I'm standing in the parking lot gazing into the exact same eyes. They hold more confidence now, but they also leave me with so many questions.

Roger slaps the back of my head. "You are such a dumbass. Go chase her and start groveling. Get on your knees if you have to."

I would have chased her without Roger's prodding, but his slap to my head does jolt me into action faster. She's halfway to her car before my feet are pounding the pavement. I don't call her name – it'll only make her run. I don't want to pull the same dick move the x-ray asshole did by grabbing her shoulders, so I do the only thing I can. I sweep her off her feet – literally – bridal style. Not typical for a fireman, but I'm not working. Damn, I'm glad I didn't throw her over my shoulder. Never have I been happier with my style of transport, because that's when I see it.

She's crying.

This is a first for me. Don't get me wrong, I've seen women cry. Tears of gratitude when we've done our job, little old ladies when we've rescued their cats, even some when CPR saved their husbands. Hell, I've caused a few by delivering epic orgasms. But again, those are in appreciation. However, to my knowledge, I've never been the reason for them through sheer idiocy and insensitivity. She thinks I called her impossible. She had just gotten done watching her best friend find her long lost love, and I was whispering a daddy kink proposition in her ear. Roger is right. I am such a dumbass.

But I'm still going to murder Tanner Carson.

I'm prepared for her to fight, kick, scream, maybe scratch my eyes out. But it doesn't happen. Instead, I feel my chest tighten when I hear her voice, broken and small, as she states, "Just put me down, Reece. I don't need rescued."

"Maybe not." I boost her up and hold her closer, relishing the feel of her body next to mine. She's so light, so right, such a perfect fit. "You do, however, need a ride because I'll be damned if I let you drive in the state you're in."

"M-my car," she stammers and swipes at her tears. "I can't leave my car."

"We'll get it taken care of." As if by reflex my lips find her forehead where I leave a soft kiss and continue the trek to my truck. "Let's get you taken care of first."

She wriggles in my arms. "I can take care of myself, Reece. Please put me down."

"No can do, Sugar. I feel responsible," I utter and press the button on the fob to unlock the doors of my truck. Using my free fingers under her leg, I pull on the handle of the door and yank it open. "Don't fight me on this, okay?"

She sighs heavily, tired and exhausted. "You are bigger than me."

I frown and huff, "I'd never use my size to my advantage."

She attempts a wry look through her tears as she looks up at me. "You'd better not. I'd have to desuscitate you if you did."

A full blown hearty laugh escapes before I can stop it and I hesitate before plopping her down on the seat. "You are so special."

She slaps at my chest, a combined giggle and a sniffle catching in her throat, making for a *giffle*? A *sniggle*? "Don't say that. That's what they call mental patients when they can't diagnose them."

Pulling the seatbelt across her belly, I buckle it securely. "You are one of a kind, Mallory Tompkins." I brush her hair away from her face with gentle fingers. "Hardly mental. And there is no diagnosis, because there is no cure. A smart man would never want one. Definitely special." I point to the dashboard. "Plug your address into the GPS. I'm taking you home."

"I need my car, Reece."

Pulling my phone from my pocket to retrieve the text I was expecting, I open it and show her the screen. We came prepared . . . somewhat. If we can get Liberty's vehicle back to their place, we can get hers as well. It'll simply take two trips. She reads the text after wiping her eyes once more.

"Good enough?" She nods. I close the door and hop in behind the wheel on the other side. I squeeze her thigh and shoot her a wink. "I promise I won't do more than 110 on the freeway with it."

She narrows her eyes; a pitiful attempt to appear tough, or a desperate reach for our normal. "95 tops or I will anesthetize your most important body part."

I bob my eyebrows and wet my lips slowly. "My tongue?"

"Just drive, Mr. Callahan," she grinds out through clenched teeth as her thigh tightens and moves inward toward the other under my grip.

"So special." I laugh and pat her thigh gently before putting the truck in gear and pulling out of the parking space.

I've wondered where Mallory lived for a while now. I

could have been nosy. Wanted to be for a long time. But I respected her space. I'm not a stalker. However, I definitely did not expect to see Tanner's ex-girlfriend's address on the GPS. Mallory and Liberty live together; that much I knew from Liz, my informant at the hospital. But this could definitely be a problem for Tanner. I cannot imagine Mallory being friends with Miranda, unless gasoline and hot sparks have found a way to mix without combusting.

Five minutes of arguing in the truck as to whether or not I should accompany her up to the apartment and wait for Roger – hello, he has Liberty's keys and I need to get hers in order to pick up her car – is almost fun. I could argue with her all day; the fire in her eyes, the rasp in her voice, the clench of her fists. Good grip. Perfect prelude to angry sex. I'd bet my left nut on it.

"What are you staring at?!" she demands.

I really wish I could remember what she was saying. Honest to God, I listen to every word she says on a general basis, and I'm pretty sure I'll recall it. But at the current moment I'm too busy imagining angry sex and the look in her eyes as she comes. Would they lighten, darken, roll back in her head? More importantly, would she purr? For the first time in my life, I want to look a woman in the eyes in the midst of ecstasy and listen to the sounds she makes. Hear her whisper my name. Or is she a screamer? I'll bet she's a back scratcher.

Throwing open the door of my truck, I remove myself from behind the wheel in one swift move and hop out to the ground below, taking one for the team. Damn Levi's! Gonna be feeling that for a while. "Let's go, Mallory or I'll carry you over my shoulder this time."

"Good evening, Ms. Tompkins," the elderly gentleman greets her as we enter the elevator.

"Told you before, Ray," Mallory says with a smile as she pushes the button for the tenth floor, "you can call me Mal.

We're pals. Did you get your cookies?"

"They were delicious, thank you." He nods enthusiastically. "And Buster loved his biscuits. If you continue to spoil him, he's going to want to live with you instead of me."

She giggles, as if the last hour hadn't taken place. "Well, I'll just have to take you both in, won't I? I'll be down tomorrow to take him for a walk. I'm off for the next three days."

The elevator opens to the eighth floor and the old man steps off but holds the door for a moment. He turns and gives me a scrutinizing look then arches a brow to Mallory. "Are you sure you won't be too busy?"

"With what, Ray?" Her mouth twitches as she lifts her brows and virtually ignores my presence.

"Oh, excuse me," I dive into the conversation in an effort to save her virtue, moving to the panel on the wall. "Guess I forgot to push the button for the eighteenth floor."

He clears his throat and narrows his eyes as Mallory's soft chuckle sounds by my side. "You must be new in the building."

"That I am, sir. Brand new." I smile brightly. "Still gettin' a feel for things."

"Mmhmm," he hums, eyeing me skeptically. "Let me know how it *feels* when your head hits the concrete at the top." He smirks. "We only have sixteen floors in this building, young man. You'd better be a gentleman. She's a gem."

Without hesitation, I wrap an arm over her shoulder, feeling the silky hair that brushes against my hand, and take a few strands between my fingers. "No doubt about it. She is special."

"Don't you forget it," he warns with a pointed finger and lets the doors go then grumbles as he turns, "Eighteenth floor. At least he called me sir."

She unlocks the door and we enter what feels like

home. It's warm and inviting with no particular shock value anywhere. It's . . . cozy. Muted colors on the walls, a few paintings that add color but nothing that screams audacious. The furniture looks comfortable – something you could sink into instead of lean on for questionable stability and fear is going to fall apart under the weight of a normal man's size. Throw pillows big enough to rest your head on versus throwing on the floor to get them out of the way. An oversized chair that could swallow her whole or be used for bending her over and . . . Of course, my head went there.

"You want something to drink while you wait?" she asks, waving her hand toward the kitchen. "I'm going to pack a bag for her."

That's what we were talking about in the truck! I had informed her Roger, Tanner, and I live in the same building, and she immediately thought to pack a bag for Liberty and have us drop it at Tanner's place. Talk about being a friend. Had it been one of us, our advice would have been to turn the underwear inside out for the second day . . . or go commando.

"Something tells me she's not coming home for a while." She turns toward the hall as if she's forgotten what she's just offered and her voice cracks, but I hear it. "If ever."

"Hey." I'm across the room in seconds, my hands on her shoulders, but before I spin her around, I let go and step in front of her, bend at the knees so as not to overpower her and take her hands in mine instead. It's a comfort measure my dad instilled in all of us years ago: *"Never make a woman feel vulnerable. Use your height and size for protection. Otherwise, you stay on equal ground."* At heights ranging from 6'1" to 6'4", he felt it a good lesson to pass on to his sons. Mallory barely reaches my shoulder. I can see where it could be intimidating.

"What's going on? Is it something I did or said?"

She shakes her head and drops her chin, her shoulders folded inward. "No, Reece. It's not you." She pulls her hands from mine and swipes at her tears. "It's not anybody. I'm tired. You don't have to pick up my car, I'll take a Lyft in the morning. Now, let me go pack a bag for Libs. I just want a hot bath, a gallon of wine, and to sleep for a hundred hours."

I take her cheeks in my palms and turn her face up, rising to my full height. Her eyes hide nothing. She's afraid of change, losing her best friend. "You're not gonna be alone, Mallory. You've got me. I'm not going anywhere."

Her mouth opens and closes, then opens again as the buzzer for the lobby sounds. She snaps her face away from my hands and moves toward the door where the intercom is. "That must be Roger." They exchange a few words and she buzzes him in after giving him the apartment number. "I'm going to pack her bag and then you can go."

She tries to rush past me toward the bedroom, but I'm faster. Rather than bend to match her height, I simply snatch her up by the waist and hold her close; her back to my front. What the hell, it feels better. It also feels familiar. Her hair smells so damn good I nearly bury my face in it, but instead simply inhale a little deeper. "I need your keys and your phone number."

"Why my phone number!?" *And she's back. The sass, the stubbornness, the little fireball that has kept me out of any bedroom but my own and from looking at another woman since that day in the OR.*

"In case there's a snag in picking up your car. Quit being stubborn."

She wriggles in my hold, her ass brushing against my raging asset, so I use both arms to hold her still – one over her ribs, my palm on her belly – and as I do, my palm flattens. Against all my better judgment, my little finger searches – and quickly finds – a memory. The tiny barbell piercing above her bellybutton.

No fucking way.

Chapter 18

Mallory

The knock on the door is solid and heavy, though Reece doesn't move to answer it. I'm a foot off the floor, ready to kick him in the shins, but I swear he's not breathing. He's frozen. My Danskos probably wouldn't hurt him that much, though I'd rather not maim the firefighter. He's been through enough this year. Maybe it's the raging hard-on against my ass that's keeping him, and me, from moving. No doubt about it, the man is packing. And while he may not use his size to his advantage, I'm sure getting some ideas how to use it for my own.

Not now, Mallory!

"Put me down, Reece. Your buddy is at the door." Then add with a touch of snark, "The one that's not saying hello to my *back* door."

He gently lowers me to my feet and whispers in my ear, "Go pack the bag. We'll wait."

I feel his eyes on me as I walk to Libs' bedroom and turn one last time before entering to see him watching. "You okay there, big guy?"

His head does that funky little tilt again before a roguish grin smatters his lips as if he's sussed the puzzle. "More than okay."

The knock on the door is harsher this time and Roger's voice follows, "Reece, unless the lady has cut your daddy balls off, open the damn door."

Rolling my eyes, I wave a hand toward the door then turn back to the bedroom. Roger's impatient voice is clear when Reece lets him in. "Well, your balls must be intact, you're not bleed . . . whoa! Did I interrupt something?"

"Fuck off," Reece growls. "I'm waiting for Mallory to pack a bag for Liberty. Then you and I are going to pick up her car at the hospital and bring it back here."

"Sounds good," Roger agrees. "You got keys?"

"Not yet," Reece says, then raises his voice as he aims his comment at me, "She's being difficult, aren't you, Sugar?"

Topping off the overnight bag – scratch that – three nights' worth of overnight things, I zip it and tote it out to the living room. It took a little longer than anticipated, as I left a note addressed to *Liberty's Vagina* on top of the clothes inside. She has found her soulmate, but it may take a little encouragement.

"Keys and phone number." Reece holds out his palm as if noncompliance isn't an option as I set the luggage by the sofa.

130

"I told you I can . . ."

"Now," he demands gruffly, though I don't feel threatened in the least.

I glare in defiance, fists on my hips, and he simply raises expectant brows. His hand remains outstretched as if waiting for me to plop something into it. So, I do. My own, with a hard palm slap against his. "Good game, bro," I say cheerily as I try to pass him. "I prefer high fives, but . . ."

My shriek is loud as he once again snatches me around the waist and lifts me off the floor. "Grab her purse, Roger. Find her keys and her phone."

Roger holds up a hand and snort-laughs. "Not on your life, buddy. Two things a man never does and plans on getting out of alive, and that is getting into a woman's purse and sneaking up behind her when she's on a scale." He wrinkles his nose. "Make that three. Answering the question, 'Does this dress make me look fat?' There is no right answer."

This time I do kick him with the heels of my Danskos . . . hard. Both shins. Previous injuries be damned.

"That's it!" In one swift move – don't ask me how – I'm thrown over his shoulder. "Stop it!"

In all my self-defense classes, I can't say as if I've been taught how to get out of a fireman's hold. Maybe it's because you're not supposed to. But I do know how to squirm and pull off a major coup. My nails are short due to my job, so drawing blood is not an option. I'd smack his ass, but knowing Reece, it would probably turn him on. His grip on my thighs is strong and makes it so my bottom half is virtually unmovable but my hands know exactly what to reach for, so they do, and I yank . . . hard.

SMACK!

"Ow! You asshole!" I shriek as my butt cheeks clench. That stung. My scrubs are not thick. Quite thin, actually. I felt that all the way to my . . . *oh!*

"Uh, guys," Roger says with a touch of playfulness in his voice. "Do I need to step out for a minute?"

"No!" Reece snaps. "She's going to get her keys and give me her phone number." He does a fast 180 spin so my face is turned toward Roger, then gently rubs the ass cheek he just slapped as he nearly groans, "Aren't you, Mallory?"

"Mm-m-mhm . . ." I stammer, enjoying the ass massage a little too much. *Damn you, Reece!* "Y-you c-can put me down. I-I'll get them for you."

"Nope." He backs up to the counter, continuing to rub my ass in gentle circles as Roger opens the fridge and pulls out a beer, twisting the cap off. "You can get them out of your purse, hand Roger the keys and call my cell. I'll wait for your happy little ring. Area code 602 . . ."

"Wait until I get my phone out, you moron!"

SMACK! This time to the other cheek. *Oohh.* His slow southern drawl sounds nearly musical as he warns, "Be nice, Sugar."

"Damnit, Reece. I am going to castrate you in your sleep!"

"Does this mean we'll be sharing a bed?" He chuckles as he starts rubbing the other cheek that he's probably left a nice pink mark on. I'll have to check it before that hot bath I've yet to pour.

"I'm gonna step out into the hall to finish my beer while you kids finish your, uh . . . bartering." Roger holds up his beer. "Cheers."

"Take the keys with you," Reece orders. "Grab the bag, too."

I hold the fob out after ripping it out of my purse and Roger snatches it from my hand on his way past, then picks up the luggage by the sofa. "Good night, Mallory. Good luck, Reece.

Sleep with one eye open."

"He's not staying!" I scream after him.

"I'll be right out, Roger," Reece says then turns his attention back to me. "Now, call me. 602-555-0126."

I don't call him – I send a text instead. The chime of the phone in his pocket appeases him and he sets me on my feet, but only after one last squeeze to both ass cheeks. "Happy?" He reads the text and grins.

Smack my ass again and I will desuscitate you.

He laughs and winks. "I prefer kissin' it, Sugar. Maybe leavin' a nip or two." As he saunters toward the door, he doesn't look back. "Do you need to have dinner sent?"

"It's in the fridge. I only have to heat it up. Someone sent Italian food last night to bribe me."

He turns and shrugs, a soft smile lighting up his eyes. "It worked."

"Thank you, for not letting me miss that." I feel the tingle behind my eyes and my nose starts to burn. "I've watched her suffer for years. Tell me he's a good guy."

"Who, Tanner?" He chuckles and nods over and over. "He's the best. I think he's suffered just as much. It's amazing what memories of your own can be stirred while watching someone else's dreams come true."

"What do you mean?"

He tips his chin. "Eat first. Make it a glass of wine and not a gallon. Don't fall asleep in the tub. I'll be back with your car. May take a while."

"Just lock the fob in the glovebox. I've got another one."

"So stubborn," he snickers, his mouth tipping on one side, then winks, "but so damn special."

The door closes and moments later my phone pings.

Would you really smother me?
I said desuscitate you.
By sitting on my face?
Reece . . .
Mallory . . .

Chapter 19

Reece

"The lady is going to murder you." Roger slams his door closed after climbing into my truck. "You got a death wish?"

I chuckle to myself as I push the button to start the truck and pull out of the lot. "You want to grab a quick one before we go get her car? I think we'd better let Tanner know where they live. The last thing he needs is a run-in with the psycho."

"Isn't Mallory expecting her car?"

"I doubt she's going anywhere. She told me to lock her fob inside it." Though the more I think about it, an idea is forming. *Leave the fob in her car, my ass.* Let her eat, take her bath, give her time.

"Alright, I'll follow you back and pick you up," Roger agrees. "We don't have to be in until eleven tomorrow."

"Where did you park Liberty's car?"

"They have passes for the parking garage. Specific spaces on the third floor in the ramp. Liberty is 3D. You can text and find out which one Mallory's is. Probably C or E." He blows a low whistle. "Nice place. They keep the passes above the visor. Slide it over the monitor at the entrance."

And that idea continues to form.

"Cranky's for a quick beer before we get her car?"

He shoots me a grin. "It's on the way. Why not? But only one."

"Do we ever drink more when we drive? Wait a minute. You had one at Mallory's."

He laughs. "I dropped it down the trash shoot. It was my excuse to get the hell out of there. You were spanking the woman's ass, Reece. Good God, it was walk away or start filming and put it on the internet. I could have made a quick buck or two." He spreads his hands to the limit of what the cab will allow. "Beginner's guide to daddy kink."

"She doesn't have a daddy kink," I snap.

"No shit," he says incredulously. "I believe half the damn parking lot and the entire lobby of the hospital knows that now. Maybe you should make the video. 'How to piss off a woman in ten seconds or less'."

"Tanner set me up for that!"

"He was joking, Reece! She's a higher class of woman."

"She sure as hell is," I mutter, pulling into the parking lot of Cranky's, my mind still racing as I scheme. *Passes for the garage. I would only be borrowing it.*

We take a seat at the bar and Roger texts Tanner. He switches to speaker when Tanner doesn't return a text and instead graces us with an actual call. Liberty is in the shower so we have a short period of time to inform him of the disaster that is Miranda and advise he stay away. We never could stand that woman, but Tanner is smart. He would have eventually figured out it was us who murdered her.

Roger takes a pull from his beer and sets it down on the bar. "Have you considered her position if you pursue her?"

"What are you talking about? What position?" My head spins. I've considered many positions with her – under me, over me, on her knees, me on mine.

"She treated you as a patient, Reece." He leans back on the barstool and folds his arms over his chest. "I believe there are rules against medical professionals and their patients hooking up. Did you not notice how your surgeon got a little prickish when you asked for her?"

"He's probably got a hard-on for her!" I spit, waving a fast hand through the air. "He wasn't being a professional, he was being a prick, like stakin' a claim. He could have been being a dick too. Just like the asshole in the restaurant. Besides, I'm not lookin' to just hook up." Oh shit! I really had not meant to disclose that.

The look of shock is followed quickly by a disbelieving chortle. "Reece Callahan isn't looking to fuck and duck the sexy little OR nurse?"

"She's a nurse anesthetist." I tip my chin. "There's a difference."

"Ah," he nods and grins, "lest you forget, the desuscitating kind. You still met her in the OR. She drugged you and got you ready to go under the knife. You were smitten by her," he air quotes, "silver eyes and pillowy lips."

"We didn't meet in the OR," I grumble, my voice low and

severe, though I'm not sure why. I'm not positive . . . yet. *Impossible.* Though impossible is leaning toward improbable, which is still a step closer to *maybe.* Navel piercings aren't exactly a rarity, but hers felt familiar. "I told you I knew her from somewhere."

"You told me she was Karma come to bite you on the ass." He leans forward on the bar once more and lifts his beer to his mouth, drawing a long pull. "Has it changed or did the bite feel good?"

Hesitant to share details – I'm not sure myself – I blow a deep breath and nod with slight unsurety. "I think I might have it figured out."

"You think," he says wryly. "Motel or her place?"

"I didn't sleep with her."

He waves his hand in a circular *anytime now* motion. "My beer is about empty and I ain't getting any younger, Reece. Is this going somewhere?"

My hand takes a slow trip from my forehead to my chin in a painful scrub. "I'm pretty sure I gave her a ride on my horse."

Roger's cackle is so loud it turns heads of fellow customers. "I know you consider yourself well endowed, Callahan, but most of us still call it a dick. Is that code for you let her take the top?"

"No, dumbass." I scowl. "My actual horse. Back in Texas."

He sticks his finger in his ear and wiggles it vigorously then tips his head as if to shake something out of it. "Say that again. This is fucking hilarious. You've lived here for years and you're sporting a hard-on from a college horsey ride?"

"High school," I grumble and polish off the contents of my beer. "I was her first kiss. And she apparently doesn't remember it or me."

He laughs so hard he nearly falls off his barstool. "This

isn't about the girl, Reece. This is about your ego! She truly is Karma." His eyes dip to the seat of my barstool. "Need some antibiotic for the bite on your ass?"

I stand, the sudden pang between my ass cheeks probably a residual from the wedgie that Mallory mastered when I had her over my shoulder. The little shit reached under my jeans, grabbed the band of my jerseys, and yanked hard. *Titillating and painful at the same time.* Hence the reason I smacked her ass. The second smack? Purely for my own pleasure. It gave me an excuse to rub the other cheek. Firm, round, fit. Perfect palm full.

"I thought you were my friend, Roger. I was hoping you'd give me a little insight."

He drains his glass, rises from his seat and we head for the door. "Don't know about insight, but I'm always good for a little advice. Let's see, I suppose you could go home and shave. Maybe leave a few scraggly patches reminiscent of pubes if it was in high school."

"Not funny, asshole."

He ignores me and continues his self-entertaining, unhelpful advice. "Lose thirty pounds. Wear a cowboy hat and boots. Ooh, I know," he spins and walks backwards and snaps his fingers, "grab a lasso. Might come in handy for later." He smirks. "Or, just go tell her who you are. You know, the old fashioned way."

Stopping at the door of my truck, I hesitate before opening it. "I'm not positive it's her. That girl was from North Carolina. Mallory said she and Liberty are best friends, grew up together. Tanner and Liberty are from here. Doesn't make sense."

"Makes perfect sense." He opens his door then shrugs. "She's obviously not *that* girl. Doesn't mean she's the *wrong* girl. And if you let the *right* one go, you're an idiot." He stares out into the night, deep in thought. "You'd better not be in this just to get laid, Reece. Things are different. Don't make promises you can't keep. Remember her best friend is part of our circle now. Tanner is going to put Liberty first. Don't fuck it up."

I lift a brow before posing the question. "Is that the voice of experience?"

"We're not talking about me," he grunts before virtually throwing himself into the truck. "Let's go get the lady's car."

Five minutes into the ten-minute drive to the hospital lot, my curiosity gets the best of me. He had told me he had a steady girl once and once was enough, but he never elaborated. I've never had a steady girl. Had plenty that wanted to be, but the constant touching and clinging always made my skin crawl. Irritating, like an itch I couldn't scratch. It's why I leave before they wake up, why I don't *snuggle*. But for some reason I picture myself staying with Mallory. I can see her with mussed hair, sleepy eyes, wearing my shirt as we share a cup of coffee and breakfast. Hell, I'd even fix it for her.

Approaching it from another angle this time, as my perspective has changed, "Doesn't it ever get old, Roger? Different beds, different faces?"

He sighs heavily as he stares out the window. "It numbs the pain, Reece." In my periphery I see him turn toward me. "And no, I never look them in the eyes, either. Hers were green."

Progress. The remainder of the drive is silent – me considering what he's said and him either wishing he hadn't said it or relieved it's over. The parking lot is at half capacity now that visiting hours are over and her Nissan Rogue sits alone with vacant spots on either side.

"Is your plan to stay with her tonight?" Roger's question catches me off guard. Maybe he can read my thoughts.

My shoulders lift and I shoot him a grin. "I was kinda hopin'. Depends if she wants to castrate me or desuscitate me.

Thinkin' I might fix her breakfast in the morning if all goes well."

He chuckles as he stretches one leg to reach into his jeans pocket and pulls out the fob, tossing it to me. "You are so whipped. I'll take your truck home. Text me if it doesn't work out and I'll pick you up tonight. Text me in the morning if it does and I'll pick you up at ten. We gotta be in at eleven. Try and get a couple hours sleep. The chief is going to kick your sorry ass if you come in dragging and un-showered."

What a brain waste of scheming. I don't need to borrow – aka steal – her pass to get in the building and I'll have an a.m. chauffeur service versus a Lyft.

"You're not going out?"

"Nah." He shakes his head before opening the door to come around to the driver's side where I meet him. "Figured I'd better be on-call in case you need a trip to the ER to get your balls reattached."

Shoulder clocking him on my way past, I growl, "You are not funny."

"I'm funny as hell," he retorts, laughing at himself, because it really wasn't funny. I have no idea what I'm walking into, but I'm about to find out.

Chapter 20

Mallory

My fingers are prunes by the time I climb out of the tub. I did almost fall asleep; carbs from leftover lasagna and a glass of wine can do that. Today's emotions probably played a large part as well. Libs sent a text a while ago.

"Going to stay with Lucas. If you need anything, call me."

She must not have received the bag and note that I had packed yet. She'd better be staying with him. What are the chances? I picture the poor lost girl at the beach shack as we ate hamburgers and fries the day we met. She wasn't afraid to cry, didn't hesitate to warn me about regrets; all because she had them, lived with them every day. I had taken the first step to welcome her, but we have walked together ever since. We know each other's secrets, pitfalls, shortcomings (like she has any), and we've spent fourteen years of lifting each other up when we fell and celebrating each other's wins. She was a lesson in my life for which I will be forever grateful. I'd never had a bestie before Liberty, but it turns out I'd never needed one. Her timing was perfect. She deserves all the happiness.

Finally, I'm settled into my overstuffed chair with another glass of wine, in a tank top and PJ shorts, and an Ava Mynx book in hand. *"The Baron"* Yes, I could grab one of the new medical magazines I picked up last week, but it's Friday night. This is *me* time. No TV, no music in the background. Silence. Pure bliss. Concrete between floors in our building – no footsteps from above. No thumping music through the walls on either side.

"You know what happens when you're naughty, don't you, Bella?"

"I-I didn't mean to be. I thought you wanted . . ."

His chuckle is deep and taunting. "You knew exactly what you were doing. And now, it's time to put you over my knee."

The knock on the door is soft but solid. I roll my eyes as I place the bookmark, and struggle to rise from my comfy chair. "Lovely," I mutter to myself. "Probably Ray, either intentionally trying to disrupt what was never going to happen or bringing Buster up to say hello." I take pity on Buster. When a dog is so homely even kids run away in fear, he needs a friend. Tempted to pretend I'm not home, I ponder those thoughts before giving in and utilizing the peephole in the door.

"What the hell?" I whisper, shocked to see Reece Callahan on the other side. I told him to leave my fob in the glove compartment. Now I'm really tempted to pretend I'm not home. I've been reading Ava Mynx, in the middle of a *punishment* chapter, and the ass-spanker is standing outside my door. No, I'm not a fan of dominance – doesn't mean you can't read about it. It's fiction!

"Mallory." His voice is so deep, I swear the walls rumble. The way he says my name is droolworthy – always has been. The way he draws it out, that sweet southern twang with a touch of playful spice. *Damn you, Ava Mynx!* "I know you're in there. The peephole darkened. Open the door, Sugar."

"Why, you want to spank me again?" Why the hell did I say that? Wait! Was that said with fervor or snark? Can I get a do-over? That was too breathy. *I swear to God, Ava, should I ever meet you in person, I'm going to murder you. After you sign every book of yours that I've purchased, of course.*

Peeking through the hole once more, I watch his chin tip and he stares at the ceiling, as if seeking strength from a higher power, before lowering it and uttering, "I forgot something."

A quick glance around the room reveals no stray items left behind that I can see. Throwing the latch on the door, I open it wide. "What did you forget?"

He steps forward slowly, confidently; the twinkle in his eyes and the softness of his smile startling me. I take two cautious steps back, my neck being stretched to its limits to gaze into those dazzling blue eyes. The door closes behind him with a quiet click.

"This." His mouth crashes to mine in synchrony with a hand in my hair and a strong arm lifting me off the floor. Gentleman Callahan has left the building. Foreplay be damned; he is having sex with my mouth. He's not testing depth capacity though. It's a languorous tease that results in my legs wrapping around his waist, my arms around his broad shoulders, and my tongue matching his strokes in a slow dance. He tastes of mint and a tiny hint of beer – not unpleasant at all. His scent is masculine – a woodsy warmth with a touch of oriental spice. The kind you could spray on your pillows to incentivize dreams.

We both pant between lip locks, a valiant attempt to suck air into our lungs. I've never been kissed like this. There's no rush, no tearing of clothes . . . yet. He samples and savors as if enjoying every moment. My moan escapes in quiet desperation as my body heats with the need to have him rescue a particular kitten.

"There she is," he whispers against my jaw, as if anticipating the sound I made. My hands travel to his hair, guiding him to move those kisses along my neckline, find that sweet spot. God, I could climb this tree of a man.

"One night, Reece," I murmur breathlessly, the warning bells in my head being silenced with every brush of his lips across my skin.

"At a time, Mallory," he returns, as if he plans on more.

"That only applies to days," I argue, craning my neck to give him better access. I don't know why I bicker. It's in my nature. "One day at a time."

"We can do days too." His tongue swirls at my pulse point and he nips lightly on my collarbone. "All the days, all the nights. You sure about this?"

"Down the hall, last door on the left."

He chuckles, the vibration tinged with the soft and bristly facial hair against my skin driving me crazy. "I'll take that as a yes."

My hands in his hair, I pull slightly until his eyes meet mine. "Now, Mr. Callahan, before I change my mind."

His eyes light with mischief. "You gonna call me that in the bedroom?"

My eyes narrow. "It's that or moron."

He squeezes a butt cheek and laughs heartily as he carries me through the living room to the hallway. "You are so special."

Once inside the bedroom, things change. There is no

more laughter, no more banter. It's a queen size bed – not one I'm accustomed to sharing – and looks pretty damn small right now when considering the mountain of a man in front of me.

All thoughts of bed dimensions or how we're going to fit comfortably go right out the window when Reece sets me on my feet and takes my cheeks in his palms, tipping my chin with this thumb. "Do you have any idea how beautiful you are?"

My cheeks flush. I'm in a tank top and shorts, no makeup, fatigued from a long day. Pretty sure there are remnants of dark circles and red rims from the tears I've cried. Definitely not at my best. "You don't have to say that, Reece." I shake my head against his palms. "We're already . . ."

His kiss is harsh as he grasps the nape of my neck with one hand and removes the scrunchie from my hair with the other, letting the locks fall. "You can say thank you, Reece, kiss me with gratitude, or jump my bones. I don't say things I don't mean, Mallory. Understood?" I nod in concession. He smiles puckishly as he slowly lifts the hem of my tank. "Good. Now, you ready to show me more, Beautiful?"

Okay, there's something you have to understand about me. I am intelligent, street smart, book smart, not exactly *in*experienced, and I'm fast on my feet. But Reece makes me nervous, and sometimes those feet make a trip to my mouth, at highway speed. "You wanna see my boobies?"

His jaw drops for only a moment before his burst of laughter follows. He lifts me with no effort, a hand on each side of my waist, and tosses me on the bed, following on his hands and knees. "So fucking special."

The laughter dies quickly as he hovers above me, burdening his weight on his elbows, eyes on mine. "Touch me," he whispers a soft plea. "Anywhere, Mallory. Just touch me."

My hand reaches for his beard, the perfect blend of soft and bristly, finely trimmed facial hair making my fingertips tingle, and I watch as his eyes close as he leans into it, relishing the contact. He breathes in deep and lets it out slowly. "I knew it." I don't think he meant it to be audible – more an inner thought. Doesn't matter now because he doesn't give me the chance to inquire as his mouth takes mine in a fervent kiss. He palms my breast and I arch my back into it as his thumb brushes over a stiff nipple.

"Reece," I whimper with need. So much better than my comfy chair, a book and a glass of wine.

He slides his arm under my back, lifting and turning me to reposition me on the bed so my head is on the pillows, taking advantage of the lift to remove the flimsy tank. His heated gaze is enough to stoke a flame I haven't felt in, well – ever, but also enough to cause a bit of self-consciousness. He catches my wrists before my arms can shelter my chest. "Don't ever hide these. They're fucking perfect."

"Tit for tat." I narrow my eyes as I pull my wrists from his hold and reach for the hem of his T-shirt labeled PFD stretched over bulging biceps and tight pecs, and yank it from his jeans. "We're in this together."

He grins and winks, reaching behind his neck to grab his T-shirt to pull it off. *Oh God, just like in Ava's books.* "We sure are."

Skin on skin from the waist up as his knees slide down the mattress, he finds purchase on top of me, mouth on mine before beginning a slow, torturous journey from my jaw to the pulse point in my neck, then giving attention to each nipple with a gentle nip of his teeth followed by a soothing lap of his tongue. His journey continues on a path straight to my bellybutton.

"Pretty," he murmurs, stopping to run a slow circle with his tongue around my barbell piercing. "How long have you had this?"

"Ree-ee-ece," I whine impatiently, running my fingers through his hair and tugging a little harder. Conversation is the last thing I'm looking for at the present time. The man has me ready to crawl out of my skin and he's interested in a piercing that I use as a reminder for strength. "Who cares?"

He chuckles against my skin, causing a rumble through my most sensitive parts, and runs his tongue in a circle around the diamond studded barbell. "Just admiring your bauble, Mallory."

Yanking his head up by his hair, I threaten with a glare, "If you don't get to work, I will cut your baubles off and pull my little buddy out of the drawer to finish the job."

Chapter 21

Reece

Forget every teenage dream I had about her – she is every man's fantasy. The flawless silky skin, curves I want to study for days – yes, *days* – and nights then start all over once I reach her toes. Her sharp intake of breath and the way she arches her body as every second of anticipation builds is incentive to deliver more. With the first swipe of my tongue, every flavor I've ever savored takes a backseat to my new favorite: *Mallory Tompkins' pussy.* She's spicy, tangy, and sweet; a perfect match to her personality.

Her hips rise as she plants her heels on my back, but I plant one hand on her lower belly to hold her in place, my little finger seeking that unique memory from so many years ago. My tongue works its magic as my fingers find that special spot and curl, coaxing an explosion that causes her thighs to flex and her heels to dig in so hard it's painful. Pain has never felt so good. As the pressure from her heels decreases and she begins to relax, I indulge myself one last teasing nip on that swollen bundle of nerves.

"Reece!" She tugs on my hair to pull me back, then tightens her thighs around my ears to hold me in place. "Too sensitive."

I blow light whispers of breath on the heated area, causing her thighs to tremor and me to chuckle. "Calmer?"

She throws her head back on the pillows and breathes a deep sigh, followed by music to my ears in the form of a soft purr. "Yes."

Sliding off the end of the bed, I stand and toe my socks off, snatch my wallet out of my back pocket and grab a condom. The wallet falls somewhere near the nightstand as I toss it in the general area. I'll find it later for more – I'm here until morning. My belt and jeans are undone in seconds flat, dropped to the floor along with my jerseys, and I'm climbing back in on my hands and knees.

Mallory eyes the goods with furrowed brows before looking up at me, a hint of unsurety in her voice. "You're uh . . . gifted."

"A man can't hear that too much." I chuckle and tear open the condom, a secret part of me wanting to pound my chest with the compliment. Take that Mr. X-ray. *Big wallets do not compensate for a tiny dick.*

"You want help with that?" she offers sheepishly.

"Sugar," I warn, rolling it on and pinching the end to prepare the reservoir for what is sure to be a bounty of babymakers, before positioning myself above her, "if I let you

BUT I KISSED A COWBOY

touch me, I'm gone. Next time, okay?" I don't give her a chance to tell me there won't be a next time, that this is one night only. It's not, one night will never be enough. I won't rush her. I saw the apprehension in her eyes. The last thing I want to do is hurt her. Her pleasure is more important than mine. For the first time in my life, I want more. I want the connection. I want to look in her eyes, see her come undone for me. "We'll go slow," I reassure her, brushing a wayward strand away from her face while rubbing my desire against her wet, warm, welcoming heat.

It's working, quite well I might add. First one leg, then the next wraps around my hips and she joins me in the movements. Her hands slide up my biceps across my shoulders and lock behind my neck. That touch. Two dainty, masterfully crafted hands that hold so much magic. My name sounds like a prayer as it whispers across her lips, "Reece, please."

"Eyes on me, Mallory." I wait until she opens them before sliding in gently, slowly, inch by inch until she winces. "Breathe," I whisper, pulling back and moving forward again. She's nervous, tense, tight as hell. I'd kiss her, but eye contact would be lost and I'm not sure we'd get it back.

In one fell swoop, I plant one hand on the mattress and ease my other under her back, lifting her with me as I rise to my knees and lean back on my heels – being careful not to lower her onto my dick any more than she is. In this position, it's not as easy to bury myself balls deep and risk causing her pain. She'll get used to me, eventually.

"You're in control this way," I tell her, bringing her mouth down to mine, delivering a kiss I only hope lets her know I mean it. I can resist my propensity to be in charge. She needs to call the shots after the day she's had, be in charge.

Her eyes fill with wonderment and something else I can't quite decipher but swear I remember – innocence or maybe a lack of confidence. "You'd do that for me?" It makes me want to hunt down every man who's ever made her doubt herself and make him a patient in the OR – so long as she's not an attending.

"Of course I would," I whisper against her lips. "Your pleasure is mine. I'm not even inside you yet, and you feel so good I'm fantasizing about the next time."

Confidence boosted, a look of sheer determination in those beautiful silver eyes, her voice a sexy promise that makes my skin tingle, "Then get on your back, Mr. Callahan, I plan to take all of you." *And there she is.*

I wind my hand in her hair and bring her mouth to mine once more, and mutter against it, "So fucking special."

She's on full display as she rides me. Inhibitions gone; perky, full breasts that will play on a reel in my head until the day I die. That tiny curved barbell looped through the skin above her bellybutton, diamond studs on each end. She's managed to take all of me. I'm a big guy; homegrown and proud. But with a well-placed thumb, the right pressure, and circular motions that had her purring like a kitten, she sank to the base.

And now?

"Mallory, baby please. Meet me in the middle." My groan is so desperate it's a near cry as I plead for mercy. Her pleasure is mine – I meant it. She is enjoying herself. But damn, somewhere along the line, I'd kinda like a release too. A major eruption, a little respite, and I'd be up to the task again in no time.

Using my pecs for balance, she grinds relentlessly on what is bound to be a bruised dick. I don't think I've ever felt so used in all my life. She pants hard, "So close, almost there."

Almost? For a third time? She has been squeezing my dick in a tight vise with pulsations more powerful than an Aquacare showerhead. But the sounds she makes are so delectable, I want to hear them again. She's not a screamer. Her displays of passion are mine and God's names whispered on her lips with a mix of shuddered breaths and sexy moans every time she lets go.

My propensity to be in charge reappears like a long lost friend as I flip her onto her back without warning and grind through a clenched jaw, "Think you can give as good at you take?"

She grins impishly and her eyes light as she wraps her legs around me and squeezes. "I can be charitable."

I drive into her hard; the sensation almost too much bear. One stroke, two strokes, three strokes, four . . .

"Fuck….yes. Mallory." For the first time ever I've spoken the name of the woman underneath me and never has anything felt so right. My release goes on and on as she pulses around me. I wasn't this out of breath on the last mountain relays we had to trek. A fifty-pound backpack for three miles in thirty minutes feels like a piece of cake right now. "You're tryin' to kill me, aren't you?"

"Just taking advantage of all I can before the clock runs out," she says breathlessly, though giving her best effort to keep it light.

I don't know if I should be hurt or pissed. Our clock isn't running out. We could be timeless.

Rolling onto my back, I take her with me and tuck her close to my chest. "We don't need a clock, Mallory. I don't want a timeline."

"One night, Reece," she reminds me, a clip in her voice that makes me cringe.

"Then I guess I have until sunrise, don't I?" *To convince you otherwise, I think to myself.* I gently remove myself from the bed and head for the bathroom to remove the condom and collect a warm washcloth. I've never done this, only read about it.

Aftercare.

Two more rounds before we're both fully sated and tired as hell – the lady gives as good as she gets. Once she gained her confidence and I gained her trust, we were the perfect match. Mallory rolls onto her side, facing the outside of the bed and I climb in behind her. I slide a bent elbow under her pillow and wrap an arm over her belly, placing my little finger over the barbell piercing for my own comfort. She hasn't reacted to any of my attempts of stirring a memory for her, so apparently it's all in my head. Her hair smells so damn good – not quite what I remember, more of a warm vanilla and coconut – but then, she's not *that* girl, just the *right* girl. Guilt washes over me as I recall Roger's words. At the same time I want a connection with her, I need to disconnect from a memory of long ago. But I'm struggling.

"You plan on staying?"

I breathe her in a little deeper and brush my finger over the piercing. She is the right girl. "The sun isn't up yet, Mallory."

"Do you snore?" she asks with a touch of snark. *So damn sassy.*

"Do you purr?" I kiss the tip of her shoulder and chuckle.

She tugs the blanket tighter to herself. "Good night, Reece."

Brushing my finger over the piercing once more, I taunt, "You never did tell me how long you've had this."

"Why are you so curious?"

"It's pretty, delicate like you." I tap it lightly, obsessing over the piece of jewelry that feels so familiar. "I'd like to know the inspiration."

"Now you want pillow talk?" she huffs.

"I'll take anything I can get."

"Rebellion," she admits reluctantly. "Caused my first grounding as a teenager, but didn't prevent a trip I didn't want to make. My cousin let me borrow her ID so I wouldn't need parental permission. My mom didn't find out until it was healed over. Grounded me for a month but rescinded it when I finally told her why I got it, and she even let me keep it after."

Teenager. A trip. Impossible, I remind myself. Tread carefully, Reece.

"Are you going to tell me why?"

She heaves an impatient breath. "I chose the barbell because I felt the weight of the world on my shoulders. It's what happens when a parent ruins a kid's dream. The barbell reminded me it wasn't my weight to carry. It's a good reminder now of what I want and what I won't ever tolerate."

Whoa! That was heavy. A kid's dream? I can't imagine my parents holding me back or causing me pain in any way, shape, or form.

"What is it you want and won't ever tolerate?"

She groans as if more questions might be the answer to the latter of my two. "World peace and peanut butter without jelly. Are we done?"

God, I love her sass...and wit...and humor.

"You said you and Liberty grew up together," I continue cautiously, ignoring the warning. "What part of Phoenix did you grow up in?"

"Last question?" she grouses.

"Mmhmm," I lie.

"We didn't technically grow up together. We kinda grew together. We met our first year of high school. Liberty's dad died a couple years after she lost Lucas."

"Damn," I utter. "That sucks."

"Yeah," she whispers sympathetically. "It did. She and her mom moved to the east coast a year after that. Libs and I went through high school and college together and then came here for our masters. We ended up staying."

Whoa, whoa, whoa. Back the horse up. My heart starts to thump in my chest as *impossible* takes a sharp swerve toward *are.you.fucking.kidding.me?* "The east coast?"

"That's another question, Reece," she grumbles, shifting and pulling the blanket tighter. *Not only is she an orgasm thief, she's a blanket hog as well.* "Curiosity killed the cat."

A low sexy groan leaves my throat as I chuckle against the crook of her neck and drop a kiss to the sweet spot that makes her shiver. "Nah, I'm good at rescuing pussy, wouldn't you agree?"

She brings her shoulder up to move my face away. "More like wearing them out. North Carolina," she says with a yawn, her voice drifting toward the deeper side of slumber. "Is the inquisition over now?"

Thank God I'm laying down, because my head is spinning. So tempted to bring her over on top of me, tell her she's welcome to take another horsey ride before sunrise, but instead I rein it in – pun intended – kiss her shoulder and utter, "Yeah, all done. Good night, Mallory."

She is *that* girl. The *right* girl. *She's My Kitten.*

Chapter 22

Mallory

The smell of pancakes and coffee fills the air as it wafts into my bedroom. Libs must be up earlier than usual. If I didn't think it rude to ask for room service, I'd call out and ask her to bring it to me, on a tray. Full service with syrup, butter, and cream for my coffee. A little orange juice wouldn't hurt either. A glance at the clock reveals it's not as early as I thought. Half past nine?

As I throw off the blanket and move to climb out of bed, every muscle in my body revolts in stiffness as if they haven't been used in . . . Oh shit! That's not Libs in the kitchen. Liberty is with Lucas – unless it didn't work out. The thought dissipates as fast as it formed. That guy was near tears.

Rising to my feet, I'm reminded once again why I should return to yoga three times a week versus the two classes I've been attending – sort of. Don't judge! I still do my Kegels every day and run the treadmill in the gym downstairs, on a somewhat regular basis. Priorities! Sometimes a pint of Ben and Jerry's and an evening of Netflix outranks exercise. Oh! Let's not forget the wine . . . and Ava Mynx.

Slowly making my way across the bedroom, I sneak a tentative peek through the partially open door toward the kitchen. The Adonis, otherwise known as Reece Callahan, stands in front of the stove, shirtless, jeans slung low on his hips, *barefoot*, flipping pancakes. My mouth waters, though I'm not sure if it's hunger or . . . hunger. A quick squeeze of my thighs provides the answer: it's food. Two days, six soaking baths, and maybe I'll consider the other kind.

"Good morning, Gorgeous," he sings a little too cheerily for my taste as he flips another cake. I'm not a morning person. If I didn't love my job so much, they'd be lucky to see me by noon, still in pajamas. Syrup, butter, coffee mugs, plates, and silverware are already set at the breakfast bar. As I make my way into the living room, he sets the skillet off the burner to the side, glances up at me and frowns. He shakes his head and moves toward me, grabs my hand and leads me back to the bedroom. "Nope. This won't do."

"Reece!" I yank against his grip, assuming he wants a morning round before leaving. "I can barely walk as it is! I'll be on a donut pillow for a week."

"You're welcome." He winks as an impish grin that I want to wipe off smatters his face. "Happy to be of service." He snatches my hand once again and leads me into the room where he picks his T-shirt off the arm of the chair and holds it above my head, neck opening stretched and ready to slide over me. "Arms up."

"What? Why?"

"Indulge me," he says, then plops the T-shirt over my head. I stand frozen, staring at him. "It works better if you put your arms through the sleeves, Sugar."

Sliding my arms into the sleeves of the soft cotton that smells just like him; a scent that is going to linger in my senses, my memory, and in my dreams for who knows how long – because this can't happen again – I look up. "There, happy?"

He taps my nose. "I am. Now wait ten seconds and come out. We'll start over."

Before I can question his motives, he's gone. I wait the allotted time and enter the living room, watching him in the same spot he was the first time I found him. At the stove; this time plating pancakes then setting them on the breakfast bar. His T-shirt sits at my mid-thigh, much like a shapeless mini dress.

"Good morning, Gorgeous," he starts again with a slow perusal from my head to my toes. "I like you in my clothes. Hungry?"

"Why are you still here?" I ask, eyeing the spread on the counter. "We agreed to one night. In case you hadn't noticed, the sun has risen."

He ignores my question. "Sit, eat. I fixed it for you. Figured you might need some sustenance. It was the least I could do. We'll talk."

Pressing the heels of my palms to my eyes, I let out an exasperated breath. I had a feeling this was coming. *"At a time, Mallory".* "Reece, there is nothing to talk about. You don't . . ."

He pulls out one of the backless barstools for me. "Sit down and eat, Mallory." He arches an expectant brow and nods at the food. "Please. Roger will be here in half an hour to pick me up. We don't have much time."

We eat in silence until Reece has finished his pancakes and I've managed half of mine. They're not bad, a little fluffier than I'm used to, and he fixes a damn good cup of coffee.

He sets his fork down and wipes his mouth with the napkin, takes a sip of his coffee, and turns on the stool. "Okay, why are you stuck on one night only? I was under the impression you enjoyed yourself."

"It has nothing to do with that." I stand, the ache in certain areas reminding me that I did in fact enjoy myself, maybe too much. Gathering the dishes, I carry them to the sink. He joins me, carrying his own and sets them on the counter by the sink, then begins to collect the condiments. "Do you have any idea what's at stake for me, Reece? I treated you as a patient. Our first encounter was in the OR! It is against all ethics and principles, not to mention the rules. I could lose my job! This was a mistake! The best I can hope for is you will not mention this to anyone!" I tip my head back, running a fast hand through my hair and stare at the ceiling. "Oh God, tell me your buddy Roger will keep his mouth shut."

"Roger would never say anything. For God's sake, we're not teenagers!" He shoots me a scowl as if insulted. "Let me ask you something, Mallory. If you treated a friend, an old acquaintance, maybe a family member in that OR, would you have to cut off all communications after? No claim to them? No chance of future relationships?"

"What!?" I huff indignantly. "No! That's ridiculous. But you don't develop relationships after and you certainly don't sleep with patients. It's not allowed!"

He leans against the counter on his hip. There's a wistfulness in his voice as he tilts his head, brows slightly lifted as if waiting for me to solve a puzzle. "You still have no clue, do you?"

"No clue about what?"

"We didn't meet in the OR, Mallory. And we are hardly a mistake." He sounds disappointed, as if I should remember him. I've only been in Arizona a couple years. I'm not that brain dead and my dating life hasn't exactly been a free for all, despite my last ginormous mistake with Eric. I'm kinda picky.

Oh shit! He did tell Rory he had kissed me before. Though I'm pretty sure I would have remembered it. Men like Reece Callahan are not easily forgotten. And I don't do one night stands. At least I didn't prior to last night.

My nose crinkles in confusion. I don't want to be a blow to the man's ego, but the first I knew of Reece, and his reputation, was the OR . . . by way of Trish. "You're going to have to refresh my memory."

"Come here." He takes my hand and leads me around the breakfast bar to the stools on the other side. "Sit here." I take the seat I vacated not long ago, and he pulls his behind it. He sits with his thighs on each side of mine – though his feet touch the floor while mine rest on the mid bar six inches above – and scoots as close as he can. His right hand rests on my stomach while his left brushes the hair away from shoulder. "Close your eyes."

"What are you . . ."

"Sshhh," he whispers softly. "Close your eyes and clear your mind."

His right palm spreads on my stomach until his little finger dips into my bellybutton, and an old familiar sensation niggles at my brain. His left hand tips my chin up and turns my head. I open my eyes to see his bright blue ones twinkle before he plants a slow, gentle, sweet kiss on my mouth. No tongue, no sucking, no biting. Be it alpha Reece or gentleman Reece, the man knows how to kiss. Exactly how to draw out the quiet moan from the depths of my throat – the rare subtle purr of pleasure that only he has mastered with a simple touch of his mouth to mine. I feel the length of him stiffening against my backside, though he doesn't acknowledge it, or press it tighter against me, just like . . . *Oh my God.*

When the kiss is over, he smiles so sweetly my heart swells a little with the long forgotten memory. "There she is," he whispers then winks. "As much as I hate to leave, I need to get to work. Keep the shirt, consider it a memory."

He rises from the stool, heads for the door, and slides his feet into his boots. His hand on the doorknob, he hesitates. "To this day, Kitten, it's still the best kiss I've ever had," he says softly, opening a safe of treasured memories I had locked away so many years ago. My head whips up in his direction, slack-jawed, eyes wide with shock, as he turns to face me. He knows he's won. It's in his eyes as he flashes that award winning grin. "Lady Luck would be pretty pissed if I didn't tell you she's missed you too." The door opens and closes behind him with a soft click, and he's gone. Like magic, for the first time in over a decade a clear vision of the face of the teenager on the horse colors my memory. His features are sharper now, the young man replaced by rugged masculinity and experience, but his eyes are the same.

You know that line you read in every book: *And I find the breath I hadn't realized I was holding.* Yeah, total bullshit. I'm hyper-freaking-ventilating. Reece Callahan was my first kiss? He remembers me? Keep his shirt? I still have his hat! Lady Luck is still alive? How long do horses live? Apparently longer than most dogs.

I need to call Libs. She's the only one who knew about that kiss. Oh wait! I can't call her. She's with Lucas.

Chapter 23

Reece

I had texted Roger when I woke up at half past eight to let him know I would be ready at ten, per the plan we had settled on the night before.

Him: Balls intact or do we need to make a pitstop at the ER before work?

Me: My boys thank you for your concern. I'm fixing her breakfast and you're not invited. Be on time. I gotta go home and shower. I've got news.

Him: You're pregnant, aren't you?

Me: Possibly triplets. Fuck off!

Roger's truck sits in the parking lot as I exit her building at ten o'clock. His burst of laughter would be audible if his window were down, but the open mouth and thrown back head is pretty indicative of the humor he finds in my appearance. The reactions of other residents coming and going through the lobby were varied. The ladies were appreciative, as is the usual, though the urge to wink and smile, as is my usual, escaped me. The men weren't quite as entertained; Ray included. Now I know what Buster looks like and quite frankly, after the little prick tried to take a chunk out of my ankle, my best hope is there is a nasty-ass cat out there gunning for him. Damn, that is one fugly dog. It's no wonder Mallory walks him; everybody needs a friend. It's out of pity, I'm sure.

"Sooo..." Roger eyes my shirtless state before putting his truck in gear and backing out of the parking space, ". . .did you have to sneak out before she woke up or was she chasing you with a knife and you couldn't grab your shirt fast enough?"

Tossing the paperback I had found on the side table by her chair and hidden outside her door in the hallway onto the dashboard, I buckle my seatbelt and grin. "Everything's fine. No knives, no sneaking out. You can't tell anyone I was here."

"What we do isn't anybody's business but our own." He glances over at the first red light. "And by our own, that doesn't mean we can't tell each other. What's your news?"

"She is *that* girl," I tell him, an overwhelming sense of achievement for recall making me puff my chest. "The one I gave a ride on my horse."

His nose scrunches. "The North Carolina girl?"

"The one and only."

He laughs heartily. "Okay. Just one question. Did you give her another ride on your horse?"

I point my finger hard as he turns into our parking lot to drop me off so I can grab a quick shower and get my truck before we head to the firehouse. "Only because it's you and I know you won't repeat it, because I'll kill you if you do," I grab at the crotch of my jeans and groan a little, "I think she broke him."

He grabs the paperback from the dashboard and turns it over. His lip curls in disgust and his face fills with mortification. "What the hell are you doing with one of Ava's books?" He tosses it in my lap as if it's bitten him. "The woman is the queen of kink!"

"It's Mallory's, you dumbass! I temporarily stole it so I could get Ava to sign it for her. It's a surprise."

He stares for the longest time before his lips tip in a devilish smirk. "So, she did call you daddy?"

"No!" I deny vehemently in her defense, then let out a pitiful sigh. "She's not like that, Roger. She's – she's just so," I search for the right word, "special."

We exit the truck and head for our building. "Just remember what I said. She's gonna be part of the circle now that Tanner's . . ." he pauses at the door before punching in the code, ". . . got the woman he's always wanted. Best friends are hard to find. Finding one woman you can see yourself with forever? Once in a lifetime, Reece." He gives me a cold stare. "If you think that's what she is, go for it. Don't play with her. Men bend, women break. Don't fuck this up."

"I don't plan to!" I snap defensively.

"How many relationships have you been in, Reece?"

"I've never wanted one." I scowl, my skin heating with the very thought of my past. "I've been a mattress jumper for a reason. No responsibility for anyone but myself. But for the first time in my life, I want something more. Mallory makes me want more."

"Exactly," he says with a lift of his brow. "And the Hotshots?"

"What do the Hotshots have to do with anything?"

"Say it again, Reece. No responsibility for anyone but yourself." He punches in the code for the door and opens it with a fast pull. "I'll let you sit on that for a while. If you can't figure it out on your own, you're well on your way to fucking it up."

"We've been Hotshots for years!" I follow his fast pace, the subject apparently a sour one and one he wants to avoid, though I don't know why.

Roger and I are both Hotshots. Not fulltime – part of a backup specialty team called out for wildfires when they get extremely large or there are a high number of them throughout country, and auxiliary teams are called upon. That's where we come in. Accessories. A bit like the second string of a basketball team. It's bitchin' work, the toll on your body and exposure to the elements definitely challenging. Digging fire lines is no picnic – makes putting in new fence at the ranch seem like a day in the park. But we do our part: extra hours every year for specialty training, geographical mapping of the landscapes, education of new equipment. We're not interstate; we are intrastate.

Bypassing the elevators as usual, he heads for the stairwell and I follow on his heels. "We're already firefighters, Roger. What the hell's the difference? It's just another method of fighting a different kind of fire."

He spins on the step in the middle of the second flight to the third floor where we both reside, one hand on the rail, the other pointing a hard finger. Admittedly, the fire in his eyes at the present time does not look easily extinguishable.

"You know damn well what the difference is. It's why we specialty train. The risks are higher, winds are unpredictable, control is questionable, and there's no way to know how long you'll be gone. No communications. It's not exactly a day job, Reece." He rolls his shoulders and heaves a deep sigh before he turns to continue his ascent. "Relationships are impossible. Just ask all the guys that are divorced, why most of them are single. Like I said, men bend and women break. Get your shower. We're due in forty minutes."

Damn, he's touchy this morning. I call out to the pair of boots on the stairs above me before he can open the door to the third floor, "You ever gonna tell me who she was?"

The door slams hard; the sound of it echoing through the empty stairwell. Nope. Not ready to talk about it.

My shower is short – having been sated to a point of euphoria I haven't felt in ever – there is no need to boost Reece junior before rinsing and toweling off quickly. Clothes on, hair still damp, I'm out the door twenty minutes before I'm due at the station. It's a ten minute drive from home and on my way, thoughts drift to last night. What are the chances? From the moment I saw her in the OR, she knocked me off my feet – metaphorically. I was already laid out on the table. But I felt that immediate attraction, the inexplicable pull. The touch on my arm that took me to a place I wanted to stay.

Over the years, I've always considered the girl on the horse a pleasant memory – the one that got away. The girl I might someday model my wife after, at the age of forty or so, to appease my mother and give her a grandkid or two. The way she felt under me, over me, around me. One night, my ass. I could do nights like that for-fucking-ever. I wanted her to touch me. I needed to see her in my T-shirt. I would have preferred naked underneath it, but I took what I could. It was a test of sorts. Fixing her breakfast was another. I was in no hurry to leave. I would have fixed bacon and eggs, had there been any bacon in the fridge, but improvisation is a sport for me. I could have done a veggie omelet, but when I found the pancake mix in the pantry, it seemed like the perfect sweet treat for breakfast. Women like those, don't they? Good God, don't ever tell my mother I made premix pancakes. She has a five-ingredient scratch recipe I've made many times for the guys at the firehouse, but I wasn't going to rummage through Mallory's pantry to find the necessary items.

And my method of delivery? I couldn't just tell her. I wanted to know if it was a memory for her too. Strange, I know. But how do you inform the woman you took six ways to Sunday just hours prior, and rode you like the cowboy she was saving the horse from, that you were her first kiss on your actual horse years ago? It was a candid moment though; one I'll never forget. She remembered alright. The flash of amazement in those beautiful eyes was priceless. Leaving her my T-shirt seemed fitting.

I wonder whatever happened to my hat.

Hopping out of my truck, I snatch my phone from my pocket.

"You didn't sleep with your patient, Kitten. You slept with your cowboy, though I don't remember much sleeping. I thought it was "impossible" when you kissed me in the parking lot. The only thing impossible for me is one night with you. My biggest regret back then was not getting your name or your phone number. This time, I know where to find you. Last night was not a mistake and we are not over."

Chapter 24

Mallory

I read the text once, twice, then once more. *"We are not over"*. When did he figure out who I was? Moreover, *how* did he figure out who I was? We didn't exchange names in Texas. I was his *kitten* and he was my *cowboy*. The more thought I give it, the clearer the memory becomes. His eyes are still as blue, his smile is cockier than I remember, but confidence will do that. He was slimmer and firm back then, but I swear I counted an eight-pack last night while I was using his pecs for stability.

"Watch out for him, Tompkins, he's a player". Dr. Evans' words echo in my head. Tossing my phone on the counter before heading to the shower, I mumble to myself, "Yeah, doc,

as if I didn't know by his initial invitation to sit on his face." I snicker as I pass the unmade bed on the way to the ensuite, recalling the activities of the night before. "Not gonna lie, best beard I've ever sat on."

Utilizing my day off with inside chores due to the rainstorm from hell – it's monsoon season – I turn out loads of laundry from machine to machine. Sheets have been changed; unfortunately removing the scent of Reece from my pillows. Funny how I missed his T-shirt in the load of colors. Maybe next week. *One night.* That was the agreement. After the emotional events of yesterday, I was a bit of a trainwreck, and he was . . . handy. And if I tell myself that enough times, maybe I'll believe it. How was I to know we had history?

My phone sounds on the counter and the temptation to let it go to voicemail is strong, but a quick peek at the screen and seeing Savannah's number makes me smile. I could use a night out. The storms in Arizona exit as fast as they enter. Flood the streets for a couple hours and dry up even faster. By later this evening, the city won't even remember it.

"Hey, what's up?"

"Oh my God!" she breathes hard. "Are you at home?"

"Yeah, why?"

"Close to a TV?"

I resist rolling my eyes. We have one in the living room and each have one in our bedrooms. How close would I have to be? "Yes," I drawl. "Any particular one you want me to choose?"

"Mallory!" she huffs impatiently. "Hurry up!" Savannah is generally well composed – the bathroom incident a perfect example – hushed and discreet.

"Why would I need a TV?"

"Channel 14. Turn it on."

Great. That's the local news channel. I'll probably be

called in to help with an emergency because the hospitals have been inundated with injured patients. Why can't people just stay home in inclement weather? Snatching the remote off the coffee table, I turn the TV on and study the screen, anticipating a freeway full of smashed vehicles.

No. No, no, no. Instead, I find myself suddenly a bit . . . amused by the view I'm being gifted. My bestie on full display, soaking wet, totally oblivious to the hard peaked nipples saluting every soldier from here to Virginia from under the sky blue sports bra I packed for her. She stands next to a gurney holding the hand of a man stretched out on it, as the EMTs strap him down. It makes total sense to me. Libs has tunnel vision; job first, vanity last. Although I am going to de-nut the cameraman when I find out who he is – the angle is totally unnecessary. He's homed in on her boobs, assuring he captures a shot that will grab the attention of the usual bored audience. Probably a shitload of horny men and teenage boys in the process as well. It won't win him any journalism awards, but pretty sure it'll get him a few pats on the back and free drinks at the bar.

The reporter gives a compelling story of a heroic rescue by two *unidentified* bike riders on the trail. Thank God for anonymity. Otherwise, the ER would soon be loaded with those men and horny teenagers seeking treatment for self-inflicted wounds if they thought it would get them closer to those boobs.

"Are you watching?" Savannah asks, her voice but a distant echo in my ear. "That's Liberty, isn't it?"

"Yup, sure is." My answer is curt, because my giggle is surfacing, and I'd rather save it for an empty room or a simple reminder to Libs you gotta tuck them babies away or wear a T-shirt over the sports bra. Wouldn't hurt to stay dry while wearing it as well. Wicking material is intended to catch moisture from the inside. But you live, you learn. Maybe I'll gift her with nipple covers for Christmas this year. We'll get a good laugh out of this . . . ten years from now. Maybe. She's got pretty good long term memory.

"She's going to be so embarrassed," Savannah says angrily. "That cameraman should lose his job."

"That cameraman should lose more than that," I growl in disgust, pondering which scalpel I can lift from one of the ORs. "What do you think, left or right?"

"Better question is with or without anesthesia?" She giggles.

"Geez, Savannah." I snort-laugh. "I didn't know you had it in you."

"You guys are rubbing off on me."

"You up for dinner and drinks tonight?"

She releases a frustrated sigh. "I wish. I'm working. That's how I knew about this. We just got done with the guy they rescued. He got hit by a deer. Left a hole in his leg the size of a golf ball."

"A what?" I can't have heard that correctly. How does one get hit by a deer? I thought we hit deer with our cars.

"It's a long story, but that guy was kinda funny. I think he fell in love with Liberty a little." She laughs, sharing the man's story. "The little gal with two colors of eyes. He warned all the men in the OR to stay away from her because 'that boyfriend of hers is a mean fella'. Who is he?"

"That," I hesitate, "is a story for another day accompanied by lots of tacos and even more margaritas."

"Can't wait," she says. "We'll do it soon. I gotta get back to work. Just had to let you know what was going on."

Giving Libs a few hours to dry up, dry off, maybe take a hot shower and calm down from the heroics of the day, I make the call. After the note I left in her overnight bag, it's apparent she didn't heed my advice. Riding bikes on her first day with her lost love after eighteen years apart? Damn! The man was a fine specimen. I advised her to ride *him!,* not a bike.

"Hey, what's up?" she answers on the fourth ring. She doesn't sound out of breath, so I must have chosen a good time.

"You know, Libs," I start slowly, teasingly, "there are much better forms of exercise to make you walk crooked. Like, oh, I don't know," my voice rises, "fucking his brains out!"

Soft chuckles in the background start before she stammers, "Excuse me." A few moments later a door slams and she shrieks, "I am going to murder you! I was on speaker phone."

"Why in hell would you answer a call from me on speaker phone? You should know better. Twenty filters and a muzzle can't keep me from making my point."

"I hit the wrong button!" she snaps. "And you made your point perfectly, thank you."

"Not yet. You didn't let me finish. Nice headlight show today. You're lucky I didn't pack your white sports bra. At least you left a little to the imagination. They don't know the color of your nipples."

"Oh my God!" she whines. "You're kidding!"

"Nope," I pop the P. "Not even a little. Don't worry, Savannah and I have you covered. We're going to castrate the cameraman as soon as we find out who he is."

"This is so humiliating."

"No, it's not. Remind that asshole of what he lost." My laughter bursts forth before I can contain it. "Arseen is going to be green with envy. Tell me, how does sweet revenge taste?"

She heaves a deep, long sigh that sounds a lot like . . . happiness. "You know, it just doesn't matter anymore."

"Perfect," I reply softly. "It's about damn time."

"Do you have any idea who I'm with right now?"

"Well," I say as if she needs reminded, "since I'm not there, I can't say as if I do. Care to enlighten me?"

"Ava Mynx."

I nearly choke on my own spit. "*The* Ava Mynx? My idol?"

"The one and only. She lives in Lucas' building. We're about to sit down and eat pizza."

"Just one question," I blurt out, rushing down the hall toward my bedroom to gather my collection, knowing she wouldn't dare turn me down. It's why she told me. "Do you have enough pizza for one more?"

"I can always order more," she reassures me.

"Pin me the address! I'll be there as fast as I can."

"With a rucksack full of books, no doubt," she says wryly.

"Quit wasting time!" I shriek, filling said rucksack with more paperbacks from my shelf. "Tie her up if you have to. Do not let that woman go anywhere!"

After stuffing my rucksack with every single Ava Mynx book I own, I lock the door and head for the elevator. Unfortunately, as the doors open, Ray and Buster greet me with a healthy dose of enthusiasm.

"Sorry, guys." I sigh with feigned disappointment. "No walk today. I'm afraid we might get washed away."

Ray holds out what looks to be a piece of clothing. "Oh, we didn't come up for a walk, Ms. Tompkins. Buster isn't one much for the rain. I brought a shirt for the gentleman from the *18th floor*." He arches a stern brow. "Thought maybe you could give it to him the next time you see him. That way he wouldn't have to walk through the lobby half naked on his way out." He waves his hand to invite me into the elevator, eyebrow still lifted as he smirks. "Going down?"

My lips tip and I stifle a giggle as I step on. "Ms. Archer get an eyeful, did she?"

He scowls and tips his chin. "She got two eyes full."

"You're not jealous, are you, Ray?"

"Tell the man to put a damn shirt on," he nearly growls. "The competition around here is stiff enough."

Pinching the bridge of my nose with the one free hand I have, I release a sigh. The man wrote the book on petty revenge – it simply hasn't been published yet. "Ray, did you sic Buster on him?"

"Buster is his own man, quite intuitive," he replies indignantly, then fights back a sly grin. "It was only a little love bite."

Chapter 25

Mallory

After the debacle outside Lucas' condo with his ex-girlfriend from hell, and the even more unpleasant task of removing her taped underwear from his door – she's a psycho – I'm gifted a proper introduction to the visitors in his condo.

Ava Mynx is everything a reader could want in a writer inside the pages and in person. She's funny, beautiful, and almost motherly. Fifty-three, writes books that would make some hookers blush, yet so proper she eats pizza with a fork. And her friend-with-benefits is a truckdriver!

As luck would have it, John – the truckdriver – is related to the man Liberty and Lucas rescued this afternoon on the bike trail, and he and Ava brought pizza and beer this evening to say thank you. They both live in the building and it turns out they are good friends with Lucas.

Ava signed every one of the books I brought over, took her time and added a little extra note to each one. On top of all that, she has a pre-release author's copy ready to send home with me.

She is also a good friend of Reece! He overheard me speak of her and her books in the Mexican restaurant, but never said a word. Could have used it to his advantage but didn't. After last night, I can't help but wonder if he's one of her avid readers. The man has moves and drive, but at no time was he selfish. He definitely gave more than he took and seemed to enjoy every last minute of it.

And this morning? The way he took me back to my youth was poetic. He didn't simply tell me who he was, he gave me an aha moment, sans the horse of course. That kiss was just like the first – soft, sweet, unforgettable. Who would have thought Reece Callahan is a diehard romantic?

For the first time in a long time, I spend the night in the condo by myself. I would have done it last night, had it not been for Reece showing up at my door. It's a restless sleep and I bury myself in the clean linens when the sun shines through the crack in the curtains, thoughts running through my head. Finding a new place suitable for one had been on my to-do list, before Michael cheated on Libs. I was in no hurry back then – my intuition telling me that wedding was never going to happen. Now, the plan is back on the list, as Libs has found Lucas. It's only a matter of time. I don't need a three-bedroom condo. I like it here, but I don't love it – not enough to spend what I would to keep it. There's no big hurry, but good housing in Phoenix is not easily found. It also costs an arm and a leg. They do have some two-bedroom units in this building. Might be worth a looksee.

Throwing the blankets off, I make my way to the kitchen to plop a pod in the coffeemaker. A protein shake is as good as it's going to get today. The memory of pancakes is almost enough to light my olfactory sense. I swear I can smell them, maybe even taste them, as I recall yesterday's breakfast and the man who fixed them. My phone pings, and I smile as I read the message:

Reece: *I wish I was there to fix breakfast for you this morning, Kitten. That was my first sleepover, outside of a fire station full of coworkers. Can't say as I've ever had the urge to cuddle with them or see them in my clothes. I look forward to our next time, soon.*

Staring at the screen, my feelings are scrambled. *"We didn't meet in the OR, Mallory".* But then Evans' words haunt me once again. *"He's your patient. Watch out for him, Tompkins, he's a player".* Would our history make a difference? Does it erase the ethics clause? Am I another notch on the bedpost?

Me: *What happened to one night?*

Reece: *You must have missed that memo, Mallory. IMPOSSIBLE. I have two more days on my shift. Make room on your schedule.*

That doesn't sound like a request, and I don't like orders. As I ponder what to write back – be it "bite me" or "screw you", either of which he would take as an invitation – the lobby buzzer sounds. Before I make it to the pad by the door, my phone pings once more.

Reece: *Please, Kitten? XO*

Better, Mr. Callahan. Laughing to myself, I set my phone on the counter. He'll learn. The art of patience and asking. He is funny. He could put the alphas in Ava's books to shame yet at the same time has this irresistible boyish charm. Pretty sure he's been melting panties for years with that impish grin as well. I've experienced all three. However, I did not anticipate him asking for a repeat. Players don't do that, do they?

Mr. and Mrs. Mason, aka Liberty's parents, are not who I expected to be greeting at my door on a Sunday morning unannounced. Libs and I have covered each other's asses for years regarding our virtue, at least where our parents were concerned. It's a little hard to convince Libs' mom that her daughter simply stepped out for a while when there are multiple Amazon packages sitting on her made bed.

Lauren Mason is a wise woman, and she knows me well. A little too well. She's like a bloodhound with the teeth of a grizzly and the jaws of a pit bull. I also have never had the desire to be the recipient of her wrath. She loves her daughter and she loves me. But rules are rules. She asks, you answer. However, this morning, she doesn't ask.

Folding her arms over her chest, she simply states, "Address, now."

"Hey, Mrs. M., how are you?" I pull her into an involuntary hug, stalling for time, that she resists for only so long before she sighs, uncrosses her arms and reciprocates.

Tom Mason stands behind her, rolls his eyes and grins, mouthing, "Don't push her." Tom is more easygoing than the missus. Her rock when she's ready to roll – off the edge. He's also used to my tactics, even enjoys on them on occasion.

"Address, Mallory," she singsongs as she releases me from the hug, though how she can give a warning with a lilt in her voice is magical. It must have something to do with Tom and having sex on the reg. Come to think of it, my own mom has been sounding a bit more lighthearted recently. Maybe it's time I checked on her.

I point to my phone on the counter. "Are you going to let me send her a heads-up to make sure they have their clothes on before you arrive? Maybe put on some jammies?"

Tom chortles from his spot just a few feet away as he

scrubs his face. "Sweetheart," he says, scratching his temple, "she does have a point."

Lauren lifts an expectant brow. "Text, address," she demands then turns to Tom, "and then we're out of here."

Folding my hands in a praying position, I bat my eyelashes. "Are you coming back to fix me your world famous waffles tomorrow morning?"

Her lips stretch in the most artificial smile I've ever seen. "We'll see how things go."

Four hours later, I receive a phone call from Libs with an invitation to join them all for dinner this evening. All, as in her, the parents, Lucas, and his father. Not the one that murdered his mother years ago. Turns out that one wasn't really his dad. Long story short – it's a helluva story. Not mine to tell.

I don't get Mrs. M's famous waffles the next morning. Nor am I spending my last day off with company. I'd stay in bed, if given the option, but I do have a few things I'd like to get done today. The first of which . . .

"Hey, Bug! How's my little girl?"

Nearing thirty years old and I'm still his little girl. Actually, I'm his only girl, and kid. His second wife and I never grew to be friends. My mom was number one in my life, and no "step" or "bonus" was going to take her place. I didn't need a fill-in and time spent with my dad was just that – with my dad. The preferred and agreed upon arrangement by all of us. I was three years away from leaving home for college and I really sucked at pretending. Good thing too. That marriage lasted all of four years and he hasn't been married since. She was a time thief for my dad and a wish thief for me. What was her name?

"Hey, Dad," I return his greeting, my lips tipping at his sentiment. Pulling my cup from under the Keurig spout, I top it with creamer and take a seat at the breakfast bar. "How is the east coast?"

"Good, good," he reassures me, sounding quite chipper. "How's the desert dust?"

"Dusty." I laugh and take my first sip of coffee, feeling the hot liquid wet my throat. "Watching the waves roll in this morning?"

My dad's house is on the beach in North Carolina, not far from my old neighborhood. Two stories with balconies off two bedrooms on the second story and a beautiful patio on the ground floor. Peaceful. Unless the sound of the ocean stimulates your bladder and you're up two or three times a night. Yes, it can do that to some people. *My aunt's biggest complaint when she visits.*

"You know it, kiddo. Still putting people to sleep?"

"With needles, gas masks, and my bad jokes, Dad."

He laughs heartily. "That's my girl. You coming home for a visit anytime soon? Got some vacation time you want to use up?"

"Don't have anything planned. But speaking of vacations," I pause, because we've never spoken of it, "I wanted to thank you for taking me to that horse ranch in Texas when I was a kid. I had a lot more fun than I ever admitted."

The silence is nearly unbearable before his broken, shocked response comes through. "You-you did? I-I thought I ruined us on that trip. You didn't speak to me for months."

"You were doing the best you could." Taking a deep breath, I close my eyes to fight back the tears, and search for the right thing to say. "You never walked away from me. No matter how impossible I was."

"I could never walk away from you, Bug. You were, and still are, the light of my life. But sometimes you can't always fix what's broken." He heaves a sigh so heavy, it whistles through the phone. "Or maybe we could have, but I was too stubborn back then. Got two strikes against me now, so . . ."

"I've heard the third time's a charm . . ."

"I'm still in love with her, you know," he says solemnly.

"Who, Marjorie?" *Damnit! I knew I'd remember her name. The bitter taste on my tongue is going to take three tooth brushings and six Tums to get rid of it.*

He lets out what sounds like a pitiful laugh. "No, your mother."

I'm stunned, so much so I nearly face plant into my coffee cup. I've never asked exactly how long my parents have been *legally* divorced, but my dad left shortly before my seventh birthday. Mom never remarried, and my dad remarried eight years later – short-lived as it was. They're still young; both having turned fifty earlier this year. I've also never asked *why* they divorced – assuming since dad is the one who left, it was his fault.

"Why did you and Marjorie divorce?"

"She wasn't the right one," he offers up a little too quickly, too easily.

"Is that why you didn't have any more kids?" I ask, surprising myself at the boldness of my question.

He lets out a heartfelt chuckle I know is aimed at me. "I already had the perfect kid, Bug. Marjorie was a square peg I was trying to fit in a round hole that had been carved out years before. It was a mistake."

Swiping tears from my cheeks that I only note once they start to fall onto the counter, I ask the one question I've never allowed myself, "Why did you and mom divorce?"

"Mallory." He draws out my name as if stalling for time. "The reasons don't matter. It was a long time ago. I have trouble remembering why myself."

I hear the denial and the pain in his answer. Oh, he remembers exactly why. And if he were to blame, he'd be 'fessing up to me, God, and every angel within hearing range.

"It was her," I whisper so softly, I'm not sure he hears it. Nearly twenty three years I've blamed my dad for everything. I listened to my mom sob night after night. She never showed anger. She never painted him as the bad guy, but she certainly didn't go out of her way to put him on a pedestal either. She was *Switzerland.* Small wonder. She would have had to admit to being the fault line in the broken home. It all makes sense now – guilt.

She let me keep the piercing, because it was her weight to carry.

"Don't you blame her," Dad warns, his voice stern. "I was responsible for the end result. I was in med school, then residency; gone more than I was home. I wasn't good at prioritizing the way I should have been. She was virtually doing it on her own. She was alone a lot."

"Apparently not if I'm understanding correctly!" I snap harshly. "They have toys for that, you know. Some perform better than the real thing."

"Mallory Grace!" he scolds, slamming the sliding door behind him as he enters the house; obvious due to the sound of the ocean waves disappearing from the background. "Was that called for?"

Probably not. Gathered around a table of tacos and margaritas with Libs and Savannah, it may have even been funny.

Humbling myself, I keep my voice low. "Sorry. I'm a little bitter with this new information. Do you know what it was like? Waiting for you to come home, change your mind. All these years I've blamed you, Dad."

"I told her to keep it that way, Bug. She was the one you

were living with," he explains. "It made life easier for the both of you."

"Why are you telling me this now?"

"Your mother insisted you know the truth," he hesitates, "and because we're back together again."

Nearly dropping the phone onto the counter, I shout, "Wh-what?!"

"Mallory, what made you call me?"

Well, since he's spilled the beans, I guess it's my turn. "Do you remember the boy who took me on that horse ride at the ranch we went to?"

"Ah, the one who gave you his hat." He chuckles. "The Callahan Ranch. I don't know the family or *the boy*, but I could call your Aunt Madeline and see if she knows who he is. She's the one who recommended the place. I guess they're a pretty big deal in those parts."

"No, no, no," I rush to say. "Dad, I called to tell you we met up again. He lives here in Phoenix."

"And you recognized him? After all these years?"

"No," I admit sheepishly. "He recognized me."

"Small wonder," he says, as if he knows something I don't. "That young man looked ready to cry when you got in the car. I was counting my blessings we lived on the other end of the country. I had enough boys to deal with back home."

"Dad," I groan. "You did not."

"You never give yourself enough credit, Bug. You are beautiful. Your eyes are stunning, your spunk and your smarts are phenomenal, but your compassion is your best feature. Once experienced, it makes you unforgettable. Now what the hell is the cowboy doing in Phoenix?"

I giggle. This is my dad. "He's a firefighter."

"Wow," he reacts with surprise. "Huh, long shifts instead of longhorns. So long as you don't let him put out your fire. You deserve the best."

"I love you, Dad."

"Love you too, Bug."

Chapter 26

Mallory

It's nearly noon before I'm out the door for my next venture. I'd had it planned before his texts came in, but between the sweet goodnight I received before bed:

Reece: Sleep tight, Sugar. Wish I was there to tuck you in

And my greeting this morning:

Reece: God, I'd love to wake up next to you. See your mussy hair, tired eyes. We'd have slow, sleepy sex and I'd fix you breakfast. Make time for me, Kitten . . . please

I knew I was doing the right thing. I hadn't answered any of his texts – they weren't exactly questions. Besides, I like surprises. And I felt like I owed him.

The station door is wide open, one of the bright red engines being hosed down in the drive out front. The small bag of takeout from the street vendor two blocks back is nestled in the warming bag that hangs from my shoulder.

"Is Reece Callahan available?" I ask the stocky, dark-haired, uniformed firefighter brandishing the water hose as he rinses the suds from the front fender.

He turns suddenly, startled at the sound of my voice, and nearly douses me with water. "Whoa there, sweetheart." He bobs his eyebrows and smiles playfully as he helps himself to a quick appreciative perusal from my head to my toes, then winks. "Did I just make you a little wet?"

I shoot him a wry look and deadpan, "Not even a little. Is Reece in?"

He narrows his eyes before recognition dawns then grins. "You're the nurse from the hospital."

"Something like that."

He turns the nozzle on the hose to shut it off and rounds the truck, shouting at the top of his lungs toward the inside of the station. "Callahan!"

"Yo!" Reece's booming southern twang echoes from inside.

"You got yourself a visitor," he yells back. "And it ain't your mama. But if she's got a sister, we got some talking to . . ."

"What are you . . . Hey, Gorgeous!" Reece's face lights up so bright he makes me feel like a gift. His long legs carry him in strides I'd have to run to keep up with and he's in front of me in no time, so close I could kiss him. "Well, my day's just been made. You came to see me?"

I shrug sheepishly and lower the bag off my shoulder. "I brought you some lunch. I didn't know what time you ate, but you can always warm it up later."

God, he's beautiful when his bright blue eyes widen in surprise and those dimples deepen with his smile. "You brought me lunch? Baby, I could have just finished a smorgasbord and I'd still eat it, because you went to the trouble."

My mouth twists as I confess, "I didn't cook it, it's just takeout. You fixed me breakfast, so I thought it was only fair to bring you something."

He runs his tongue over his bottom lip slowly before biting it and teases, "Tit for tat, huh?"

Our shirt-for-shirt trade off. "You remember that?"

The backs of his fingers brush my cheek and he whispers so low it makes goosebumps break out on my skin, "I could walk you through the whole night minute by minute. It's all I've thought about."

"Really?" Not gonna lie, I've put some pretty good time into the memory myself. My Ava Mynx book has sat untouched on the table by my chair; same page I left it the night he knocked on my door. Who needs fiction when you've had the real thing? Oh shoot! I neglected to get that one signed.

His smile is so genuine it makes me weak in the knees. "I've thought about you for years, Kitten. The girl that knocked me on my ass with a single kiss." He taps my nose and grins. "Now, what did you bring me for lunch?"

I hesitate, reconsidering my food choice. What he just said was romantic and so damn poetic. So far, we've had a tendency to lean toward the humorous edge in our interactions. Maybe a public spot isn't appropriate for this, but damnit, it seemed fitting at the time.

My nose crinkles as I hold the bag out. "Tacos?"

His burst of laughter can be easily heard throughout the

firehouse behind us, where I now note there are a number of fellow workers watching us. He grasps the back of my neck and lowers his mouth to mine, muttering before landing a kiss that takes my breath away, "So fucking special."

The horns blare from inside the firehouse, signaling the call to action. Reece releases his hold on me as if on autopilot and the methodical chaos starts inside the station. He plants a kiss on my forehead and murmurs, "Sorry, baby. Gotta go." In his rush toward the open doors of the station, he turns quickly one last time and points his finger. "You're my girl, Kitten. Always were, always will be."

Stepping off to the side, far away from the doors and engines gearing up to drive away, I wait until two engines and the rescue truck have left the station house – sirens blaring and horns honking – and watch as they make their way down the street out into traffic; Reece blowing me a kiss on his way past.

Dedicated heroes.

The warmer bag hangs from my hand. Six soft shell tacos inside, wrapped individually, the toppings in separate containers, a dozen or so sauce packets, ranging from hell-fire hot to medium, tossed in. I smile to myself as I round the corner of the open door to the fire station in search of the nearest living being.

An older gentleman with shock-white hair and dark brown eyes stands in the doorway entrance to another part of the building, as if he were waiting for me. He wears a simple button down, blue jeans, and a welcoming smile. My silent joy nearly bursts at the seams. He looks fantastic compared to the last time I saw him. No skin pallor, his cheeks are a healthy rosy color, lips and fingers show no signs of cyanosis.

"Hello there, young lady. Can I help you?"

Holding up the understandably forgotten bag, I make my request, "Can I leave this for Reece Callahan? The contents need to go in the fridge."

He eyes the bag with interest and his bushy brows head for his hairline. "You brought Reece bagels all the way from New York?"

Turning the bag in my hand to see the logo printed on the front, I'm reminded of what the man is looking at. *Zabar's.* I own three of the sturdy bags. Bought them on a trip to the Big Apple from the popular café on 80th and Broadway years ago. Handy little buggers. Had lunch there twice in the week I stayed. *Addictive.*

"Oh, no." I chuckle, handing it over, amused at his knowledge of the famous bagels – now hungry as I remember how good they were. "They're actually tacos. Don't know how well they'll keep, but . . ."

"Man, I used to love Zabar's bagels. Haven't had one in years," he says wistfully. He takes the bag with his left hand and extends his right to shake mine. "I'm Burkey. An old timer here, retired. Still hang out when I get bored. You must be the lady that's put a twinkle in Reece's eyes lately."

My cheeks flush in embarrassment. Don't know about a twinkle in his eyes, but he did mention a tingle in his spine the other night right before he . . .

"I – I don't know about that," I stammer, the flush in my cheeks deepening with the naughty thought.

"I've known Reece for years. Never seen him the way he's been lately," he says with a headshake. "Reminds me of the way I was when I met my wife. The Zabar's bag is a good reminder too." He winks. "Had a little spat over the last blueberry bagel. I told her if she let me take her to dinner, I'd share the bagel with her and buy her the coffee to go with it. Married her six months later."

"You're from New York?"

He nods as a melancholy smile stretches his mouth. "We

were. Moved here years ago and the kids and grandkids are all here. I hate to travel, so no reason to go back." He pretends to shiver. "Too cold up there anyway."

"I hear you," I agree easily. "That bagel story was wonderful though. One you might want to share with those grandkids."

He studies my face for an extra moment and his eyelids flicker as if recalling having heard it before. "We're having dinner on Sunday. I just may do that."

"Well, it was nice meeting you, Burkey. I should get going." I point to the bag. "You can keep the bag if you want. A little reminder of back home."

He laughs boisterously. "I'll think about it, but it may make me miss those bagels even more."

Once back at my condo, I collect my laptop from my desk in the spare room and bring up the website for Zabar's. I had a feeling it was possible.

Aurthur Burke. He was in the operating room approximately six months ago for open heart surgery – quadruple bypass. Retired firefighter. Widower. I watched Dr. Michael Knight remove the man's heart from his body and put him on a bypass machine while he performed the repairs. I don't remember every patient that comes through our ORs, but some leave a lasting impression that hold not only a memory but a piece of your heart as well. Mr. Burke was one of those. He loved his wife very much and missed her terribly. His desire to be with her again was a bit unsettling. He needed a little convincing his kids and grandkids weren't done with him here; that there were still memories to make and anecdotes to share about a mother and grandmother they missed as well. Instead of the conventional counting backwards from one hundred, I had him hold his palm against mine and asked him to count off his five grandchildren by name, and with a smile on his face he made it to the last one before his eyes closed and he was fast asleep.

Ordering a gift package of lox and various bagels, as well as ten extra blueberry – a heart patient's dream of allowable dietary foods – shipped in care of the firehouse to one Aurther Burke, two-day delivery to ensure it's here in time for the weekend, aka giving the delivery service time to screw it up, I smile to myself. Taste and smell are the two strongest senses to stimulate recall. It should help him tell the story and plant a good picture in the minds of children while he tells it, as they share the treat that brought their grandparents together.

We seldom are kept in the loop regarding a patient's outcome. I'm in the OR, manage pain control for a day or two, and then I'm gone and on to the next patient. We usually find out if they make it through the entire hospital stay, but beyond that? It's in the surgeon's and cardiologist's hands.

First rule of thumb: *Never get attached to a patient.*

As I close the laptop, the *rule* plays through my head. Reece was my patient after. *After* half my life of a pleasant distant memory. *After* he gave me my first kiss. *After* he gave me the souvenir I still have packed in my closet. *After* he made that ride on a horse so special, I've never gotten on one since.

Maybe, *I shouldn't have kissed him,* but I can't say I'm sorry I did.

Chapter 27

Reece

Shift over, I'm anxious to get home. I downed those tacos like they were dessert when I got back to the firehouse; sharing two of them with Roger. A minute in the nuker, fresh toppings, a dab of hell sauce, and they were good as new. Burkey passed on my offer – heartburn and dietary restrictions – but he couldn't say enough about Mallory. He wouldn't let me take the bag home to return it; said she told him he could keep it. Then he had half a dozen questions about her. Not sure how I felt about that, but I answered them the best I could, leaving him with the impression our first encounter was the hospital. He simply smiled as if he had a secret – or had solved a puzzle.

However, he did tell me if I didn't marry her, he had a single son that would be interested. *Not funny, Burkey!*

Odd as it may sound, my balls didn't shrivel and I didn't run for the door to pack my bags and head back to Texas at the mention of marriage.

And here I stand outside my condo door, staring at a note attached to it with tape; eye level for all to see:

Didn't think the crabs you keep catching would get along with the scorpions so I let you off the hook...this time. Might want to get those critters treated.

Tanner

Tanner Carson is a dead man. At my feet lie two cans of Raid bug killer from one neighbor, a premade home remedy crab treatment from another, and a basket from Mrs. Thompson, complete with a safe sex pamphlet, a supply of condoms, and a shaving kit with a note offering to help me treat the "critters". She's 73 years old!

Tearing the note off the door and collecting the unseemly items at my feet, I open my door and head for the trashcan. Offering to be his proxy for sex with Liberty because he took her for a bike ride versus giving her the ride of her life was said in jest. Geez, some people just can't take a joke. But this? Too far, Tanner. He knows of my phobia of scorpions. They're mean little bastards. Fast, furious, and those pincers are meant for killing. Designed for death. An early curse sent to earth in preparation for the final countdown. The grading scale for sinners. Worse than rattlesnakes and black widows.

My phone pings with a message from Roger:

"Pizza and beer at Tanner's in an hour? Thought we could welcome Liberty into our world the right way. Pregame on tonight. Wiley's in."

Hmmmm. Cockblocking Tanner Carson. I'd rather kill him at the moment but teaching him patience might not be a bad idea. If I didn't have plans of my own for later, I'd pass out on his couch, snore like a freight train, piss with the door open while I whistle a tune in the morning and leave the seat up. Vengeance is mine, sayeth the Callahan.

"Sounds good. Order the pizza and grab the beer. I'll spot you when we get there."

A hot shower, change of clothes, and one unanswered phone call later, I'm on my way down the hall to Ava's condo.

"Reece!" She smiles brightly when she opens the door, then glances at the paperback in my hand. Her smile turns puckish and she chuckles. "I didn't know you were a fan, dear. Learn anything new?"

Feeling the heat on my neck as it rushes upwards to my cheeks, I clear my throat. "It's, uh, not mine. I need you to sign it."

She opens the door wide and waves me in, taking the paperback from me in the process. "Generic signature or to someone in particular?"

My brow furrows. How the hell should I know? I'm more of a Sports Illustrated kinda guy. I suppose personalization would make it more special. "Could you make it out to Mallory?"

"Mallory," she repeats slowly. She holds out a flattened hand, palm side down, indicating approximately five foot-six. "About yeah tall, gorgeous brunette, eyes the color of molten silver? That Mallory?"

"You know her?!" I huff what sounds more like an accusation than a question.

"We met the other night at Tanner's. Lovely girl. Quite feisty." She nods as if she hasn't burst my balloon, deflated my tires, or knocked my ego into the next millennium. This was supposed to be something special for *my* something special. She studies the cover for a moment. "I don't remember this one in the collection she brought for me to sign. Hang on, let me get my pen."

"You signed a collection for her?"

"I did," she says proudly. "I'll make this one extra special."

Taking her sweet time, she blows on the scribble to ensure the ink is dry before closing the cover. "Now, don't peek," she singsongs before handing it back, a slyness in her tone that has my spidey senses on alert. Maybe I should just burn it and buy Mallory a new copy. Ava is known from one end of the country to the other – to some as an erotica writer – to others as the queen of smut. She's well off but chooses to live a simple life, and her boyfriend is a truckdriver. She has a heart of gold, fits well into our group of friends, but yes, sex tips from her truly would be like advice from your mother. Roger was not kidding.

I simply tell her, "Thank you. I appreciate it."

"She's your kitten, isn't she?"

I can't help my smile. "Yeah, she is."

"Enjoy the book, Reece."

Laughing, I shake my head and remind her, "I'm a fan of yours, Ava, not your books. Self-taught and never had any complaints."

Back down the hall I stop at my condo to drop the book off before meeting with Roger and Wiley. I hesitate before setting it on the counter. "*Now, don't peek*". It's only a little note and a signature, right? No one will know.

Mallory,

Meeting you was such a delight. I recommend Chapter 3, pages 22-27 for some new ideas. Chapter 21, pages 89-96 for a finish he'll never forget.

All my best,

Ava Mynx

Unable to help myself, I flip through to page 22. By the third paragraph I'm squinting. By the second page, I'm biting my lip. By the third page, I've drawn blood. By page 26, I slam the book closed. Sweet Jesus! I will never be able to look Ava – or John, for that matter – in the eye again. I'm a fun guy, creative, adventurous – to a point. But I'm a homegrown Texas boy. Getting a woman to bend to my will applies to flexibility, nothing more. A glance at my watch indicates I have approximately two minutes to go bleach my brain.

Roger and Wiley open their doors in unison and step out as I approach. "You look a little pale, Reece," Roger says as he holds out two six packs.

"I'm fine," I mutter, reaching for the beer, hoping he doesn't inquire further. I might confess and end up being the brunt of every "Ask Ava" joke he can think of.

"I gotta run down and grab the pizzas. Delivery guy should be here in a minute."

We wait in the stairwell for Roger to return with the pizza then start our trek one more flight up to Tanner's condo once he joins us. The stairs are always the chosen path over the elevator – a little extra security check for the residents as well as the cardio it provides. The exception made for the night we removed Miranda from the premises was to avoid the temptation to knock her down them, and to avoid the accusation that we did if she intentionally took a fall. Lawyer, remember?

"Did you call Tanner and tell him we were coming?" Wiley inquires.

I shoot him a side-eye. "This is pregame night. He knows the drill." My unanswered phone call earlier was to Mallory. Tanner doesn't deserve one.

"Things are different, boys," Wiley says with a warning

lilt in his voice. "There's a woman involved now."

Roger snort-laughs as he reaches the top step. "Woman advice from the man who's three-times divorced. Yeah, I think I'll pass on that, Wiley."

"Don't say I didn't warn you," Wiley mutters.

Knocking in the typical three-taps fashion, we wait for footsteps. Instead, we hear muffled voices followed by a woman's giggle and Tanner's moan. The side of my fist pounds hard as I yell, "Open the door, you prick!" I proceed to shout through the barrier, informing him of the items left at my door, reminding him of Mrs. Thompson's age, aka you succeeded in humiliating me, asshole. The moans coming from inside grow louder before Liberty screams, "Lucas!"

Wiley snickers and shakes his head. "Told you, you should have called first. Let's go put the pizza in the oven at my place to keep it warm. We can shoot back a beer or two until they're done." He shrugs at my seething glare. "Some things can't be rushed. Patience is a virtue. Lost love is stronger than young love. What can I say?"

"Nothing, Wiley," I deadpan. "You can say nothing."

Chapter 28

Reece

Disappointed that *my kitten* hadn't shared the information about meeting Ava is one thing. Not returning my phone call yet has me jumpy. But not informing me of Tanner's newfound parentage this afternoon is inexcusable. This kind of news is of epic proportions.

Somewhere along the line, I suppose we should tell her best friend that we're sleeping together; that I'm her cowboy from Texas. Wait a minute! Did she ever tell Liberty about her first kiss? Best friends do that, don't they? That's fodder for slumber parties, isn't it? I knew the minute Ryder and Ronan got laid the very first time. They couldn't shut up about it, until the next time, then the next, and the next, ad infinitum. *Three counties, people.*

Slamming Tanner's bedroom door behind me, I pull up my contacts and press *Amor.* Spanish for love; passion. It was that or *Fireball.* Either/or would fit. But I wanted her first on the list.

"Hey," she answers groggily. "I was going to call you back."

"Were you now? Did you forget to share something with me this afternoon, Kitten?" I ask accusingly. "Something big?"

"The only one with something *big* to share is you, Reece." She snort-laughs. "What are you talking about?"

"Nice try, Sugar, but flattery will get you . . ." Damnit! She did it again. One reminder of our night together and this woman has me on my knees. I sigh. "Fine. Flattery will get you everywhere. But right now I'm a little pissed at you. Why didn't you tell me about Tanner and . . ."

"It's not my story to tell!" she yells indignantly. "It should come from him. You guys are friends."

"As are you and Liberty. Pretty strong connection, don't you think? We're connected. You could have told me," I argue, then confess, "I want you to be part of our circle, Mallory. My circle. What are you doing right now?"

"Curled up on my sofa with a bowl of cereal and a Hershey bar, getting ready to watch Netflix."

"Sounds . . ." I hesitate, "cozy."

"Don't make fun of me, Mr. Callahan. I'm in a mood," she growls in warning, so unlike the woman I kissed outside the station this afternoon. *Ah, Mr. Callahan. So, we're back to that. What kind of mood? Was that an invitation?*

"Would you join us here at Tanner's? We have pizza, beer, pretty sure there's wine. Liberty's here. I know she'd love to see you."

"Pizza?" she whimpers. "Do you guys ever eat anything other than pizza?"

"You don't like pizza?"

"Not tonight," she grumbles. "I already feel big as a house."

She's gotta be kidding. The finest ass I've ever seen, the perkiest tits I've ever held in my palms, curves that women pay plastic surgeons to carve on them. And the sexiest, most tasteful barbell piercing that only the luckiest bastard (me) gets to see when she's naked.

"Your body is perfect." I open the door to make my way out to the others. "Now, get your skinny little ass over here before I paddle it so hard you won't be able to sit to eat pizza." The words in Ava's book come to me like a movie script in my mind. I lower my voice so only she hears, "If that's not good enough, I can think of something calorie free to feed you while you're on your knees."

Did I really just say that? Damn you, Ava! I'm burning that fucking book.

Her gasp is audible before I end the call with a simple push of the red button only to look up and see four gaping jaws, one paired with narrowed blue and green eyes that meet mine. Maybe she wasn't the only one to hear it.

Shrugging casually, I lamely explain, "What? We call it word play."

Liberty's cold, hard stare leaves no room for doubt as she makes herself clear. "I have access to scalpels and the morgue, Reece. Hurt my friend, and you will be the victim of one and a resident of the other."

Holding her cold gaze with my warm one, I answer without hesitation, "And if I ever do, I will give you permission."

Standing outside the door of the complex, I wait for the Rogue to pull into the parking lot. It's been over half an hour and she still hasn't shown. Now I fear I pissed her off. *But they were words out of her book!* Ten minutes later, headlights finally barrel through the main drive and she whips her vehicle into a parking spot like a pro. Dead center between the lines from front to back. One more thing to admire. I've watched some of the residents take aim, start, stop, back up, try again, then again, and eventually take up two spaces because they can't hit their asses with both hands. But my girl aces it on the first try. I'll bet she could break a horse in a day. He wouldn't dare buck her off. Probably let her ride him bareback . . . or bare naked. Wait, that's my job.

Reaching her car before she can climb out, I open the door and hold out my hand to help her down. She slaps my hand away and hops down, slams the door, and locks it with the fob. Her silver eyes flare with a heat I've never seen and my hopes rise – until she says, "I want my book back. I'm not Bella, you're not the Baron, and the only *paddling* you'll ever be doing is trying to swim to shore after I throw your ass overboard."

In the millisecond that follows, I wait for her to further comment on my offer. *Knees, Mallory. What about the knees?*

She spins on her heels and charges toward the door of the building. I should have never opened that damned book! *But still – the knees.*

"Mallory, wait!" I plead, my steps half the count of hers to catch up. Just like in her condo, she ignores me and continues on her mission. So, just like in her condo, I pick her up, throw her over my shoulder and trek toward the door. Wedgie be damned; my boys can take one for the team tonight. Good luck, sweetheart. I went commando.

Heading for the stairwell versus the elevator, I climb the

three flights to the third floor, down the hall, and stop when we get to my condo. "Put me down, you moron." Her voice is weaker than usual and she sounds tired, but I wait until we're inside before setting her on her feet.

Taking her hand in mine, I lead her to the counter and pick up the book, opening the front flap to show her the signature inside. Wincing, I tell her, "I didn't technically steal it. I borrowed it so Ava could sign it for you. I had no idea you'd already met her. It was supposed to be a surprise."

She reads the inscription on the inside cover, then looks up at me. "You did this to surprise me?"

My shoulder lifts in a defeated shrug. "I told you in the restaurant that night if you ever wanted the real thing to let me know. My original plan was to introduce you to her."

Her teeth sink into her bottom lip as her cheeks flush and her nose crinkles. "Um, thanks?"

"You really into that stuff?" I question with a quick nod at the book in her hands. I only scanned a couple pages and I'm not sure if it's because I know the author, or if I'm simply a sound believer in my own creativity, but I can't imagine *my kitten* getting that down and dirty. A little tap on the ass is one thing, but . . .

"No!" she denies vehemently then rolls her eyes and shakes her head. "It's fiction, Reece. The medical journals get a little boring, so I have a tendency to step out of the real world sometimes. Ava adds a story; it's not just smut." She bursts into a fit of soft giggles as she wags her finger. "You shouldn't have peeked at her specified pages."

"No shit." I swallow hard to hold down the bitter taste that threatens to rise. "Still mad at me?"

She eyes me skeptically. "You done being a moron?"

Wrapping my arms around her shoulders and holding my lips to her forehead, I murmur, "Is that a requirement?"

"I suppose it is part of your charm." She pulls back and tips her chin up. "Are you done trying to quote Ava's books?"

"God, yes," I groan. "Can we just never mention it again?"

"Might come in handy as blackmail." She shrugs. "Barter for Chinese instead of pizza."

Her impish grin is irresistible and with her chin already tipped up, easy access is but a breath away. My mouth fits hers perfectly. I swear, every kiss is as good or better than the first. Kisses are intimate; the reason I've never been a fan . . . until Mallory.

"Stay with me tonight," I whisper across her lips.

Her head is shaking before she pulls away. "I can't. I work tomorrow and need to get up at five. First surgery is at 6:30."

"I'll get you there on time," I promise her.

Her hands come up in front of her like a shield. "All my stuff is at home. I've got a routine. This is only the start of my week."

"Then let's stay at your place again," I proffer, reaching to bring her close once more. "I can get up early. I'm a firefighter, Mallory. Dressed and climbing into a truck in three minutes or less is a requirement. Come on," I prod softly. "I'll fix you breakfast while you get ready."

"I need more than three hours sleep, Reece!" she protests, apparently recalling our night together. "I can't spend half the night having sex with you and expect to function properly in the OR."

A quick glance at my watch reveals it's not quite seven o'clock. If we leave now, we could get two good sessions in, she'd be passed out by ten, and get seven hours of sated slumber. Sleep is always better after sex. If I drive her to work, that might possibly get her an extra half hour of sleep. *Hey! I'm a planner.* Come to think of it though, it was her who woke up three hours into the night and rubbed that peachy little ass against me and fired up another round.

"I promise to not keep you up late." I tip her chin up, leave a soft kiss on her mouth and whisper, "I've missed you."

She squeezes her eyes closed, pulls her chin away from my fingers, and blows an exasperated sigh. "Reece, I'm bloated, grouchy, and the timing sucks."

I drop my hands to her hips and gently squeeze. "I bet I could take your mind off every one of those things."

Had I put a tablespoon of vinegar on her tongue, her expression would be less sour. "I am not having sex with you when I'm on my period!"

Well, color me stupid. "Oh . . . *oh*."

The urge to palm-slap my forehead is strong, but I'm afraid I may knock a few more brain cells loose. Being raised in a household of six boys, the education of female bodily functions wasn't high on the list. After Ronan's stunt of tossing my mother's purse through the air in the restaurant, I was under the mistaken impression she was a closet smoker of white wrapped cigars . . . for a while. *I was twelve! Give it a rest!* That was one birds and bees conversation with my dad I could have passed on – or waited for. Mind you, finding out my mom didn't smoke was a relief, but I could have lived without the details. Ronan paid for it over the years though. My big brothers loved me and felt evening the score on my behalf was only fair. Ketchup on his sheets (River). A very rare and bleeding hamburger served to him from the grill, complements of Russ (thank you, bro). Beet stains on his saddle (good job, Reid). Waking one morning with red food coloring stains from the tip of his nose to his chin, greeted with a horrified gasp, "Good God! Tell me that's from eatin' Skittles and not . . . Skittles." (a popular barfly) (Ryder). But mine was the classic when Ronan was stomping around the barn in a fit of anger and Russ asked what his problem was. I answered before Ronan could with, "*It's his time of the month.*" My real win that day? When Russ clapped my shoulder and congratulated me for making it into the big league. Being the youngest wasn't always easy, but even my small wins felt trophy worthy, because of my brothers.

"I'm sorry. I really suck at hints." I draw her to me once again and kiss her forehead. "It's the moron thing. Part of my charm, remember?"

She chuckles against my chest when I wrap my arms around her shoulders and hold her close. Her arms around my waist partnered with her laugh balance my world. No sirens, no alarms, no flashbacks of the last three days. Just peace.

She rests her chin on my chest as she tilts her head up. "I'm going to go see Libs for a bit and then head home."

"You're not gonna let me stay with you?" Damn, I really do suck at this. The other night with her was the best sleep I'd had since I can't remember when. I didn't toss and turn. She fit me like a glove; her feet tucked between my calves like they belonged there. The scent of her hair matching the softness of the woman.

Her brow furrows as if truly questioning my memory . . . or sanity. "What part did you not understand?"

"I like Netflix." Tucking a strand of hair behind her ear, I smile. "I'd love to curl up on that sofa with you. Haven't had a Hershey bar in years, outside of s'mores with my nieces and nephews. Captain Crunch was always my favorite, but I'll take what you've got."

She tries to hide her surprise but fails – a stellar moment for me. I pay attention. When people describe life events, you lend them an ear, maybe laugh, and then move on. When Mallory shares even the tiniest event, she paints a picture. I could see her tucked into the corner of her sofa, a bowl of cereal in her hands, Hershey bar on the coffee table. Yeah, yeah, I know. Totally screwed up on the cycle thing, but I was mad at Ava and waiting for Mallory to refuse that calorie free offer on her knees, *which she has yet to do.*

She narrows her eyes. "You know we're not having sex, right?"

"I know."

"But you want to stay the night." I nod. "Why?"

"I can still hold you, can't I?" I'd love to confess the comfort she gave, the peace I felt with her next to me, the perfect fit when she folded into me. But it's too soon. She's as skittish as she was the day I put her on Lady Luck. I need her trust.

She looks wary, but I see the moment she lowers the shield the tiniest bit and she arches her brows. "Do I get to choose the movie?"

"Is this forewarning for a chick flick?"

She closes one eye in contemplation. "I was thinking something along the line of a cowboy adventure."

She is perfect. Sassy and sweet, smart, quick witted; everything I never knew I wanted. My laugh can't be contained as I wrap my fingers in her hair and bring her mouth close to mine, muttering before I taste what I crave, "So fucking special."

Sending her ahead to the fourth floor while I pack an overnight bag, I pull my phone out and text my trusted source for a little guidance.

"What do you do with a woman on her," my finger on the button, I hesitate, considering the best way to word it so it doesn't sound tacky, and switch from the P to the M, *"monthly?"*

My phone rings moments later with a call from the same number I was texting. I was expecting a short list of suggestions, not a vocal response.

"Hey," I answer, "You didn't have to . . ."

"Not a thing, you idiot," he enunciates with a growl. "Put your dick away and give the woman a reprieve. What the hell's the matter with you, Reece?"

"I didn't mean my dick! I meant what can I do *for* her! She doesn't feel well. Don't be such a judgy asshole."

"You said *with* her. Not *for* her."

"Semantics. You should have known what I meant."

His laugh starts as a low rumble but soon turns into a full blown cackle. I imagine him throwing his head back, rolling his eyes; probably sharing this with Reid in the morning. "Little brother, I'm never sure what you mean."

"Are you gonna help me out or not, Russ?"

"Ibuprofen, heating pad, foot rubs, Godiva chocolates, and wine," he says easily, as if it's an old school recipe. "I keep a special stash for Abbie so I'm always prepared."

Small wonder the woman looks at him the way she does.

"No cereal?"

"No what?! Uh, Reece, how old is she?"

I do a quick calculation in my head. If she was almost sixteen when I was . . . "Around thirty. Why?"

He groans. "I swear to God mom dropped you on your head. Get the woman some real food. Make it something hot. You cannot be that dense."

"I've never done this before!" I holler in my own defense. "How am I supposed to know this shit?"

His chuckle is soft, once again revealing just one of the many reasons why he is my favorite. He gets me. "Special, is she?"

"So fucking special, Russ," I utter, then head to the bedroom to toss a few things into a duffle. "I'll give you the low down another time."

"You ever gonna bring her around?"

"She's been there once before," I tell him. "Fourteen years ago. Took her for a trail ride on Lady Luck. Thanks for the tips, bro. Gotta go."

"What?! Hang on a minute!"

I disconnect before he can inquire further. We discussed a nurse in the OR and the girl on the horse at my last visit. He's a smart guy. He'll either figure it out or blow up my phone sometime tomorrow, after giving me a chance to prove myself.

Chapter 28

Mallory

The door flies open as soon as I knock; Liberty on the other side with a hand outstretched, aimed for my elbow and I'm soon being pulled down the hallway toward Lucas' bedroom.

"Spill it," she demands as soon as the door closes, her synchronous lifted brows and narrowed eyes so reminiscent of her mother's it nearly makes me laugh. She's going to make a great mom someday. "I thought you hated him."

"Eh, hate is a funny word, Libs." I shrug. "Things change."

Her brow drops as she furrows it. "Isn't he the same

fireman from the airport who offered to . . ." she air quotes, ". . . rescue your pussy?"

"One and the same." I glance around the room, taking in the fine furniture, tasteful colors, and the massive, unmade, king size bed. "How did your cop do? I don't see any handcuffs."

"Mallory!" Her teeth are clenched so tight, I swear her jaw is going to lock. I simply meet her glare with a smirk. She softens and whispers, "He's wonderful, Mal. Better than everything I ever dreamed of." She snaps her fingers then points one. "I see what you did there. Not so fast. Your turn, bestie."

"Picture it," I start with my best impression of a beloved actress in an old TV series both of us still watch over and over. "Denton, Texas. 2011. A huge horse, me on the front of a saddle with a studly hot cowboy behind me. The horse we're riding suddenly dips her muzzle to munch on grass and a strong hand grips me around my belly to keep me high in the saddle and pressed against his hard body, not to mention his, well, you know. Using his stronghold and rugged good looks, he coerces me to leave him with a kiss he'll never forget, and the first one I ever got. Lo and behold, fourteen years later, here we are again."

Libs blinks twice, thrice, four times before her jaw drops. Good thing too. I'm reassured it didn't lock after her clenching it so hard. "Reece is your cowboy from the dude ranch?" I nod slowly. "No way. How did you figure it out?"

"I didn't. He did."

"Mallory," she whispers in astonishment then sucks in a deep gasp. "Wait! That's why he called you kitten. Did you tell him you still have his hat?"

"No," I hiss with a scolding glare. "Geez, Libs. How would I explain having memorabilia without having a clear memory of him?"

She shoots me a look of empathy that tugs on my heart. She didn't recognize Lucas either, but we're not even in the same ballpark for circumstances. "So where do you think you two will go from here?"

I snort-laugh. "With my luck? Probably back and forth from his place to ours for as long as it lasts. Don't worry about me."

"Mal, give him a chance. If you had seen the way he reacted when I . . ."

The light tap on the door draws our attention away from the conversation, and Lucas sticks his head in the opening. "Everything okay in here?"

Libs literally beams as she smiles at him. *So damn happy.* "We're good." She turns to me and slips her arm through mine. "You ready?" I let her take the lead back out into the living room where Reece waits, duffel bag in hand. Huh, guess he really does plan to stay the night.

"Saved you some pizza," Roger offers as he waves at a closed box on the coffee table. "Still hot. Just took it out of the oven. Better hurry, Wiley's a bottomless pit." He smirks at Reece. "It's all meat. Reece won't eat anything with veggies on it because he thinks it might be . . ."

Reece narrows his eyes in warning, as if that were one cat to be left in the bag. "We're gonna grab something else." He extends his hand for mine. "Ready?"

"You don't want pizza?"

He winks. "We're bartering."

Oohh, I think I just got Chinese!

I grin impishly and whisper, "So, I can't tell them about . . ."

He lifts a stern brow and that deep growl I'm growing quite fond of lets loose in my ear as he leans close, "Let's go,

Kitten."

Once at my car, he opens my door and waits for me to get buckled in and started before telling me, "I'll be about half hour behind you. I need to stop and grab a couple things and then I'll be right there, okay?" He leans in, leaving a soft, sweet kiss on my mouth. "Pick out a movie. Doesn't matter what. I'll be too busy watching you, anyway. Now, drive safe." He closes the door and waits, hands in his pockets; his image in my rearview mirror until I turn to leave the parking lot.

Reece arrives forty-five minutes after I get home; two Walgreen's bags in one arm, the duffel bag thrown over his shoulder, and a bunch of flowers in his free hand. I'm so taken aback by the unexpected view, I'm not sure whether to laugh or tend to the burn behind my eyes. The only man who has ever given me flowers is my dad, other than a corsage for prom from Trenton Weller, and his plan was to *de*flower me before the night was over. Pretty sure the poor guy wouldn't have found my clit with a navigation system. I never did find out, because when he pinched the side of my boob in search of my nipple it was game over. Left a quarter-sized bruise in its wake. His game was football. I only hope he's learned to loosen his grip over the years because he never made it to the NFL.

"For you." Reece holds out the cellophane wrapped flowers. They really are pretty – fresh – still chilled from whatever cooler he'd chosen them from. A colorful mix of daylilies and irises; some that haven't opened yet. He drops his duffel in the foyer and makes his way to the kitchen counter where he lays the bags. Removing the items one by one, he announces each as if they need an introduction. "A heating pad for comfort, ibuprofen if you have any pain, lotion so I can rub your feet." He pauses before extracting the items from the second bag and I study what's been laid out so far. Did he Google remedies? Helpful hints? It's not like I'm dying. It's one or two days of cramps and discomfort, another day of inconvenience, and it's over. Which it almost is.

He pulls out a bottle wrapped in a brown paper bag from Hootie's Liquor store and peels the paper back. Pinot! He then removes a rectangular box and grins sheepishly – the familiar little man in a military uniform on the front making me laugh. Captain Crunch! He shrugs one shoulder as he rattles the box. "Told you it was my favorite. We can either save it for breakfast or munch on it while we watch a movie." The man has a sense of humor. My favorite trait and so hard to find. "Last item from the bags," he says as he pulls it out and presents it with both hands. "Hershey bars are for kids. A true lady deserves Godiva chocolates."

That's it. I'm done. The burn behind my eyes is sliding downward, causing a tingle in my nose, making it hard to swallow. Maybe it's the hormones, maybe it's emotion. I can take goofy Reece, moronic Reece, sexy Reece. But sweet Reece? That one is a little harder to contend with. He sets the chocolates on the counter, bends at the knees and takes my cheeks in his palms. His thumbs wipe away tears. "You don't like Godiva chocolates? I can run out and get Hershey's. Hell, I'll buy you M&Ms if you want. Just don't cry, Sugar."

How I do it without destroying the flowers in my hand is a puzzle, but I do. I don't think I've ever put so much effort into a kiss. But then, no man has ever put so much effort into me. He lifts me off my feet to ease my struggle to reach and his need to bend.

"The Godiva is perfect," I murmur against his mouth. "Thank you."

"Oh, I'm not done, Kitten." He chuckles. "You haven't told me what your favorite Chinese food is yet."

I bury my face in his neck, a choked sob leaving my throat. "General Tso's chicken. Maybe some hot and sour soup?"

Keeping one arm around my back, the other wrapped in my hair, he kisses my temple and breathes in deeply, as if savoring my scent. "Let's hope the General and the Captain can get along. Chicken and soup it is. Go put on some jammies, get comfy. I'll put the flowers in water and order dinner."

"Why are you doing this, Reece?"

He draws my head back, his grip strong but gentle in my hair. "I'm going to make you understand someday, Mallory Tompkins. This is nothing compared to what you do for me." He seals his mouth over mine for another delicious kiss, a trace of tongue, a tiny nip of my bottom lip, before he breaks away and winks. "Still the best kiss I've ever had." He sets me back on my feet, lightly taps my butt, and turns me in the direction of my bedroom. "Go change, I'll order food."

Halfway to the bedroom, his low voice sounds strained behind me as he nearly pleads, "Mallory, please put on some long pants and a T-shirt. I'm doing my best here, but a man can only take so much."

Well aware, Reece. You couldn't hide that thing behind a concrete wall. Those Levi's are not keeping a secret for you.

Chapter 29

Reece

I do a quick adjustment after watching her walk down the hall toward the bedroom to change clothes, then chastise myself as Russ's words ring in my head, *"Not a thing, idiot. Give the woman a reprieve."*

First things first. I place the order for dinner at the same restaurant we all use on a regular basis, and confirm it will be approximately thirty minutes for delivery. Searching her cupboards for an appropriate container, I finally find a vase, then fill it with water. There's a packet tucked inside the rubber bands wrapped around the stems that I assume should be added to the water, so in typical Reece style – and stupidity – I open it . . . with my teeth.

PSA: Do not do this.

"Thun of a bith!" I sputter as the grains of whatever the shit is in the packet virtually explode onto my tongue and teeth, as well as half my beard. Rushing to the sink, I turn on the water and collect handfuls of the lifesaving liquid to suck into my mouth to rinse and spit. As I'm spitting into the sink, Mallory arrives at my side.

"Are you okay? What happened?"

"I think I just poisoned myself," I breathe hard after a gargle and spit. "I accidentally swallowed the powdery shit that was supposed to go in the vase for the flowers. Would you check the label and see if I need a trip to the hospital?"

She picks up the now empty packet, her eyes wide. "This?" she inquires, holding the packet between her fingers.

"Yeah." I snatch a paper towel from the holder and bring it to my mouth. "I probably should have looked for scissors, but I used my teeth instead."

"Well," she says slowly, "the symptoms probably shouldn't be too bad. I doubt you'll get a sugar high from the carbohydrate, the citric acid probably tasted a little tangy, and if you have any internal bacterial overgrowth it should actually be helpful. It's harmless, Reece. If you don't settle down though, I might have to take you to the hospital for a Valium." She squints to read the fine print. "Oh wait, it says here in rare cases it can cause tulip sprouting between the butt cheeks." She shrugs. "Good bathroom freshener, I suppose." I stare for a moment, until she clamps a hand over her mouth to hide her grin, but her giggle wins.

The two steps it takes to reach her are almost too many. Lifting her off her feet once more, she wraps her legs around my hips. I gaze into the most beautiful silver eyes I've ever seen, the tiny flecks of green highlighted by the playfulness reflected in them. "I love your laugh. It is literally music."

"Keep doing things like this and I'll be singing all night long."

"It wasn't my best moment, was it?"

She runs her fingers through my beard before she pats my cheek gently and giggles. "You are so charming."

I swallow that giggle with a kiss. If I could only bottle that sound, carry it in my pocket and pull it out when I need it most. Maybe I could record it and add it to my playlist. Sleep with it under my pillow at night. Cancel out the noises that haunt my dreams. She is such a breath of fresh air. I've seen her tough side, experienced her compassion, anger, shyness, and unsurety. I've watched her cry, enjoyed her spark and spunk, felt her come undone for me. With every tiny chunk of armor she lets go of, I want to pry the next one off. Know everything there is to know about her. For the first time in my life, I want the whole woman.

"And you are so special."

The intercom buzzer sounds to indicate dinner has arrived and I set her back on her feet. "The general is here. I'll run down and get dinner."

"I'll grab the silverware and plates."

I head for the door and turn at the last moment. "You don't use chopsticks?"

Her brow arches and she smirks. "Do you?"

"God no. I hate those damn things. Silverware only." I roll my eyes. "It's no wonder those Chinese people are so small. They're half starved."

She releases an exasperated huff. "Reece."

"Yeah?"

"Go get dinner."

Mallory has everything set up by the time I get back to the tenth floor, my hands full of delicious smelling Chinese food. Silverware, two bowls, two plates on the coffee table, replete with a pile of napkins. At home, I'm a straight-out-of-the-carton kind of guy. Why do dishes if you don't have to?

The TV is on pause, movie ready to go. After serving our dishes, we sit back, get comfy, and Mallory hits *play*. The credits roll for "*Hear My Song*" with Ned Beatty and Shirley Ann Field – a movie I have never even heard of – and the first scene opens . . .

Holy shit!

A bite of Hunan beef goes down the wrong way as I watch a very busy young couple on screen, both on their knees, panting hard as the female clings tightly to the bed railing, breathlessly screaming, "*Mickey!*" as he takes her from behind. It's virtual porn!

What the hell?! I thought we were watching a cowboy flick! It's hard enough to be in the same room with the woman and fight off a permanent semi. By the time I clear the stuck piece of food from my throat, the scene is over.

"Uh, Mallory . . ." I start slowly, wiping my mouth with a napkin and adjusting my position on the sofa. I can't watch this – not tonight anyway.

She backhands my bicep. "Settle down. It's the only sex scene in the whole movie and there's a purpose behind it." *No shit there's a purpose behind it. It's called an orgasm!* She hits pause, then reaches for my beer and holds it out for me. "Here, wash it down and get over yourself." She grins puckishly. "Unless you want me to play it again."

"No," I grind out slowly, the picture on the screen burning a hole in my brain while the heat in my crotch slowly simmers. "Once was plenty."

She pushes play and the movie continues; the sex scene

having come to an end. Turns out it's a romantic comedy based on the story of the Irish tenor, Josef Locke, and actually a damn good movie. International tax evasion, lost love, and loyal friendships that some people would kill for – like some of my own. It wasn't sappy or predictable. And yes, the opening scene was the one and only snippet of nudity in the whole movie. It was literally the whole package. Something for both of us. With my Irish background – a heritage we were raised to be proud of – the scenery was perfect. Just like her.

"So, what did you think?" she inquires as the ending credits roll. It's nearing ten o'clock and I know our night is almost over. She sounds tired – can't say it bothers me at all. I've looked forward to the next seven hours as much as the last few we've spent together. *I get to hold her.* Not that I haven't during the movie. She's been tucked under my shoulder for the last hour; the soft scent of her hair filling my senses. Couldn't get her to accept the offer of a foot rub, but all in good time.

"Perfect choice. Never been a big Ned Beatty fan, but I liked him in this." I begin to collect the now empty cartons and stack them on the plates.

"I've got these," she protests, rising to her feet and snatching her wine glass and my two empty beer bottles at the same time.

"One trip," I tell her as I make my way to the kitchen behind her, my hands full. "You have a bedtime, Sleeping Beauty. I'll finish up here. You go get ready for bed. This will only take a minute. I'll join you as soon as I'm done."

She sets the glass on the counter and the bottles in the sink to be rinsed before going into the recycling bin. She turns to me, her nose crinkled in that same adorable way it does when she giggles. "You're really going to stay? Knowing there's no advantage?"

Thumb and finger on her chin, I tip her head back so she can't look away. "I thought I was the moron. Mallory, it doesn't matter what we're doing, where we are, or whether or not we have our clothes on." I chuckle and wink. "I do love it when we're naked, but it's not a requirement. My *advantage* is being with you." I plant a soft kiss on lips I've remembered since the first time I had the pleasure. "Have a little faith in me, please?"

"I'm just trying to figure out what you want, Reece."

"That's easy," I whisper. "I want you. But I want you to want me, too."

"But what if . . ."

My finger is over her mouth before she can continue. "No ifs, no buts. I'm in this to win you. I've never done this before and I'm a shit loser, Kitten. I'm not like Liberty's ex-fiancé or that asshole you were with. I'm loyal to a fault. I haven't been with, thought about, or even looked at another woman since the OR. Unless you tell me to walk out that door right now, I'm not going anywhere."

Her eyes widen in surprise; the entire irises surrounded by white. "You haven't been . . . That was months, Reece."

I press my lips to her forehead and groan softly. "Believe me, I know."

"What did you do for . . ." she winces, ". . . release in the interim?"

Holding up my left hand, I wiggle my fingers. "This guy gained some pretty good dexterity and grip strength," then wiggle my right fingers, "while this guy was out of commission. But once I got him back, my trusty friend was good as new. You know, I could save the physical therapy department some money on those squeeze balls, but I wasn't sure they would appreciate my home methods."

"Oh my God!" she squeals and slaps my chest. "That was more than I needed to know."

"A little more than I wanted to confess, Sugar. Now go get

ready for bed."

Chapter 30

Mallory

As I stare at my reflection in the mirror after brushing my teeth and tossing back two ibuprofen, his words bounce around in my head. He hasn't been with another woman in months? But why?

Admittedly, I never spent another night with Eric after the Mexican restaurant incident either. Being anonymously gifted with timestamped pictures and video of him and Michael revisiting *The Tempest* after we declined their offer of drinks was enough to piss me off and convince Libs we needed the Vegas trip. If I knew who gifted me with them, I'd send them a thank you card.

I fail to see anything spectacular staring back at me in the mirror. I'm not exactly ugly. No warts on my nose and I haven't sprouted chin hairs, though I do take a moment to examine every angle carefully. Those pesky little buggers can pop up overnight. I truly believe the masks we wear in surgery rub against the hair follicles and encourage a sprouter on occasion. Nothing like the dental assistant offering, "Oohh, here, let me get this for you." I wasn't sure if I should have slapped her or expressed gratitude. She really didn't have to hold it up to the light and display the inch-long strand between her fingers.

But I digress. Yes, I'm stalling. Four nights ago, we were both blissfully sated and extremely exhausted before landing on the pillows. Tonight, I'm ready for sleep physically, but mentally I feel as if I drank two cups of coffee versus the two glasses of wine I actually did imbibe. My heart skips a few beats, and my mind flits from thought to thought so fast I swear you could put me on the spectrum.

Rinsing my toothbrush and setting it in the holder, I glance in the mirror one last time. *What you see is what you get.* Reece's PFD T-shirt over a pair of skimpy shorts. For someone who usually sleeps in next to nothing, aka tank top and shorts, the T-shirt is burdensome enough. Pants? Impossible. I'd probably slip them off, unknowingly, somewhere around midnight.

Reece is sitting on the edge of the bed when I open the bathroom door, duffel bag at his feet. He eyes his T-shirt in appreciation and smiles. "All done?"

I only nod and pull back the never-used comforter, folding it in half at the foot of the bed, and climb in under the waffle blanket and sheets. He closes the bathroom door behind him and as he does, a spectacular idea strikes. I throw back the covers and hurry to the other door in the room. He's been so sweet and thoughtful and needs to know it wasn't all one-sided.

As he steps out of the bathroom, bare chested and clad in navy gym shorts, mere seconds after I've climbed back into bed, I sit up tall and proudly display my own proof of the memory of us. "I may not have recognized you, Reece, but I didn't forget you."

He stops short mid-way between the door and the bed, shock and awe enveloping his eyes before a tooth revealing smile lights his face, and he whispers, "You kept it."

In my best – though lame – southern drawl I respond as I tip the hat on my head, "Complete with a little bit of Texas dirt and cowboy sweat."

His laughter rings throughout the room as he dives for the bed and topples me, burying his face in my neck as the hat falls off my head, lost somewhere between the pillows and the headboard. "It did mean something and you do remember," he whispers as if he's been given a gift.

"Most of it," I confess. "It was a really bad day for me. You gave me something I could hang onto, the same day my dad took away my biggest hope. One canceled out the other and by the time I let that anger go, I guess I had moved on from hopes and dreams to my version of reality, and let go of some memories."

He nods against the crook of my neck before lifting his head and burdening his weight on his elbows. "I know. My brothers told me about it."

"Your brothers?"

"Your dad told them he was worried about you. Had some news he needed to share and was trying to give you something to enjoy on your vacation before breaking it to you."

"That's a helluva confession to make to strangers," I grumble, remembering my introduction to *what was her name?* Oh yeah, Marjorie. "Did you know about it before we went out on . . ."

"No," he answers quickly. "I only found out a couple months ago when I visited back home." My sour expression must be enough to beg the question for me. He rolls his eyes. "I might have mentioned the gorgeous nurse in the OR with the beautiful eyes while I was there. Ryder made fun of me for my obsession with the girl on the horse that I couldn't shut up about years ago."

My lips roll between my teeth to hide my smile. "You talked about me after I left?"

"For months," he admits. "You haunted my dreams in a good way, and bad. My silver-eyed girl and the regret I never got your name or number." He brushes a wisp of hat hair away from my face. "I didn't want to date any other girls. Their kisses would have tainted the memory of yours. The cotton candy flavor. But then my football coach insisted I get a date for homecoming."

My nose crinkles before I put two and two together – *of course he was* – and the question slides out before I can stop it, "Why?"

He grins wryly. "Gotta have a queen to go with the king."

I roll my eyes. "You were homecoming king."

"Crown and all," he replies, his voice laced with overtones of boredom.

"Did you kiss your date goodnight?"

"Nope," he says cockily, then laughs so hard his chest bounces on top of me. "But I got my first blowjob."

"Oh my God!" I giggle underneath him. "You suck!"

"No, Sugar." His eyes light with mischief and he bobs his brows. "But she sure did." His expression softens and he holds my gaze, burdening his weight on his elbows as his thumb grazes my bottom lip. "I've never been a fan of kissing, Mallory. It's intimate, intended for lovers; not hook-ups. You ruined me.

No one has ever come close to that perfect kiss since, so I gave up a long time ago."

"You realize the chances of us ever meeting again were . . ."

"Apparently one hundred percent." He drops his mouth to mine but doesn't get too carried away with the kiss. "We're here, aren't we? And in case you haven't noticed, kissing you is one of my favorite pastimes." He grabs the hat before rolling off of me. "It's after ten and past your bedtime. I made you a promise." He lifts the hat to his nose and sniffs. "Damn, I do miss home sometimes, but this definitely needs a trip to the cleaners."

The sharp sound of skin on skin as I slap his shoulder only makes him laugh. "I've had it stored in plastic."

"I'll get it cleaned, but no more storing it away, Kitten." He winks and shoots me a sexy grin. "You're gonna need to keep it handy to ride your cowboy."

"Can I ask you something?"

"Anything, Sugar." He sets the hat on the nightstand and rolls back, propping up on one elbow.

"How did you figure out who I was?"

He brushes a thumb across my eyebrow. "From day one, your eyes haunted me. Even with the drugs from the surgery, I knew these eyes."

"You did tell Rory you'd kissed me before."

"I also begged Roger to go find you." He nearly growls, "I told the surgeon I wanted to thank you personally, but he said he would take care of it himself."

"He did." I neglect to elaborate that he also warned me about Reece being a player and reminding me of ethics rules.

"How nice of him," he deadpans then moves his thumb in a pass over my bottom lip. "The kiss in the parking lot, the taste on your lips and looking into your eyes. And then you purred. It was like a step back in time. It's why I said *impossible*.

"The day at your condo, when I snatched you up by your waist as you tried to run away." He places his hand on my stomach and plays with the piercing over my bellybutton and smiles sweetly. "This right here. I couldn't help myself. My little finger fell into place like it had found a home. I came back that night, still not positive, but determined. You were so damn resistant to tell me how long you'd had it. I had to ask so many questions before you finally admitted to being from North Carolina. That's when I knew for sure you were my kitten."

"It was so long ago," I whisper, as if time changes everything.

"Then I guess we have a lot of catching up to do." He kisses me softly, rolls me over onto my side and tucks himself in behind me. "And we will. But I promised you a bedtime. No more stories tonight, angel. You need your sleep. I'll be right here and I'll fix you breakfast in the morning."

"You don't need to . . ."

"Yeah, I really do, Mallory. Goodnight."

Chapter 31

Reece

She kept the hat. My treasured, fit-to-my-head-like-a-glove hat. Had one of my brothers tried to borrow it, I would have tackled them to the ground and fought them to the death for the sake of that hat. But placing it on my kitten's head that day felt like sharing a part of me, putting a claim on her – my hopes high that maybe her dad would bring her around the next year for vacation again. I was young, naïve, and totally smitten.

Now? I'm older, not as naïve, yet still totally smitten. Yeah, I'm horny too, but I'll take care of that once I get home in the morning. Tonight, I'm proving myself.

Which is proving to be a challenge, as she's snuggled so tightly against me that you couldn't slide a piece of paper between us. Yet, she's sound asleep; her breaths even and deep. I'd be asleep too – if my dick were as tired as the rest of my body. But that asshole seems to be suffering severe insomnia at the present time. Mallory stirs slightly and adjusts herself, gifting me a slight reprieve with some air space between her delectable ass and my raging hard-on. I gently back away to put a bit more space between us. But the asshole is like a heat-seeking missile, taking advantage of the looseness of my gym shorts, and homes in on his target. The inches between us disappear in seconds and the greedy bastard is at it again. I really should have worn jerseys under my shorts, but my boys have a thing for freedom when I sleep, and old habits are hard to break.

"Would you sleep better if I help relieve some pressure for you?" *Damnit! I thought she was asleep.* She rolls over to face me and places her hand on my shoulder to move me onto my back, then tips her chin up and kisses my jaw. "You seem a little restless, Reece."

"Mallory, no." My voice is raspy as my physical need usurps my conscience and I make a silent vow to put numbing cream on the disobedient asshole in the morning as his punishment. "That's not why I'm here. I told you . . ."

"I know," she whispers and kisses my chest. "You didn't ask."

Her magic fingers play with the hair on my chest, trailing them down my belly before slipping her hand under the band of my shorts and grabbing the greedy asshole, as if punishing him, and giving him a good squeeze. Her thumb brushes the tip then teases the sensitive underside of the head while those delicate fingers grip what seems more than physically possible. My moan can't be contained as my hips jerk forward. I want to tell her no, tell her both of us or neither of us, but her touch is my kryptonite. And damn, the woman knows what she's doing. I couldn't do it this well, and it's *my* dick. Is it science? Do the medical journals she reads teach handy dandy methods? Is it advice from one of Ava's . . . *You had to go there, didn't you, Reece?*

I need to feel her mouth on mine, feel as much of her as I can. I'll make it up to her, in spades, as soon as I can. Tipping her chin to the perfect angle, I capture her mouth to collect more of the kisses I've deliberately avoided with other women. Their lips wouldn't have been as soft, wouldn't have fit mine like they were made for them, wouldn't have tasted like hers. I wrap my hand in her hair, tugging and pulling her closer at the same time, coaxing that ever familiar purr from her throat. That's all it takes. The rush in my spine is so powerful I lose myself in the sensation as I explode. Her hand holds me tight in a vise-like grip – tiny pulses as she flexes her fingers around my dick – much like the simulation of your partner's release with a final thrust. It's now I note she has both hands wrapped around me. Her shoulder is buried into the mattress next to my chest and probably tingling from the blood supply being depleted.

"Come here," I whisper and roll her on top of me then start to rub the shoulder that was buried under her weight to help with circulation.

She chuckles against the crook of my neck. "My hands are messy."

"So are my shorts, baby." I match her laugh, though more breathless and broken, as I drop kisses to her temple. "Good thing I packed an extra pair. Don't make me let go yet. I'll take care of the mess."

I could ask her where she learned to do that, but if she were to answer, "Ava's books" or "experience", I would never be able to enjoy another one. It doesn't matter, Reece; that was the best hand job you've ever had.

The alarm on her phone starts to play at five a.m. on the nose; the time displayed on the ceiling beaming from the clock on her nightstand confirms it. What I had not anticipated was waking to the sound of Marvin Gaye singing "Let's Get It On". My wish for slow, sleepy, morning sex – something I've only ever dreamed of – vanishes as soon as she slips out from under my arm and climbs out of bed. She's on autopilot. Every move is deliberate, gauged, bordering mechanical. *She'd make a helluva firefighter.* Not as speedy as we are, but definitely as methodical.

Pretending my peaceful slumber hasn't been disrupted, I keep one eye slightly open and watch as she enters the closet, returns with chosen attire, and slides a drawer open silently to retrieve her underwear and what looks to be a sports bra.

"Are you going to get your ass out of bed and fix me breakfast like you promised, or lay there and stare at me?" *Not a morning person. Got it.*

I'm out of bed in seconds flat and she is in my arms, lifted off her feet, legs wrapped around me as I grab two hands full of ass cheek. "You gonna kiss me good morning first?"

"No tongue," she orders, her nose crinkled. "I haven't brushed my teeth yet."

"You got a guy on your phone singin' about gettin' it on and you're worried about whether or not you brushed your teeth?"

She narrows her eyes. "It's a hygiene thing."

I smirk. "Did you forget where my mouth was right before I kissed you four nights ago, Kitten?"

Her reaction is exactly what I was hoping for – eyes wide, jaw agape – and I take full advantage with an open mouth kiss, my tongue tangling with hers as we start our day the way it should be started. Well, when you're not still on the mattress and geared for slow, sleepy, morning sex. I'm looking forward to that, as soon as our schedules allow.

"Now, go get ready," I tell her as the kiss ends and set her on her feet. "I'll get your breakfast and take you to work."

"Why would you take me to work?"

"So I can pick you up," I say easily. "We'll go to dinner. Our first official date. You choose the restaurant. I'll make reservations."

"I don't know when I'll be off. My schedule depends on surgeries. I'm with Evans this week." She smirks and reminds me, "Your favorite surgeon. Ortho is unpredictable. Sometimes we get quirky cases . . . like firemen who put their arms through car windows."

I cock a brow and smirk. "Have any of them ever offered you a seat on their face before, Kitten?"

She clears her throat loudly and scowls. "Mancusso's. I'll need to come back here for a shower and to change."

"Mancusso's it is." I nod toward the bathroom. "Get a move on. Your first surgery is at 6:30. You don't want to be late."

That beautiful little nose crinkles. "How do you know when . . ."

"I listen, Mallory, because everything you say is important to me. Now, go get ready. I'll have breakfast when you come out."

Her mouth twists as she considers what I've told her. "I only drink a protein shake before work, otherwise it's too heavy on my stomach. There's a container of chopped fruit in the fridge along with spinach leaves. Almond milk on the top shelf. The protein powder is in the cupboard above the Ninja mixer. Vanilla, please."

"You didn't like my pancakes?" I ask, my chef ego a bit

bruised. My firehouse buddies rave about my cooking skills. My Texas chili has them licking their bowls. Mind you, the sleeping quarters are uninhabitable until the windows have been opened and the fans run for a while – okay, a long while – but it's so worth it.

She swipes both hands through her hair and that soft purr I've grown to love is replaced by a slightly feral growl. *Buster! It sounds just like the fugly dog when he tried to bite my ankle!* "Your pancakes were good, Reece. Never mind. I'll fix the shake when I come out." She charges toward the bathroom, clothes in hand, and the door closes behind her. The water for the shower starts, and I stare at the closed door. I know just how to fix that owly mood. *Next time, Reece. When our schedules allow.*

In the kitchen I find all the ingredients she named: the container of chopped fruit, spinach leaves, almond milk, and protein powder. I rub my hands together in anticipation – or confusion – doesn't matter, this concoction cannot be appetizing. I've never been one much for protein shakes – having been raised in barbecue country. However, in our line of work we've been trained to utilize prepackaged ones for efficiency purposes. The Hotshots practically survive on them and Gatorade when necessary. If they came in BBQ or pizza flavors, I just might enjoy them. Nah, scratch that. If you can't chew it, forget it.

I know how to use a Ninja. I own one. This morning, however, after adding all the ingredients to the container, putting the lid on before pressing the start button might have avoided the Vesuvius eruption that has left fruit and spinach bits spewing all the way to the ceiling, and splattering every surface available to include counters, cupboards, and the floor, not to mention my upper body and face. Even the fridge and dishwasher are painted in various colors of apple, peach, pineapple, and a perfect green to match whatever came out of Blair's mouth in *The Exorcist*.

Mallory appears in my periphery as she takes in the mess. Standing on the other side of the breakfast bar, her breaths are long, slow, and deep, as if she's counting with each one in, each one out. The silence is deafening as my heart rate spikes and I wait for her to demand my exit, never to return.

"I'm sorry," I mutter, too ashamed to face her. "I forgot to put the lid on."

Her footsteps are slow, each one with purpose – probably in order to avoid sliding on the fruit and milk covered floor – but she hasn't grabbed a knife yet so that's a plus. Once by my side, she gently takes my elbow and turns me toward her. She's in scrubs, her hair in a messy bun, no makeup, a slight sheen to her Chapstick coated lips. *Beautiful.* She stares up at me, her face blank as she takes in my remorseful grimace. Her gaze turns thoughtful, maybe a bit resigned – much like my mother's used to as she considered what to do with me when I screwed up. One slow blink before her tongue slips out and she slowly runs it from my sternum to my throat, then steps back and licks her lips.

"It would have tasted really good," she says softly.

This moment in time will forever be etched in my brain, because it's the exact moment I realize I am in love with Mallory Tompkins.

Scrubs be damned; she has to have more in the closet. I hoist her into my arms, our bodies meeting as tightly as possible when she wraps her legs around my waist and I kiss her, with everything I have.

"It's the moron syndrome," I murmur against her mouth.

Her lips are soft against mine and I taste the cherry flavor as she mutters back, "You're still going to call the cleaning service and have the place spotless before I get home. I'll leave you my keys."

"Done. You're not mad at me?"

She shakes her head slowly as if resigned then smiles. "You're too charming. Now drop your shorts at the breakfast bar and use them to wipe your feet so you don't track through the living room, then go shower the fruit off."

"You want me to walk through the living room naked?"

She cocks one eyebrow. "Yes, Reece, yes I do."

Doing exactly as told, I wiggle my ass on the way through to her bedroom.

"And that, Mr. Callahan," she laughs behind me, "is why it's so hard to get mad at you."

Turning before crossing the threshold. "What about your breakfast?"

"I have some store-bought ones in the back of the fridge. Now hurry up so I'm not late. I have to change my scrubs as it is. I'll drink the shake on the way." She eyes my crotch and scowls. "Go put the soldier away."

I wink and treat her to a double salute. "Yes, ma'am."

Chapter 32

Mallory

Ever seen a sexy bare-chested man splattered in pieces of fruit, spinach leaves, protein powder, and almond milk standing at your kitchen counter? No? Still billboard material. As I eyed the damages – splashes of yellow, white, and green from my appliances all the way to my ceiling – my muscles tensed, the thought of strangling Reece hung heavy in the air. *"There's no use crying over spilled milk"* echoed in my head. *But what about the food bits?* Then I noted all the ingredients laying on the counter. Every last item I had mentioned to go in the shake. Moreover, the look on his face and agonized tone of his voice as he apologized. My kitchen may have looked like a kindergarten classroom after fingerpainting mayhem, but the man in front of me looked more like the little boy who'd put the most effort into his artwork, only to have it fall to the floor and be stepped on.

He is trying so hard. Something tells me Reece Callahan has never been met with resistance – not in the mating department, anyway. He's suave but lacks the finesse component. But that's okay because he's killing it in the masculine department. Definitely charming. He's confident as hell but seems to have a deep-seated need to please. He's not stupid by any means. I only call him moron because it tickles me and gets a rise out of him. And last but not least, he enjoyed a movie that's pretty near and dear to me. The camaraderie, romance, comedy, lifelong friendships. Ireland is on my bucket list and the scenery in that movie is breathtaking. My maternal grandparents were Irish, and visiting their homeland has always been a dream of mine. I want to visit those pubs, view those landscapes, and walk the edges of those cliffs.

"Ready?" Reece sounds cheerful as he exits the bedroom, freshly showered and fully dressed. "Think I got all the fruity bits off." He glances around the kitchen from the floor to the ceiling and grimaces. "I'll make sure it's spotless before you get home and I will be here while they do it, okay?"

"Yup," I say slowly, holding out the keys and the number for my cleaning lady, then head for the door where my Danskos sit.

"Hang on." He reaches for my hand and pulls me into a tight embrace before pummeling my mouth with a kiss I'm going to feel for a few hours. "We're early. Didn't think you'd appreciate that with an audience at the hospital and I wasn't going without it, so . . ." He cups my cheek, brow slightly furrowed as he inclines his chin. "Still my girl?"

I rise up on my tiptoes so I can plant a kiss on his jaw. "So long as you get my kitchen cleaned up."

He chuckles and presses his lips to my forehead. "There she is."

"Emergency entrance or staff lot?" he asks when we're nearing the hospital.

"Staff lot, please. It'll save me a couple thousand steps and ten minutes," I answer without thinking. It may save me the steps, but I hadn't considered what it may cost me in inquiries. Reece's truck isn't exactly subtle. Bright red, built for industrial size men, and custom license plates to identify his emergency service capabilities. I also hadn't considered the climb up into it might not have been as challenging as the break-neck high jump out of it may be.

He smiles and bobs his eyebrows. "Still got fifteen minutes to spare if you want to pull over and make out."

I roll my eyes and shake my head. "Next time, horndog."

As I hold my badge attached to my lanyard out for security to check, I greet the guard in my usual manner, "Morning, Sean."

"Hey, Mallory. Got an escort today, I see. Car troubles?" *And here we go. He may not be the hospital's best source for gossip, but he is the first line for gossip. He has a tendency to be chatty, but I generally limit our conversations to a simple salutation and "Have a good day".*

Before I can respond, Reece shoots him his million dollar smile. "No car trouble and not an escort. Just spending every last minute I can get with my girl. I'll be back to pick her up at quittin' time."

"Hey!" Sean's eyes go wide as he points his finger. "Aren't you the firefighter all the women in the ER . . ."

Reece rushes to stop him as my flushing face turns toward the side window. "Only one woman I'm interested in. Have a good day." The truck moves forward before Sean can inquire further and we make our way through the lot toward the entrance doors.

My seatbelt is off and I throw my door open at the crosswalk approximately thirty feet from the door. What the hell, if I break an ankle, I'll use a walking cast in the OR. How could I be so stupid? *"Watch out for him, Tompkins. He's a player".* I just got done dealing with one, I sure don't need to go rounds with another. This one hurts, though. Really hurts.

Reece snatches my bag out of my hands, sets it in his lap, and slams the gearshift into park. "Not a chance."

"Hand it over, Reece. I'll get out here!"

"No," he snaps. "You're mad, Mallory. Rule of thumb. Two things a couple never does. One: never leave for work or go to sleep mad at each other. Two: If you can't work it out right away, you still kiss goodbye and kiss goodnight."

My face squirrels into fifty shades of confusion as I stare at him. I mean, really, those are pretty good rules, but right now I don't want to hear the voice of reason. I'm too pissed . . . or jealous. Wait a minute. A couple?

"Close the door," he orders.

"No. Just give me my bag."

"Now, Mallory."

"No!"

He glances around to check for pedestrians, puts the truck in drive, gently grabs my arm, and pulls the truck forward quickly until the door swings shut, hits the child lock, turns left into a parking lane and stops. He reaches across the console, grasps the back of my neck and pulls me toward him at the same time he leans toward me, bringing our mouths so close we're exchanging the same air.

He squares me straight in the eyes, his voice harsh. "I'm no saint, not gonna lie, but I have never fucked one of your coworkers. Hospital personnel are off limits. I have never mixed my job with my *former* extracurricular activities. And those activities became *former* the moment I saw a *future*. That future is you." He seals his mouth over mine in a desperate kiss, the kind that gives and takes; Reece Callahan style. He leans his forehead on mine and takes a slow breath in, his eyes closed, as if searching for the right words. "You were my best kiss, Kitten. I want you to be my last. My past and my future. My only. Why can't you get that?"

"I'm not good at letting my guard down. I've never done this, Reece."

"Neither have I, but I've never wanted to until now. I think I was waiting for you. So you tell me, Mallory, do you want to do this?" He squeezes my nape a little firmer. "Would you just have a little faith in me?"

I do want to do this. I want it all. And I want it with him. Nodding against his forehead with mine, I sniffle. "Yeah, to both of those."

"Still my girl?"

I stifle a sob and attempt humor instead – because it's who I am. "Are you going to have my kitchen clean?"

He chuckles and murmurs against my mouth, "So fucking special." He delivers one last kiss to my mouth, a few to my cheeks to claim the tears with a whisper, "Salty and sweet." He reminds me I'm going to be late, which would be a violation of rule number one because it would make me mad again and it would be his fault.

Running to the locker room to drop my things off, I swipe my cheeks to assure they're dry. Savannah is at her locker as I step inside.

"The Hennessey surgery has been moved back at least an hour. Had a ruptured spleen come in two hours ago. GI took our OR and cardiac already had claim to the others. Seems bypasses take precedence over knee replacements." She adds sarcastically, "Who woulda thunk it?" She does a double take and squints when she turns toward me. "You okay?"

"I'm fine. Is Evans pissed?" I ask regarding our favorite anal retentive physician, my hopes dwindling for any semblance of notoriety beyond *"You didn't suck at your job today"* as I shove my belongings into my locker.

"Haven't seen him yet. Don't know if that's a good or a bad thing."

"Tompkins!" Evans' low demanding growl sounds from the door opening, making Savannah and I both jump. "A word."

"Asshole sounds fitting," I mutter as I slam my locker door shut. Savannah muffles her giggle. "Be right there," I call out to him.

"Now, Tompkins!"

"Can I pee first?" I antagonize him. I don't really need to go, I simply enjoy being a pain in his ass. What's he going to do? Report me for insubordination due to a potty break?

"Cross your legs. My office. You've got one minute."

Tapping on his door *three* minutes later, I roll my lips between my teeth to hide my smug grin after hearing him sigh and a resigned, "Yes, Mallory."

"Sorry, bladder was full. You wanted a word?" I ask sweetly through the ten-inch opening I've created.

"Get in here. Close the door." *Ooh, someone's in a mood.* He's not behind his desk; instead leaning on it, arms folded over his blue scrubs covered chest. "I thought we discussed Mr. Callahan."

My stomach dips. We had . . . for all of a nanosecond. But that was before Reece and I discovered we had a history. We were friends long ago – sort of – reunited by chance. No one needs details.

"We did. What's the problem?"

"I saw you in the parking lot, Mallory." He arches a brow and inclines his chin. "Looked pretty damn cozy to me."

"Eh, I don't know if cozy is a good description. Broad daylight in a pickup truck isn't quite the same as candlelight and satin sheets." I shrug. "Is there a point to this, Dr. Evans?"

"He was your patient," he says slowly as if I need reminded.

"He was also my friend before that, going all the way back to our childhoods. We hadn't seen each other in years so recognition was a little slow, but we caught up quickly."

"I would say damn quickly," he mutters. "You got any proof of this?"

"You could call my dad and ask him," I proffer. "You may have to wait until he's out of surgery, but I'm sure he'll answer any questions you have."

He looks skeptical, which actually was my goal. *Semantics.* My personal life has never been anyone's business. That, and I don't appreciate my honesty and integrity being questioned.

"Your dad has surgery today?"

"No," I answer confidently with an added touch of snark. "My dad is a surgeon who's *in* surgery today. Wednesday is his golf day though. Might be able to catch him before tee-time tomorrow. I think he's playing the greens at Hilton Head."

His fixed glare is usually nothing to be toyed with, but I stay the course – pun intended – because every word I've told him is truth. The tension eventually leaves his shoulders as the tic in his jaw relaxes. His chin drops and he shakes his head. "So you chose the player, huh?"

His words bite; the sharp sting causing a pang in my chest. How would he know about Reece? It's probably rumor,

243

or assumption. The sting doesn't last long as Reece's words play in my head. *Former* extracurricular activities. Recalling the conversation with Eric regarding the good doctor's own thoughts about me, I can't help myself. Tongue in cheek, I tilt my head and ask as if I'm actually curious, "Am I to understand you've never taken a trip or two to Candyland, Dr. Evans?"

If I were truly concerned about his welfare, I would slap him on the back to ensure he doesn't choke on his own spit. But at the present time, he deserves to. Pretty sure the guy has played more than 18 holes in his lifetime as well, and it wasn't on a golf course. Unless he likes to do the dirty outdoors.

"Thanks for your concern," I say lightly. "But the only thing Reece plays these days is me . . . like a fine-tuned instrument. Are we done here?"

His pager vibrates on the top of his desk and he grabs it to read the message. "Surgery in thirty, OR-4. Be ready."

"Got it." I take my leave, neglecting to close the door behind me just to piss him off a little more.

"Should have taken my shot when I had it," he grumbles right before something hits the wall.

Nah, I think to myself. I have a thing for cowboys. Always have. And now, I remember why.

Chapter 33

Reece

"Did a pressure cooker blow up in here?" the lead member of the cleaning crew asks as she observes the mess in the kitchen and studies the ceiling.

"Uh, no." I scrub my hand over my face then move it to the back of my neck and squeeze. "It was the Ninja."

"The Ninja?" She looks at me in surprise then begins to unload her supplies. "You know you're supposed to put the lid on those before you start them, don't you?"

"Yes, ma'am." My cheeks flush as I nod. "Lesson learned."

"The hard way, I see." She snorts and shakes her head.

"Something tells me this is your mess. No way Ms. Tompkins or Collins did this. They're smarter than the machines they own."

Feeling thoroughly chastised, I nod. "Yes, ma'am. I take full responsibility."

She blows an exasperated breath through puffed cheeks. "You probably can't cook either." She rolls her eyes and holds up a hand. "Never mind. That drawl of yours makes me think you're probably one of those grillers anyway. Barbecue country. It's for the best. Keeps you out of the kitchen." She waves toward the sofa. "Just stay out of the way and we should be done here in an hour or so."

As I'm heading toward the sofa, she inquires, "Out of curiosity, which one of the girls did you screw up with?"

"Beg your pardon?"

She rolls her eyes again as if already frustrated with the conversation. "Which one of the girls are you dating?"

"Uh, Mallory?" I don't know why it sounds like a question.

She snickers, as do the other two that have started to clean the ceiling with long handled mops. "And you're still alive? With your manhood intact?"

"Um," I stammer. "She actually licked my chest and told me it would have tasted good." *Oh shit. Why? TMI, Reece.*

Three sets of shocked, wide eyes stare at me from the other side of the breakfast bar. Somebody say something, please. No wait! Don't say anything . . . especially to Mallory. Some things are best left unsaid. Wish I'd thought of that before I opened my big mouth.

"He must be good under the sheets," she says to her assistants. They titter and nod in agreement. "Easy on the eyes, too."

Never in my life have I felt so objectified.

She cants her head to the left as if thinking. "What do you

do for a living?"

"I'm a firefighter, ma'am," I say proudly. "92ⁿᵈ district."

"Aha!" She points a stiff finger as her face lights in recognition. "You were April, holding those two little bunnies yet your full chest and rippled abs on display. Thought I recognized you. What month are you doing next year?"

Lowering my head in humiliation and pinching the bridge of my nose, I contemplate how I'm going to murder Roger. When the asshole told me I was going to be posing with a couple *bunnies* on my lap, I immediately pictured big tits and long legs spread across my thighs. Instead, I got two furry little creatures with long ears – one helping itself to a bite of my nipple and the other leaving a gift of pellets on my pantleg. I should have known better. They never place women with men on the calendar. Kinda defeats the purpose. However, since then I've been honing my skills with Photoshop. Paybacks are a bitch. A diaper for Baby New Year in January. An arrow to the crotch straight from Cupid's bow for February. An exploded firework to the same for July. You get my drift.

"To be determined," I grumble, though determined mine will be the most innocuous and uneventful month of the year. Randomly choosing the nearest reading material to occupy myself, I note it's one of Ava's books and drop it like a hot potato. *I'm done.* Rising from my seat, I head for the bedroom. I hadn't made the bed. Had she? I can be useful – and less humiliated – somewhere else. Apparently these ladies know Mallory and Liberty. *Still alive? Manhood intact?* Yeah, I'd say they're familiar with *my Kitten.*

The bed is already made, laundry collected and in the hamper, bathroom neat and orderly. I double rinsed the shower earlier. Not needed in here either.

Taking a seat on the edge of the bed, I ruminate this morning's conversation. Two rules of thumb. They were drilled into us like a fiery Sunday sermon.

"Never go to bed mad or without a kiss goodnight. Besides, that kiss may lead to forgetting what you were mad about to begin with."

"Never part angry or without a kiss. Not work, not shopping, not even errands. You will never forgive yourself if your loved one doesn't come home."

Lessons better observed than experienced. My uncle Ron died in his sleep. My aunt Janine woke up in bed alone, still mad from the night before. Got up to start the usual routine of coffee and breakfast before sending him out the door to join us at the ranch. When he didn't rise to the sound of her banging around in the kitchen, she tried to roust him from slumber on the sofa where she had banished him the night before, only to find his slumber to be permanent due to a cerebral hemorrhage. She never forgave herself. She followed him into the ever after a year later. Perfectly healthy – no determinable cause of death. Natural causes. AKA, a broken heart.

The other? A neighboring rancher whose wife insisted on going into the city to shop instead of waiting a day, after the forecasted storms had passed, as her husband had pleaded she do. She threw a hissy, stomped out the door – without a kiss goodbye – never to return. That one, I've always credited to stubbornness plus stupidity, but it didn't change the fact that he loved her, and it broke him. Never did ask if the dress chosen for her final farewell was one she had purchased that day.

My dad was a one-armed kind of hugger. However, the pats on our shoulders, the reassurances in his words, and the kudos we received on a regular basis made us never doubt his love for us. But you can bet your sweet ass we never left the house without a full hug and a kiss on the cheek for our mom. It was requisite, and we never minded.

I knew Mallory was upset over the security guard's stupid remark at the gate. I wasn't letting her get out of the truck with any doubts about us, about me. Hell, Dr. X-ray would be all over that like flies on shit. No way am I going to let fat wallet/ tiny dick near her. I'll bet he stalks vulnerability and eats it for breakfast.

Yes, the ladies in the ER – some nurses, some intake personnel – can be quite flirtatious, and admittedly we play into it but we never play *with* it. To be honest though, I've been nothing more than cordial with those ladies on the rare occasions I've been there since the day of surgery. My favorite female in the ER has always been Liz; a motherly type in her sixties who reminds me of my own.

"We're all done out here, April," the cleaning lady hollers down the hall.

The urge to groan is strong, but a laugh escapes instead. It's no wonder she's familiar with Mallory. She's a smartass. They probably drink wine and tell dirty jokes if the regularly scheduled cleaning is the last one of the day.

Entering the kitchen, I glance at the ceiling first and follow the path I remember being covered in various colors of the shake that didn't make it. Spotless. Reaching for my wallet, I extract my credit card and six twenty dollar bills; handing two to each of them and the card to the woman who's been extremely *chatty*. "It's perfect. Thank you."

She slides the card through the small reader, presses a few buttons, hands it back, then holds the reader out so I can sign. $430.00!!! For an hour's work? That's . . . that's $7.16 a minute!

She must read my thoughts as I reluctantly scratch my name on the small space. "Ms. Tompkins texted earlier." She smirks. "Told me to add a 30% tip."

"B–but," I stammer, my jaw loose. "I just tipped you each forty dollars."

"Thank you." She nods as if it's nothing then turns to collect what's left of the supplies and heads for the door with her crew behind her. I stare at their backs, nonplussed at their lack of gratitude. Having been raised to be grateful for a roof over my head, delicious food at every meal, and the best *tip* in life being "Don't take any wooden nickels", I find this all a bit insulting.

"Hey, April," she says with a playful lilt in her voice before she's out the door. "I've got a tip for you. Put the seat down or you will be history."

The door closes and I'm free for the rest of the day... *After* I run back into the bathroom to double check. Damn glad I did, too. I glance around the living room to ensure everything is in place. Looks good. I turn back once more before locking the door behind me, that irritating voice inside my head telling me I forgot something. Oh shit! I used the guest bathroom this morning while Mallory was in the shower.

Maybe the cleaning lady was worth the extra tip.

"Ah, so you do remember where you live." Roger is exiting his condo as I arrive at mine. "I was getting ready to call the movers for you."

"Not yet. I'll be sure to let you know." I enter the code to the lock into my phone and the deadbolt slides open. "You had lunch yet?"

"Nope. You want to grab some?"

"Sure." I open the door and set my duffel bag inside, closing it behind me. "Where to?"

"Cranky's serves lunch. I could go for a burger and a cold beer."

Never in my life did I think the mention of our favorite bar would send a shiver up my spine, but it does. *Former* extracurriculars. Not that I would be tempted, in the least, but wouldn't that include avoiding the temptation, reminders, old faces? Sex with Mallory was the best I've ever had – and I've had a lot. Watching her come undone was my undoing. I looked into her eyes. Kissing her isn't something I *like* to do – it's my *favorite* thing to do.

Roger claps my shoulder and rolls his eyes, apparently reading my thoughts. "Never thought I'd see the day. Reece Callahan has traded in his freedom for one pussy. I'll double up in your honor the next time I'm at Cranky's. *Five Guys* it is."

"Might as well," I grumble as we saunter down the hall. "Already spent 500 bucks to have her kitchen cleaned. What's another thirty for a burger."

"You did what?!?"

"It was my fault. Long story."

He laughs as he opens the door to the stairwell. "Better start now, Reece. This sounds like a good one."

Stopping at the threshold, I narrow my eyes. "Only if I get March, June, or August for the calendar next year."

He stops short at the top of the stairs and turns around, his forehead scrunched in confusion. "What the hell does her kitchen have to do with the calendar?"

"Nothing," I snap harshly. "It was the cleaning ladies."

"Ah," he drawls, enlightened. His mouth twitches. "So did they inquire about the bunnies or ask you to pull a rabbit out of your pants?"

I flip him the bird and sneer. "You're buying lunch for that, asshole."

He only snickers. "Thirty bucks to hear how you fucked up? So worth it."

"Forty," I retort. "You forgot my beer."

After humiliating myself and entertaining Roger with this morning's mishaps, we breathe in our food in silence long enough to take the edge off our appetites.

"You are aware of the fires that started out west?" Roger asks warily as he sets down his mug and wipes his mouth. I nod. "And the two we already got going down south here?"

"Yeah." I pick up my own mug and take a long pull. "But they're getting the two out west under control, aren't they?"

"Reece, there're five out west as of this morning. When's the last time you checked your monitors? The two that *were* have spread another five thousand acres *each,* and the three new ones are a hundred miles apart, at least a thousand acres each, and the winds are only expected to get worse."

I'm not sure what shoots up faster – my eyelids or my eyebrows – not to mention the pit in my stomach that opens. "What's it lookin' like down south?"

He lifts his burger to his mouth but hesitates. "Not good."

I pull my phone from my pocket and open the monitoring app, checking the latest update. It's a morning ritual of mine – unfortunately, one I neglected today. "Roger," I look up from my phone, "they're gonna be pulling the inter Hotshots out west if they can't get a handle on it."

"I'm well aware," he speaks around a mouthful then swallows and nods at my phone. "Which means . . ." he arches a brow, ". . . our number's up for going down south. They've already pulled some full timers in from the north and the upper east."

"Fuck," I groan before an indignant gasp comes from the table next to us. If I hadn't already spent my morning apologizing and being humiliated, I might just have two fucks to give and apologize. But I don't, so I ignore it.

"You haven't told her yet."

"Exactly when was I supposed to slip that in, Rog?" I narrow my eyes. "Between her delectable purrs of ecstasy or my growls when I'm coming?"

The mug of beer that was on its way to his mouth stops midair as he stares. Okay, maybe that was a little TMI. Silverware drops on the table next to us as the woman rises from her chair. "Well, I never!" she huffs and throws her napkin at me, hitting me in the face, before stomping toward the hostess stand.

Roger sighs. "Yup. My bet is she has never." He gulps the remainder of his beer and sets the mug down hard. "Anybody ever tell you, you talk too much. Let's go, idiot, before they throw us out. One more restaurant we gotta mark off the list."

Downing the rest of my beer first, then snatching the last quarter of the sandwich from my plate – hey, it's eight bucks worth of burger! – I head for the door while Roger takes care of the bill.

Standing outside my truck in the parking lot, I feast on the last of my sandwich. It's not that I eat slower than Roger, it's that I was the one with the story to tell. "You did tip the waitress, didn't you?" I ask as he approaches.

"I did, and she asked that I not bring you back." He smirks. "However, she is interested in a threesome if you're game. She said she doesn't purr, but she'd be willing to bark. You in?"

Staring at him in disbelief, my jaw drops. Sonofabitch. I do talk too much. Why would I divulge her purrs?

"Take it back or you will be a pedestrian." I hit the button on the fob once to release the lock on the driver's side only.

"Hey!" He points his finger accusingly. "I wasn't the one announcing my sexual kinks to the restaurant. Time to grow up. Peter Pan is officially six feet under, Reece. Keep it to yourself."

I tap the button to release the lock for the passenger's side and we both climb in. "Did the waitress really offer that?"

"Shit no!" He pretends to shiver and scrubs his arms. "She was probably sixty. I was trying to make a point. I don't want to know what your girlfriend does in bed. More importantly, I doubt she wants anyone to know. Jesus, Reece, there are things you just don't share."

"It's not a kink. It's this sweet little sound that . . ."

"Reece!"

"What?"

"Shut the fuck up and drive." He holds up his index finger. "One more thing. Don't ever call her *Kitten* in front of me again. I thought it was just a nickname."

"It is! It's from way back . . ." His glare is enough to silence me. I'll explain it to him – someday.

Chapter 34

Mallory

"I'll be ready in half an hour."

My text to Reece is short, but my day has been long. I really wish I had driven myself. This morning's ruptured spleen set us back an hour and, to his credit, Evans never rushes and is not a fan of postponing a waiting patient to the next day. *"We're here until the job is done".* It's admirable but doesn't make him any more likable. Particularly today.

More than a few times he raised eyebrows when he barked my name – all for sport, I'm sure – and even Savannah muttered a quiet *asshole* when her back was turned. Four surgeries and it didn't dawn on me until the third was over, it wasn't that I poked the bear this morning, it was that the bear didn't get to poke me.

"Can you come through the emergency department? Can't get into the staff lot. No pass, Kitten."

Oh shoot. I hadn't thought of that this morning. It's already six o'clock, my feet need an Epsom soak, and I need wine. It's only an extra thousand or two steps.

"On my way."

To say I'm surprised to see Reece standing in the ER waiting area when I arrive is one thing, but Reece in dress slacks and tucked in shirt that fit him like they were tailor made? He won't need to nip my lip with a kiss tonight; I just bit through my bottom one. *Oh shit! Our date.*

His face lights with that thousand watt smile as he steps forward and takes my cheeks in his hands, drops a kiss on my mouth and says none too quietly, "Hey, Gorgeous. How's my girl?"

I know what he's doing. He's not staking his claim – he wants me to stake mine. The intake staff behind the counters and the nurses who've come up to the front to collect files are all getting a full show. The grapevine will glow brighter than network wires as word spreads. The gossip will travel from room to room. By the time midnight rolls around, rumor will have it that Reece and I had sex on the floor in the middle of the waiting room.

"Better now," I whisper softly. "But my feet hurt." I don't add that the last thing I feel like doing is going out this evening.

"I can fix that." He slides my bag off my shoulder, turns his back to me, and squats. "No saddle, but I promise you a good ride. Hop on, Sugar."

"Reece! Get up!"

"It's this or I throw you over my shoulder," he teases as he glances back and winks. "Get on my back, Mallory."

"Damn girl, ride that cowboy or I will," one of the ladies behind the reception desk hollers. "Giddy up."

Rather than suffer any more heckling, I place my hands on his shoulders. "Nope, wrap 'em around my neck. Squeeze me like you mean it, baby." His voice drops to a low sexy growl, "I know you know how."

Oh, I know how. I know exactly where your trachea is, and the jugular, as well as . . . *Oh, he's talking about . . .* Damnit, Reece! I dive forward and wrap my arms around his neck, probably tighter than is necessary, and as I do he hitches his forearms under my thighs, rises to his full height, and pulls my legs around him.

Liz from reception hands him my bag and laughs. "Goodnight, kids."

"I am going to murder you," I threaten close to his ear, so as not to make more of a scene than we already have as we approach his truck.

He merely chuckles. "I've told you before exactly how to do it. As long as I have a face, you will always have a place to sit. I'll die a happy man."

For the first time today, I giggle. He is incorrigible. "Best seat in the house."

His footsteps falter slightly and he groans. "Say the word, baby. Theatre's open."

"Do I get popcorn and Mike and Ike's?"

He drops to a squat, sets me back on my feet, then stands and turns to face me. With one brow lifted and a devilish grin full of promises, he answers, "You get orgasms and Reece Callahan."

I tip my chin and slowly lick my lips. I don't feel like I'm poking a bear with Reece; more like scratching the ears of a lovable but horny stallion. "What if I'm hungry?"

Oh, he's fighting it. He swallows hard, his jaw tics, his eyelids flicker, his fingers twitch before he finally takes a leap and taunts me, "Calorie free or do you need sustenance?"

"Is there protein in it?"

He slides his hand to the back of my neck and brings his mouth close to mine. His voice is low, the playfulness gone. "Depends. Do you spit or swallow?"

"I gargle."

He sputters, unable to maintain his composure as he grips my neck harder and leans his forehead on mine. "So. Fucking. Special."

"Do you mind if we don't go out tonight?" I've waited until we got back to my place. The original plan was for me to come home and get a shower, but now that we're here, I really don't want to leave again. It's been the day from hell. I don't need to be wined and dined; simply fed. If it were just me, I would fix a salad and be happy, but Reece doesn't strike me as the salad type. Think more meat and potatoes. Or pizza. Maybe barbecue.

"You don't want to go out? No date?" His disappointment doesn't seem mountainous, but there is still that shadow of uncertainty that crosses his eyes. "Do you still want company?" *And there it is.*

"Of course, I do." The tension leaves his shoulders immediately and he smiles, confidence restored. "How about you order some dinner and I'll grab a shower. I'm open to anything. Menus are in the drawer on the left side of the breakfast bar."

"I could still order Mancusso's."

"I'd rather save it for an actual night out, if you don't mind. There's a Greek menu in there that's really good."

"That sounds good to me. Unless," he hesitates, face lit with an idea from the depths of hell, "I could fix us something." *Yup, eager to please. Unfortunately, the memory of a gnat.*

My eyes lift toward the ceiling and inspect the area that was covered in a virtual fruit and spinach salad this morning, then back to him. He snaps his fingers. "Greek food it is. Fixed by the hands of others, in a kitchen that is not yours."

"Good idea. I won't be long."

"Take your time," he tells me. "I'll get things set up. Red or white?"

"There's a bottle of Reisling in the fridge. That'd be great, thanks."

By the time I return from my shower, in satin shorts and camisole under a matching short robe, the lights are off and Reece has candles lit, silverware and plates with napkins set on the breakfast bar; two glasses of wine poured.

"What's all this?"

His eyes sweep over my nightwear in appreciation, but then he shrugs. "Couldn't take you to the atmosphere, so I thought I'd bring the atmosphere to you."

He's done it again. Reece doesn't hide anything. He's rugged, masculine, confident in so many things. Open and somewhat painfully honest. Playful, funny, a little clutzy when he tries, but he *tries!* This isn't just sweet and thoughtful though. This is romantic Reece. How many more sides does he have?

He picks up his phone from the counter and presses a few buttons. "Dinner is ordered. Forty minutes away." With the press of a few more buttons, soft music begins to play, and he sets the phone back down. He gathers me in his arms and whispers, "And now, we dance."

"Dance?" I don't know whether to laugh or cry. I haven't danced in ages. Never in my pajamas, unless you count the typical teen years practicing in front of the mirror, or at home when the beat is too good to pass up. You know how it is. Turn on some music while you clean house and it gets done in half the time. That, and nobody's watching.

"I'm improvising, Mallory," he explains, swaying me in perfect time to the music in the background. "Our time is regulated, limited. I want to do all the things with you. Make every moment memorable so that in another fourteen years from now you can recall them like they were yesterday."

My nose tingles and my eyes start to fill with stupid tears. How I couldn't keep a crystal clear vision of the boy on the horse is far beyond me. He was my best kiss too, locked away in a closet with a cowboy hat, deemed to be a simple pleasant memory. A fuzzy one, but a memory just the same.

His lips land on my forehead in a soft kiss. "Don't cry, Kitten. Just dance."

If I never see another side of Reece Callahan, I will die a happy woman, because it doesn't get any better than this. But you can bet I'll never forget it. Not this time.

Chapter 35

Reece

We were all taught to dance at an early age. It was generally to country music, but mom insisted we learn more than a two-step and barn dances. At the current time, I'm appreciative of her demands. Never been a big fan of holding women close on a dancefloor. Boot scootin'? I could handle it. But slow dancing for me has always applied to rhythm changes on a mattress. I'm not a club guy. The last time I danced was at my brother's wedding, and I can guarantee it did not feel like this. This is perfection.

Mind you, the space we have is limited, there is no resin on the floor – no fruity bits or almond milk either, thank you very much – but we don't need it. What I do need is for her to remember it.

The fires out west are not being contained, the winds are only expected to increase, and the crews down south near the canyon are about to be split up. Which means the auxiliary units are about to be called for duty. They've already set up our replacements to fill in while we're gone. For the first time ever, I've given consideration to my responsibilities beyond the Hot Shots. Not sure if it was Roger's reminder or if it would have dawned on me eventually. We've only been called in three times in the last ten years, and I've never had an ounce of hesitation, but I've never considered what I might leave behind if I didn't come back, either.

I'm well aware of the hazards, the dangers, the long term health risks and repercussions. But for some reason, I am overcome with a feeling of dread this time. Hence the need to give her a memory; something to hold onto. My original plan was to take her to dinner and then go dancing, but plans changed and here we are.

I would have come up with the idea on my own, but the phone call from Burkey today asking me to stop in at the station for a minute may have played a part. The woman is incredible. He thought he may have recognized her – the reason he had so many questions the first time – but the package that came brought the man to tears. He shared the story of what she did for him in the operating room; naming his grandkids instead of counting backwards. He felt it important to let me know what a prize I had landed and what an idiot I would be if I blew it. He then told me if I did get called down south, I'd better come back safe and give up the Hotshots. That Mallory was a much better risk than an urn.

"Dinner's here." I kiss the top of her head, then part us gently. The slight leftover dampness on the front of my shirt from her tears feels like a grip on my heart. I know she feels a sense of guilt not remembering like I did, but my guilt is coming from a place I myself don't wholly understand. I am trying to give her a memory. But at the same time I want to make a million more with her, the sense of urgency to give her at least one before I leave is overwhelming. How can I convince her everything will be fine when I can't convince myself of it this time? It's the dead of summer, the heat index killer. I'm healthy as a horse, but I'm not flame retardant. What the hell has gotten into me?

I unpack the spanakopita, place a slice onto each plate, and bow slightly. "The spinach you missed at breakfast this morning, madam." She giggles as I continue to unpack the rest of the food and set each container on the counter. "Couldn't find any specialties with fruit or almond milk, so gyros meat will have to do."

She giggles once again and pulls the tray of lamb and beef toward her. "You're crazy, you know that? Do you even like spinach?"

My efforts to avoid grimacing are failing miserably. *The menu said it was a specialty!* I shrug. "Uh, sure. Who doesn't like spinach?"

She nods at my plate. "If you can eat that whole thing and actually chew without gagging," she leans close, drops a kiss to my jaw, and whispers, "I will gargle."

My eyes nearly bug out of my head and my fork tines scrape the plate as I dig into the delicate phyllo dough layers. I study the massive bite I've put on my fork – the faster the better. Right? If I hold my breath, I can chew and swallow. Maybe if I chew with my mouth open and breathe through my nose, my tastebuds won't be tainted. Maybe if I don't chew at all . . .

I relent and stuff it in my mouth, chewing slowly; thoughts of my girl's promise numbing every sensory perception but one – touch. Wait a minute. This isn't half bad.

There's tasty, flaky dough and cheese, and . . . oh shit. There's the spinach! Tiny strings of green material hidden amongst delicious goodness. *My fucking brothers.* The entire bite rolls out of my mouth and into my hand, soon swept into my napkin, which is then used to swipe at my tongue. I rise from my chair and work my way to the sink, where for the second time in as many nights, I rinse, gargle, and spit.

"I take it you didn't like it?" Mallory asks from her position at the breakfast bar as she cuts off a bite from hers, places it in her mouth and moans in delight.

"It wasn't so much the taste," I grumble, planning two particular brothers' demise in my head. "More the texture."

"Just a wild guess, Reece, and something that Roger said. Same reason you don't take veggies on your pizza? Meat only?"

Narrowing my eyes, I inquire, "How would you know that?"

She shrugs as she forks another piece. "Brothers can be really cruel."

Damn! She's hitting a little close to home. I'm not sure I would agree with *cruel*, but Ronan and Ryder could definitely get under my skin. "What would you know about my brothers?"

"You're the youngest of six boys, right?"

"Yeah."

"I used to babysit for two boys. The older one was horrible." She sets her fork down. "They're not boogers, Reece. Any more than veggies, olives or mushrooms are." She takes a sip of her wine and grins mischievously. "The youngest and I got revenge though. Dipped his brother's hand in warm water while he was asleep. He nicknamed him B-dub. Short for bedwetter. Threatened to tell the whole neighborhood if he wasn't nicer. It's good to see the little guy come out on top."

I stare at her in amazement as her eyes light in amusement. That is exactly what Rone and Ryder used to tell me. Anything with a weird texture or the color of green was an additive they put in special just for me. Eventually, I knew it wasn't, but some things scar you for life. The power of suggestion. *Assholes.*

"Compassion," I whisper, picturing the little boy she befriended, the tears in Burkey's eyes today, and remember her calming touch in the OR with me.

"Eh," she scrunches her nose, "more like one-upsmanship."

Rounding back to her side of the counter, I take her hand and lift her from the chair. We're toe-to-toe, her chin lifted high so our eyes meet. "Compassion, Mallory. Burkey told me what you did for him, in the hospital and the package you sent today. You didn't even sign the card. *"Tasting what you shared with their grandma makes the story authentic for them and more memorable for you"*? He had tears in his eyes."

"I didn't mean to make him cry." She worries her brow, so I smooth it with my thumb and kiss her forehead.

"They were the best tears I've ever seen." I wrap my arms around her shoulders and gently squeeze. "He told me to give you a hug and say thank you."

She shrugs against my chest. "The way he lit up when he saw that Zabar's bag and was so quick to share that memory, he needs to share those kinds of things with the kids. I was just giving him a little push."

Tipping her chin up, I speak the truth. "Something tells me if you wanted to, you could move mountains."

"I don't know about moving mountains, but I know of a volcano I can cause to erupt." She flashes a grin as she squeezes my dick – greedy asshole that he is. "I won't hold you to eating the spanakopita."

A long, heavy groan leaves my throat. It would be so easy, but so one-sided. My pleasure is in pleasing her as well. Two nights in a row? She went without last night. We haven't eaten dinner. I haven't rubbed her sore feet yet. This entire night was planned to give her a memory she won't forget – sex or not.

I remove her hand from my now stiff and aching hard-on; the loss of her touch feeling as if the Band-Aid has been ripped off. "Nope. Both or nothing."

She grins impishly. "I didn't say I was letting you off the hook."

My grandmother was a huge fan of those stupid little dogs people put in the rear windows of cars. You know the ones. The heads would bobble with every bump in the road but the bodies stayed firmly planted on the dash. That's me right now. My feet are frozen where I stand but my head wobbles as I wait for her to confirm. Must be a pug and rottweiler mix though, because my eyes are bugging out of my head as I fight to contain the drool puddling in the corners of my mouth.

"You – you're done with . . ."

"Mmhmm."

"Hang on." I nearly run to the pantry where I saw the aluminum foil the morning I was rummaging for breakfast ingredients and made pancakes. Tearing off an approximate length of three feet, I lay it over the food and blow out the three candles on the counter. *Fire hazard.*

My initial inclination is to throw her over my shoulder, stalk down the hall, and toss her on the bed. I have missed her, missed being inside her. But that nagging feeling strikes once again. If I tell her I'm leaving, where I'm going, the night will be ruined. She'll worry or be upset. I'll ruminate the what ifs. I can't pretend either. We could do fast and hard, playful, heated. Slow is best though. I want her to remember this, to know, even if I don't tell her, she was always my first thought upon waking, my last thought before sleeping, and will be last thought when . . . *if, Reece, if,*

Chapter 36

Mallory

Reece blows out the last candle and turns to me. "I think reheated sounds good right about now, don't you?"

"You're not hungry?"

He picks me up as if I weigh nothing and carries me toward the bedroom. "Starving."

Once inside he sets me on my feet at the side of the bed. Reaching for the belt of my robe, he torturously takes his time pulling the long tie to release the single bow and watches it fall open, then slides it off my shoulders and lets it fall to the floor. "Damn, you're beautiful," he whispers.

"You should see what's underneath," I return with a grin, reaching for the buttons on his shirt.

"Oh shit, shit, shit. We can't," he nearly whines, taking my hands in his, halting my efforts.

"What?"

We can't? After his speech this morning I was determined to dip my toes in the water, put more effort into this, give him the chance he'd asked for. Earlier in the ER was his subtle way of making a statement; the piggyback ride simply adding to the chivalrous trait I find so damn irresistible. He hasn't said a word about the cleaning lady's teasing or the bill – of which she is refunding half. Her text was quite amusing. I really should hunt down a copy of that calendar.

"I don't have any condoms." He winces as if in pain and his throaty groan reverberates throughout the room. "I just assumed we wouldn't be . . ."

And yet he's still here. A planned date with no expectations. Improvisations to still make it romantic when I didn't want to go. He lit candles. He danced with me!

Take a leap, Mal.

"Are you clean?"

His brows furrow. "I've never not been."

"I'm on the pill." I shrug slightly. "You told me to have a little faith in you."

As God is my witness, his eyes glass over as he stares at me. There's a warmth I've never seen before, as well as something I cannot describe. The playfulness is gone. "You'd be my first. Just like you were my best." He slides his hand into my hair, grasping it tightly, but not to the point of pain. "And come hell or high water, Mallory Tompkins," he whispers against my mouth, "you will be my last." The kiss is demanding, but not harsh. It gives but it takes at the same time, just like a generous but needy gentleman.

My knees bend, ready to drop to the floor and deliver what I had promised him, but he holds me firmly in place. "Not tonight, Sugar. I want my first time bare from start to finish inside you." He palms my cheeks and lifts my gaze to meet his. "It's not fair to ask, and you don't have to answer if you . . ."

"It's my first too," I volunteer before he can finish.

"So fucking perfect," he mutters.

"I thought I was special."

He chuckles softly, slowly peeling the straps of the camisole off my shoulders. "You've been upgraded."

There is definitely a difference between latex and velvety skin. I'd always been told condoms created a little more friction. The barrier that not only served as protection from those little babymakers but also mimicked the little buddies in our nightstands. Someone should have told me they also serve as another kind of barrier: that 0.07 mm gap of true intimacy.

The gap that disappears the moment Reece enters me slowly, eyes on mine, and whispers my name like a prayer, "Mallory." He swirls his hips as if searching for any and every sensation to make it enjoyable for the both of us. Slow, sensual, passionate; grinding with each pass as he moves in and out. "I never knew it could be like this."

Digging my heels into his back, I whisper, "Faster."

"Patience, baby. It feels too good. I need this to last."

"W-we can d-do it again. Please," I plead breathlessly.

His fingers weave with mine, raising them above my head. "Eyes on mine, Mallory." Speed becomes my friend as I indulge him and he drives hard over and over again until my voice is so hoarse I don't recognize it and he groans so loud, Ray probably heard it on the eighth floor. He's careful to burden his weight on his elbows as he drops, but we're breathing so heavily our chests clash and we're exchanging the same air. "We are never using condoms again. So fucking perfect," he breathes against my mouth before claiming a kiss that allows me air through my nose – barely – but feels so good.

I close my eyes and run my fingers through his facial hair, that perfect blend that feels so good against my skin. The nuzzles in the crook of my neck, the brushes against the insides of my thighs. I've fallen, so far and so deep, I may never recover.

"I love it when you touch me." I open my eyes to find him gazing down at me, a slight twitch in the slowly deflating appendage that hasn't quite lost its zest for life, and quite possibly seeking resuscitation. "I wish I could explain it. I knew that day in the OR you were special. You scared the shit out of me because I'd never been so desperate to get close and run away at the same time."

"Are you glad you didn't run away?"

"I couldn't if I had wanted to." He squeezes his eyes closed and breathes deep, hesitating. "I meant every word this morning. I do want this. But I should have told you from the beginning, I'm a Hotshot, Mallory."

As I giggle, his now deflated appendage slowly slips out, but he doesn't leave his position on top of me. "I know you're a little full of yourself, Reece, but I'll deflate your ego when you need it."

He leans his forehead on mine. "You don't know what a Hotshot is, do you?"

"I know it's what we used to call the smartass kids in school. Is it different for adults?"

"Hotshots are specialized tactical crews that respond to wildland fires." He eases off of me and scoots over to the side of the bed where he sits with his back to me. "When the need arises, auxiliary crews are called in to help out. With the new fires out west, they're pulling some of the full-time crews from down south near Antelope canyon and calling in the auxiliaries to help. I'm on an auxiliary team. We're on alert to leave soon. They're not making enough progress out west and they've already called in teams from three other states."

"Y-you fight wildfires?" My voice is shaky, picturing Reece out in the middle of nowhere amongst the raging flames that I've only ever experienced the horror of viewing on the television screen. Not to mention the lives lost a couple years ago in the midst of a canyon fire. "Who – who does your job here?" I don't know why I asked. I couldn't care less. It's hard enough knowing the risks of his job – I'm not naïve – but this, this is beyond my scope of comprehension.

"Guys throughout the districts who take on extra shifts." He shrugs. "That's why it's done a particular way. There are multiple crews across the country who are full-timers, but we stay intrastate while they travel wherever they're needed."

"Who is we?"

"From our station, it's Roger, me, and Chauncy. I don't think you've met him. There are seventeen others we travel with when called out."

"Are Hotshots the guys that drop out of planes?"

"No," he offers quickly. "Those are smokejumpers. We go in on the ground and stay on the ground."

His phone sounds from his pants, which are lying in a crumpled pile on the floor. The lyrics from Deep Purple's *Smoke on the Water* – how apropos – fill the room, sending a chill up my spine.

"That'll be Roger."

I sit frozen as he takes the call; phone to his ear, forehead on his free palm. "Got it. Pick you up in an hour. We'll leave my truck at the hangar so you can leave yours for Ruthie if she

BUT I KISSED A COWBOY

needs it."

"Hangar?" I ask once the call has ended. "I thought you didn't jump."

"They fly us down close to the area and drop us off, Mallory. On the ground, near the fires, not in the fires."

"Is it dangerous?" Yup, Darwin award for stupid questions goes to . . . me.

"We specialty train for these, baby." Yup, academy award for evasiveness goes to . . . Reece.

"How long will you be gone?"

His shoulders deflate with a soft sigh. "Until the fire's out." Done with the inquiry, he rises off the bed, disappears into the bathroom, and the shower water starts.

An icy chill runs down my spine with a memory from long ago. *"Never neglect to tell the people you love how you feel, Mal."*. On the beach, four days after I arrived back from Texas. Those words of wisdom from Liberty Collins the day we met. The advice has served me well with the loss of three grandparents, maybe even some lonely and scared patients who really needed a friend.

Tossing the blanket off, I slip out of bed and into the bathroom. The steam is thick in the air, but I see his silhouette through the glass. He stands with both hands on the tile wall; head bowed, the hot water from the massage head above pelting his skin. I silently step in behind him and collect the bottle of vanilla and coconut body wash, filling my palm with a generous dollop. I might not be able to tell him, but I can show him.

Tapping his shoulder gently, making him jolt and turn, I hold my soap-filled hand out. "Not exactly your usual manly scent, but clean is clean."

He smiles softly, hair hanging wet on his forehead over

273

sparkling, ocean blue eyes, water droplets clinging to long lashes and his beard. He's so beautiful. "I'll smell like you. I'll get to keep you with me longer. You do the honors, so I can remember how it feels when you touch me."

Starting with his chest, I spread the soap slowly to his shoulders, massaging the tension in the tight muscles, moving to his biceps. I'm suddenly lifted off my feet and pinned against the shower wall, sharing lather with Reece via the hard press of his body against mine.

"Need you again, Mallory." The desperation in his whisper matches his swift thrust – so unlike the usual patient Reece – but it's the strangled urgency that follows; each consecutive thrust in sync with "Just...one...last...time" before he buries himself deep and releases so powerfully his legs shake.

He slaps the tile wall above my head in seeming frustration. "I'm sorry. That was selfish," he pants remorsefully into the crook of my neck.

This isn't how I want our last moments before he walks out that door. I don't think he wants to go any more than I want him to leave. I feel like I'm sending him off to war. I don't want the memory – I want the man.

"You owe me one, Mr. Callahan," I whisper against his ear before nipping it gently. "You'd better come home, so I can collect."

If it weren't for the shower water, I would swear he has tears in his eyes when he lifts his head. "That's the plan." He leaves a kiss on my mouth I won't soon forget – slow, passionate, deep – before he leans his forehead on mine and whispers, "So fucking special. Perfect wasn't because of the lack of condoms, Mallory. It's because it was you."

Chapter 37

Reece

By the time I'm at the door, duffel bag at my feet – dress pants and shirt tucked inside – back in my usual jeans and T-shirt, I want nothing more than to crawl back into bed and hold her all night. Slow, sleepy sex in the morning. As it is, I've got twenty minutes to pick up Roger.

"You didn't get dinner." Mallory holds out a *Zabar's* bag identical to the one she left with Burkey the day she brought me lunch at the station. "Gyros sandwiches. They'll stay warm until you're ready to eat. I heated them up. I packed an extra for Roger so you wouldn't have to eat alone."

Always thinking of others. Who's going to take care of her? Is

Liberty going to be so busy with Tanner that she neglects her best friend? Will Ray check on her? Will Buster hear her if she screams for help?

I stare at this wonder of wonders, wishing the last fourteen years had been ours. Would we be like Russ and Abbie? Reid and Corrine? River and Gina?

"Thank you. He'll love it. Communication is nearly impossible where we'll be, but I'll be thinking of you every waking minute, dreaming of you when I sleep."

She places a hand on my chest, her forehead crinkled and her eyes narrowed. "Don't you dare. You concentrate on the job. Stay focused and be careful. I'll do the thinking, and dreaming, for the both of us."

"Best kiss I've ever had," I murmur against her mouth before diving in for one last taste. Sacrificing the taste of cherry for those gyros sandwiches is going to be hard. I hold her close, resting my chin on her head and breathe in the soft scent that is hers and hers alone. "Still my girl?"

She nods against my chest. "Still your girl, Reece."

I take the bag from her hand and pick up the duffel from the floor. The door closes behind me and I stand in the hallway, staring at it. The whisper is so soft I barely hear it myself as I aim it toward the barrier between us, "I love you, Kitten."

A knuckled hand reaches from behind me and raps loudly on the door I'm staring at. It flies open immediately and a teary-eyed Mallory takes in the two men standing in front of her, then glances down at the fugly dog sniffing the *Zabar's* bag.

"Mr. 18th floor has something to say, Ms. Tompkins." The arrogant stuffed shirt rolls his eyes and shakes his head at me before turning to leave and grumbles, "Buster's been neutered and he has more balls. Just tell the woman."

I drop the duffel and the food bag at my side and step

forward without hesitation, my fingers in her hair, palms on her cheeks. *Silver eyes and pillowy lips.* It really is a perfect description. "I want to do all the nights, all the days, all the things with you. Watch more movies, snack on Captain Crunch. Dance with you to every slow song ever written. I want to take you to see Lady Luck, kiss you under a Texas sky again. I love you, Mallory Tompkins."

Her tears fall so fast they pool between the edges of my palms and her cheeks. "Don't cry, Kitten," I whisper, then kiss away the salty moisture beneath her eyes.

"I-I c-can't help it."

Selfishly, I claim one last kiss – probably a breath or two – then reluctantly tell her, "I'm sorry, but I've got to go." I back out the door, stealing every last memory I can on my way before I grab the bags and bolt for the elevator.

"Reece!" she cries out as the elevator doors open. Turning one last time, I see her standing just outside her door; hair still damp from the shower, in my T-shirt, tears rimming her eyes. "I want to do all those things, because I love you too. You'd better come home, cowboy."

I force a smile and wink. "That's the plan, Sugar."

As soon as I'm in the truck I yank my phone from my pocket and text Tanner.

"Would you make sure Liberty checks in on Mallory at least once a day, please? I know it's a big ask as you've got a lot going on, but long story short, Hotshot duty down south. If anything happens, will you be the one to deliver the news and please make sure Liberty is with her when you do."

It doesn't take more than a minute for his reply.

"You got it. Nothing is going to happen! Stay safe. Things are replaceable, Reece. You're not! See you when you get back. Beers are on me."

Typical Tanner. The only material things in life that ever meant anything to that guy were the items left for him by Liberty. A note, bubble gum, bracelet, and a picture. Mallory kept my hat, I kept the memory of a perfect kiss.

Roger's waiting at my door when I return to our building. Glancing at his wrist, he checks his watch. "Good thing I lied and gave you half hour leeway."

My head whips in his direction as I enter the code into my phone. "You what!"

"You've got ten minutes, loverboy. I knew you'd be late. Let's roll." He sniffs the air as he leans toward me. "Jesus, you smell like a tropical forest. What the hell did you roll in?"

"Fuck off," I grumble and open my door. "We took a shower. I didn't have my soap. And it smells like a tropical beach."

His brows lift as a puckish grin lights his otherwise smug face. "*We* took a shower? I didn't think kittens liked to get wet."

I glower as I stand in the doorway, debating if I should slam it in his face or invite him in while I grab what I need. "Tell me you got laid while I was gone so I don't have to listen to this the whole trip down."

"Told you I'd do doubles in your honor next time I was at Cranky's." He winks. "I'm in a really good mood."

"You're lucky." I hand over the bag with the gyros sandwiches. "Because one more smartass comment and you will be watching me eat instead of enjoying the gyros sandwiches Mallory was kind enough to pack for the both of us."

His face lights up like a damn Christmas tree. "Tzatziki?"

"Pretty sure. She's nothing if not thorough."

He unzips the bag and fills his nose with the delicious scent, and I head toward the bedroom to drop my laundry and duffel and snatch the emergency one I had ready. "Hurry your ass up," he calls after me. "Damn! She put cottage fries in here, too. Out of curiosity, she got a sister for rent?"

For rent. Of course, because the one with green eyes ruined him.

I volunteered to drive, the usual for our long trips away, so Roger can leave his truck for his little sister, Ruthie, should she need it. She's finishing her masters in physiotherapy, works at a diner, feisty as hell, and kickboxes at the gym like a champ. Tanner coaches her on a regular basis, as Roger seems to think his dick is more trustworthy than anyone else's. That, and Tanner carries a gun. I wouldn't touch her with a ten-foot pole because, well – bro code. Ruthie's ultimate goal is to work for an NFL team. Roger's goal is to keep her tied down and a virgin until she's thirty. We haven't bothered to tell him because, well – bro code. Big brothers wear blinders. Smart friends of big brothers wear muzzles.

"Here." Roger hands me a half-wrapped gyros sandwich that I can hold with one hand while driving with the other. Still warm, dressed with all the goodies: lettuce, tomato, onions, tzatziki sauce, and smells fan-freaking-tastic. "You spill it, you wear it." We moan in unison with the first bite. "Holy shit, this is good," he says over a mouthful. "So much better than the pussy I had earlier."

I nearly choke on my mouthful. I have no idea if he's serious, but I do know his intentions. Keep the mood light, avoid the subject, don't mention the incident two years ago when we lost a few men. Not as huge as six years ago when nineteen were lost. So much controversy, so much bitterness. We go in knowing the risks, believing *when* – not *if* – we come out alive. Then we gear up for the next time. Because there is always a next time.

The sky is pitch black when we board the small craft. A flight crew of three, and twenty Hotshots. It'll take an hour and a half and then . . . showtime.

"Did you tell her?" Roger asks, once we're seated and buckled in.

"Yup." I fold my hands together across my stomach, lay my head back against the seat, close my eyes and hope he'll take the hint.

"What'd she say?"

"Be careful. Come home to her." I shrug.

"Did you tell her the rest?"

I roll my eyes under closed lids, then turn my head and open them. "What else was there?"

He chuckles. "That you're in love with her, dumbass."

A slow smile spreads across my face as I nod. "Yeah, I did."

"Good. You've got something to look forward to when we come back." He zones in on the back of the seat in front of us, narrowing his eyes. "Don't get in your own way, Reece."

"You ever gonna tell me who *green eyes* was?"

His grumble is so low I nearly miss it. "Off limits."

Since I know he won't punch me in front of a plane full of coworkers – that and the doors to the plane have just closed – I push my luck a little further. "The subject or the girl?"

"*Former* best friend's little sister," he mutters reluctantly.

Whoa. I'm not sure what's open wider, my gaping jaw or my eyelids. I mean, Roger isn't exactly a tower of virtue – who of us are – he simply leans a bit. But the man has principles. I trust him with my life on the daily. If I had a sister, she could do a whole lot worse than him. I might demand STD testing, but . . .

"When you say little . . ."

"For God's sake, I'm not a pervert," he snaps indignantly

and scowls. "She was twenty-two."

"And you were . . ."

"Twenty-nine."

"Seven years isn't so bad, Roger." Turning in my seat, I squirrel my face. "Wait a minute. Twenty-nine? That's when you joined us at the 92nd. Transferred in from Scottsdale. You were as hellbent on getting laid as I was. That's where we found our common ground."

"Like I said, Reece, it numbs the pain." He stares at the back of the seat once more. "I limit my alcohol, don't do drugs, work out like a demon, and I love to fuck." He slowly rolls his head in my direction and smirks. "I call it grief therapy."

"God, I'm sorry. You didn't say she died."

"She didn't." He squeezes his eyes closed and heaves a painful sigh. "Her brother did."

Well, that explains *former* versus *ex* best friend. "So what happened with you and green eyes?"

His chin drops to his chest as he shakes his head, his voice remorseful as he admits, "I got in my own way. Don't be an idiot, Reece."

The Supe rises from his seat at the front of the plane and turns to capture our attention. He's new; a total opposite from our longtime supervisor, and the name sewn on his shirt is *Oujiri.*

"Where the hell is Timmons?" I mutter under my breath as I feign scratching my nose and turn my head toward my comrade.

Whether or not Roger heard me is of little concern at the moment, as I would hate to be on the receiving end of the proverbial daggers he's throwing at him. *"Sonofabitch."* It's a near silent utterance, but the white-knuckled fists next to me indicate there just might be a history here.

The pensive look on the Supe's face causes immediate tension and all conversation stops. "Looks like we've got our hands full," he warns as his gaze slowly moves from one team member to the next, pausing as it lands on Roger. "They upped the hazard level. Seems we're dealing with arson, and they ain't done. Got ourselves a new one south of the canyon. That's where we're going with another team."

"Fuck," Roger mutters so low I'm the only one to hear. "That's how he lost 'em last time. They got caught in the middle."

"So we stay away from the middle," I mutter back.

"You guys got questions?" Supe tips his chin as he aims his inquiry at us, though his eyes are on Roger.

"Yeah," Roger sneers with a cold, hard stare. "Tell me you learned something from six years ago."

The Supe's eyes narrow but neither one break eye contact. "Fire's headed south with the winds, Bellamy." *Ah, so they do have a history.* "You guys will be digging the lines and doing firebreaks from below it. They need the jumpers out west and we can get in on foot."

Roger waits for the Supe to blink, and once having won the stare down, he sits back in his seat. Not sure if it's confidence regained or resignation. His hands aren't folded together, so I doubt he's praying. But his leg is bouncing with nervous energy. Supe's plan seemed to make sense. Admittedly, that was one helluva standoff, but in the end I trust Roger as much as I trust any one of my brothers.

"You got an uneasy feeling about this one?"

"We stay together," he murmurs. "We're both going home. Got it?"

"Roger that," I say with a chuckle, tipping a finger from my forehead in mock salute.

He snorts. "It's no wonder she calls you moron."

See? Pretty much a carbon copy of Russ.

Chapter 38

Mallory

Nine days later

I've heard nothing from Reece, which shouldn't be surprising as he did warn me, but hope is my seed of possibility. Glued to the television every evening seeking updates, and the most I can ascertain is size, location, high winds hampering their efforts, the fact there is another fire south of the two that already were, and they have now determined arson.

The door opens and closes harder than usual. "Why wasn't the door locked?" Libs demands as she sets her keys on the counter. "And the deadbolt wasn't latched. What are you thinking? Any Tom, Dick, or Harry could have walked in." *Our mothers' warning.*

Given my sour mood, I can't find the energy to retort with my usual, *"Or Tom's hairy dick."* It is our golden rule. Doors locked at all times. Our building is highly secure, but people are crafty. We've had safety precautions drilled into us since long before we went to college.

"Sorry," I mutter, then chomp down on another bite of celery. "Musta forgot."

Libs rounds the sofa and grabs the stick of celery out of my hand, snatches the remote out of the other, and powers off the television.

"I was watching that! Give it back!"

"Hit the shower. We're going out for dinner. Savannah's meeting us for tacos and margaritas. You've got an hour."

Throwing my head back on the cushion, I groan, "I don't want to go out."

"I didn't ask."

"Libs, I've just come off a ten-day rotation so I could keep my mind busy. My feet hurt, my ass aches, and I'm bitchy. I'd make lousy company." I hold my hand out. "Now, give me back the remote. Have fun and eat enough tacos and drink margaritas for the both of us."

"Fine. I'll call Ray and have him and Buster come keep you company," she proffers slyly. "Maybe you two can discuss the meaning of life while Buster drools on the furniture and farts in your lap."

My eyes are narrowed slits as I scowl. "You wouldn't dare."

She laughs. "Oh, but I would. Now get your achy ass up, walk your sore feet and tired body into the bathroom and get a shower. Hurry up."

Resigned and grumbling, I rise from the sofa and make my way for the hall. "You forgot bitchy."

She snorts. "No I didn't. That's a given. You never leave home without it."

An hour and a half later, we're seated in a booth at our favorite Mexican restaurant with our first round of margaritas half gone, order placed, listening to Savannah tell us how Dr. Arseen has been placed on disciplinary leave. It pays to lock doors while you're giving head when donors are making the rounds. Rather it would have, had she been discreet, or smart enough to do so. I always knew she'd get caught.

"When did this happen?" I ask once she's done giggling.

"Day before yesterday." She huffs indignance, "If you weren't running out the door so fast your shoes were burning rubber, I would have told you before now. What's going on with you?"

"Mal's got a date with the television every night," Libs volunteers before tipping her glass to her lips and peering at me over the rim. "She's obsessed."

Savannah scrunches her nose. "Please tell me you haven't converted to watching porn instead of reading it. You've already got me hooked on reading Ava."

"Ava is erotica, and I'm not watching porn, you idiot," I snap harshly. "I'm watching the news."

The waiter interrupts the conversation, setting three large plates on the table filled with a mix of soft and hard shell tacos on each, as well as the standard Spanish rice and beans.

"Can we get more chips and salsa, please?" Savannah asks him. "Oh! And another round of margs?" He nods and walks away. "Okay, why are you watching the news?"

"Mal's boyfriend is fighting the wildfires down south," Liberty says, then offers me a sympathetic grimace. "She's worried . . . understandably."

"Boyfriend?!" Savannah's eyebrows shoot skyward before they furrow. "And he's a Hotshot? Have I been living under a rock? Who's the lucky guy?"

Libs grins puckishly. "Weren't you in the OR the day the firefighter was brought in with the arm injury? The one that told Mallory if she kissed him he would whisper all sorts of things in her ear . . ."

My scowl only makes Libs' grin grow as Savannah gasps. "The sexy one that pissed Evans off? Didn't he offer you a seat on his face too?"

As I glower at Savannah and demand, "How do you know about that?" Libs huffs, "You didn't tell me about that!"

Savannah winces, pondering confession or betrayal before she says weakly, "Trish?" Her lips twitch. "Oh come on. It was kinda funny. Did you take him up on the offer?"

My eyes flit back and forth between the two of them before I tip my chin high. "A lady never tells."

Libs rolls her eyes and picks up her hard shell taco. "Oh please, if you were a lady, we would have never asked."

Half an hour later, our plates are clean. I've only had one margarita and refused a second, instead ordering water in its place, the intention to keep my head clear. If Reece calls, I want to hear every word.

Liberty's phone rings on the tabletop and the face of her past, present, and future appears on the screen. Her smile alone could light up the restaurant.

"Hey you," she answers, her voice a tone she uses with no one but Lucas. "Yeah. We're at the Hacienda. We just fin . . ." *Pause.* She pales and her brow furrows within seconds. "Okay. Sure, we'll wait. See you soon." Her mouth twists as she sets the phone back on the table.

"Lucas?" I ask, though I don't know why. I saw who was calling.

"Yeah," she answers almost reluctantly as she studies the phone then sinks her teeth into her bottom lip, the way she does when she's worried.

"Isn't he working?" She nods slowly, avoiding eye contact. "Libs?" I plead as the sickening roil starts in the pit of my stomach. "What did he say?"

"To wait here, that he's on his way and will meet us outside."

Ten minutes later, a very pensive Lucas climbs out of the passenger side of a squad car driven by his partner. Liberty pulls him into a hug that reaches far beyond *hello* and deeper into the zone of *comfort*, as she squeezes tightly. He turns to me and that's when I see it. *Dread.*

"Mallory." He takes my shoulders in gentle, shaky hands, his face contorted and red eyes rimmed with moisture. "I'm sorry, but there's been an incident. Reece and Roger got caught in what they call a merge. Another guy from their squadron got caught in it too. I don't know how else to tell you, but they lost them."

"You–you mean th–they can't find them?" I study the forlorn face in front of me before I grasp his shirt and yank hard. "Right!? They just haven't found them yet. That's what you mean."

"I'm sorry, Mallory." He shakes his head slowly as his eyes fill with tears.

"No!" I scream in denial. "You tell them to keep looking! Make them keep searching. This is not the plan!"

"Mallory," he starts again. "I don't know the details, but they sent word to notify family. Reece had asked me to notify you if anything happened and to make sure Libby was with you. I'm sorry."

"No! Tell them to keep looking, Lucas!" My knees crumple as hands reach under my arms and hold me up. "Lady Luck and a Texas sky. We haven't done those things."

Liberty whispers as she pulls me into a hug, "We've got you, Mal."

"Libby, I'm sorry. I've got to get to Roger's sister," Lucas says from somewhere close. "I came here first because I knew Mallory had you. I need to wait with Ruthie until her family gets in from Scottsdale. I'll call you later."

"Ruthie?" Savannah gasps. "Ruthie Bellamy?"

"Yeah," Lucas replies. "You know her?"

"Not as well as I know her brother," she says coldly. There's a sudden determination in her voice as she tugs me away from Liberty's arms. "Mallory, you sober enough to drive?"

"I'll take care of Ruthie," Lucas tells her in no uncertain terms. "It's my job."

"I wasn't offering." Savannah glares through icy, narrowed green eyes then pulls out her phone and enters info. "I'm going to find her dumbass brother. Roger's one of the best Hotshots in the country. He's not dead. But I may kill him myself when I find him." She takes my elbow and turns me toward the curb. "Lyft is three minutes away. We can take my car or yours. Let's roll. Liberty, you coming?"

"Where the hell are you going?" Lucas spits angrily.

"Mallory and I are going to ground zero. We'll make sure Liberty gets home safe first." Savannah spins back and points a hard finger into Lucas' chest. "Tell Ruthie *Peaches* says hello and you'd better only inform her that her brother is *missing*. Do *not* tell that poor girl he's dead. Got it?"

"Libby?"

"I'll be at home, Lucas." She leaves a soft kiss on his

mouth.

"All right," Libs starts as soon as the car door closes and the driver takes off. "Somebody better tell me what's going on." She scrunches her nose. "And who the hell is Peaches?"

"I'd like to know myself." I look to Savannah and wait. Between crusty tears on my cheeks, the roiling in my stomach, and the ache in my chest, I can't think straight.

Savannah rolls her eyes. "I'm originally from Georgia. Conceived in the Hostess City of the South after a broken condom, a horny soldier, and too much booze. Mom and Dad thought it was cute. If there were time, I'd be happy to indulge you both." She aims her gaze at my bestie. "Liberty, I'll explain later, but you'll have to wait. Mallory, do you have hiking boots?"

Libs and I exchange a telepathic look of *where the hell did this version of our friend come from* as I answer, "Yeah."

"Good." She nods curtly and continues to text on her phone. "Grab those. Put on comfy jeans and a long sleeve T-shirt. Bring a jacket. We'll need to stop at my place so I can grab my creds and clothes. We need to hurry. I'm sure the helicopter will be ready by the time we get to the airbase."

I whirl my head toward her. "The what?!"

She holds up a finger when her phone rings. "Hey, General. I need your superpowers. Can you help your girl out?"

Chapter 39

Mallory

"Fatigues or not, General, you're getting a hug," Savannah says to the staunch, stern looking, salt and pepper-haired gentleman waiting for us at the security gate as she hops out of the car – my car – and jumps into his arms.

The general's mouth twitches before breaking into a full blown grin. "Hello, Trouble," he says gruffly and lifts her off her feet, delivering a loving hug. "What's my girl gotten herself into this time?"

It's taken us an hour to get from my place to Savannah's to here – a military base – an excursion that has left me in a state of confusion that I hadn't planned to travel to. She's reassured me over and over that *they* may have lost Reece and Roger; *we* haven't. No vast details – just trust her. I've also never seen Savannah take charge the way she has this evening.

A soldier in fatigues opens my door and matter-of-factly states, "I'll take your car from here, ma'am. Grab your personal items." I follow orders, grabbing both Savannah's things and mine because, well – he's in uniform, then join Savannah and the man in green.

"This is my good friend, Mallory Tompkins. She's a nurse anesthetist at Banner," she introduces me. "Mal, this is the General, otherwise known to me as Dad and to civilians as Dirk Mitchell."

I extend my hand. "Hello, sir."

"Ms. Tompkins," he returns with a nod and a firm handshake, then looks to apparently his daughter. He crosses his arms over his chest, a formidable stature of strength and authority, as he inclines his chin and arches a brow. "Now, young lady, explain. Antelope canyon? It's a disaster down there."

"Well aware, Dad." She squares her shoulders as if gathering strength to present her case. "Mallory's future husband has been reported *lost*."

The general turns to me and frowns. "My condolences."

"She doesn't need condolences, Dad," Savannah scolds. "He's not dead. They just don't know where he is."

"How do you . . ." He stops short when their eyes meet and he sees something in hers that he's obviously all too familiar with.

"Because he's with Roger," she says curtly, then takes her duffel and jacket from my hands. "Can we go now?"

"Savannah," he pleads on a whisper. "You've got this poor girl's hopes up. You can't keep living in the past."

"No, Dad," Savannah snaps bitterly, "I'm not letting her *give* up, and I'm going to go find my future and kick his ass when I do. He made a promise and broke it. Had I known where he was, I would have been happy to roast his ass for him. Now, is the chopper ready?"

"It's waiting," he grumbles. "Spencer will take us out. I'm going with you. I have better creds and it'll be faster to clear us for landing close to ground zero."

"Can we take Granger?"

"You don't ask for much, do you?" He scowls though there's no real heat behind it, then heaves a sigh at the ceiling and shakes his head. "I'll have them gear him up."

She tips up onto her toes and kisses his cheek. "Thanks, Dad. Let's fly."

"Are you former military?" I ask after we've climbed into an army green utility vehicle on our way to wherever the hell we're going.

She nods. "Yup. Four years. Dad's a career man."

"How did I not know this?" I hold up a finger and whisper, "One more question. Future husband?"

She shoots me a mischievous grin and none too quietly quips, "How many faces have you sat on?"

My gasp is less audible than the snicker from the man behind the wheel, but a whole lot less than the extremely audible chastising from General Mitchell, "Savannah Leigh!" He then reaches over the gap between the seats and backhands the driver across the bicep. "Drive, soldier."

Savannah giggles then winks. "Like I said, future husband."

Where in the hell did my quiet and shy OR tech go?

"There he is!" Savannah shouts as we approach the enormous whirly machine on the helipad. *Tacos, we had to eat tacos.* Too preoccupied with the metal beast in front of us, I had neglected to note the hairy beast in a bright orange jacket being loaded onto it.

"You ever flown in one of these?" the general asks.

"No, sir," I reply weakly. "I've flown plenty, but never in one of these."

"Barkley!" he shouts to one of the soldiers at the open door. "You got barf bags in there?"

"A few of them, sir," the soldier reassures him.

"Make sure they're easily accessible." He looks back and forth from his daughter to me. "Let's go, girls."

Savannah pats my leg in reassurance as the blades whir above us. Headphones are on, we're buckled in snugly, as is the dog. My heart is pounding in my chest. "Remember what we're doing," she shouts as she lifts one side of the headphone from my ear. "Close your eyes if you need to, breathe deep. If you need to puke, just use the bag. Wouldn't hurt to ask God for some help." She places the headphone back over my ear and gives me a thumbs up gesture and we're rising off the ground.

I wonder if God minds redundant prayer.

Chapter 40

Reece

"Holy shit, that was close!" My breaths are staggered between gasps, coughs, and wheezes once deeper into the cavern where the water pool is cooler and the air is fresher and untainted by the smoke. The headlamps on Roger's and my helmets are the only light guiding our way. Chauncy is semi-conscious, but time was of the essence as we dragged him to safety.

"I think the heat singed the hair off my balls," I pant through heavy breaths as we wade through the near waist-high water, dragging Chauncy's limp but alive body through the cooling liquid. "Good thing they shriveled inside my taint out of fear."

"Be glad you still got balls. That was too fucking close." Roger coughs, breathless and tired, propping himself along the edge of the rock wall, keeping a strong grip on Chauncy's shoulder while I hold the other. His body weight has become less cumbersome the deeper the water has gotten, but he was virtual deadweight before hitting the river water. The choice between life and death doesn't leave a whole lot of time to check for injuries. "We gotta stop here. Too much farther and the water gets shallower and starts seeping back into the ground. Help me get his turnout off him."

We work together to remove the heavy coat and Chauncy groans without resisting as we do, but then his head falls forward as his body goes totally limp. We dunk him to his shoulders in the cool water and bring him up; the only shock method available to revive him. It's not like we can perform effective CPR in water and there's no place to lie him flat. There are no ledges; just water and walls.

"Chauncy, come on, man!" Roger orders with a harsh shout. "Wake up, you fucker! I refuse to sing Amazing Grace at another funeral for one of you assholes." He grasps his chin in his hand and stretches his neck back to flex the throat muscles then massages them to cause a reaction. "Cough!" As if obeying orders, Chauncy sputters and coughs. Roger applies one of the two oxygen masks we've managed to rescue and I adjust the portable tank. "Breathe, damnit!" he commands.

"He's coming around." I take the mask from Roger and hold it to Chauncy's face, giving Roger respite and time to collect a few deep breaths himself. Chauncy's panicked eyes finally open under a nasty gash on his forehead and he sucks in air as if it might be his last breath. "Slow, Chaunce," I soothe with a calm voice. "Slow deep breaths. We gotcha. It ain't your day to die, buddy."

"It shouldn't be anybody's day to die." Roger swipes a

rugged hand over his face.

"How did you know about this cavern?" I ask once Chauncy has relaxed and his breathing has calmed.

"I didn't, but we were at the edge of the river and I could smell the accelerant. Pattern of the smoke," he explains, "east edge of where the fires merged had an empty pocket. Had to be something here. We had nowhere else to go." He rubs his eyes with the heels of his palms, clearing some of the soot away. "Damn, if Chauncy hadn't tripped and lost his gear, we would have gotten here sooner. I think he may have broken his leg."

"Pretty sure he did. It's useless. You could smell the accelerant?"

"Oh yeah," he sneers.

"From way up there? How could you smell it? I couldn't smell anything."

"You smell death once," he hesitates, "you don't forget it."

"We smell accelerants all the time, Rog. Hell, I can smell the gas when I fill my truck. I don't think of death when I do."

"They didn't use gasoline, Reece." He looks me dead in the eyes and I swear I see murder in them. "They used kerosene. Pour that shit in a lengthy trail and you can be long gone in one direction while it burns the shit out of everything in another."

"It doesn't evaporate as fast," I remind myself out loud.

"Not in a cool canyon, it don't," he mutters. "And still burns hot as hell. These fuckers knew exactly what they were doing."

"So why do you relate specifically kerosene to death?"

"Long story." He rests his head on the wall of red rock behind him and closes his eyes. "What do you relate to death, Reece?"

Damn, that's a tough one. I know what prompted me to

choose my occupation. The *Jaws of Life* and the magic they perform. But I don't relate death to every car accident I'm called to. Not every house fire results in it. Not every medical emergency ends with it. I've seen death, more times than I'd like to recall. It goes with the job. But the peace I've found from the disquietude of it all comes in the form of a warm, compassionate, silver-eyed beauty who hides it under a sassy, fiery personality. *So damn special.* God, I want to get home to her; do all the things.

"No one thing in particular. What's your point?"

Lazily, he rolls his head against the rock and opens his eyes. "You're lucky. But the one unavoidable truth is life inevitably leads to death. You get one shot. Decide what you want out of it and then figure out a way to get it."

"You talking about getting in your own way?"

He snort laughs. "I couldn't get out of my own way."

"What's that got to do with kerosene?"

Chauncy coughs and shoves the mask off before I can get my answer. His voice is raspy and dry, but audible. "Where in hell are we?"

"It ain't hell, Chaunce," I say with a pathetic chuckle. "You still got time to redeem yourself." My eyes flit to Roger and my brows lift. "We all do."

He doesn't acknowledge what I've said, but a little food for thought is the best I can give him at the present time. "We have no satellite communication down here," he grunts instead, staring at the one radio we didn't lose in his hand. "We're going to have to wait this out for a while."

Trying my best to keep it light yet knowing we are far from guaranteed survival, I shrug. "I can think of worse company."

Chapter 41

Mallory

I made it without throwing up . . . barely. Don't get me wrong; I like dogs. I like them even better when they don't look at me as if I'm a pork chop and they haven't eaten since breakfast. I also prefer a low-drool canine. Granger is the former and not the latter. He's a shepherd of some sort. A duty dog – his bright orange vest fits like it was made for him.

The fires are all but extinguished; the glow of embers spread for miles as we fly above on our way to the landing spot on the east end of the disaster. I only know this because I've been listening. Now that we're here, the smell of lingering smoke and burnt ash is overwhelming and quite nauseating.

I do find out rather quickly when Savannah and her father are on a mission, you fall in step and keep up. We deboard the chopper and virtually run to an area with a makeshift station surrounded by multiple tents, water tanks, and a shitload of flood lights. There are multiple personnel walking around, but it's nearing three o'clock in the morning and there is only one thing, one person, on my agenda.

The General speaks with some men at the station while one brings masks to Savannah and me while we wait in the distance.

A dark haired man approaches the two of us, eyes glued to Savannah. "Savvy, what are you doing here? Haven't seen you in ages. You look amazing."

Judging by the look on her face, she's not happy to see him. "Call me Savvy again and I will remove your tonsils via your asshole."

He smirks. "Sassy as ever and still bitter, aren't you?"

"Some things will never change," Savannah snarks. "Now, who's the Supe on Roger's crew?"

"I was," he says bitterly.

Savannah takes the two steps forward that closes the gap between them, her voice but a low growl. "Was? Not *is*, Oujiri? You don't seem too remorseful about men you reported dead. A little too fast to make that call, isn't it?" She jabs her finger into his chest. "Why aren't you out there looking?"

"It's dark!" he hollers mere inches from her face. "We wouldn't find anything and you know it. The search is over. Been looking all day. There's no way they made it. We'll move to recovery tomorrow. Roger disappeared from his manned post. Took two men with him." He arches a brow. "Not like it hasn't happened before."

Savannah rears back and instead of the typical slap you'd expect a woman to deliver, she throws a full blown, closed-fist punch to the man's face; hard enough to knock him back a few paces. "You will pay for that, you asshole."

The sound of heavy machinery can be heard in the distance as engines are started. Savannah's eyes fill with horror as she turns toward the makeshift station and shrieks, "General! Tell them to shut down the machinery! They can't move dirt before search and rescue, and that can't be completed before dawn! What the fuck are they thinking!!?"

"Savannah, we found melted satellite radios, a helmet," the man spits through a bloodied lip. "There is no way . . ."

"Shut the fuck up, Oujiri!" She snarls and grabs the front of his shirt. "Until I find teeth and knock yours out, there is no proof. Where did you man them?"

His chest heaves as he narrows his eyes. "Lower canyon on the south side."

"The whole team?"

"Of course, the whole team!"

"Where did the fires merge?"

"Between the crews." He runs a hand through his hair. "They were too far apart. Roger and two others ran for the east end. We lost two that ran to the west with the others and had some pretty hefty injuries. We can't save them all, Savannah. Shit happens."

As the sound of the heavy machinery dies, she sneers, "Seems to happen more under your watch. Who ordered the heavy equipment?"

"I did! We gotta smother the embers." He throws his hands in the air. "I also don't need to stand here and explain myself to you."

"Maybe not to me," she says threateningly. "I only lost a brother, right? But my dad lost a son, and the General is waiting." She nods toward the makeshift station. "Right over there. Stick around, I'm sure he'd love a chat. Best get ready with your explanations." The man's face pales as Savannah snatches the sleeve of my jacket and pulls. "Let's go, Mal."

"Where are we going?" I ask apprehensively as we walk toward the General who waits for us in the passenger seat of a Jeep next to the driver.

"Shoes on him?" She looks to the soldier behind the wheel of a Jeep next to ours where Granger sits tall in the backseat. There's a soldier beside him and another in the front passenger seat.

"Yes, ma'am." He nods. "He's ready to hunt."

"Hunt?" I inquire.

"He's a search and rescue dog. Don't want him burning the pads of his paws so we put special protection on him." She hikes a booted foot onto the top of the rear tire of our Jeep and hops into the back effortlessly, sliding over to the other side. "And we are going to find Reece and Roger and whoever the other guy is. Hop up. You can do it. If you can sit on the man's face and not smother him, pretty sure your thighs have worked up some good muscle strength."

"Savannah Leigh!" her dad scolds from the front seat.

"Oh, come on, General." She giggles. "I've seen the smile on mom's face."

A quiet round of snickers comes from the vehicle beside us as well as the driver in our Jeep. I know what she's doing. I've held back tears countless times since we left home. Maybe this is simply her way of dealing with stress or helping me deal with mine – not that she's explained her vested interest in Roger. I sure wouldn't want to be the soldier up front though. That bicep has to hurt, but he doesn't flinch as the General takes a whack.

The adrenaline kicks in once again as I hike my booted foot on top of the wheel, boost myself up, and swing my other leg into the Jeep. It's not as stealthy nor as graceful as Savannah's moves were, but as my ass lands on the seat; one foot flailing in the air and making contact with the driver's head, the Jeep begins to move.

"Be glad they're hiking boots, Barkley," Savannah teases the soldier. "I could have loaned her my shitkickers."

Chapter 42

Reece

"Sonofabitch!" Roger yells as he tilts the light on his helmet down and looks back in the direction from where we've entered the cave. "We gotta go. Turn on your headlamp. Grab his shoulder. Move!"

I hadn't noted the murky water that is now coating our already filthy turnouts. We've alternated using each headlamp to save power. Floating pieces of tinder soon join it as a slow current carries them into the cave. We've been in here for what seems hours; not sure exactly how many. Don't know if it's day or night. Exhausted, Chauncy has simply propped on the both of us, a consistent state of drifting off, but stable. He's in a lot of pain, but alive.

"Aahh!" Chauncy yelps in pain as we shift him in the water and throw his arms over our shoulders and begin to drag him back toward the entrance.

"Hang in there, Chaunce," I reassure him. "We haven't come this far to give up now."

"Keep your headlamp aimed low. Watch out for drifters," Roger orders as we wade through the water. "Some pieces could be heavy and hit hard."

The air becomes filled with the acrid stench of burnt forest and wet ash, and the depth of the water hits our knees as we approach what has to be the opening. Still no daylight ahead, pitch black. We're no longer wading but rather stumbling through debris. Chauncy's weight is once again cumbersome as his dependence on us is nearly a hundred percent. He can only put weight on one leg and every time his right one is compromised, he screams in pain. It's gut wrenching, *but he's alive.*

The sound of heavy equipment rumbles in the distance and I swear I feel vibrations under my heavy boots.

"Earthmovers. That motherfucker," Roger mutters angrily. He tightens his grip on the arm hanging over his shoulder. "Chauncy, I'm sorry, man. But if we don't move fast, we're dead men. Reece, grab his leg and hike him up. I'll grab the other."

I don't question his orders, the motives, the *who* he's talking about. He got us here, out of the flames, and we're alive. I would definitely trust him with my sister, if I had one – after some STD testing.

The entrance to the cave seems so far away, and Chauncy's pain feels like my own with every howl, as we race toward the opening where the sounds of the machinery grow louder, then suddenly come to a stop. The heavy rumbling and vibrations are no longer felt beneath our feet. We pause, welcoming the deafening silence that surrounds us and peer through the opening ahead to see a blinding bright light, and then . . . a dog's bark. *It's true. Animals are in the afterlife.*

Distant shouts ring out in the dark. "Roger, get your ass out here!"

"Reece! Where are you?"

I look over a slumped Chauncy between the two of us, my body drained of all energy, my hopes and aspirations sucked out of me at the sound of the desperate screams of the woman I love calling me back from the depths of hell. *Impossible.* Our struggle and efforts put into survival an exercise in futility. This was all a dream.

"We died, didn't we?"

"Yup," Roger says, casual as can be. "Now, let's go toward the light."

My feet stay frozen in the muck and mud, unable to move. The dirty water flows slowly around my boots, some dead and burnt twigs make their way through – some don't – gathering around my boots. I don't want the light; not yet. I want my Kitten. This wasn't the plan.

"I thought there would be angels," I utter, sorely disappointed.

"Jesus, Reece," Roger scolds impatiently. "You ain't dead. We wouldn't end up in the same place anyway. Your angel is out there." He finishes on a grumble, "Though I think my demons have come to haunt me. Let's go."

The welcome sound of barking and whining bounces off the walls and echoes throughout the cave. *Search and rescue!*

There's a thick half wall of dead limbs built up at the entry to the cave that has washed down – or been pushed by the earthmovers – as we reach it. It's not the workers' fault, it's what happens when you're collecting dirt to cover the embers so they don't get blown around; starting a fresh disaster.

That bright light? Not heaven after all – just the high beams on the machinery so the men can see what they're doing in the dark.

"Need some help over here!" Roger hollers over the crisscross limbs blocking our way to freedom. "Got a man injured! Bring a stretcher!"

A bright light shines directly on the blocked entry nearly blinding us as shouts break out amongst the crew. "Over here! Get more light! Move some dirt to catch that water flow, fast! And get Granger outta here! Move it! Move it!"

Water flow? Shit! Timber from up the river must have broken loose after having worked like a temporary dam. They're buying us time.

The heavy machinery starts up again immediately and the earthmovers are literally *on the move.* Hands are everywhere as they yank the logs and limbs away from the opening of the cave. The end of a long safety strap is passed over the top and fed to us as one man shouts, "Figure eights! Wrap it quick. We got water coming down the canyon. Do not let go!"

It's tricky, but we've been trained. Wind it between us – they've got one end, we'll be wrapped like sausages – approximately six hundred pounds of humans.

"Sorry, Chaunce," we say in unison as we gently lower his legs to the ground. We'll lift him again – if possible. Otherwise, we'll drag him. *But he's alive!*

"Do what you gotta do," he groans. "Just get us the hell outta here."

We're wound together by the heavy safety straps by the time the timber has been moved enough to maneuver around it, and Roger and I lift Chauncy by the backs of his thighs as his arms round our shoulders once again. The distant rush of raging river water sounds like thunder as it makes its way down the canyon, bringing full tree trunks with it.

With one man on each side of Roger and me, we're virtually run through the mud of the riverbed; all of us strapped together, with the main harness being three leads attached to the bucket of a bulldozer lowered over the edge of the bank.

Roger and I lift Chauncy first and climb in with him as close as possible without tearing rib cages or shoulder joints apart. The guys on each side of us quickly follow and the dozer lifts the bucket high in the air and backs away from the river's bank. It's mere seconds before the roar of water and breaking timber rushes past, approximately twenty feet below where we sit in the bucket, and exactly where we were just moments ago.

Chauncy squeezes my arm so hard I feel his fingertips through my turnout. "You were right, Reece. It ain't my day to die." He looks back and forth between Roger and me. "Thanks, you guys."

The dozer slowly lowers the bucket to the ground after moving us away from harm's way. "Hang on," the guy next to me says, "we gotta get your straps off." He chuckles. "Unless you want to remain attached at the hip."

Two Jeeps sit aimed at us, headlights on high beam, so bright it makes my head hurt. I put my hand up, palm out to shield my eyes, and ask, "Is that our ride?"

The guy on the other side of Roger snort-laughs. "I'd say that's one helluva ride. The General had to hold them back. I wish you the best, gentleman. If you both still have your balls by the time you're forty, be sure to call me. I'll throw them a party." He nudges Roger. "Is yours the redhead or the brunette?"

Roger swipes a dirty hand over his face. "Fuck," he groans low and long, "the one time I needed a hallucination."

The straps binding us together release as an ambulance arrives for Chauncy. The crew empties out of it, unloading a stretcher from the back to load him up.

My head whirls toward the man at the end of the bucket, my hopes high. I'm not dead, so maybe, just maybe. "Did you say there's a brunette in there?"

Roger mockingly adds, "Don't forget the silver eyes and pillowy lips."

The guy snickers. "Not to mention a few other assets."

"Chaunce," I turn to my injured partner as the EMS workers approach, "you're gonna be okay. I'll check on you as soon as I can."

"Go get her, Callahan. I'll be fine." He reaches for my shoulder, gently shoving me forward. "If you don't marry her, Burkey's son will. He's been waiting for you to fuck up." He wrinkles his forehead – or maybe winces in pain with his laugh. "Just kidding."

Helmet in hand, I hop out of the bucket and march toward the Jeeps, my heart pounding in my chest as I keenly eye each one to try and determine which one she occupies. My efforts are unnecessary as she hops to the ground from the one on the left; my helmet long forgotten on the ground as she runs into my arms. I'm filthy; covered in soot, river water, mud, and probably smell like a week's worth of sweat, grime, and God only knows what else. She's silent as I lift her off her feet, and she wraps her legs around my oversized turnout, clinging tighter than the straps we had just removed. This is my Kitten; a quiet crier, my private sentimentalist, a bundle of emotions wrapped in the prettiest package I've ever seen that only I get to unwrap.

"You came for me?"

She breaks when she buries her face into the crook of my neck, her body wracked with sobs so powerful she trembles in my arms. "Th-they said you w-were d-dead. But it w-wasn't the p-plan."

It wasn't the plan. I had told her that. I had left her with hopes and dreams to go play Smokey the Bear. *Men bend, women break*.

Sliding my fingers into her hair, I tug gently to pull her away from my neck to look at the face I want to wake to, the eyes I want to gaze into as she comes undone for me, the lips that delivered the best kiss I've ever had.

"Because we haven't done all the things," I whisper and smile at the memory.

She nods shakily and whimpers, "Yeah, that. Now kiss me."

"No tongue," I warn, forcing a grin. "I haven't brushed my teeth yet. It's a hygiene thing."

She steals my thunder as another tear spills and she narrows her eyes to match my sass. "I hadn't finished wiping my chin when you . . ."

"So fucking special," I murmur against her mouth, fighting back tears of my own. "I love you." Then deliver a kiss neither of us will ever forget.

"You irresponsible, selfish, bullheaded, arrogant ass!" The shriek comes from somewhere close by, though it didn't need to. It could have come from halfway across the canyon and still been audible. We turn our heads in unison to see Roger and the redhead in a standoff.

"Tell me how you really feel, Peaches." Roger has stripped his turnout off, helmet at his feet, and he stands with his hands in the pockets of his soaked uniform.

"If I told you how I really feel, my dad would wash my

mouth out with soap," the redhead snarks and tips her chin.

"Oh, sweetheart." Roger chuckles sinisterly. "Your dad has much better reasons to wash your mouth out with soap."

"Oh shit," Mallory whispers. "Is he aware her dad is a general? He probably has a gun."

"Does she by chance have green eyes?"

"Really pretty ones. Maybe we should go distract the general for them."

"Not on your life, Sugar. I need popcorn and a beer for this."

The redhead steps close, edging toe-to-toe with him. Roger's hands leave his pockets and his fists clench at his sides, battling restraint, as he pleads, "Don't do this, Savannah. Keep your distance."

"Or what, Roger? What are you going to do?" she challenges, reaching out to run a teasing finger through his beard. "Kiss me? Hold me like you used to? Fall in love with me again?"

My friend looks agonized as he utters, "Not again, Savvy," then grabs a handful of auburn red hair, stares into the eyes of its owner and confesses, "I never stopped." Their mouths disappear as Roger seals them together.

"About time," I whisper, more to myself, then tell Mallory, "*Now* we'll go distract the general." Apparently, not fast enough as a man in his near sixties wearing fatigues, looking a might bit angry, approaches at a fast pace. And now I fear I've been derelict in my duties to warn my friend.

"General Mitchell!" Mallory calls out to him, her panicked voice pitched two octaves higher than normal. "We were just on our way to see you."

"Save it, Ms. Tompkins," he spits, though his anger is not aimed at her. No, I recognize that glare. Ronan was the recipient of one just like it the night his *date's* father was approaching the woods they had snuck off to. In keeping with the code we boys had to warn of incoming danger, I tuck Mallory's face into my neck and raise my head high; letting out three loud, rapid, high-pitched whistles.

There! My job as a best friend is done. Unfortunately, little did I know it was also a signal call for the orange-vested German Shepherd.

Fuck. my. life.

Chapter 43

Mallory

"Granger!" The soldier's shout takes us by surprise, and Reece and I both turn to see what the calamity is all about. As the dog charges, I instinctively climb higher on the tree of a man I'm already attached to, but it doesn't take long to realize I'm not his target. Seems Savannah is his goal, or maybe the man she was wrapped around before disentangling herself with the commotion.

The general certainly doesn't seem to be in any rush to stop him, though the soldier I remember as Barkley lets out a succession of whistles as another runs past the general to catch the canine. Unfortunately, none of it is successful before the dog tackles Roger to the ground and stands on his chest, teeth bared as they go eye-to-eye. Or is that muzzle to nose?

"Granger, nein!" Savannah scolds, tugging at his collar to pull him off a seething Roger. *"Es ist okay, junge."* By the time she has the dog removed from Roger's chest, and back in the hands of the soldier, a fuming Roger is on his feet.

"German commands, Savvy? Really?" Roger snaps.

"Don't start with me, you stubborn ass," she warns. "He saved your life. You haven't even thanked him yet."

"Who whistled?" the soldier demands, eyes flitting from them to us as I shimmy down to the ground out of Reece's arms. "And how would any of you know our attack code whistle for a military dog?"

Judging by his expression, Reece had no clue. I'm not sure what compelled him to whistle, but I'm sure he had his reasons. "Reece whistles when he's happy, or . . . excited," I volunteer on his behalf in an effort to be helpful. "Kinda like, you know . . . He does it all the time." I shrug and wince as my cheeks heat. *Where the hell was I going with this?* "It had nothing to do with the dog."

Eyebrows raise and furrow in unison – some in confusion, some in suspicion – on every single face as they stare at Reece. With the exception of Roger, who sneers. "Whistles, huh? Is that before or after he growls?"

"Shut it," Reece grinds through a clenched jaw.

Before I can inquire, the general bellows, "Bellamy, you and I need to have a discussion."

"Dad," Savannah protests, "I don't need you to . . ."

"Savannah Leigh." His growl alone is enough to make us all draw a deep breath.

Savannah simply rolls her eyes and huffs, "Not here, Dad."

The EMS workers approach with a loaded stretcher containing the other Hotshot that was rescued. His leg is splinted and an oxygen mask covers his face. Roger and Reece both make their way to his side before they can load him up.

"Where are you taking him?" Reece inquires.

"The hospital in Page. It's the closest," one answers. "Where he goes from there is up to them. They'll take good care of him. We've already transported some over there."

"How many?" Roger demands, his eyes narrowed.

The guy looks sympathetic as he slowly shakes his head. "I can't say for sure, but we'd rather take them to Page than the morgue. Chauncy here told us what you guys did. Good job."

"How many to the morgue?" Roger asks so slowly, it sounds painful.

I can't hear the answer, but it's given with a bowed head and a deep sigh. Roger stiffens before he reaches out and lightly pats the arm of the man on the stretcher. "You hang in there. I'll see you back in the city, Chaunce." He grumbles as he storms past me toward the Jeeps, "Once they let me out of jail."

Roger freezes as a third Jeep rolls up behind the two we rode in and the same dark-haired man that confronted Savannah when we arrived climbs out of it.

"Good call, Savvy. Glad to see you boys made it out safe. That merge caught us all off guard." He speaks with authority on his way to us, as if he's privy to exactly what has gone down over the last hour, though he was nowhere to be found. "Bellamy, Callahan, you both need to be checked out at the hospital for injuries."

Roger halts the man's journey to us by stepping in his way, his voice so filled with venom it's downright scary. "The only one gonna need a hospital is you, Oujiri, and that's only if you don't need the morgue. You incompetent motherfucker." His fist flies before Reece or the general can stop it, but it doesn't end there. The two are on the ground in seconds, Roger winning the battle as he pummels Oujiri over and over again.

Reece tries to step in, but the general holds his arm out to stop him and calmly orders, "Let him be. He needs this."

Savannah is over him before her dad can stop her, and yanks on the material of his wet shirt. "Roger, enough. Please stop. It's not worth it and it won't change anything. You can't bring him back."

As if her words have struck a chord, Roger stops his assault as he straddles the bloodied man beneath him. His breaths are charged and heavy as he stares at his enemy. "You will never be in the field again, Oujiri. I'll see to it myself," he pants through harsh breaths. "Kerosene. You never even fucking checked. Two dead men today and how many injured? We should have never been where you put us, just like we should have never been where we were six years ago. This one's for Silas, you asshole." He rears back with his right fist and lands one last hard hit.

He gets to his feet and looks to the general, his eyes brimming with moisture and a ton of regret. "I shouldn't have said that in front of you. My apologies, sir. I need to go check in. Thanks for your help."

"Roger," Savannah pleads as she grasps the front of his shirt – the desperation in her voice palpable. "Don't do this again. Please. Don't shut down on me."

He takes her wrists in his hands and gently unwinds her fingers from his shirt as he looks over her to the general once more, his eyes as cold as a New York December. "I'm sure you'll see to it Savannah gets home safe and sound?"

They exchange icy glares – Roger's hard and unmoving, the general's a mix of anger and disappointment, as he takes a crying Savannah in his arms.

The body on the ground starts to groan with signs of life

as Oujiri regains consciousness. "Might want to call a bus for him," Roger says dryly as he heads toward the Jeeps. "Looks like he tripped over something."

"Barkley!" the general orders. "Call for a bus and get his ass outta here. He was in a restricted area after dark. Rolled down an embankment and got pretty busted up." His hard gaze runs the circuit of every man and soldier in the perimeter. "Anybody got a conflict with that?"

"No, sir" rings out from approximately a dozen obedient voices around us as the Jeep Oujiri was driving starts up, and Roger turns it around to drive back toward the encampment with the makeshift station and tents. The brakes squeak as he comes to a sudden stop and calls out loudly, "Reece! Got two seats open. Hurry your ass up!"

Reece takes my hand in his. "Let's go, Sugar. The man is not known for his patience."

"Wait!" I turn to where the general is trying to soothe a broken Savannah. If not for her, Reece and Roger might be dead. "I can't leave her, Reece. She fought for you. Savannah brought her dad and me and these soldiers, and the dog to search for you!" I burst into tears as the weight of the past seven hours comes crashing down. "I can't abandon my friend. Don't make me choose. Please."

He takes my cheeks in his palms and tilts my teary gaze up. "This is just one of the reasons I love you so much." He kisses me softly and gathers me in my favorite kind of hug. The one that is all encompassing, all consuming; the kind that makes the rest of the world go away. "I'm going to go get checked in with Roger, and then," he props his chin on my head, "we'll get the hell outta here. Together. Okay?"

"Yeah." I nod under the weight of his chin.

"Don't be too mad at him, baby. He hasn't learned how to get out of his own way yet. There's apparently a lot of pent up anger there, but a helluva lot of pain too. He's like a brother to me. He's the reason I'm alive. Please don't ask me to choose, either."

"I won't. I'll see you at the station."

"You bet you will," he reassures me. "I'm not going anywhere without you. We still have to do all the things, Kitten." I sniffle against his chest as he kisses the top of my head then tips my chin up and shows me a smile that renews my hope for that kiss under a Texas sky. "All the things."

Chapter 44

Reece

Roger puts the Jeep in gear and takes off the moment my ass hits the seat. These are military style Jeeps; no doors, a rollbar, and seats that feel like cafeteria chairs. However, they do have seatbelts.

"Where's the fire, dumbass? Let me get my belt on! Wouldn't hurt for you to do the same." He ignores me, shifts into third gear and increases the speed once he hears the click of my belt. "Put your fuckin' belt on!" I yell. "You damn near died once already today. This one's avoidable. And slow down!"

He downshifts and eventually comes to a full stop, yanking the seatbelt around himself and latching it. The sun is making its slow appearance on the horizon, casting a much more welcome orange glow than the one we've been battling for the past nine days. Roger rests his head on the back of his seat and looks up at the lightening hazy sky and releases a deep breath.

"They didn't have to die." He rolls his head slowly toward me and that's when I see his tears. "We should have been at the bottom end of that, not in the middle."

"Hindsight," I mutter, though now remembering our conversation on the plane. *Stay out of the middle.*

"Hindsight, my ass. Negligence. And that is what kills, Reece." His knuckles turn white as he grips the steering wheel tighter. "He knew it was arson, but never had the bottom quarter checked. It came up behind us. That's where we got fucked . . . again." He swipes at his cheeks, then puts the Jeep in gear and we move forward.

"You want to talk about the redhead?" I ask.

"Nope."

"I'm here if you change your mind."

"Appreciate it, but you ain't the kind of therapy I need, Reece."

We ride in silence until we reach the encampment where a team greets us with cheers of congratulations for surviving, as well as large bottles of drinking water. It doesn't take long to discover they had spent a portion of yesterday searching, recovered two melted satellite radios, Chauncy's helmet, and Oujiri had prematurely reported us amongst the dead.

Roger pales as he stares at the crew manager. "Tell me you haven't contacted my family."

"Oh shit," I mutter to myself. Why hadn't I thought of that? Mallory would have been notified by Tanner; per my request. And if Tanner was notified, my whole family is sitting in Texas mourning me, and I'm not even dead! My mom and dad are not young people. This could have devastating effects. How long have they thought I was gone?

"Give me a phone!" Roger and I demand in unison.

We're each handed a satellite phone and scatter a few feet apart as we enter numbers as fast as we can to a loved one. Russ sounds like death warmed over as he answers his phone in a gravelly whisper, "Did you find his remains?"

My heart nearly rips in two at the sound of my big brother's brokenness. The air catches in my lungs and the lump in my throat gets caught as stupid tears roll from my eyes. "Wouldn't you rather have all of me, bro?"

"Reece?!" His voice cracks and he doesn't even try to hide his sob as he pleads, "Sweet Jesus, tell me that's you."

"It's me, Russ. They fucked up."

"He's alive!" Russ announces with a loud relieved, but broken sob to whoever is there to hear it, and disruption erupts in the background.

"Reece!" My mom's shriek is the loudest, quickly backed up by my dad shouting, "He's okay!" The chaotic chorus continues, indicative they were all gathered at the family home, mourning as a unit.

The phone call ends only after my mom has verified I'm still alive by hearing my voice and those three simple words every mother lives for – *I love you.*

I knew when I saw Mallory get out of that Jeep – the look on her face, the sobs as I held her in my arms, that Roger was right. *Men bend, women break.*

Roger hands the phone back to the crew manager and studies the ground in front of him. "Ruthie and your folks okay?" I ask.

He nods slowly over and over before a defeated smile

spreads across his face and he pinches the bridge of his nose. "Of course she did."

The two Jeeps we'd left behind pull up to the encampment and the love of my life hesitates before she climbs out. Never do I want her to hesitate with me. My arms will always be open; ready to hold her when she cries, catch her before she falls, wrap her in a cocoon so tight she never feels threatened, yet give her the freedom to fly and be the independent, awesome woman she is.

"I'm signing out," I tell the chief at the shack then make my way to the side of the Jeep where I extend my arms and offer her silent assistance. She accepts without hesitation and flies into my arms; right where she belongs.

The chief from the shack calls out, "You guys more than deserve to be dismissed, but I need Oujiri to sign off on this."

"Didn't you hear?" I call back and slide a quick glance at Roger as another ambulance pulls in to the area. "Oujiri got injured. Took a tumble down the embankment after dark. He really should follow the rules."

"We've got a couple seats open on the chopper," the general informs the chief. "We can take them back up north."

"Sir, I can . . ." Roger starts to protest.

"I said," the general interrupts on a growl, "we have a couple seats open. I highly recommend you take my offer, Mr. Bellamy."

There's a silent exchange between them as they coldly stare at one another before Roger concedes and grumbles, "Let me change and grab my stuff and I'll be right with you."

"Speakin' o' which," I tell my girl. "I'm a little chafed myself. I'd like to get out of these. I'll be right back."

Once inside the sleeping quarters, Roger pulls the footlocker we've shared from under his cot and opens the lid, removing the duffels from inside and tossing mine to me. "What about Chauncy's?" I ask. "I think we ought to take it with us so it doesn't get lost. We can send word to let him know we have it."

"Good idea." He nods toward Chauncy's cot. "Grab it, will you?" Our heads whip toward each other in unison as the *oh shit* realization dawns and Roger groans, "Oh fuck. They would have reported him dead, too. Hurry up and change. We've got one more call to make."

I strip my wet clothes off as fast as I can – not easy when they're caked with mud and soot. What I wouldn't give for a long hot shower right now. "You got a contact number for his family?"

"Nope," he says, zipping his duffel and leaving his wet, skanky clothes on the ground and heading for the tent opening, "but the chief will. He can handle it. The faster they get word to them, the less they have to suffer."

By the time I'm changed and carrying two duffels out of the tent, Roger is halfway back to the shack. Two minutes later, he's connected with the chief, trying to explain the sheer clusterfuck, as well as Chauncy's injuries and the urgent matter of contacting his family to let them know he's not a heaping pile of ashes amongst the ruins.

"They took him to a hospital down here in Page," he tells him. "That's all I know, Chief. Reece and I gotta go or we're going to miss our ride back." He rolls his eyes and nods, listening, then responds, "Yeah, yeah, I know. Good to hear your voice too. I will. Tell 'em the beers are on them. See you soon."

Handing the satellite phone back to the manager, he smirks at me. "Chief says they were grieving me more, but they're happy you made it too."

Flipping him the bird, I storm toward the sound of music

to my ears, AKA the military chopper waiting to take us home. "Asshole."

He rushes up behind me, tossing his arm over my shoulder. "Aw come on, Reecey. Lighten up, it was a joke. You just stared death in the face and won."

"So did you. So I gotta ask, why the hot and cold with green eyes?"

He claps me on the back and coaxes me forward. "Ask me no questions and I'll tell you no lies."

"Ah, typical avoidance. Let me throw your own words back then. Get outta your own way." Before the noise makes it impossible, I add, "I also need to tell you thanks. You saved my life out there. If not for you . . ."

"Don't," he interrupts. "We're a team. We got lucky this time. Let's go home."

Chapter 45

Mallory

The ride back in the chopper might have been a whole lot more comfortable had I sat next to Reece, but as weight distribution determines seating – so I was told – I sat next to Savannah while Reece and Roger occupied virtual bench seats on the outer edges on opposite sides behind us. Even if conversation had been possible, the tension radiating off three people on board was enough to make the silence golden. Probably better that way. My greatest desire was to slap Roger, knock some sense into him, and let him know the gorgeous redhead sitting next to me saved his life. She got her dad down to the site, shut down the heavy machinery, fought for him.

She punched Oujiri before he did. Instead, I reached across the way, palm up, waited for Savannah to place her hand over mine, and squeezed. She mouthed, "Thank you" as I rolled my eyes. I mouthed "left or right one?". It earned me a halfhearted smile.

Stunned she had a connection to our circle, I was chomping at the bit to hear the details on our flight here. Conversation in the helicopter was limited between the general and the pilot, unless you consider the one between God and me. But He doesn't have a tendency to speak so it was pretty much one-sided, and silent. Besides, Savannah's story sounds like one to be shared over tacos and margaritas. Lots and lots of margaritas.

And now, we're on the ground back at the military base waiting for my car to be brought to us. Full daylight has broken and the sun is shining high. The temperature is already in the eighties and a shower, air conditioning, not to mention a good eight hours of sleep, sounds pretty good.

"Thank you for staying back with my daughter, Ms. Tompkins," the general quietly utters to me. "She's had a tough time."

"No thanks needed, sir. She's my friend," I return. "I owe her a lot. And thank you. If not for you guys, I'm not sure they would have made it out."

He nods, but I don't miss the acquiescence in his voice as he mumbles, "Roger would have tried his damnedest. It was nice to meet you, Ms. Tompkins."

"I'll see you later, Dad." Savannah stands on her tiptoes and kisses his cheek before he pulls her into a bear hug.

"It's going to be okay, Trouble," he reassures her. "We've been down this road before. Got a couple officers here that would make good prospects."

She sniffles against his shoulder. "I was an army brat and

BUT I KISSED A COWBOY

a soldier myself, Dad. Not about to be an army wife. I love you."

"Love you too, Kiddo. Call your mom. She misses you."

As the Rogue pulls up to the security entrance where we stand, Roger pulls his cell from his pocket. "Uh, guys, I'll call a Lyft."

Our first stop is near the airport to retrieve Reece's truck from the hangar located somewhere on the outskirts. From there I need to take Savannah home. I'm dirty, exhausted, hangry, and not in the mood. Worse yet? It's too early for wine and too late for a full eight hours sleep in order to avoid circadian rhythm ruin. As Reece opens his mouth to either protest or agree, I step between them.

"I've got this," I tell him. "Go keep Savannah company." His eyes dance between the two of us before his lips twitch, and he only nods. I hold up two fingers to Roger. "You've got two choices, buster, and a Lyft is not one of them. Plant your ass in the backseat of my car and take the ride or end up in my OR where I'll remove them without anesthesia. Five seconds to choose. Five...four...three...two..."

He storms past me toward the car and grumbles, "That explains what happened to his. Where did you put them?"

"I let him keep his," I sass with a tip of my chin. "They're too pretty and I like playing with them."

He shoots me a scathing glare as Reece and Savannah laugh, then yanks open the rear passenger door and slides inside.

"Uh, Savannah?" Reece grimaces as Sav pulls open the passenger door. "Any chance I could ride up front with my girl?"

"Oh for God's sake," Roger groans from his seat in the back. "Are you sure she doesn't keep them in her pocket and squeeze them at will?"

"It's all yours, Reece." She pats his arm before rounding the car and opening the back door on the driver's side to climb inside. After I've climbed in and buckled up, she scoots forward on her seat and giggle-whispers in my ear, "When I grow up, I want to be just like you."

A sudden shriek comes from the backseat as Savannah's red hair moves from one side of the seat to the other in my rearview mirror. "You are all grown up and don't you ever fucking change." The low growl is quickly followed by moans I could not creatively imagine while deep inside the pages of one of Ava's books. Reece and I exchange a furtive glance and I start the engine.

"Everybody buckled up?" I inquire with a slight lilt in my voice.

"Just drive, Mallory," Roger orders, his gruff voice a bit garbled, as if his lips are otherwise occupied.

"Alrighty then," I singsong, shifting the car into gear. "Safety is not the top priority. I can turn the music up if you like. Do you prefer classic rock, jazz, or blues? Just don't make a mess on my seats."

"Jesus Christ," Roger sputters as Reece and Savannah burst into spontaneous laughter. "Put your seatbelt on, baby. Reece, mind if I take your truck? I'll make sure Savvy gets home."

"You know the code," Reece says easily. He twists in his seat and quips, "And your way. Try and stay out of it this time. Fob is in the console."

"Yeah, we made it," Reece tells a still shaken, but very relieved Lucas after we've dropped Roger and Savannah at the hangar. Loud cheers and shrieks of joy come through clearly as Reece moves the phone away from his ear. More words are spoken from the other end before Reece responds, "Let me get some sleep first. I'll show you proof of life when I'm sure of it myself." He laughs and listens once more. "Really? I'll let her know. Tell Liberty thanks."

He ends the call and tucks the phone back in his pocket. "Liberty is staying with Tanner. Said the condo is all yours for the next three days. So, Kitten," he reaches across the console and brushes his fingertips over the curve of my jaw, sending goosebumps up my spine, "are we showering at your place or mine?"

My mouth spreads in an impish grin, remembering our last shower together. "You do owe me one, Mr. Callahan."

"I owe you everything, Mallory," he says softly. "We can start with one, but I'm an overachiever. Buckle up, baby."

The door to the condo closes hard as we drop our bags and shoes in the foyer. Reece turns to latch the deadbolt, drops his forehead against the door with a thud, and takes a few deep breaths. "Give me a minute, Kitten. I gotta slow down."

Stepping forward, I place a hand on his shoulder. "You need sleep. How about a shower, some food, and then . . ."

He turns suddenly, one hand in my hair, the other around my waist, and I'm off my feet. Dark circles beneath dilated pupils, heart beating fast against my chest, his breaths increased. "Runnin' on adrenaline, Sugar, and I don't want to hurt you. I've missed you so damn much." His kiss is restrained, the moan mimicking pain rather than desire. "Give me three minutes in the shower to wash off the first layer of grime. Please. I shouldn't even be touching you."

"Okay." I brush back a lock of dirty, soot covered hair from his forehead. I don't care about the dirt, the smell of smoke and whatever else it is that clings to him. *He's alive!* This was the plan.

He sets me back on my feet and reaches for his duffel.

"Hope you don't mind me using your soap again."

"I bought some for you while you were gone." I shrug at his surprise. "It kept me company until you got back."

He stares in wonderment, his jaw slightly slack as his forehead creases. His whisper is soft and sincere as he smiles, "So fucking special."

Making my way to the bedroom after hearing the water turn on, I sit on the edge of the bed; the first minute to myself since leaving for the pits of hell last night. *The plan.* The original white picket fence life with a husband and a couple of kids that I've dreamed of since the age of ten flits through my mind. *My* hopes and dreams. *My* plan. At nearly thirty, I'm no closer than I was at ten. Libs has finally found Lucas. I couldn't be happier for her. Risky enough that he's a cop, but if she's okay with it, who am I to judge?

Last night's events run a fast replay through my mind. The unfathomable nearer to death experience none of us would want to suffer, word that some actually did cross over to the other side, the injured firefighter being loaded onto the ambulance. *This is not my white picket fence dream.* My dream wasn't just a man to build a home with; it was a man who would actually come home. In the real world, accidents do happen, but in Reece's world, he's an accident waiting to happen.

A cowboy was perfect. A firefighter was risky enough – they're everyday heroes. But a Hotshot? Now that I know what they are, and got an up close glimpse into their world, there is not a snowball's chance in hell. I can't sign up for this.

I sink to the floor in a crumpled mess, my head in my hands, quiet sobs wracking my body so violently it's hard to breathe.

Of all the opportunities in life, I had to fall in love with a Hotshot.

Chapter 46

Reece

Scrubbing my skin raw twice doesn't feel sufficient, but a vat of industrial cleaner wouldn't remove it. It's not on my skin. It's in my nose, my brain, my very soul. Lives lost – carelessly according to Roger. Can't say the residual effects of damn near dying aren't still lingering either. I've never come that close. Finally have the adrenaline rush settled though. I couldn't take her when I was ready to jump out of my own skin; that's what punching bags are for. No, when Mallory and I have angry sex, it will be after some silly little argument. A mutual battle of edging to see who wins. Breathless pants with narrowed eyes, scowls with smirks just under the surface, daring the other to concede to the passion we share. And when it's over, the winner will get a bonus orgasm. Oh hell, who am I kidding? I'd be willing to lose every single time. Anything for my girl.

Damnit! Where is she?

The three minutes I'd asked Mallory for have come and gone at least twice over. Sliding the glass door open, I stick my head out and peer through the foggy bathroom, seeking the naked creature I was hoping would join me, but find the room empty. Please tell me Ray and Buster didn't come knockin' for a visit. Shutting the faucet off, I grab my towel and wrap it around my waist.

"Sugar?" I call out as I open the door. "Did you forget to join me?" Ready to step out into the hall and investigate the whereabouts of my very reason, I catch a glimpse of her on the floor at the side of her bed; her body folded in on itself as she sobs. This is Mallory: hide the pain with sarcasm and humor while others are watching and let loose like Niagara Falls in the quiet of solitude. The stress of it all has caught up to her.

Taking a seat on the floor next to her, I gather her in my arms and place her on my lap, hold her head to my chest and just let her cry. I'd do anything for her. Crazy to think that one glance in an OR four months ago could stir a memory from years before and eat away at my conscience, put a padlock on my dick, and consume my every thought since. My brunette, silver-eyed beauty who stole my heart with one kiss and never gave it back. She is magic. And I'm the lucky bastard who gets to keep her.

"I don't think I'm strong enough for this, Reece," she whispers once her sobs have calmed.

"Mallory Tompkins," I murmur and drop a kiss to the top of her head, "you are the most amazing woman I've ever met. Your compassion knows no boundaries, heart like a lion, loyal to a fault. It's who you are. People who love you and are willing to return those qualities is where you find strength and help you flourish. I want to be one of those people."

She trembles in my arms, her voice wobbly. "Your risk is too high. I need stability. You can't be my picket fence, Reece."

Tipping her chin up, I gaze into red-rimmed, bloodshot eyes, encompassed by dark circles. "I will be your Fort fucking Knox. No more Hotshots. I will never put you through that again, and I'm sorry I ever did. When I saw you get out of that Jeep, I'd never been so happy to see anyone in my life. But at the same time I could see I'd dimmed your light a little. I don't ever want to do that again. I want to help you shine, be one of the reasons for your smile." I swipe a thumb across her wet cheek. "Never be a reason for your tears. You came for me. I want to be here for you."

I swear I see the same look in her eyes I saw years ago – innocence, unsurety, that tiny lack of confidence. "You're giving up the Hotshots for me?"

"I'm not giving up anything. I'm *quitting* the Hotshots for *us*. How would we do all the things if I'm not here?" She sniffles. "Still my girl?"

She wraps her arm around my shoulder and buries her face in my neck – the perfect fit, the perfect woman. "Still your girl."

"How about I go pour you a hot bath? Your preferred treatment." Before her parted lips can beg the question how I would know that, I place a finger over them. "I listen, Mallory." I wink before I lift her off my lap. "If you're a good girl, I'll rub your feet while we share it."

"Reece!" she gasps as I stand to my feet then quickly follows, reaching for my bare skin, smoothing gentle fingers so lightly over my back it almost tickles. "You're bruised from your neck to your feet! What did you do?"

Her touch alone makes everything feel better, though I'm

sure whatever it is she's noted will be rearing its ugly head in a day or two. Don't think I broke anything, but when you've got flames licking the underside of your ass, the only thing on your mind is your next step and how fast it can carry you.

"Rough terrain." I take her hand and lead her into the bathroom. "A week or two and I'll be good as new."

"You need to be checked!" she demands, pulling her hand from mine once inside. "Something could be broken."

Leaning over the large jacuzzi tub, I flip the stopper and start the water. "I know what isn't broken, Sugar." Turning back, I strip the towel from my waist, and grin impishly. "And he's begging for a little attention. He's grown quite fond of you."

She glances at the attention seeking beggar between us then back up at me, narrowing her eyes. "And still growing as we speak."

"He's homesick." I reach for the hem of her T-shirt and pull it over her head, then tug the scrunchie from her hair. "Anxious to get back where he belongs." The hook and eye closures of her bra are next; one flick of my thumb and fingers doing the job. Straps peeled from her shoulders and she is exposed to me as I toss the white cotton cups off to the side. The button of her jeans pops open easily and the zipper slides without resistance. Sliding my palms between her skin and the clothing over her hips, I notice it. In the time I've been gone, she's lost weight she didn't have to spare. I swear there's a little less ass cheek for my grip, a little less fullness between the diamonds on my favorite bauble, and guilt washes over me.

Pizza, pasta, ice cream, and Godiva chocolates every night for the next month.

"The water!" she shrieks when I have the jeans and panties to her ankles.

Talk about being caught with your pants down, because

that is exactly how I leave her: backed up against the vanity, jeans to her ankles, watching me shoot to my feet and scatter to shut off the faucet.

"It's not even half full." Though I do proceed to shut off the valve.

"Well, I don't know how much to put in for two people," she snaps, yanking her feet out of the jeans. "The only water I've ever shared with anybody is in a swimming pool . . . or the ocean."

A smile tips the corner of my mouth as I cross back over to where she stands. All those years of one night stands just may have paid off. No showers, no tubs, no repeats. "So, I'd be your first?"

She crosses her arms over those perfect C-cup fillers, and scowls. "Yes, but I doubt I'm yours."

"As a matter of fact, you are, Kitten." I brush back a lock from her face then lift one shoulder and scrunch my nose. "Unless you count the doubling up my mother did with us boys when we were little. Saved her time and trouble."

The giggle I've grown to love and missed so much is music to my ears. "You're crazy."

"About you I am," I murmur against her mouth. "Wanna be my tub buddy?"

"Think your mother would approve?"

"I'll be sure to call and ask her when we're done. Now, get your ass in the bath."

Chapter 47

Mallory

Reece certainly does make up for lost time . . . three times over. I'm a noodle; tucked into him like a second skin with my back to his front, ready to sleep for hours, though knowing mine should be limited in order to sleep tonight. I have two more days off and I want to utilize them to the fullest. I've been up for thirty-three hours.

It's two o'clock in the afternoon; the room darkening blinds closed to the daylight outside. I set the alarm on my phone to six PM, vibration only, so as not to wake him, and slip it under my pillow. I have no idea how long he's been up, but I get the feeling he could sleep until tomorrow morning and it still might not be enough. His bruises are deep and ugly, but his lungs are clear. I rubbed arnica cream on his bruises – despite his protests – and made him eat a sandwich.

"I love sleeping with you. You make it all go away," he whispers against my neck. "The noise, the commotion, the wreckage." His warm breath on my shoulder feels like the sleep aid I've been missing for the last nine nights. "You're my bubble, Mallory. Stay inside of it with me."

"I'm pretty comfy too."

He moves his little finger to my belly button and brushes my piercing. His groggy voice trails like it did before he went under the anesthesia, "I . . . love . . . you." Soft snores follow and his breathing deepens. He's out and shortly after, I join him in peaceful slumber.

My body rebels when the buzz under my pillow starts. Dry eyes – check. Mouth filled with cotton – check. Massive body still wrapped around mine – check. Ten more hours sounds like heaven right now. Fighting the deep groan that begs to leave my throat, I slide my phone from under the pillow and shut it off. Deftly removing myself from under Reece's arm, I slip out of bed and sneak into the closet to grab something to wear.

Before leaving the room, I take a quick peek back at the silhouette of the man in my bed, and note he's moved my pillow to hug it against him. I smile to myself as I quietly close the door behind me. He felt my absence.

Coffee! It's been thirty-seven hours since I've had coffee. I'm literally running on empty and refueling is necessary, despite the time of day.

They did offer us some at the encampment along with water. Desperate for it, I accepted – immediately regretting it with the first sip. I was polite though – *accidentally* spilling the cup of battery acid while unscrewing the cap on the water bottle. But I didn't spill it *on* anyone. It probably would have burned a hole in their clothing.

Plopping a pod in the Keurig, I snatch my usual mug from the cupboard, add a splash of cream, then place it under the spout and push the button. As I'm checking my phone, seeing a dozen missed messages, arms wrap around my waist from behind and a deep southern twang rumbles in my ear.

"You popped my bubble, Sugar. Got a second cup for me?"

"Reece!" I slap a hand over my heart and whirl to see him in black jersey underwear. "Don't sneak up on me like that. What are you doing up?"

"Restless," he mumbles. "I'll sleep tonight. Probably should get back into a regular rhythm anyway."

The Keurig sputters with the last drops so I reach for it and hold it up for him. "Cream okay?"

"You take the first one. I can get it." He kisses my forehead, reaches above me and opens the cupboard to grab another mug. He pulls the old pod from the machine, opens the tray for a new one and pops it in, collects the cream from the fridge and pours a dollop into his mug, then sets the mug in the holder. He studies the set up as he points his finger from place to place, as if going through the motions a second time, then nods firmly before pressing the button. He turns to see me staring and shrugs. "You didn't like salad green the first time I decorated your kitchen. Wasn't sure you'd be too fond of coffee color either. Just being cautious."

This is Reece. Sexy, a little goofy, always entertaining, mischievous like there's a bit of kid left in him, but so damn strong.

I set my mug on the counter. "Kiss me."

He clicks his cheek and shakes his head. "Oh, Mallory. You know what that's going to lead to."

Clamping my molars tightly, I grind out slowly, "Kiss . . . me."

He towers over me, a devilish smirk painting his gorgeous face. "Here?" He brushes his thumb over my bottom lip then drops a soft kiss to it. "Here?" Another to my jaw. "Maybe here?" That sweet spot behind my ear. "How about here?" My collarbone. He lifts me off my feet and carries me to the countertop where he sets me down gently. *Libs would kill me if she knew.* "So many choices," he whispers across my skin as he lays me back against the granite slab. "Hope you don't have any plans, Kitten. I'm going to be busy for a while."

Yup, Libs would kill me – if she knew – so we're not going to tell her.

"No, we're having pizza." Reece pulls the menus for Thai and Chinese food from my hands. "With the most fattening and greasy combination we can find. Hot wings and dressing too. We're also ordering stuffed crust."

"Stuffed crust!" I scowl and reach for the menus in his hand, but he holds them above my head. "I don't eat greasy pizza and I never eat stuffed crust!"

He throws the menus on the floor and picks me up, by my butt cheeks, and gives them both a good squeeze. "You're gonna eat whatever it takes to stuff the filling back into these. How much have you lost?"

Admission of weakness is nearly as difficult as weakness itself. "I'm not a stress eater. I had no appetite."

"I'm home, Mallory," he whispers against my forehead then leaves a soft kiss. "And I'm not going away again."

"Promise?"

"Promise." He meets my gaze. "I'd be an idiot to walk away from the best thing that's ever happened to me. Now, Sugar," he winks as he squeezes my butt cheeks again, "We're going to stuff your upper cheeks so we can fill out these lower ones. I like my palms full."

Not one to take orders, I tip my chin in defiance. "Fine. I may as well forgo any exercise so I can achieve faster results. No cardio, no stretches, no heavy breathing–" I poke a finger in his chest and arch a brow, "– no exertion whatsoever. I'll just sit and do nothing."

"I can live with that," he grins cockily, "so long as it's on my face." He smacks my butt lightly and sets me on my feet again. "Now, go set up the movie and I will order dinner."

Turns out dinner is actually pasta and two orders of cheesecake with an extra dessert of tiramisu from the same Italian place Reece bribed me with the night before Libs and Lucas reunited outside the hospital. Still carbs, still fattening, but *he knew* it was my favorite.

"When can you get some vacation time?"

The movie is running needlessly, because conversation seems to be the only thing keeping us awake, and quite frankly, much more interesting.

"I have a couple weeks available." I shrug and tease, "I was saving it for a trip to a dude ranch in Montana."

"A what!" If he was sleepy, he certainly isn't now given his wide eyes and the scowl on his face.

"It's on my bucket list," I say casually.

"Well now you can put it on your fuck it list," he growls and pulls me onto his lap to straddle him. "You're comin' to Texas with me. Lady Luck needs to know I finally won. I'm gonna kiss you under those stars." His forehead creases as he acquiesces, "The same ones I stared at night after night for weeks on end after letting you go without ever knowing who you were." He grasps the nape of my neck and draws me in for a soft kiss. "All the things, Mallory."

My voice breaks as the man brings me to tears once again, "Do I get a new cowboy hat?"

He chuckles against my mouth. "So fucking special."

Chapter 48

Reece

Six weeks later we're driving down the gravel road that will take us to my youth, and our short history. She's nervous; evident by her hands twisting in her lap and the slight bouncing of one knee. We flew into Dallas early this morning – the only family member aware of our pending arrival is Russ.

"They're gonna love you," I reassure her, placing my hand on the bouncing knee and squeeze.

"Don't be so sure. I've only met family once before and it didn't go so well."

"Only once?"

BUT I KISSED A COWBOY

"Once." She scrunches her nose. "After that, they all chose better."

"Whoa, whoa." I pull the truck over to the side of the road and slam it into Park. "What do you mean they chose better? What the hell could be better than you?"

She rolls her eyes and shakes her head. "I meant wise enough to *know* better. I have . . . *filter* problems. It started with my first homecoming date when Gavin's snobby mother told me my dress wasn't proper. I informed her neither was her husband, but if her son behaved himself he was safe for the night." She turns her head slowly and shrugs. "I didn't go to homecoming, and Mrs. Dobbs found out what a skirt-chasing asshole she was married to."

I don't doubt her story for a moment. I can almost picture it. "What did you do instead?"

"Sat on the beach with Libs, drank two beers each that my cousin supplied. She babysat us as well." She smiles at the memory. "Got a little tipsy, made our final plans for our futures, got home by curfew, and went to bed."

Laughter bursts out of me before I can contain it. "My mother is going to adore you."

"No time like the present to find out." She heaves a sigh. "Let's get the show on the road."

The homecoming this time hits hard. I hadn't expected to be hugged so tightly and as long by each of my brothers. I certainly didn't expect the watery eyes nor turned heads as they swiped their chins; the sniffles they tried to suppress. Not one hair tousle this time. The mix of *"Never too late to change careers"* (Russ) *"Damn, bro"* (Reid) *"Good to see you"* (River) *"Don't ever fuckin' do that again"* (Ryder) and *"Stick to rescuin' pussy, you dumbass"* (Ronan) squeezes my lungs.

But the one that sends a knife through my heart comes from the broken cry across the yard as my mother flies out the front door; my dad not far behind. She looks ten years older than she did just months ago. If guilt had a scale, I'd be the heavyweight. I put forth the effort to save her the steps, and hopefully a broken hip, and meet her halfway.

"Hey, mom."

She cries in my arms, squeezing my middle tighter than I would expect for a woman in her sixties. "Parents go first, Reece. Stop trying to break the rules."

"I'm sorry," I whisper against the top of her head. "No more wildfires. I already promised . . ." *Oh shit! Where did I leave her?* I turn to see my five brothers hovering; two assholes with cocky grins plastered ear-to-ear, while two ask questions and Russ simply smiles. Mallory doesn't seem too overwhelmed, but as usual, it's Ronan's lack of diplomacy that earns him a thwack to the back of his head from Russ and my mother's attention when he hollers,

"No fuckin' way! You're the Kitten?"

Mom simply stares as I stomp toward them and Russ gently leads her my way. Placing my arm around her shoulder, I kiss her forehead. "I'm sorry, baby. Got a little caught up in . . ."

"Don't apologize," she warns softly. "How a man treats his mother speaks to his character."

"How did I do?"

"A+. Have you asked her if we can be tub buddies yet?"

A low groan leaves my throat and I mutter so no one hears, "I am stripping every stitch of clothing off of you the minute we get the door closed." She giggles with our last few steps. "Mom, Dad, this is . . ."

"Mallory Tompkins," Mom whispers in astonishment and steps forward, taking her cheeks in her hands. "Oh my goodness. You were so pretty then, but you are just stunning."

My dad smiles and shrugs when I look to him for answers. "Mom? You know Mallory?"

She chuckles, slightly shifting Mallory's face toward me. "No, dear. But who could forget her? Look at these eyes. You pined after this girl for months."

"You knew about that?" I then note my poor girl's cheeks in my mother's hands, pillowy lips pressed into a pucker I want to kiss.

"A mother knows everything, Reece." She releases Mallory's face and softly caresses her cheek. "Where did he find you?"

Mallory grimaces and shoots me a look of unsurety. "Actually, it's quite a funny story."

Dad laughs and claps my shoulder. "It usually is when Reece is involved."

"Mom," I try once again, "how did you know her name?"

"Records," she says without hesitation. "Everyone who rode that trail had to sign waivers. Insurance liability."

"And you remember Mallory out of all those people?"

She smiles at me, then winks at my girl. "You gave her your hat, Reece. For a cowboy, that's the same as your heart."

I grin at my girl, relishing the slight flush in her cheeks. "Sure was."

"Hey, Reece!" Ronan hollers teasingly. "Did she take that seat you offered, or you want me to saddle Lady Lu . . . Damnit, Russ!" The shriek is only slightly louder than the slap to the back of his head. "I was just jokin'."

Apologizing silently with my eyes as I watch her slight flush turn beet red, I contemplate where I can hide my brother's body and try to recall the sentence for murder in Texas, just in case they find him.

"Unca Wees!" The shouts ring in unison as Abbie, Corrine, and Gina release the munchkins from the two SUVs as they run to greet me. And the questions begin:

"Did you meet Smokey the Bear?"

"Did Big Foot get out okay?"

"Did you rescue Goldilocks and the three bears?"

"Did you get to keep the bunnies on the calendar? I want one."

"Can we fix s'mores tonight?"

I look to Mallory who's laughing at the questions, and wink. "Priorities."

Lying in the double hammock under the canvas of black sky lit by glimmering stars, we take deep, relaxing breaths together. She has met every single member of the family, plus some extended kin who joined us for a barbecue once word got around. Not sure if it was because they thought I was involuntarily cremated six weeks ago, or because I brought Mallory with me. The only sound around us is a few crickets who haven't called it a night.

"You really love it here, don't you?"

"I love the peace of it, Mallory," I tell her. "I miss it sometimes, but I love the busyness of the city too. You love it by the ocean in North Carolina, don't you? What made you stay in Arizona? Go from fishbowl to dustbowl?"

"The master's program initially. Then Libs, I guess," she says, tucking herself in closer. "It was the best part of her life there, and I supported that. They did have offers that were hard to refuse at Banner. I'm not sure if it was ever my intention to stay, but things fell into place and there hasn't been any reason to leave."

"I'm sure glad you stayed." Taking her chin between my

finger and thumb, I tip it for the perfect fit. "Now, about those kisses under the Texas sky."

Chapter 49

Mallory

Lady Luck was getting too old for two people to ride her, so Reece boosted me up into her saddle while he rode next to me on a beautiful Palamino named Cinnamon. Same trail, same grove of trees we'd stopped at years before, where he dismounted and helped me down.

"Ring any bells?"

Glancing around at the scenery, it seems picturesque; typical of a landscape portrait. But when Lady Luck dips her muzzle and starts to graze on the overgrown clover, I'm taken back to the near nosedive off the front of a saddle that all led to my first kiss.

"Lots of bells."

He takes my cheeks in his palms and tilts my face up. "Where it all started. All the things, Mallory. And I want to make more, so many more with you." It might not be our first kiss, but I swear it is our best kiss. Everything he doesn't say, he puts into this kiss.

Five days later, we're saying goodbye to his entire family on the front lawn of what I've deemed to be a virtual mansion in dude ranch country. It's massive. But I suppose having raised six boys under one roof was no easy undertaking. The house has wings! Not literal ones – the sectioned kind: an east wing, a west wing. Apparently, two of the sons, Ryder and Ronan, haven't grown wings yet, because they still occupy one of them.

Hugs are in abundant supply as well as pleas to come back soon, often, and to bring our entire group from Phoenix with us. I can see that, actually.

I've been to the spa with all of the ladies, sat around campfires in the evenings, heard some pretty hilarious stories about Reece's childhood. Knowing he shared the story of his offer of a seat on his face, I shared the story of his kitchen disaster with them, sans the naked walk, ass jiggle, and double salute in my living room, but I'd only had three beers at the time. That changed the night we went out with his siblings and their wives, when he got up to sing karaoke and chose Bob Seger's *"Come to Poppa"* in the overcrowded bar – the hidden innuendo with his sexy eyes, winks, and eyebrow waggles. *I don't have a daddy kink* but I can give as good as I get. It shows too, as all five brothers stand shoulder to shoulder, as we reverse out of the driveway, and toss him double salutes. One from the forehead, the other an exaggerated hip jiggle. Thank God they kept their pants up. Reece only laughs and honors them with double finger salutes then waves a final goodbye.

"Told you they'd love you." He squeezes my thigh as we make our way down the gravel road that will lead us to the highway out of Denton and back to the airport. "You willing to come back?"

"Of course I am. I had a blast."

"Good," he says, reassured. "North Carolina next?"

My head spins so fast, my neck cracks. "What?!"

"I showed you mine. It's your turn. You're not ashamed of me, are you?"

"No!" I protest, then admit, "I already told my dad about you. He also remembered you." I turn toward the window and grumble, "Better than I did."

He squeezes my thigh again. "Hey, we talked about this. Stop it. Do I want to know how your dad remembered me?"

Recalling the conversation with my dad – "*That boy looked ready to cry*" – I smile to myself. "Probably not."

Reece groans loudly. "Sweet Jesus, tell me it wasn't the hard-on from hell. I'll never be able to look the man in the eyes."

Oh, this is gold. I eye his crotch playfully and watch him squirm in his seat. "It is one of your best features."

Reece veers the truck off the gravel onto a dirt road and shuts off the engine. His seat moves back with the push of a button and he narrows his eyes. "One that you haven't gotten to enjoy the entire time we've been here."

"I was not having sex with you in your parents' house! You would have pounded that headboard through the wall."

His eyes twinkle in horny delight. "We're not in the house anymore." He slides his belt from the confines of its buckle, pops the button on his jeans, and lowers the zipper. "Start strippin'. We just moved that fuck it list to Texas. Literally. Time to ride your cowboy, Sugar."

"Tompkins!" As God is my witness, if that man yells my name one more time, I'm going to box his ears. My day is over. Five surgeries, five pain management follow-ups, and one grumpy surgeon who seems to think I have a hearing problem. He should have chosen proctology for all the times he's been up my ass lately. I've been back two months from my vacation with Reece, and in need of another one already.

"Right here, Dr. Evans," I reply from around the corner of the locker room, collecting my personal belongings. "You don't have to yell."

He appears at the end of the aisle of lockers, arms folded over his chest. "My ears have been plugged lately."

I know I shouldn't, but sometimes I just can't help myself. "Music too loud at the strip club?"

Ooohh. Yup, I poked the bear. His low throaty growl and steely glare are pretty much a dead giveaway. "You're on my roster tomorrow. Check in at five in the morning. Double knee replacements on a single patient. Needs some hand holding."

"Five!" I nearly shriek. I loathe double replacements. They're usually done when a patient is afraid they won't follow through with the second due to the pain from the first. I also would love to know why I'm coming in so early when our usual start time for surgeries is six thirty to seven. Not to mention . . .

"I'm on Dr. Knight's rotation for the next three days in cardiothoracic." Michael isn't my favorite person either, but he's an excellent physician, and I love cardiothoracic. Arseen is a distant memory, so that helps.

"You get the pleasure of my company instead, Mallory." He smirks. "For the rest of the week."

Slamming my locker closed, I shoulder my way past him. "Pleasure is hardly the word I would use. I'll see you at five."

Maybe I'll check with the gastro clinic to see if they have

any openings. It may be a decrease in pay, but if I have to deal with assholes all day, it'll be due to colonoscopies and not personalities.

Chapter 50

Reece

"My wife and kids are in there! You gotta get them out!" the man on the front lawn of the two-story house engulfed in flames screams. "They're all in there!

It's midnight, he's in pajamas and barefoot, as he stands and stares at the inferno while we rush to hook up waterlines and aim hoses at the house to douse the flames. Smoke pours from every window and door while flames lick the frames of the openings.

"How many? Where are they located?" the chief hollers, seizing his shoulders in a hard grip to gain his full attention. "Where are they located?" he shouts again.

"Up-upstairs," he finally answers. "Three kids, my wife. In the back. We were sleeping. There wasn't time for me to . . ."

"See if there's access in the back!" Chief orders as he points to the rear of the house. "Four people on the second floor."

Roger and I both run for the rear of the house, axes in hand, only to find there is no access . . . anywhere. The windows and glass on the sliding doors of both levels have shattered due to the heat. Flames shoot and smoke billows from every opening possible. Hoses are soon turned on the flames as they're strung between the houses and brought around the back, and what feels like forever later, we're frantically searching through the remains of what used to be a home.

These are the jobs that will forever haunt me: the baby crib, the toddler beds, the scorched body in the hallway that never made it to the room that held them. But this one is different. There's something niggling in my brain that I can't let go of. Both stories were fully engulfed when we got here. Four bedrooms, but the kids were all kept in one. Seems . . . odd.

The hoses are rewound, equipment is loaded back on the trucks, fire hydrants sealed up. It's five o'clock in the morning before the last of the black body bags – varying in size from tiny to standard – are loaded into the coroner's truck. The fire marshal arrived hours ago to start his investigation.

"I'll be back in a minute," I mutter to Roger before making my way back toward the house to find the marshal.

"We're ready to go, Reece," he says, stripping his turnout off. "There's nothing left to do here."

"I'll be back in a minute!" I repeat angrily and continue my trek toward the lifeless frame and roasted timber. "Take off if you want. I'll walk back."

The marshal is inside what used to be the living room

when I find him. "Find the accelerant, Bernie." It's not a question, but I hadn't meant to make it sound like an order either. I'm simply observant. I'd observed that man watch his family being loaded into the coroner's vehicle. I'd overheard him spout his story over and over – word for word – without missing a beat, as if it were rehearsed, planned, scripted.

Bernie lifts a brow then furrows it. "If there's something to be found, I'll find it, Callahan. You becoming the expert now?"

"Not at all," I tell him, my eyes set in a cold, hard stare. "But I will tell you this, I would die trying to save my wife and kids before I'd ever stand back and watch them burn to death. He said, *'we were sleeping'*." I arch a cynical brow. "More than a few times. I don't see any evidence of blankets or pillows on that sofa. Where the hell was he sleeping that he couldn't get to any of them and leave *every.single.one* of them behind?"

He narrows his eyes in thought and nods slowly. "That's a damn good question."

I head out for the truck but pause as I reach the opening that was once a threshold. "Bernie, if you can't find anything here, have them do a tox screen on the remains."

"Drugs? Didn't you find the mother in the hallway?"

I turn back slowly and shoot him a wry look. "Don't ever underestimate the power of a mother's love. They've been known to kill bears and lift cars off their kids. Where do you think they got the name *Her*cules?"

He rolls his eyes and shakes his head. "I'll give the detectives a heads up now. Good call."

"Might want to get a hold of the coroner's office PDQ, too." Forcing a smirk I don't really feel, I finish, "Make damn sure the husband doesn't order a complete cremation before the investigation can be completed."

"Anything else you can think of before you leave?" He

arches a brow, his voice tinged with a touch of sarcasm. "Sounds like you've been reading true crime stories."

I can't help myself. "Nah, see enough of that shit in real life. My girl reads smut. Much more interesting and a helluva lot more fun."

"Get outta here, Callahan," he grumbles.

"See ya around, Bernie."

"What was that all about?" Roger asks as I slide into the backseat of the truck.

"Somethin' ain't right about this." I hang my hat on the hook and toss my turnout on the seat next to me.

"No shit, something ain't right," he retorts. "We got four people dead and a house in ruins."

"Like I give a flyin' fuck about a house. We got three kids and a mom dead." I yell to the front over the sound of the engine, "Boonie! Got a question for you. Would you die tryin' or let your wife and kids burn?"

"That's the dumbest damn question I've ever heard, Reece!" he shouts back, his hands gripping tighter on the wheel. "I'd go up in flames. I ain't got no life without my wife and kids."

"Good answer, Boonie." I look out at the rising sun in the Arizona sky; the one that mother and those babies won't enjoy today. I can't unsee them. The devastation of losing your home is nothing compared to losing your everything. But whose everything were they? My brothers would die in a heartbeat for their wives and kids. Hell, Ronan and Ryder would burn long before they would watch a house go up in flames with their nephews and nieces inside. My father would shed his own blood to extinguish flames for all of us. And my mother would have done exactly what that one did: her best to get to us . . . or die trying.

"You okay?" Roger backhands my bicep when the truck pulls to a stop outside the station after reversing into the drive, prompting me to move.

I only nod before snatching my turnout off the seat and hopping down. Thirty six hours to go. No, I'm not okay. It's always the little ones that are the hardest.

I need my bubble.

Burkey is already cooking breakfast for us upon our return. I think it's pancakes, maybe oatmeal – the smell of which is turning my stomach as I pass through on my way to the showers. It's not his fault. It's not necessarily the smell either. It's the . . . residual. Residual thoughts, residual bitterness, that gnawing feeling in my gut. But just as strong is the fear that I'm nearing my breaking point. It's getting worse with each incident. I'm like a stretched rubber band ready to snap. Rescues, health scares, mishaps, emergencies, *accidents*. I'm there for them, happy to be of service. But with every criminal act of intent, I lose a bit of myself with every loss of life.

"Hey, you've been awful quiet. You wanna go throw back a couple before we go home?" Roger follows me out of the station the following afternoon. "Or, we can drop the vehicles at home first and throw back a gallon or two? Call a Lyft. It's been a helluva shift." He claps my back and chuckles. "If you're in for self-inflicted punishment, we can call Wiley to chauffeur us."

"I'm good," I grumble on the way to my truck. I haven't called my girl in two days as it is. Misery does not always love company and I did not want to bring her mood down with mine. "I'd suck as company anyway. I'm beat."

"Isn't Mallory going out with the ladies tonight?" He smirks. "Or does she really keep your balls in her back pocket and squeeze them at will?"

The sigh is long and heavy as I pinch the bridge of my nose. The ladies are out tonight, and Roger is still battling how to handle his free time. Yeah, his are being squeezed too. What he really means is dinner and liquor at a condo of our choice. Seems Cranky's holds no appeal for him since our near-death experience – not that I've gotten the story – but I've been a little occupied myself.

"Order the damn pizza and grab a couple six packs. Give me an hour. We'll watch the replays at my place."

"That's the spirit." He claps me on the back again and laughs. "Want to call Wiley and John to join us? Tanner's on night shift this week."

My chin drops to my chest as I release a pitiful laugh. "Might as well. Anything to put this week behind us. Guess I'd rather hear Wiley plan trust funds for future grandkids than relive the horrors of this week."

"We can't save 'em all, Reece," he says solemnly. "I know this one was tough, but they were gone before we got there."

Staring at the ground, I quietly admit out loud what I wouldn't to anyone else, "I've been at literally hundreds of calls due to stupidity or negligence, but never once have I truly felt like puttin' my hands around somebody's throat." I look him in the eyes, maybe seeking vindication for my feelings. "I wanted to kill him, Roger. What kind of man stands by and watches his family burn to death?"

Firm in his answer, he lifts a brow. "The kind we will never be. Let Bernie do his job and if there's anything to find, you know he'll find it."

"I love bein' of service to the people, Roger, but my tolerance level is shit. I don't know if I can do this anymore."

"That, my friend," he says with a reassuring pat to my back, "is your call. You've got ten years in. You're not the first to feel this way. Nothing is worth your sanity or peace of mind,

Reece. Or your freedom. And let's face it, you're too fuckin' pretty for prison."

He laughs, I don't, and grumble instead, "See you at mine in an hour."

Once inside the door, I throw my keys on the counter and pull up my contacts. He should be done with work by now, and either teaching one of the kids to ride a bike, or pinching Abbie's backside with one hand and tossing back a beer with the other, while smelling the delicious dinner she's cooking.

"Hey there, little bro." He sounds cheery as hell, so it could be the former, could be the latter, as either of those two exercises make him happy. The noise in the background has me guessing. "Needing more womanly advice, or are you gettin' the hang of it?" Ah, he must be pinching Abbie's ass.

Holding a nervous breath – as of late I haven't suffered any massive screw-ups, but I could be well on my way to destroying that record – I finally pose my question, "Russ, are there still three available with five squared for each?"

"You know there are," he says confidently. "Wait a minute, are you . . ."

"Somethin's gotta give. I really have no clue what I'm doing."

The background noise on his end grows quiet as he obviously slips away to another area – most likely his office – and I hear the door close. "You sound stressed. Wanna to talk about it?"

"Nah, I got two more calls to make." My insides quake as I consider the number I stole from her contacts weeks ago. "There's an order to this. I gotta do it right. Talk later, bro."

This isn't a rash decision. I've spent months rolling it around in my head, picturing various scenarios, but only one truly fit. Something she said the night we got back from the canyon fires, and her words from the night in the hammock play in my head as I enter the numbers. *"I'm not even sure if it was ever my intention to stay, but things fell into place and there hasn't been any reason to leave."*

I look up to the ceiling and whisper as I enter the last number into my phone, "Let me be her reason. Please."

Chapter 51

Mallory

My phone sits on the restaurant table, fast becoming an unwelcome distraction as I impatiently wait to see the screen light with Reece's face. He got off at five today and the plan was to see each other tonight after dinner and drinks with Libs and Savannah. At least it was before he started his shift. The last I heard from him was a text wishing me a good day and an *I love you* that same day. He usually texts me every day – and night – and often calls when he has the chance.

Tonight, we ladies are discussing the finer details of Libs' upcoming wedding over tacos and margaritas. It's nearing eleven o'clock and I still don't know where I'm going.

"Don't you think Mal is going to look fabulous in lime green and orange?" Liberty asks Savannah. "My mom was so afraid if we put her in the sheer lavender, she'd walk down the aisle braless and we'd all be getting a nipple show."

The phone loses my attention as the conversation gains it. "What!?"

They both giggle as Libs smirks. "So you are listening."

"Newsflash." I dip a chip in salsa and pop it in my mouth and chew slowly, then tip my chin. "I'm wearing black, just like my soul. The real show comes at dance time when you all find out I wore no panties."

We hold a steady glare until Savannah breaks it with a throat clearing. "Why are you watching your phone?"

"I haven't heard from Reece." I check it once more before turning the phone facedown. "It's not like him."

"Lucas gets off at eleven," Libs informs me. "I'm headed over there. You want to ride with me? We can share a Lyft."

"Make it triples," Sav adds, a slight slur in her voice. "There's a fireman's pole in that building I've been having a lot of fun with."

"You ever going to give us the story?"

She stares at her margarita glass and her mouth twists. "Someday, when it's not so raw. When it doesn't hurt as much."

Studying my friend, I shake my head. "I'm not Roger's biggest fan, but with the trio bromance, I have to tolerate him. I don't get it, Sav. You're so sweet and he's just so . . ."

"Intolerable?" She laughs. I nod while Libs giggles. "I don't like him all the time, either." Sav sighs. "But I always love him." Her eyes light with mischief as she wiggles her eyebrows. "Come on, let's go slide on some firemen's poles."

"Hey!" Libs protests. "Mine's a cop!"

Savannah giggles and winks. "Bet he has a helluva nightstick."

Half an hour later, I'm knocking on Reece's door as Savannah waits at Roger's down the hall. The conversation on the other side shushes as footsteps draw closer.

"The one you're looking for is down there," I tell Roger when he opens the door I knocked on, and point toward Savannah. "Where's Reece?"

"Is that my Kitten?" Reece's obviously inebriated, slow southern drawl comes from inside the condo.

Roger scowls at my arched brow, as Savannah makes her way back to us. "It's been a rough shift, Mallory. The mood's been pretty shitty the last couple days."

"And alcohol was the treatment? Where did they teach that, Roger? Psych 101 or the Frat House on Dipshit Boulevard?" I shove my way past him to find Reece with his head laid back on a cushion, navy blue PFD T-shirt, gray sweats, eyes glazed over. There are half empty liquor bottles on the coffee table accompanied by multiple empty beer bottles and the ever famous pizza boxes.

Wiley and John stand to their feet, guilt washing over their faces. Wiley mutters, "I think we'll get going."

"Not until you clean up your mess, you idiots," I snarl. "I'm not your housemaid. Trash bags are under the sink. Make it fast."

"Don't think so, Roger Dodger." Savannah pushes on Roger's chest, forcing him back inside. "You helped make the mess. Clean it up."

Short of making them polish the coffee table and wiping down the kitchen counters, because I want them the hell out of here, I do wait for them to clear every last bottle and box away, tie the bags, carry them into the hall, and slam the door behind them.

Reece has moved forward on the sofa, elbows on his knees, face planted in his palms. I stand in front of him, a tall glass of water in my hands. "Drink this." He slowly lifts his head, then takes the glass, chugs the entire contents and sets the glass on the table.

Yeah, he looks like hell. Dark circles under his eyes, the usual bright blue dimmed by lack of sleep and too much alcohol. "Want to talk about it?"

He raises his eyes to meet mine and the saddest, most pitiful whisper leaves his mouth as he rips my heart from my chest, "I suppose I should have told you first. Things have changed. I just can't do this anymore."

Months together flash through my mind as I stare at him in disbelief. *What changed? He can't do this anymore? "Have a little faith in me". He took me back to Texas! Put me on Lady Luck! Guess we ran out of all the things.*

Tossing a glance back at the door, I imagine once again having been the subject of conversation. "So instead of just telling me, you drank liquid courage with your cheering section?"

He nods slowly, guiltily. "They listened to my reasons. Agreed wholeheartedly it's for the best. I hope you'll understand too."

Understand? I want to throw something, slap him, take back every 'I love you' I've ever gifted him. But I don't. I hurt too much to be angry. This is pain, and I don't inflict pain; my job is to prevent it. I fight back the tears, but lose the battle and once the first one falls, others soon follow.

"You could have broken up with me through a text. It would have been less humiliating." Storming for the door, I turn one last time, my parting words meant to sting. "I liked you better as a cowboy." I slam the door closed behind me as hard as possible; the simple task feeling as if I've closed a chapter. A chapter I wish had never been opened. Maybe it's the epilogue. Subtitle: *Picket fences are for dreamers*

Bypassing the elevator, I take the stairwell, two steps at a time.

"Mallory!" His scream is a desperate extended three syllables. He is stealthy for being inebriated – I'll give him that – as he has the door open and is running down the stairs before I reach the first floor. "Mallory, wait!"

Chapter 52

Reece

Nothing more sobering than panic and the fear of losing the love of your life. Color me 'moron' – I think it's neon purple. Of course, it came out wrong. Details! I skipped the details! Adrenaline pumps through my veins as I chase her across the parking lot. "You misunderstood! Baby, please! I'm barefoot!"

"I don't care if you're bare-ass naked and being chased by scorpions!" she sobs as she picks up speed. "You made your point."

Oh shit! Scorpions. Sassy little vixen went for my Achilles heel. Little fuckers and their funky fluorescent glow under ultraviolet light. Can't get Arnie to install the lamps in the parking lot to make them easily detectible, but I'm working on it. Oh, screw it. The sting of losing her would be so much worse. And there wouldn't be an antidote.

This is one battle I cannot lose. She can fight me all she wants; bruise me, scratch my skin until I bleed. I deserve it. Though I prefer she not scratch my eyes out – I wouldn't be able to look into hers. The kindest, softest, most beautiful eyes I've ever looked into. And I made her cry. She is my solace, my peace, my one and only refuge in all the madness. My bubble.

My grip around her waist is gentle but strong as I grab her from behind and hold her to me. No heels to my shins this time, no threats of desuscitation or castration without anesthesia. She doesn't even fight me as she trembles in my arms. Keeping her upright so I don't lean into my compromised state and take us both down the ground, I breathe into the soft hair that tickles my nose and heightens my senses. "It was moron syndrome. Will you let me explain?"

"You were pretty clear, Reece," she cries. "I don't need details or excuses. You want out. Just let me go."

"Never. I don't want out. The only thing I'm letting go of is my job." I bury my face in the crook of her neck as my own body starts to tremble for the first time since the incident. "I can't do it anymore. Some of the human race and I are havin' a problem. I'm gonna die a bitter emotionless man, or in jail, if I keep doin' this."

She goes slack in my arms. "What happened?"

"House fire. If he'd just tried, I might have understood. But he did nothing." My voice cracks as the wretched vision returns. "When I saw those bodies, the little beds, the mom, all I could picture was you and our kids. It gutted me. I woulda died tryin' to save you, but he just stood there, watchin'." I hold her tighter to me. "A man has a breakin' point, but what would truly break me, Kitten, is losin' you."

"Would you put me down?"

"Not if you're gonna run. It took too long to find you."

"I won't run. I promise." I reluctantly set her down gently, and she spins in my arms before I've let go. "I'm sorry you went through that."

I lift her into my arms again and she wraps her legs around my waist. "How in the hell could you think I'd ever give you up? I'd be lost without you." I wind my fingers in her hair, tugging and tilting her head for the perfect fit, the kind of kiss that changed my whole world.

"You taste like booze," she murmurs against my mouth.

"And you taste like heaven." I draw back and lick my lips. "A little bit of tacos and margarita too. Stay with me? Be my bubble?"

She sniffles. "Will you brush your teeth and sleep naked?"

Even through her tears she sets my world back on its axis. Taking one handful of ass cheek, I squeeze it gently and begin the trek back inside. "So fucking special."

Standing in the hall are Roger and Savannah – her arms folded over her chest – him glaring as we make our way toward them.

"Happy now, Peaches?" he grinds impatiently.

"I was watching out for her!" Savannah snaps. "She did the same for me!" She pokes a finger in his chest. "Because you were being a dumbass."

He snatches her wrist into his grip. "Well, if you're waiting for Reece to stop being a dumbass, you're going to grow old and gray because it's his favorite pastime."

"Reece is not a dumbass!" Mallory protests over my shoulder. "He's a moron! And you'd better be nice to her, Roger. She has access to scalpels, and I'll help her bury your balls!"

BUT I KISSED A COWBOY

"Not a chance." Roger laughs cockily. "She likes playin' with 'em too much."

"They don't have to be attached to play with them," Mallory warns. "You up for a game of golf next week, Savannah?"

The thumb I was pretending to use for the code on my phone to unlock my door fumbles. Her quick wit is killer. She's feisty, strong, hilarious, and loyal as hell. She backs down from no one. We have three days off together. *Finally.* This wasn't my original plan, though I've covered all my bases. Pretty sure Dr. Tompkins would have preferred a face-to-face visit, but he trusts his daughter's judgment. He also let me know in no uncertain terms that, as a surgeon, he would use my body for organ donation and no one would ever be the wiser, should I Ever. Hurt. His. Daughter.

"Cn you gt me plan by 2 tomo?"

"I see the money for Hooked on Phonics was wasted. Are you drinking?"

"Ned the pln at 2 tmrw plese"

At the same time Mallory asks, "Having trouble with the door?" my phone rings and Russ' face lights the screen.

"It's Russ," I tell her, gently sliding her down my front and setting her on her feet. "Probably just checking in. Can you keep those two from killin' each other while I take this?"

"I can try," she grumbles as she turns toward them. "I think Roger just wants angry sex. I hope she snaps his dick off."

That's my girl. My back turned, I take the call. "Hey."

"Back here to the ranch?"

"So you did understand," I say. "Yes, please. I'll catch it at the Perry Stables." He yawns loudly. "Oh shit, did I wake you?"

"Nope." He chuckles as Abbie giggles. "Just baskin' in the afterglow. You're lucky, little bro. Five minutes earlier and I mighta kicked your ass. So, you gonna tell me what's up?"

Grinning cockily, though he can't see it, I tease, "Well, if you're baskin' in afterglow, I can tell you what's not up anymore."

"I can still kick your ass, Reece."

"I really am sorry. I wasn't paying attention to the time."

"No problem," he drawls. "I should say thank you. Now I'm awake enough for round two. See you tomorrow."

"You're welcome!" I holler into the phone, unaware if he heard, as the line has disconnected. Can't take credit for his stamina, but my timing is impeccable.

Still my favorite.

My family owns two small jets and a helicopter. With the vast amount of land to surveil and the cattle and horses that sometimes need to be recovered, the helicopter is used. For auctions, conferences, and simple getaways, the jets are used. The Callahans could also have their names plastered on half the wings of hospitals in the Dallas area as well, but they don't. They're humble, and extremely generous.

Showered, teeth brushed, and a towel wrapped around my waist, I pull back the covers on my side of the bed, drop the towel, and crawl in next to her. She smells so good; coconut and vanilla. Hair like spun silk, and satiny skin. My hand nearly covers the flat of her stomach as my little finger searches for the delicate bauble that ended my journey. The best kiss I'd ever had. Not so impossible after all.

"This is still our three-day weekend, right?" She nods against my chest. "Go away with me tomorrow."

"I am not hiking this weekend," she warns adamantly. "I want my feet up. Preferably with a glass of wine in my hand."

Rolling her onto her back, my hand latches onto one of

BUT I KISSED A COWBOY

my favorite body parts. "The wine can wait until tomorrow, Sugar. Let's get a head start on putting your feet up right now." Her giggle is my music, and I want to hear this song every day for the rest of my life.

"I'll be back to pick you up in about an hour." I lean in and kiss her once the door to her condo is open and she's safely delivered. "Pack a bag."

"What am I packing?"

"Clothes." Leaving one last kiss on her mouth, I wink and add, "Undies are optional, although I do love those thongs you wear."

"Ah, Mr. Callahan," the well-dressed, distinguished gentleman I've been dealing with for the last month greets me as I enter the store. "Ready for final inspection before I wrap it up?"

"Definitely." Due to the specificity, it's taken a lot of time, thought, and scheduling so I could get Tanner to help me with this . . . sans Liberty. He understood better than anyone, though his wishes of 'good luck' seemed a bit more skeptical than sincere. Big enough to be unmissable, comfortable so it fits like a glove, no prongs and . . . perfect, just like her.

"It's even better than I pictured." I hold it between my index finger and thumb, admiring the way the light dances off the facets. Handing it back to him, I pull out my wallet and remove the black Amex.

Once back in my truck, I tuck the little black velvet box inside my duffel, along with every hope and dream I never knew I had until her.

My phone rings, the screen displaying a number that makes my stomach roil. Reluctantly, I press the button on the steering wheel. "Yeah, Bernie."

"Not that we wouldn't have caught it," he starts with an air of arrogance, "but I did want to say good call, Callahan. Your instincts serve you well."

Hesitant to have my mood destroyed, I inquire in spite of myself, "Do I want to know?"

"He was creative." He snorts in disgust. "Rubbing alcohol. Used it in every damn room of the house. Curtains, carpets, clothes. Tox screens are weeks out, but we'll see what they show. He's already been arrested."

"Motherfucker," I mumble through a clenched jaw, my hands white-knuckling the steering wheel, secretly wishing it was his neck.

"I also called with a proposition. If you're ever interested in the Marshal's team, I got a place for you. You can give it a trial run. Got a couple guys going to be out for a few months each, due to surgery." He chuckles. "Take a walk on the wild side, Reece."

"I'm goin' home, Bernie."

"Sleep on it. Let me know," he says.

I'd already slept on it. My decision was made. And my version of home isn't exactly what he thought it was. But I don't tell him that. "Take care, Bernie."

Chapter 53

Mallory

"Callahan Stables?" I stare at the logo on the small plane that sits on a runway no longer than what looks to be a few football fields.

"Rone and Ryder's brainchild of renaming the family business Callahan *Studs* lasted all of a second," he places an arm over my shoulder and leads me toward the plane, "after dad threatened to make them geldings if they ever suggested it again."

"Your brothers aren't all bad," I wrinkle my nose at the memory of the night at the bar when we visited Texas, "for severe man whores."

"Hey, Reece!" the pilot yells and waves from the top of the stairs.

"Hey, Doobie!" Reece calls back with a wave. "Thanks for comin'."

Doobie? As in one of the musician brothers or a frequent indulger? At first glance, it's a crapshoot. Blue jeans and T-shirt, long hair, beard, and a gentle smile that makes him look a little like Jesus. At least the pictures I've seen. Due to the fact they didn't have cameras back then, I've always been a little skeptical.

"Uh, Reece? Where are we going?"

"Back to where we began, Mallory." He squeezes my shoulder a little tighter. "There's a feature I forgot to show you while we were there."

Three hours later we're on the end of a landing strip on Reece's family ranch. There must be at least a half mile of hangars that house various aircraft.

"This is what you wanted to show me?" I ask after we stretch our legs and before we hop into the waiting Jeep.

"Nope. A lot of this is used by the crop farmers who rent land from the family. Callahan deals with horses and cattle only." He points toward the many small planes on one end. "Those are crop dusters used by the farmers. We generally use the helicopter when we're looking for stray cattle or horses. The small planes are for travel and auctions." He takes my hand. "Come on. The house is five miles from here. Let's go see the family."

"Five miles? How much land does your family own?"

"How far can you see?" he answers easily, and slides his shades on. "But there's only one parcel I'm thinkin' about right now. And you're gonna have to wait until tomorrow to see it because my bet is Russ already has the barbecue going and we've got dinner and a campfire to get through this evening."

The next morning I leave a soundly sleeping Reece to make my way to the kitchen where I find Mrs. Callahan pulling bakery from the oven. The tempting aroma of fresh baked cinnamon rolls and coffee makes my mouth water.

"Good morning, sweetheart," she greets me. "Did you sleep well?"

"Very." I stretch and fight a morning yawn. "There is something about open windows and the air here that makes for peaceful slumber."

She sets a cup of fresh brew at the breakfast bar for me with a small pitcher of cream, and I take a seat. "You don't leave the windows open in Arizona?"

"Can't, really." I shake my head. "Even on the tenth floor, the sounds of traffic and sirens reach your ears."

"Tenth floor?" She giggles. "You've come a long way, Mallory. We could barely get you up on a horse for fear of falling off the back."

We share a laugh at the memory and a few more with easy conversation before arms wrap around my shoulders from behind and my favorite voice grumbles in my ear, "You left me in bed . . . alone."

"You were sleeping."

He drops a kiss to my neck – that sweet spot that sends shivers down my spine – and whispers, "I missed my slow, sleepy, morning . . ."

"You want coffee?" My voice is an octave too high as I try to lift off the stool, but he holds me firmly in place. *He knows we don't have sex in his parents' house!*

"I'll get it, baby. Looks like you could use a refill." He mutters so only I can hear, "I'll save the special cream for the shower, which we are sharing. Next time, wake.me.up." He drops a kiss to my temple and heads for the coffee pot where he pours me a refill and one for himself, then rounds the counter to sit down beside me. Planting a hand on my thigh, he squeezes it gently.

His mother beams with pride as she sets down a plate of fresh cinnamon rolls in front us. "If he gets any sweeter, he's bound to make me cry."

Reece's hand slides farther up my leg and his pinky starts to dance at the apex of my thigh. "Mallory likes me sweet." He flicks his finger against my center as he leans forward to reach across the counter then sets a roll onto my plate. He winks and flashes me a sexy grin. "But I think she likes my *salty* best."

I swear I leave fingernail impressions in his skin as I remove his hand from my thigh and shoot him a seething glare. His mother chuckles and shakes her head as she gazes out the kitchen window. "So much like his daddy."

Two hours later, we're standing in an empty field. Reece has pointed out three houses not too far away, each one belonging to one of his brothers and their families. "You didn't ask me what my plans were when I told you I was quittin' my job."

"My only concern was you, Reece. You were a mess. Are you sure the housefire is your only reason for quitting, or the final straw?"

"You seem to know me well, Kitten. Something you want to share?"

"Do you remember what you told me in the OR when I asked if you had any allergies?"

He rubs the back of his neck and grimaces. "Was it as bad as asking you to sit on my face?"

I roll my eyes. "You told me it was stupid people."

He chuckles as he recalls. "And you told me they have a tendency to give you hives, too." His chin lowers as he shakes his head. "I wish it were that simple, Mallory. I can deal with stupid. Hell, I can tolerate ignorance. But my temperament can't handle the evil anymore. I'm gonna end up in a cell next to Bubba someday."

I can't say I don't understand his predicament. We see plenty in the OR. Days we have to grind our teeth and fight throwing up in the haz mat bin. Days we fight back tears as we watch Evans repair the broken bones of an abuse victim. But I'm not on the scene to rescue those victims. I work with the aftermath. How would I have reacted to that man who did nothing to try and save his family?

Nodding slowly, I do a one-eighty turn and take in the surroundings: wide open spaces, fresh air, unobstructed blue sky. God, it's so peaceful here. It smells, looks, and feels like freedom. He didn't need to bring me here to make me understand; to break my heart. Keeping my back to him, I state the inevitable out loud, "You're coming back here, aren't you?"

"That depends. I've always thought of this as home, until I realized that's what you are to me. To put the two of you together would be heaven. You told me you've never found reason to leave Arizona. I brought you here to convince you to let me be that reason."

I turn to find him on one knee; an open velvet box in his hand, the sun reflecting off the stone inside so brightly it's hard to see.

"I told you *I* will be your Fort fucking Knox, Mallory," he says softly. "You're standing on ground we could build our house. One story, two story. Your choice." He holds up a finger. "Oh, and a picket fence around a huge front yard so our kids will have plenty of room to run – whenever you're ready for them. If you don't like this lot, there are two others to choose from. I kinda prefer this one though, as it's the closest to Russ

377

and he's the most sane out of the five.

"I know your work is important to you and it would be selfish to deny people your compassion. There are hospitals in the area that I'm sure would love to have you. We'll visit Liberty as often as you want. I'll be home every evening for you. We'll watch movies, dance to every slow song ever written, and I will kiss you under the Texas sky every day for the rest of my life. I promise to love you harder, longer, more than you ever thought possible. Marry me, Mallory."

I think my tears started at *Fort fucking Knox* and increased to a downpour at *picket fence*. He remembered.

"You forgot the Captain Crunch," I utter through tears.

"No I didn't." He shrugs. "You kinda got me hooked on Froot Loops."

"We can do both."

His lips tip in a playful grin, teasing me with the memory of our first night together. "Like all the days and all the nights?" I nod. "I'll take that as a yes?"

"You'd better hurry, Mr. Callahan, before I change my mind."

He winks. "You gonna call me that in the bedroom?"

Finishing the scene that is ours and ours alone, "It's that or moron."

"Gimme that hand," he lovingly demands then slides the ring on my finger. He stands, taking my cheeks in his palms. "You are so special. Now gimme those tears," he whispers, dropping soft kisses under my eyes and onto my cheeks. "Salty and sweet. My favorite kind."

Chapter 54

Reece

Construction on a large ranch house started immediately on the lot where I proposed, as soon as we nitpicked, argued, and eventually compromised on designs after some really fun angry sex. My sly Kitten finally figured out I didn't give two shits about design, colors, counter material, or flooring, and that I was simply enjoying the angry sex a little too much after the bickering. She then countered with becoming annoyingly complacent and said whatever I wanted was *"fine"*. After arriving home from our last trip, I showed her the *final* plans of pink appliances, blue countertops, and green walls, as well as counterfeit signed contracts for the next phase of construction

– my photoshop skills have vastly improved in preparation for my very last calendar for the firefighters' charity.

We had the best angry sex ever. I apologized profusely, *after*. I'm not stupid.

They had estimated six months for completion, but if I know Russ – and I do – it will be done early and will be perfect. Cherry cabinets, quartz countertops, slate appliances, etc. – just the way my girl wanted it. The only thing I wanted was a mudroom in which to drop my filthy clothes before I entered the house after a day of dealing with horses and cattle. We've managed to make three short trips there over the last two months to inspect the progress, but Russ is overseeing everything in the interim.

I'm still with the fire department until our move. I'm calmer now – my bubble to keep me sane, a whole new future ahead of me. Not sure what I've done in this life to deserve her, not sure I do deserve her, but I'll never take a day for granted again.

On one of the brightest days in Arizona, we stand in the backyard of Tanner's boss, Captain Sullivan. We're here to witness one of my best friends marry the love of his life. Tanner Carson and Liberty Collins fought their way back to each other through the most incredible odds one could imagine. They never stopped searching or hoping. I never knew where to start the search for my *Kitten*. She was a pleasant memory from my teens. The one that got away. But the grand re-entry she made is unforgettable.

It will make for fascinating storytelling for the kids someday; the way she stole my heart on a sunny Texas morning and made it beat faster in an OR on a hot Arizona afternoon. We can skip over the invitation of a seat on daddy's face, and instead embellish on the kiss of gratitude in the hospital parking lot when their daddy was a hero. The kiss that took their daddy back to the best time in his life; the best kiss he'd ever had, the prettiest girl he'd ever seen. As I stare at my future bride on the other side of the platform we all stand on, I can picture the scene around our dinner table. Mini Reeces and mini Mallorys demanding more of the story.

"Reece!" A distant whisper comes from somewhere on my left. The whisper is harsher the second time, followed by a quick backhanded thump to my solar plexus, "The rings, dumbass!"

"Oh!" I startle from my haze of future bliss and reach into the breast pocket of my tux, preparing to hand them to the preacher. "Sorry 'bout that."

"I told you not to call him dumbass," Mallory scolds Roger discreetly from the other side of the platform. "He answers better to moron."

Roger smirks. "He answers best when you just squeeze his balls."

Tanner is fuming as his eyes dart back and forth between them before Mallory grins evilly. "Better enjoy yours while you got 'em, Roger. There's a ping pong table in the rec room. Savannah and I plan on playing tonight. I brought the scalpels."

"Do I have to put you two in timeout?" Liberty warns through clenched teeth.

"Oohh." Mallory's face lights up. "Can it be in a soundproof room so no one hears him scream while I remove them?"

Roger turns his eyes on me and scowls. "You're gonna live with that?"

I smile at my girl and wink. "You bet your ass I am, and I'm gonna love every minute of it. Now shut up and enjoy the ceremony."

Four months later

Watching as my bride makes her way down the makeshift aisle in my parents' backyard on the arm of her father, my eyes water and I find it hard to catch my breath. She is so beautiful. Hair down in loose waves. Her lips coated with a touch of extra color that I can't wait to kiss off. White satin gown fitted to her luscious curves, ending with the perfect pair of . . . white, rhinestone-studded cowboy boots. Flashbacks of the kiss on Lady Luck, Mallory leaning over me in the OR and again in recovery, fourteen years later flit through my mind. She truly is unforgettable. That sparkle and shine. Her touch. Her taste. She didn't leave a hole in my heart that day; she left it idling, in neutral, waiting for her to come back and give it a jumpstart. Waiting for the right woman to stay the night for, to share breakfast with, to wear my T-shirt in the morning, to hold onto and never let go.

After heartfelt vows that have made my wife cry, the long awaited words from the preacher ring in my ears; "You may now kiss your bride", I glance up at the sky above, then drop my gaze to the eyes I dreamed about years ago.

I bob my eyebrows, then smile and wink. "First kiss under the Texas sky as my wife." I capture her mouth in a kiss she won't forget. Her lips are soft and pliant under mine and . . . uncannily memorable. So much so, my senses are kicked into overdrive and I'm diving in for another taste before I finish savoring the first. My dick hardens faster than morning wood as Mallory purrs and I groan. My hand fists her hair as my tongue works to lap up every last morsel of delicious . . .

A large hand grasps my shoulder. "A little decorum, bro," Russ's low, deep growl resonates in my ear. "We got elderly in the crowd."

Why I've ever wasted time trying to one-up this woman is far beyond me. I am putty in her hands and will be on my knees until the day I die.

I snap back from the kiss, my breaths heaving as I stare at my best memory and my whole future, and whisper, "Cotton candy."

Her timid smile, molten silver gaze from under thick dark lashes, and tiny touch of unsurety take me back to the best kiss I've ever had as she admits, "I never wore it again after that day, but I found out they still make it. I needed something old to go with the new, borrowed, and blue."

My laughter cannot be contained as I bring our mouths mere millimeters apart and utter before another kiss, "So . . . fucking . . . special."

Epilogue

Six years in to wedded bliss and picket fences

"When's daddy comin' home?" Rush's dejected whine matches his sagging shoulders as he rounds the corner into the kitchen.

"He was here for lunch with you. Now, when does daddy always come home for the rest of the day?" I pose my own question as a teaching tool and nod at the analog clock that sits on the end table in the family room. He's four point six, *going on forty*, and smart as a whip.

He sighs and rolls his eyes dramatically. "When the big hand's on the twelve and the little hand's on the five."

"Mmhmm," I confirm, then scoop another spoon of fruit into Rissa's hungry little mouth. She's our two-year-old – dotes on her big brother and is daddy's little princess.

"But the little hand's only on the four," he complains.

"Yup, sure is. So how long do we have to wait?"

He crosses his arms over his chest and scowls. "Too long." I see it in the little imp's eyes, but I don't stop him. His creativity knows no bounds. It'll be interesting to see what he tries this time. Crossing the room slowly, sneaking glances over his shoulder on the way, he flicks the little hand forward an hour.

Damnit! I knew we should have bought an encased face! This kid is so much like his dad. Hence his name. Delivered ten minutes after arriving at the hospital! Time waits for no one, and neither does Rush. I quit my job the moment I held him in my arms. I'll go back someday . . . maybe.

"Dad's comin', mom! Look! The little hand's on the five."

"Mmm." I nod. "How did that happen, Rush?"

"I helped it," he says proudly, chin tipped high. *Points for honesty.*

"Daddy 'ome!" Rissa squeals, whipping her head toward the door and in the process, spreading fruit from the corner of her mouth to her ear.

"Not yet, sweetie," I tell her. "In a while." And the waterworks start, as well as significant whining and a mixture of spit and food spewed onto my shirt. Firming my gaze at my firstborn, I arch a brow. "Do you see what you've done?"

"Sowwy, sissy," he grumbles and walks slowly back to his little sister, then bypasses us both to reach for a cloth on the counter. "I'll clean it up, mom."

"I'll get it." I accept the cloth he readily holds out – holding back my own tears while trying to calm his baby sister – and gently scold him, "Changing the clock will not get your dad home faster, Rush. That's not the way it works. You need to be patient."

One would think four years of motherhood with this child would make me a pro by now. Not only is Rush creative, but he loves a challenge. I should have known by his easy acceptance and daddy-like swagger as he disappears back into the playroom to wait that hope was going to kick my ass.

This is the same kid who woke us up last Saturday morning at five o'clock with a whispered, "Mornin', mom. I fixed coffee for you guys." Never had we flown out of bed so fast, knocking elbows as we threw the blankets in opposite directions, expecting either a Rush disaster in the kitchen or the need for fire extinguishers. Instead, we found the perfect pot of coffee waiting to be poured. He knew not to pour it. Never touch a hot pot. Anxious to get out for the usual Saturday morning horse ride with his dad, he was simply lending a helping hand. He had been observing for some time. His words: "I've been watching you do it."

Ten minutes later the back door flies open and a panicked Reece rushes in – mud-crusted Levis, boots still on, my favorite cowboy hat topping sweaty blonde curls, and looking scrumdillyicious despite the dirt he tracked in – followed by Russ and Ronan.

"What happened? Are my girls okay?"

A now calm and fed Rissa flexes tiny fingers, twirls her feet in circles like helicopter blades as she reaches for her main man, and squeals, "Daddy!"

Ronan chuckles. "Rissa looks okay to me, although I'd say mama don't look too happy right about now."

Without missing a beat, I eye the counter behind me where my phone is *supposed* to be, then turn to the entryway of the kitchen from the playroom and see my son, feigning innocence yet looking guilty as hell. "Where is my phone, Rush?"

"You said the clock wouldn't work!" he defends his actions and holds up my phone. "So I called him. I made Rissa cry and then you cried. I saw you, mom. Dad fixes everything."

Reece stops first at Rissa's chair, bending to kiss the top of her and head and greets her, "Hey, Princess." Then slides to his knees by my side, my cheeks in his dirty palms, before I can deny Rush's claims. "You were crying?" My bottom lip trembles as I shake my head.

"Who wants ice cream?" Russ' cheery booming voice is aimed at the kids as he reaches behind Reece to remove Rissa from her high chair. "Aunt Addie always has ice cream for Rush and Rissa."

Two squeals equals a positive as Rissa forgets her daddy's existence and Rush leaps into Ronan's waiting arms. "They can have dinner with us, too," Russ offers with a wink. "You two take your time."

"Hang on," Reece says as he rises from his knees and takes Rush from Ronan's arms. "Man hug, Bubba. Thanks for takin' care of your mom and sissy."

"Love you, Dad." Rush squeezes tightly around his dad's neck, then snatches his hat off his head and plops it onto his own. It's ten sizes too big, covers his face, and the brim nearly hits his shoulders. "Maybe when I'm five," he says through muffled giggles under the hat then plunks it back on Reece's head, backwards. Laughter fills the room and they're soon off and on their way for ice cream.

Reece pulls me to my feet, hands on my waist, a kiss to my forehead, and whispers, "Talk to me, Kitten."

"You did it again, Reece." I take a deep breath and remind myself it really does take two to tango, and damn, can we tango. Tango, two-step, rock-n-roll, foxtrot, blues, jazz. The man has rhythm, on and off his feet. But as God is my witness, the mere thought of adding to our happy little crew, and the man's sperm become Olympic swimmers. It was supposed to take a couple months!

"I barely get my body back from Rissa and you're blowing me up like the Goodyear blimp."

His mouth twitches on one side and he bites his lip so hard I wait for blood to appear as his eyes flicker in amusement. He holds up a finger. "Wait here a minute."

He throws the back door to the mudroom open. Boots thud, the clunk of a belt buckle hits the floor, clothes are being stripped off, and moments later my bare-ass naked husband reenters the kitchen. Tall and proud, the soldier makes a star-studded appearance.

"What are you doing?"

He shrugs and grins impishly; that horny sparkle lighting those baby blues. "I think he deserves a shower with his wife and an achievement award. Don't you?"

I point to the prize seeking villain. "*He* is what started this whole thing!"

He lifts me off my feet, one hand under a butt cheek, the other wrapped in my hair. "Would you trade it?"

I study the bright blue eyes I fell in love with so long ago. The boy on the horse. The firefighter that rescued me in the hospital parking lot. The Hotshot I nearly lost. Now the cowboy that traded long shifts for longhorns, prize-winning horses, slow dances, kisses under a Texas sky, Captain Crunch and movies, and a quiet life with picket fences and family.

"Not for anything in the world."

"I love you, Mallory Callahan. Now kiss me, and remind me of the best thing I've ever had and what a lucky man I am."

The End

Thank you for spending this precious time
with me. Please consider spending a little more time
and leave a review on Amazon and Goodreads, as
it gives you, the reader, a voice in the pages.

Oh! Don't forget! We still have Roger's and Savannah's story to tell. Coming November 2025

Other Books By This Author

The Crew Series:

Amazon.com: Run To Me: A friends to lovers romance (The Crew Book 1) eBook : Mick, Annie : Kindle Store

Wicked Lemonade (The Crew Book 2) - Kindle edition by Mick, Annie. Contemporary Romance Kindle eBooks @ Amazon.com.

Amazon.com: Find Another Hero: Just Make Sure He Can Dance (The Crew): 9798685424785: Mick, Annie: Books

The Attorney Series:

Tell Me Why, Jannie: Mick, Annie: 9798595087735: Amazon.com: Books

The Fresh French Connection - Kindle edition by Mick, Annie. Literature & Fiction Kindle eBooks @ Amazon.com.

Sixties is the new sexties:

Old Farts and Pop Tarts - Kindle edition by Mick, Annie. Literature & Fiction Kindle eBooks @ Amazon.com.

Amazon.com: Saari, Not Sorry eBook : Mick, Annie: Kindle Store

Amazon.com: The Chauffeur: Phoenix Rising eBook : Mick, Annie: Kindle Store

Manipulation 101: Code of Ethics - Kindle edition by Mick, Annie. Paranormal Romance Kindle eBooks @ Amazon.com.

Amazon.com: Somebody's Someone eBook : Mick, Annie: Kindle Store

A little Christmas delight for anytime of the year:

Amazon.com: Donner's Vixen eBook : Mick, Annie: Kindle

Store

Amazon.com: I Should Have Kissed Him (The Nurses of Maricopa County Book 1) eBook : Mick, Annie: Kindle Store

About The Author

Annie Mick

A diehard laughaholic who has learned to take everything with a grain of salt, Annie Mick loves to dish it out with a good dose of sarcasm.

If you can giggle while you wiggle, it's added exercise and spares you ten minutes on the treadmill.

It is true that if you can laugh while you cry, the tears are saltier and it makes the margaritas taste better.

If you can find your hero in one of her books, therein lies her success. If you can find a bit of yourself in one her characters, therein lies her joy.

Life is too short to not get lost in a fantasy; if only for a day, if only in a book, one page at a time.

Sweet dreams.

The Nurses of Maricopa County

The doors of Banner Medical are open 24 hours a day, but it's what happens behind them that just may surprise you.

I Should Have Kissed Him

Lucas

It's true what they say: you never forget your first love. Liberty Collins was mine. Problem is, I not only never forgot her, I never got over her. Liberty wasn't just my first love; she was my only love, and my last.

The very memory of her and the night we parted have served well as a cruel reminder there will never be another love of my life. We made a deal that day, one I've never forgotten. One that has factored into every decision I've made since.

She's back, and I've come to collect on her 'promise of tomorrow'.

A story of young love and best friends torn apart by tragedy and tested by time. Follow the journey of Lucas and Liberty as they struggle with adult relationships, all the while searching for the one they never forgot.

Recommended for mature audiences due to subject matter.

I Kissed A Cowboy

Long ago on a sunny morning in Texas, there was a boy who took a girl for a ride on his horse . . .

Reece Callahan, firefighter extraordinaire

Offering the beautiful nurse anesthetist a seat on my face probably wasn't the best approach, but it was the drugs speaking at the time – sort of. Old habits die hard. Those eyes and that kissable mouth were taking me to a place and time I'd been before. A place I wanted to revisit – something I never do. I could break those rules, at least once, maybe twice . . .

Mallory Tompkins

The rules and ethics are concise; contractual. My own are pretty clear as well. The hospital's? No patients. My own? No players.

Reece Callahan is well known as both. He's also persistent. But the day he rescues me in the hospital parking lot is the day that changes everything . . . for both of us.

He wasn't just a patient, and she wasn't just his attending anesthetist. Does history change the rules and ethics? Can they get past what was and move on to what can be?

Book #2 in The Nurses of Maricopa County series can be read as a standalone, but serves best as the second course in a delicious setting of spicy and sweet characters you got to sample in Book #1.

Never Kiss A Hotshot

Coming in November 2025

www.ingramcontent.com/pod-product-compliance
Lightning Source LLC
Chambersburg PA
CBHW070835260626
47170CB00007B/2385